I0577030

William Carew Hazlitt, Joseph Ritson, James Orchard
Halliwell-Philipps

Fairy Tales, Legends and Romances

Illustrating Shakespeare and Other Early English Writers

William Carew Hazlitt, Joseph Ritson, James Orchard Halliwell-Philipps

Fairy Tales, Legends and Romances
Illustrating Shakespeare and Other Early English Writers

ISBN/EAN: 9783744693752

Printed in Europe, USA, Canada, Australia, Japan

Cover: Foto ©Andreas Hilbeck / pixelio.de

More available books at **www.hansebooks.com**

Fairy Tales

LEGENDS AND ROMANCES

ILLUSTRATING

SHAKESPEARE

AND OTHER

EARLY ENGLISH WRITERS

TO WHICH ARE PREFIXED

TWO PRELIMINARY DISSERTATIONS

1. On Pigmies
2. On Fairies

BY JOSEPH RITSON

FR███████████████████SELLERS ROW

PRINTED BY BALLANTYNE AND COMPANY
EDINBURGH AND LONDON

PREFACE.

—o—

THE subject of Fairy Mythology is one which of late years has attracted a good deal of attention both here and on the Continent. German scholarship has added much to our knowledge of this peculiarly interesting branch of folk-lore, and their labours have, in some cases, found English translators. A recent writer in the *Quarterly Review* was, I believe, the first to put in print, what many must have felt, that, in "A Midsummer-Night's Dream," the fairies were the most important persons of the drama.

Two scarce books are here amalgamated, and made accessible to the student. Ritson's *Fairy Tales*, 1831, contains matter not in Halliwell's *Illustrations of the Fairy Mythology of a Mid-*

summer-Night's Dream, 1845, and Mr Halliwell's work has matter not found in Ritson. The present republication forms a union of the two, with certain additions and corrections.

I have to thank Mr Halliwell for the permission which he gave me to make what use I pleased of his volume.

W. C. HAZLITT.

KENSINGTON, *November* 1874.

I.

On Pygmies.

—·—o—

THE existence of a little nation of diminutive people engaged in almost continual wars with the cranes, is an opinion of such high antiquity as to be coeval with the rudiments of the heathen mythology. Homer, who flourished 907 years before the vulgar era, is universally admitted to be the earliest poet whose works remain, and though totally blind and unable either to read or write (no written characters being known to the Greeks till many centuries after his time), he had recourse to his invention, and with a harp in his hand, went about various countries, singing and playing, as a bard or rhapsodist, and was well rewarded for his poetical effusions, which being fabulous stories, of his own composition, of gods, heroes, wars, battles, sieges, voyages, adventures, and miracles, altogether incredible and impossible, and of persons, things, cities, and countries which never existed but in his fertile invention and ingenious fabrication, [and with] which every one who heard him was delighted; and in process of time, four or five centuries

A

after his death, when his countrymen, the learned
Greeks, possessing admirable memories, and 'having'
somehow or other got an alphabet, and being made
capable to read and write, these delightful and ingenious compositions of our blind bard have fortunately come down to the present times, in the course
of 2000 years or upward. When, therefore, translations have become common in almost every learned
language, particularly in our own, of which we are
possessed of one so excellent that it has been happily
said—

> " So much, dear POPE, thy ENGLISH Iliad charms,
> When pity melts us or when passion warms,
> That after-ages shall with wonder seek
> Who 'twas translated HOMER into GREEK :"

we are at liberty to conceive that the account of the
Pygmies, as found in the Iliad, is there given and
preserved from ancient and established tradition, and
possibly recorded in history or celebrated in epic
poetry long before the time of Homer—

> " So, when inclement winters vex the plain
> With piercing frosts or thick-descending rain,
> To warmer seas the cranes embody'd fly,
> With noise and order, through the mid-way sky,
> To Pygmy nations wounds and death they bring,
> And all the war descends upon the wing." [1]

Hesiod, likewise, had mentioned the Pygmies, in
some work now lost, as we learn from Strabo.[2]

---

[1] Homer's Iliad, b. iii. v. 3, in the lines of Pope.

[2] B. i. p. 43; b. vii. p. 299. "But for to Hesiod no one
would object ignorance, naming Half-dogs, *Longicipites*, and
Pygmies. Neither, truly, that concerning Homer to be wonderful, when also by much of those who come after many
things both have been ignorant of and monstrously feigned : as
Hesiod, Half-dogs, Joltheads, Pygmies."

[Birds] in the spring-time, says Aristotle, betake themselves from a warm country to a cold one, out of fear of heat to come, as the cranes do, which come from the Scythian fields to the higher marshes whence the Nile flows, in which place they are said to fight with the Pygmies. For that is not a fable, but certainly the genus as well of the men as also of the horses is little (as it is said), and dwell in caves, whence they have received the name Troglodytes from those coming near them.[1]

Herodotus, indeed, speaks "of a little people, under the middle stature of men, 'coming' up to certain Nasamonians who were wandering in Africa, and knew not the language of each other;[2] but does not call them Pygmies, or give them any other name. Cambyses, however, as he elsewhere says, went into the temple of Vulcan [in Egypt], and with much derision ridiculed his image, forasmuch as the statue of Vulcan was very like to the Phœnician Pataicks, which they carried about in the prows of their galleys: which those who saw not, it was indicated to him to be those in the image of a Pygmean-man.[3]

"Middle India has black men, who are called Pygmies, using the same language as the other Indians: they are, however, very little : that the greatest do not exceed the height of two cubits, and the most part only of one cubit and a half. But they nourish the longest hair, hanging down unto the knees and even below : moreover, they carry a beard more at length than any other men ; but, what is more, . . . after this

---

[1] Of the History of Animals, b. viii. c. xii. "Of the Pygmies, that is, of dwarfs, dandiprats, and little men and women, the generation is alike ; for of those whose members and sizes are spoiled in the womb, and are even as pigs and mules." —Aristotle, Of the Generation of Animals, b. ii. c. viii.

[2] Euterpe, ii. p. 32.   [3] Thalia, iii. p. 37.

promised beard is risen to them, they never after use
any clothing, but send down truly the hairs from the
back much below the knees, but draw the beard
before down to the feet: afterwards, when they have
covered the whole body with hairs, they bind themselves, using those in the place of a vestment. . . .They
are, moreover, apes and deformed.　Their sheep,
however, are equal to our lambs: their oxen and
asses approach to the magnitude of our rams: their
horses, likewise, mules and other beasts do not out-
reach.　Of these Pygmies, the king of the Indians
has three thousand in his train; for they are very
skilful archers.　They are, however, most just, and use
the same laws as the other Indians.　They hunt hares
and foxes, not with dogs, but crows, kites, rooks, and
eagles.　There is a lake among them, having the
compass of eight hundred measures, containing 625
feet each, to which, as no wind blows, oil swims
above; which truly they draw out of the middle of
it with vessels, sailing through it in little ships, and
use it."[1]

Ovid, in his "Metamorphoses," alludes to some
old story, not now to be found—

> " Another show'd, where the Pygmæan dame,
> Profaning Juno's venerable name,
> Turn'd to an airy crane, descends from far
> And with her Pygmy subjects wages war."[2]

Pomponius Mela says that "more within the
Arabian bay than the Panchæans were the Pygmies,
a minute race, and which ended in fighting against
the cranes for planted fruits."[3]

---

[1] From a fragment of Ctesias, who flourished in the 337th
year before the vulgar era, in Wesseling's edition of Herodotus,
p. 828.

[2] B. vi.　　　　　　　　　[3] B. iii. c. viii. p. 287.

According to Sir John Maundevile, the "gret ryvere that men clepen *Dalay* . . . gothe thorghe the lond of *Pygmans:* where that the folk ben of litylle stature, that ben but 3 span long : and thei ben right faire and gentylle, aftre here quantytees, bothe the men and the wommen. And thei maryen hem, whan thei ben half yere of age, and geten children. And thei lyven not but 6 yeer or 7 at the moste. And he that lyvethe 8 yeer, men holden him there righte passynge old. These men ben the beste worcheres of gold, sylver, cotoun, sylk, and of alle suche thinges, of ony other that be in the world. And thei han often-tymes werre with the briddes of the contree, that thei taken and eten. This litylle folk nouther labouren in londes ne in vynes. But thei han grete men amonges hem, of oure stature, that tylen the lond, and labouren amonges the vynes for hem. And of the men of oure stature, han thei als grete skorne and wondre, as we wolde have among us of geauntes, yif thei weren amonges us. There is a gode cytee, amonges othere, where there is duellinge gret plentee of the lytylle folk : and it is a gret cytee ; and a fair ; and the men ben grete, that duellen amonges hem : but whan thei geten ony children, thei ben als litylle as the Pygmeyes : and therfore thei ben alle, for the moste part, alle Pygmeyes ; for the nature of the lond is suche. The grete cane let kepe this cytee fulle wel : for it is his. And alle be it, that the Pyg-meyes ben lytylle, yit thei ben fulle resonable, aftre here age, and connen bothen wytt, and gode and malice, ynow."[1]

" At the north poynt of Lewis [one of the *Hebrides*, or Western Isles] there is a little ile callit *The Pyg-mies Ile*, with ane little kirk in it of ther own handey-

---

[1] Voiage and Travaile, London, 1727, 8vo, p. 252.

wark, within this kirk the ancients of that countrey
of the Lewis says, that the said Pigmies has been
eirdit thair.   Maney men of divers countreys has
delvit upe dieplie the flure of the litle kirke, and i
myselve amanges the leave, and hes found in it, deepe
under the erthe, certain banes and round heads of
wonderfull little quantity, allegit to be the banes of
the said Pigmies, quhilk may be lykely, according to
sundry historys that we reid of the Pigmies : but i
leave this far of it to the ancients of Lewis."[1]

The inland parts, in some places of the coast of
Coromandel, toward the hills, are covered with im-
mense and impenetrable forests, which afford a shelter
for all sort of wild beasts; but in that which forms
the inland boundary of the Carnatic rajah's dominions
there is one singular species of creatures, of which
Mr Grose, the author of "A Voyage to the East
Indies," performed by himself in the year 1750 (the
second edition whereof was published, by the writer,
at London, in 1772, in two volumes, octavo), had
heard much in India, and of the truth of which, he
says, the following fact, that happened some time before his arrival there, may serve for an attestation :—

Vencajee, a merchant of that country, and an in-
habitant on the sea-coast, sent up to Bombay, to the

---

[1] Description of the Western Isles of Scotland, by Donald
Monro, High Dean of the Isles, who travelled through the
most of them in 1549 : Edin. 1784, 12mo, p. 37. See a defence
of the existence of the Pygmies in Rosse's Arcana Micro-
cosmi, London, 1652, p. 106.   Martin, likewise, in his
Description of the Western Islands of Scotland, 1703, p. 19,
says: " The island of Pigmies, or, as the natives call it, *The island
of little men,* is but of small extent. There have been many
small bones dug out of the ground here, resembling those of
human kind more than any other." This, he adds, gave ground
to a tradition which the natives have of a very low-statured
people living once here, called *Lusbirdan,* that is, Pygmies.

then governor of it, Mr Horne, a couple of these creatures, as a present, by a coasting vessel, of which one Captain Boag was the master, and the make of which, according to his description and that of others, was as follows :—

They were scarcely two feet high, walked erect, and had perfectly a human form. They were of a sallow white, without any hair, except in those parts in which it is customary for mankind to have it. By their melancholy, they seemed to have a rational sense of their captivity, and had many of the human actions. They made their bed very orderly, in the cage in which they were sent up, and on being viewed, would endeavour to conceal with their hands those parts which modesty forbids manifesting. The joints of their knees were not re-entering, like those of monkeys, but saliant like those of men ; a circumstance they have in common with the ourang-outangs in the eastern parts of India, in Sumatra, Java, and the Spice Islands, of which these seem to be the diminutives, though with nearer approaches of resemblance to the human species. But though the navigation from the Carnatic coast to Bombay is of a very short run, whether the sea-air did not agree with them, or they could not brook their confinement, or Captain Boag had not properly consulted their provision, the female, sickening, first died, and the male, giving all the demonstrations of grief, seemed to take it so to heart that he refused to eat, and in two days after followed her. The captain, on his return to Bombay, reporting this to the governor, was by him asked what he had done with the bodies ; he said he had flung them overboard. Being further asked why he did not keep them in spirits, he replied bluntly he did not think of it. Upon this the governor wrote afresh to Vencajee, and desired him to procure another couple at any rate, as he should grudge no expense to be master of such a curiosity. Vencajee's answer was, he would very willingly oblige him, but that he was afraid it would not be in his power : that these creatures came from a forest about seventy leagues up the country, where the inhabitants catch them on the skirts of it ; but they were so exquisitely cunning and shy that this scarcely happened once in a century.

If the above relation, concludes our author, should be true, as there is no reason to doubt it, we have here a proof that the existence of Pygmies is not entirely fabulous, as nothing can nearer approach the description of them.[1]

---

[1] Vol. i. p. 231, &c.

II.

On Fairies.

———ο———

THE earliest mention of FAIRIES is made by
Homer, if, that is, his English translator have,
in this instance, done him justice—

"Where round the bed, whence Achelöus springs,
The wat'ry FAIRIES dance in mazy rings."[1]

These nymphs he supposes to frequent or reside in
woods, hills, the sea, fountains, grottoes, &c., whence
they are peculiarly called Naiads, Dryads, and
Nereids—

---

[1] Iliad, b. xxiv. v. 776. The word *Fairy*, as used in our
own language, is a mere blunder. The proper name of the
French Fairy is *Faée* or *Fée*, or in English, *Fay*; *Faërie*, or
Féerie, which we apply to the person, being, in fact, the *country*
or *kingdom* of the *Fays*, or what we call *Fairyland*. We have
committed a similar mistake in the word *barley*, which signifies,
in fact, the *ley* or *land* upon which the *bear* grows (ᵬeꝑe, *hor-
deum ;* lea3, a ley).

" What sounds are these that gather from the shores,
   The voice of nymphs that haunt the sylvan bow'rs,
   The fair-hair'd dryads of the shady wood,
   Or azure daughters of the silver flood!"
                                        —Odys. b. vi. v. 122.

The original word, indeed, is *nymphs*, which, it must
be confessed, furnishes an accurate idea of the *fays*
(*fées*, or *fates*) of the ancient French and Italian
romances; wherein they are represented as females
of inexpressible beauty, elegance, and every kind of
personal accomplishment, united with magic or super-
natural power.   Such, for instance, as the Calypso of
Homer, or the Alcina of Ariosto.   " Agreeably " to
this idea it is that Shakespeare makes Antony say, in
allusion to Cleopatra—

"To this GREAT FAIRY I'll commend thy acts,"

meaning this grand assemblage of POWER and BEAUTY.
Such, also, is the character of the ancient nymphs
spoken of by the Roman poets: as Virgil, for instance—

" *Fortunatus et ille, deos qui novit agrestes,*
   Panaque, Sylvanumque senem, Nymphasque sorores." [1]

They likewise occur in other passages, as well as in
Horace—

" *Gelidum nemus*
   Nympharumque leves *cum* Satyris chori ; " [2]

and still more frequently in Ovid.
    Not far from Rome, as we are told by Chorier, was
a place formerly called *Ad Nymphas,* and at this day
Santa Ninfa; which without doubt, he adds, in the

---

[1] Geor. l. ii. v. 493.   [2] Carmina, l. i. o. i. v. 30.

language of our ancestors, would have been called
The place of Fays.[1]

The word *faée* or *fée*, among the French, is derived,
according to Du Cange, from the barbarous Latin
fadus, or *fada*. In Italian *fata*. Gervase of Tilbury,
in his "Otia Imperialia" (d. iii. c. lxxxviii.) speaks of
"some of this kind of *larvæ*, which they named *fadæ*,
we have heard to be lovers;" and in his relation of
a nocturnal contest between two knights (c. xciv.), he
exclaims: "What shall I say? I know not if it were a
true *horse*, or if it were a fairy (*fadus*), as men assert."
From the Roman de Partenay, or De Lusignan, MS.,
Du Cange cites—

> " *Le chasteau fut fait d'*une fée
> *Si comme il est partout retrait.*"

Hence, he says, *faërie* for spectres—

> " *Plusieurs parlant de* Guenart,
> *Du Lou, de l'Asne, et de Renart,*
> *De* faëries, *et de songes,*
> *De fantosmes, et de mensonges.*"

The same Gervase explains the Latin *Fata* (*fée*,
French), a divining woman, an enchantress, or a witch
(d. iii. c. lxxxviii.)

Master Wace, in his "Histoire des Ducs de Nor-
mendie" (confounded by many with the "Roman de
Rou"), describing the fountain of Berenton, in *Bretagne*, says—

> " *En la forest et environ,*
> *Mais jo ne sais par quel raison*
> *La scut l'en les fées veeir,*
> *Se li* Breton *nos dient veir,*" &c.

> (In the forest and around,
> I wot not by what reason found,
> There may a man the fairies spy,
> If Britons do not tell a lie.)

---

[1] Recherches des Antiquitez de Vienne, Lyon, 1659, p. 168.

But it may be difficult to conceive an accurate idea from the mere name of the popular French *Fays* or *fairies* of the twelfth century.

In Vienne, in Dauphiny, is *Le puit des fées*, or *Fairy-well.* These *Fays*, it must be confessed, have a strong resemblance to the *nymphs* of the ancients, who inhabited in caves and fountains. Upon a little rock which overlooks the Rhone are three round holes which nature alone has formed, although it seem at first sight that art has laboured after her. They say that they were formerly frequented by Fays; that they were full of water when it rained; and that they there frequently took the pleasure of the bath, than which they had not one more charming.[1]

Pomponius Mela, an eminent geographer, and in point of time far anterior to Pliny, relates that beyond a mountain in Æthiopia—called by the Greeks the high mountain—burning, he says, with perpetual fire, is a hill spread over a long tract by extended shores, whence they rather go to see wide plains than to behold [the habitations] of Pans and Satyrs. Hence, he adds, this opinion received faith, that whereas in these parts is nothing of culture, no seats of inhabitants, no footsteps; a waste solitude in the day, and a more waste silence; frequent fires shine by night, and camps, as it were, are seen widely spread; cymbals and tympans sound, and sounding pipes are

---

[1] Chorier, Recherches, &c. Oenone, in one of Ovid's epistles, says—

" Edita *de* magno flumine Nympha *fui.*"

See also Homer's Odyssey, b. xiii. ; Porphyry, De antro Nympharum. These *watery nymphs* were likewise called *Naiades*, others were *Oreades*, &c., according to the objects to which they were attached, or over which they presided.

heard, more than human.[1] These invisible essences, however, are both anonymous and nondescript.

The *penates* of the Romans, according to honest Reginald Scot, were "the domesticall gods, or rather divels, that were said to make men live quietlie within doores. But some think that *Lares* are such as trouble private houses. *Larvæ* are said to be spirits that walke onelie by night. *Vinculi terrei* are such as was Robin Good-fellowe, that would supplie the office of servants, speciallie of maides; as to make a fier in the morning, sweepe the house, grind mustard and malt, drawe water, &c., these also rumble in houses, drawe latches, go up and downe staiers," &c.[2] A more modern writer says, "The Latins have called" the fairies "*lares* and *larvæ*, frequenting, as they say, houses, delighting in neatness, pinching the slut, and rewarding the good housewife with money in her shoe."[3] This, however, is nothing but the character of an English fairy applied to the name of a Roman *lar* or *larva*. It might have been wished, too, that Scot, a man unquestionably of great learning, had referred, by name and work, and book and chapter, to those ancient authors from whom he derived his information upon the Roman *penates*, &c.

What idea our Saxon ancestors had of the Fairy, which they called ælf, a word explained by Lye as equivalent to "*lamia, larva, incubus, ephialtes*," we are utterly at a loss to conceive.

The nymphs, the satyrs, and the fawns are frequently noticed by the old traditional historians of the north: particularly *Saxo-grammaticus*, who has a curious story of three nymphs of the forest and

---

[1] B. iii. c. ix.
[2] Discoverie of Witchcraft, London, 1584, p. 521.
[3] Pleasaunt Treatise of Witches, 1673, p. 53.

Hother, King of Sweden and Denmark, being apparently the originals of the weïrd, or wizard, sisters of Macbeth.[1] Others are preserved by Olaus Magnus, who says they had so deeply impressed into the earth, that the place they have been used to, having been (apparently) eaten up, in a circular form, with flagrant heat, never brings forth fresh grass from the dry turf. This nocturnal sport of monsters, he adds, the natives call *The dance of the elves.*[2]

> " In John Milesius any man may reade
> Of divels in Sarmatia honored,
> Call'd *Kottri,* or *Kibaldi;* such as wee
> Pugs and Hob-goblins call. Their dwellings bee
> In corners of old houses least frequented,
> Or beneath stacks of wood : and these convented,
> Make fearefull noise in buttries and in dairies ;
> Robin Good-fellowes some, some call them fairies.
> In solitarie roomes these uprores keepe,
> And beat at dores to wake men from their sleepe ;
> Seeming to force locks, be they ne're so strong,
> And keeping Christmasse gambols all night long.
> Pots, glasses, trenchers, dishes, pannes, and kettles,
> They will make dance about the shelves and settles,
> As if about the kitchen tost and cast,
> Yet in the morning nothing found misplac't." [3]

Milton, a prodigious reader of romance, has likewise given an apt idea of the ancient fays—

> " Fairer than famed of old, or fabled since
> Of FAIRY DAMSELS met in forest wide
> By knights of Logres, and of Liones,
> Lancelot, or Pelleas, or Pellenore."

These ladies, in fact, are by no means unfrequent in those fabulous, it must be confessed, but at the same time ingenious and entertaining histories ; as,

---

[1] B. iii. p. 39.   [2] B. iii. c. x.
[3] Heywood's Hierarchie of Angells, 1635, fo. p. 574.

for instance, *Melusine*, or *Merlusine*, the heroine of a very ancient romance in French verse ; and who was occasionally turned into a serpent;[1] *Morgan-la-faée*, the reputed half-sister of King Arthur, and *the lady of the lake*, so frequently noticed in Sir Thomas Malory's old history of that monarch.

Le Grand is of opinion that what is called *Fairy* comes to us from the Orientals, and that it is their *génies* which have produced our *fairies;* a species of nymphs, of an order superior to these women magicians, to whom they nevertheless "gave" the same name. In Asia, he says, where the women imprisoned in the harems prove still, beyond the general servitude, a particular slavery, the romancers have imagined the *Peris* who, flying in the air, come to soften their captivity, and render them happy.[2] Whether this be so or not, it is certain that we call the *aurora boreales*, or active clouds, in the night, *perry-dancers*.[3]

After all, Sir William Ouseley finds it impossible to give an accurate idea of what the Persian poets designed by a peri, this aerial being not resembling our fairies. The strongest resemblance he can find

---

[1] Peter de Loyer says he can no more believe the history of *Melusine* than those "olde wives' tales, and idle toyes, and fictions of the *fayrie Pedagua*," &c.—Treatise of Spectres, 1605, fo. 19. "Certainly," he adds, "if all the *nymphes* [or *fays*] of which I have spoken have at any time appeared unto men, it cannot be imagined but that they must needs be spirits and divels : and the truth is, that even at this day it is thought, in some of the northern regions, they do yet appeare to divers persons ; and the report is, that they have a care and doe diligently attend little infantes lying in the cradle ; that they doe dresse and undresse them in their swathling-clothes, and do performe all that which careful nurses can do unto their children."

[2] [Fabliaux, 12mo, i. 112.]

[3] V. Caylus, Mem. de l'Aca. des Belles Let. xx.

is in the description of Milton in "Comus." The
sublime idea which Milton entertained of a fairy vision
corresponds rather with that which the Persian poets
have conceived of the peries—

> " Their port was more 'than' human as they stood ;
> I took it for a faëry vision
> Of some gay creatures of the element
> That in the colours of the rainbow live,
> And play i' th' plighted clouds." [1]

It is by no means credible, however, that Milton
had any knowledge of the Oriental peries ; though
his enthusiastic or poetical imagination might have
easily peopled the air with spirits.

There are two sorts of *fays*, according to M. le
Grand—the one, a species of nymphs or divinities ;
the others, more properly called sorceresses, or women
instructed in magic. From time immemorial, in the
Abbey of Poissy, founded by St Lewis, they said every
year a mass to preserve the nuns from the power of
the *fays*. When the process of the damsel of Orleans
was made, the doctors demanded, for the first question, " If she had knowledge of those who went to
the sabbath with the *fays?* or if she had not assisted
at the assemblies held at the fountain of the *fays*, near
Domprein, around which 'dance' malignant spirits ?"
The journal of Paris, under Charles VI. and Charles
VII., pretends that she confessed that, at the age
of twenty-seven years, she frequently went, in spite
of her father and mother, to a fair fountain in the
country of Lorraine, which 'she' named the good
fountain to the fays our lord.[2]

Gervase of Tilbury, in his chapter " Of *Fauns* and
Satyrs," says " there are, likewise, others, whom the
vulgar name *Follets*, who inhabit the houses of the

---

[1] D'Israeli's Romances, p. 13.   [2] [Ibid .p. 75.]

simple rustics, and can be driven away neither by holy water nor exorcisms ; and because they are not seen, they afflict those who are entering with stones, billets, and domestic furniture ; whose words, for certain, are heard in the human manner, and their forms do not appear."[1]   He is speaking of England.

This *Follet* seems to resemble our *Puck* or *Robin Good-fellow*, whose pranks are recorded in an old song, and who was sometimes useful and sometimes mischievous.   Whether or not he were the fairy-spirit of whom Milton

> " Tells how the drudging *goblin* swet,
> To ern his cream-bowle duly set,
> When, in one night, ere glimps of morn,
> His shadowy flail hath thresh'd the corn
> That ten day-labourers could not end,
> Then lies him down, the lubbar fend ;
> And stretch'd out all the chimney's length, .
> Basks at the fire his hairy strength ;
> And crop-full out of dores he flings,
> Ere the first cock his matin rings,"[2]

is a matter of some difficulty.   Perhaps the giant-son of the witch that had the devil's mark about her (of whom " there is a pretty tale "), that was called *Lob-lye-by-the-fire*,[3] was a very different personage from *Robin Good-fellow*, whom, however, he in some respects appears to resemble.   A near female relation of the compiler, who was born and brought up in a small village in the bishopric of Durham, related to him many years ago several circumstances which con-firmed the exactitude of Milton's description ; she particularly told of his thrashing the corn, *churning*

---

[1] Otia Imperialia, d. i. c. xviii.   [2] L'Allegro.
[3] Beaumont and Fletcher's Knight of the Burning Pestle, a. iii. s. 1.   A female fairy, in Midsummer Night's Dream, says to Robin Good-fellow, " Farewell, thou *lob* of spirits."

B

the butter, drinking the milk, &c., and, when all was done, "lying before the fire *like a great rough hurgin bear.*" [1]

In another chapter Gervase says : "As among men Nature produces certain wonderful things, so spirits in airy bodies, who assume, by divine permission, the mocks they make. For, behold, England has certain dæmons (dæmons, I call them, though I know not but I should say secret forms of unknown generation), whom the French call *Neptunes*, the English *Portunes*. With these it is natural that they take advantage of the simplicity of fortunate peasants ; [2] and when, by reason of their domestic labours, they perform their nocturnal vigils, of a sudden, the doors being shut, they warm themselves at the fire, and eat little frogs, cast out of their bosoms, and put upon the burning coals ; with an antiquated countenance, a wrinkled face, diminutive in stature, not having [in length] half a thumb. They are clothed with rags patched together; and, if anything should be to be carried on in the house, or any kind of laborious work to be done, they join themselves to the work, and expedite it with more than human facility. It is natural to these that they may be obsequious, and may not be hurtful. But one little mode, as it were, they have of hurting. For when, among the ambiguous shades of night, the English occasionally ride alone, the *Portune* sometimes, unseen, couples himself to the rider ; [3] and when he has accompanied him, going on a very long time, at length, the bridle being seized, he leads him up to the hand in the mud, in which, while infixed he wallows, the *Portune*

---

[1] See the tale of the Maath Doog.
[2] It should rather be *unfortunate.*
[3] That is, gets up behind him.

departing, sets up a laugh, and so in this kind of way derides human simplicity." [1]

This spirit seems to have some resemblance to the *Picktree-brag*,[2] a mischievous barguest that used to haunt that part of the country in the shape of different animals, particularly of a little galloway; in which shape a farmer, still or lately living thereabout, reported that it had come to him one night as he was going home—that he got upon it and rode very quietly till it came to a great pond, to which it ran and threw him in, AND WENT LAUGHING AWAY.

He further says there is in England a certain species of demons, which in their language they call *Grant*, like a one-year-old foal, with straight legs and sparkling eyes. This kind of demons very often appears in the streets, in the very heat of the day, or about sunset, and as often as it makes its appearance, portends that there is about to be a fire in that city or town. When, therefore, in the following day or night, the danger is urgent, in the streets, running to and fro, it provokes the dogs to bark, and while it pretends flight, invites them, following, to pursue in the vain hope of overtaking it. This kind of illusion creates caution to the watchmen who have the custody of fire, and so the officious race of demons, while they terrify the beholders, are wont to secure the ignorant by their arrival.[3]

Gower, in his tale of "Narcissus," professedly from Ovid, says—

> "As he cast his loke
> Into the well, . . .

---

[1] Otia Imperialia, d. iii. c. lxi.

[2] Picktree, in the bishopric of Durham, is a small collection of huts, erected for the colliers, about two miles to the northeast of Chester.

[3] Gervase, d. iii. c. lxii.

> IIe sawe the like of his visage,
> And wende there were an *ymage*
> Of such a *nymphe*, as tho was *faye*." [1]

In his " Legend of Constance " is this passage—

> " Thy wife which is of *fairie*
> Of suche a childe delivered is,
> Fro kinde, whiche stante all amis." [2]

In another part of his book is a story " Howe the kynge of Armenis daughter mette on a tyme a companie of the *fairy*." These " ladies " ride aside " on fayre [white] ambulende horses," clad very magnificently, but all alike, in white and blue, and wore " corownes on their heades ;" but they are not called *fays* in the poem, nor does the word *fay* or *fairie* once occur therein.

The fairies or elves of the British Isles are peculiar to this part of the world, and are not, so far as literary information or oral tradition enables us to judge, to be found in any other country. For this fact the authority of father Chaucer will be decisive, till we acquire evidence of equal antiquity in favour of other nations—

> "In olde dayes of the king Artour,
> Of which the Bretons speken gret honour,
> ALL WAS THIS LOND FULFILLED OF FAERIE ;
> The ELF-QUENE, with hire joly compagnie,
> Danced ful oft in many a grene mede. [3]
> This was the old opinion as I rede ;
> I speke of many hundred yeres ago ;
> But now can no man see non ELVES mo,
> For now the grete charitee and prayeres
> Of limitoures and other holy freres,

---

[1] Confessio Amantis, fo. 20, b.

[2] Ibid. fo. 32, b. These are the first instances *faye* or *fairie* is mentioned in English ; but the whole of Gower's work is suspected to be made up of licentious translations from the Latin or French.

[3] Wif of Bathes Tale.

'That serchen every land, and every streme,
As thikke as motes in the sunnebeme,
Blissing halles, chambres, kichenes, and boures,
Citees and burghes, castles highe and toures,
Thropes and bernes, shepenes and dairies,
This maketh that ther ben no FAERIES."

The fairy may be defined as a species of being partly material, partly spiritual, with a power to change its appearance, and be, to mankind, visible or invisible, according to its pleasure. In the old song printed by Peck, Robin Good-fellow, a well-known fairy, professes that he had played his pranks from the time of Merlin, who was the contemporary of Arthur.

Chaucer uses the word *faërie* as well for the *individual* as for the *country* or *system*, or what we should now call *fairyland*, or *fairyism*. He knew nothing, it would seem, of *Oberon*, *Titania*, or *Mab*, but speaks of

" PLUTO, that is THE KING OF FAERIE,
And many a ladie in his compagnie,
Folwing his WIF, THE QUENE PROSERPINA, &c."

—"The Marchantes Tale," l. 10101. From this passage of Chaucer, Mr Tyrwhitt "cannot help thinking that his *Pluto* and *Proserpina* were the true progenitors of *Oberon* and *Titania*."

In the progress of "The Wif of Bathes Tale," it happed the knight

"In his way . . . to ride
In all his care, under a forest side,
Whereas he saw upon a dance go
Of ladies foure-and-twenty, and yet mo.
Toward this ilke dance he drow ful yerne,
In hope that he som wisdom shulde lerne,
But, certainly, er he came fully there,
Yvanished was this dance, he wiste not wher."

These *ladies* appear to have been *fairies*, though

nothing is insinuated of their size. Milton seems to have been upon the prowl here for his " Forest Side."

In "A Midsummer-Night's Dream," a fairy addresses Bottom, the weaver—

> " Hail, *mortal,* hail ! "

which sufficiently shows she was not so herself.

Puck, or Robin Good-fellow, in the same play, calls Oberon—

> " King of *shadows,* "

and in the old song just mentioned—

> " The king of *ghosts* and *shadows ;* "

and this mighty monarch asserts of himself, and his subjects—

> " But WE are SPIRITS of another sort."

The fairies, as we already see, were male and female; but it is not equally clear that they procreated children.

Their government was monarchical, and Oberon, the king of Fairyland, must have been a sovereign of very extensive territory. The name of his queen was Titania. Both are mentioned by Shakespeare, being personages of no little importance in the above play, where they in an ill-humour thus encounter—

> " *Obe.* Ill met by moonlight, proud TITANIA.
> *Tita.* What, jealous OBERON ? Fairy, skip hence ;
> I have forsworn his bed and company."

That the name [OBERON] was not the invention of our great dramatist is sufficiently proved. The allegorical Spenser gives it to King Henry the Eighth. Robert Greene was the author of a play entitled " The Scottishe History of James the fourthe, . . . intermixed with a pleasant comedie presented by

Oberon, king of the fairies." He is, likewise, a character in the old French romances of " Huon de Bourdeaux" and "Ogier le Danois," and there even seems to be one upon his own exploits, " Roman d'Auberon." What authority, however, Shakespeare had for the name TITANIA it does not appear, nor is she so called by any other writer. He himself, at the same time, as well as many others, gives to the queen of fairies the name of MAB, though no one, except Drayton, mentions her as the wife of OBERON—

> " O then, I see, Queen MAB hath been with you,
> She is the fairies' midwife, and she comes
> In shape no bigger than an agate-stone
> On the forefinger of an alderman,
> Drawn with a team of little atomies
> Athwart men's noses as they lie asleep :
> Her waggon-spokes made of long spinners' legs ;
> The cover, of the wings of grasshoppers ;
> The traces, of the smallest spider's web ;
> The collars, of the moonshine's wat'ry beams ;
> Her whip, of cricket's bone ; the lash, of film ;
> Her waggoner, a small grey-coated gnat,
> Not half so big as a round little worm
> Prick'd from the lazy finger of a maid :
> Her chariot is an empty hazel-nut,
> Made by the joiner squirrel, or old grub,
> Time out of mind the fairy's coachmakers.
> And in this state she gallops night by night,
> Through lovers' brains, and then they dream of love.
> .   .   .   This is that very MAB,
> That plats the manes of horses in the night ;
> And bakes the elf-locks in foul sluttish hairs,
> Which, once untangled, much misfortune bodes." [1]

Ben Jonson, in his " Entertainment of the Queen and Prince at Althrope," in 1603, describes to come " tripping up the lawn a bevy of fairies attending on MAB their queen, who, falling into an artificial ring

---

[1] Romeo and Juliet.

that was there cut in the path, began to dance around."[1]

In the same masque the queen is thus characterised by a satyr—

> " This is MAB, the mistress fairy,
> That doth nightly rob the dairy,
> And can hurt or help the churning
> (As she please), without discerning.
>   She that pinches country wenches,
> If they rub not clean their benches,[2]
> And with sharper nails remembers
> When they rake not up their embers ;
> But, if so they chance to feast her,
> In a shoe she drops a tester.
> This is she that empties cradles,
> Takes out children, puts in ladles ;
> Trains forth midwives in their slumber,
> With a sieve the holes to number ;

---

[1] Works, v. 201.

[2] Thus, too, Shakespeare, in The Merry Wives of Windsor—

> " Cricket, to Windsor chimneys shalt thou leap:
> Where fires thou find'st unraked, and hearths unswept,
> There pinch the maids as blue as bilberry :
> Our radiant queen hates sluts, and sluttery."

Milton likewise gives her the same name—

> " With stories told of many a feat,
> How FAERY MAB the junkets eat."

So, too, Jonson, in the above entertainment—

> " Fairies, pinch him black and blue,
> Now you have him, make him rue."

And in Milton's Allegro—

> " She was pincht, and pull'd, she said."

Again, in The Merry Wives—

> " Where's Pead?—Go you, and where you find a maid,
> That, ere she sleep, has thrice her prayers said,
> Rein up the organs of her fantasy,
> Sleep she as sound as careless infancy :
> But those as sleep, and think not on their sins,
> Pinch them, arms, legs, backs, shoulders, sides, and shins."

And then leads them from her boroughs,
Home through ponds and water-furrows.
  She can start our franklin's daughters,
In 'their' sleep, with shrieks and laughters,
And on sweet St Anne's night,
Feed them with a promis'd sight,
Some of husbands, some of lovers,
Which an empty dream discovers."

Fairies, they tell you, have frequently been heard and seen, nay, that there are some living who were stolen away by them, and confined seven years. According to the description they give who pretend to have seen them, they are in the shape of men, exceeding little. They are always clad in green, and frequent the woods and fields; when they make cakes (which is a work they have been often heard at), they are very noisy; and when they have done, they are full of mirth and pastime. But generally they dance in moonlight, when mortals are asleep, and not capable of seeing them, as may be observed on the following morn, their dancing-places being very distinguishable. For as they dance hand-in-hand, and so make a circle in their dance, so next day there will be seen rings and circles on the grass.[1]

These circles are thus described by Browne, the author of " Britannia's Pastorals "—

  " A pleasant meade,
Where fairies often did their measures treade,
Which in the meadow made such circles greene,
As if with garlands it had crowned beene.
Within one of these rounds was to be seene
A hillock rise, where oft the fairie queene
At twy-light sate, and did command her elves,
To pinch those maids that had not swept their shelves :
And further, if by maiden's over-sight,
Within doores water were not brought at night,

---

[1] Bourne's Antiquitates Vulgares, Newcastle, 1725, 8vo, p. 82.

> Or if they spred no table, set no bread,
> They should have nips from toe unto the head ;
> And for the maid that had perform'd each thing,
> She in the water-pail bad leave a ring."

The same poet, in his "Shepheard's Pipe," having inserted Hoccleve's tale of "Jonathas," and conceiving a strange, unnatural affection for that stupid fellow, describes him as a great favourite of the fairies, alleging that

> " Many times he hath been seene
> With the fairies on the greene,
> And to them his pipe did sound,
> While they danced in a round,
> Mickle solace would they make him,
> And at midnight often wake him
> And convey him from his roome,
> To a field of yellow broome ;
> Or into the medowes, where
> Mints perfume the gentle aire,
> And where Flora spends her treasure,
> There they would begin their measure.
> If it chanc'd night's sable shrowds
> Muffled Cynthia up in clowds ;
> Safely home they then would see him,
> And from brakes and quagmires free him."

The fairies were exceedingly diminutive, but it must be confessed we shall not readily find their actual dimensions. They were small enough, however, if we may believe one of Queen Titania's maids-of-honour, to conceal themselves in acorn-shells. Speaking of a difference between the king and queen, she says—

> " But they do square ; that all their elves for fear,
> *Creep into acorn cups*, and *hide them there.*"

They uniformly and constantly wore *green* vests, unless when they had some reason for changing their dress. Of this circumstance we meet with many proofs. Thus, in " The Merry Wives of Windsor "—

" Like urchins, ouphes, and *fairies* green." [1]

In fact, we meet with them of all colours; as in the same play—

" Fairies black, grey, *green*, and white."

That *white*, on some occasions, was the dress of a female, we learn from Reginald Scot.[2] He gives a charm " to go invisible, by [means of] these three sisters of fairies," *Milia, Achilia, Sibylia :* " I charge you that you doo appeare before me visible, in forme and shape of faire women, in *white* vestures, and to bring with you to me the ring of invisibilitie, by the which I may go invisible, at mine owne will and pleasure, and that in all hours and minutes."

It was fatal, if we may believe Shakespeare, to speak to a fairy. Falstaff, in " The Merry Wives of Windsor," is made to say, " They are fairies; he that speaks to them shall dye."

They were accustomed to enrich their favourites, as we learn from the clown in " A Winter's Tale :" " It was told me I should be rich by the fairies." They delighted in neatness, could not endure sluts, and even hated fibsters, tell-tales, and divulgers of secrets, whom they would slily and severely bepinch when they little expected it. They were as generous and benevolent, on the contrary, to young women of a different description, procuring them the sweetest sleep, the pleasantest dreams, and, on their departure in the morning, always slipping a tester in their shoe.

They are supposed by some to have been malignant,

---

[1] In the same play is this line—

" You *orphan*-heirs of fixed destiny,"

for which Warburton proposes to read " *ouphen*-heirs."

[2] P. 408.

but this, it may be, was mere calumny, as being utterly inconsistent with their general character, which was singularly innocent and amiable.   Imogen, in Shakespeare's " Cymbeline," prays, on going to sleep—

> " From *fairies*, and the temptors of the night,
> Guard me, beseech you."

It must have been the *Incubus* she was so afraid of. Old Gervase of Tilbury, in the twelfth century, says, in a more modest language than English : " *Vidimus quosdam* dæmones *tanto zelo mulieres amare quod ad inaudita prorumpunt ludibria, et cum ad concubitum earum accedunt, mirâ mole eas opprimunt, nec ab aliis videntur.*" [1]

Hamlet, too, notices this imputed malignity of the fairies—

> " Then no planets strike,
> No FAIRY takes, nor witch has power to charm."

Thus, also, in " The Comedy of Errors "—

> " A fiend, a FAIRY, pitiless and rough."

They were amazingly expeditious in their journeys : Puck, or Robin Good-fellow, answers Oberon, who was about to send him on a secret expedition—

> " I'll put a girdle round about the earth
> In forty minutes."

Again, the same goblin addresses him thus—

> " Fairy king, attend and mark,
> I do hear the morning lark.
>   *Obe.* Then, my queen, in silence sad,
> Trip we after the night's shade,
> We the globe can compass soon,
> Swifter than the wand'ring moon."

---

[1] Otia Imperialia, d. i. c. xvii.   This is what is now called *the nightmare.*

In another place Puck says—

> " My fairy lord, this must be done in haste ;
> For Night's swift dragons cut the clouds full fast,
> And yonder shines Aurora's harbinger ;
> At whose approach, ghosts, wandering here and there,
> Troop home to churchyards," &c.

To which Oberon replies—

> " But we are spirits of another sort :
> I with the morning's love have oft made sport ;
> And, like a forester, the groves may tread,
> Even till the eastern gate, all fiery-red,
> Opening on Neptune with fair blessed beams,
> Turns into yellow gold his salt-green streams."

Compare, likewise, what Robin himself says on this subject in the old song of his exploits.
They never ate—

> " But that it eats our victuals, I should think,
> Here were a fairy,"

says Belarius at the first sight of Imogen, as Fidele.[1]
They were humanely attentive to the youthful dead.
Thus Guiderius, at the funeral of the above lady—

> "With FEMALE FAIRIES will his tomb be haunted."

Or, as in the pathetic dirge of Collins on the same occasion—

> " No wither'd witch shall here be seen,
> No goblins lead their nightly crew ;
> The FEMALE FAYS shall haunt the green,
> And dress thy grave with pearly dew."

---

[1] They nevertheless sometimes haunted the buttery : " Have you nothing to do [quoth the *widow* to her husband *Jack*, after she had, by a trick, got him to the wrong side of the door, and locked him out] but dance about the street at this time of night, and, like *a spirit of the buttery*, hunt after crickets ? "—Jack of Newbury.

This amiable quality is, likewise, thus beautifully alluded to by the same poet—

> " By FAIRY HANDS their knell is rung,
> By FORMS UNSEEN their dirge is sung."

Their employment is thus charmingly represented by Shakespeare, in the address of Prospero—

> " Ye elves of hills, brooks, standing lakes, and groves,
> And ye that on the sands, with printless foot,
> Do chase the ebbing Neptune, and do fly him
> When he comes back ; you demy-puppets, that
> By moonshine do the green-sour ringlets make,[1]
> Whereof the ewe not bites : and you whose pastime
> Is to make midnight mushrooms; that rejoice
> To hear the solemn curfew "——

In " The Midsummer-Night's Dream," the queen, Titania, being desirous to take a nap, says to her female attendants—

> " Come, now a roundel, and a fairy song ;
> Then, for the third part of a minute hence :
> Some, to kill cankers in the musk-rosebuds ;
> Some, war with rear-mice, for their leathern wings,
> To make my small elves coats; and some, keep back
> The clamorous owl, that nightly hoots, and wonders
> At our quaint spirits.[2]   Sing me now to sleep;
> Then to your offices, and let me rest."

Milton gives a most beautiful and accurate description of the little green-coats of his native soil, than which nothing can be more happily or justly expressed : he had certainly seen them in this situation with "the poet's eye "—

> " Fairy elves,
> Whose midnight revels, by a forest side

---

[1] Thus, also, in The Merry Wives of Windsor—

> "You moonshine revellers, and shades of night."

[2] Sports.

Or fountain, some belated peasant sees,
Or dreams he sees, while overhead the moon,
Sits arbitress, and neerer to the earth
Wheels her pale course, they, on thir mirth and dance
Intent, with jocond music charm his ear ;
At once with joy and fear his heart rebounds." [1]

The impression they made upon his imagination in
early life appears from his " Vacation exercise," at the
age of nineteen—

" Good luck befriend thee, son ; for, at thy birth,
The FAIERY LADIES daunc't upon the hearth ;
The drowsie nurse hath sworn she did them spie,
Come tripping to the room where thou didst lie ;
And sweetly singing round about thy bed,
Strew all their blessings on thy sleeping head."

L'Abbé Bourdelon, in his " Ridiculous Extrava-
gances of M. Oufle," describes " the fairies, of which,"
he says, " grandmothers and nurses tell so many tales
to children ; these fairies," adds he, " I mean, who
are affirmed to be blind at home, and very clear-
sighted abroad ; who dance in the moonshine, when
they have nothing else to do ; who steal shepherds
and children, to carry them up to their caves, &c." [2]

The fairies have already called themselves *spirits*,
ghosts, or *shadows*, and consequently THEY NEVER
DIED—a position, at the same time, of which there is
every kind of proof that a fact can require. The

---

[1] Paradise Lost, b. i.
[2] English translation, p. 190. He cites, in a note, that Cor-
nelius van Kempen assures us, that in the reign of the Emperor
Lotharius, about the year 830, there appeared in Friesland a
great number of fairies, who took up their residence in caves, or
on the tops of hills and mountains, whence they descended in
the night to steal away the shepherds from their flocks, snatch
away children out of their cradles, and carry both away to their
caves : referring to Bekker's World Bewitched, p. i. 290.
These fairies only agree with ours in their fondness for children.

reviser of Johnson and Steevens' edition of "Shakespeare," in 1785, crows not a little upon his dunghill
at having been able to turn the tables upon his adver-
sary by a ridiculous reference to the allegories of
Spenser, and a palpably false one to Tickell's " Kensington Gardens," which, he affirms, "will show that
the opinion of fairies dying prevailed in the present
century," whereas, in fact, "it" is found, on the
slightest glance into the poem, to maintain the direct
reverse—

> " Meanwhile sad Kenna, loath to quit the grove,
> Hung o'er the body of her breathless love,
> Try'd every art (vain arts !) to change his doom,
> And vow'd (vain vows !) to join him in the tomb.
> What could she do, THE FATES ALIKE DENY
> THE DEAD TO LIVE, or FAIRY FORMS TO DIE."

Ashamed, however, of the public detection of his
falsehood, he meanly omitted it in the next edition,
without having a single word to allege in his defence,
though he had still the confidence to represent it as
"a misfortune to the commentators of Shakespeare
that so much of their [invaluable] time is obliged [for
the sake of money] to be employed in explaining [by
absurdity] and contradicting [by falsehood] unfounded
conjectures and assertions ;" which, in fact (unfounded
if they were, as is by no means true), though he was
hardy enough to contradict, he was unable to explain,
and did not, in reality, understand, contenting himself
with an extract altogether foreign to the purpose, at
second-hand.

The fact, after all, is so positively proved, that no
editor or commentator of Shakespeare, present or
future, will ever have the folly or impudence to assert
" that in Shakespeare's time the notion of fairies dying
was generally known."

Ariosto informs us (in . Harington's " Translation,"
b. x. s. 47) that—

> " (Either auncient folke believ'd a lie,
> Or this is true) A FAYRIE CANNOT DIE ; "

and again (b. xliii. s. 92)—

> " I AM A FAYRIE, and, to make you know,
> To be a fayrie what it doth import,
> WE CANNOT DYE, how old so ear we grow.
> Of paines and harmes of ev'rie other sort
> We tast, onelie NO DEATH WE NATURE OW."

Beaumont and Fletcher, in " The Faithful Shep-
herdess," describe—

> " A virtuous well, about whose flow'ry banks
> The nimble-footed fairies dance their rounds,
> By the pale moon-shine, dipping oftentimes
> Their stolen children, SO TO MAKE 'EM FREE
> FROM DYING FLESH, AND DULL MORTALITY."

Puck, *alias* Robin Good-fellow, is the most active
and extraordinary fellow of a fairy that we anywhere
meet with ; and it is believed we find him nowhere
but in our own country, and, peradventure also, only
in the south. Spenser, it would seem, is the first that
alludes to his name of Puck—

> " Ne let the *Pouke*, nor other evil spright,
> Ne let Hob-goblins, names whose sense we see not,
> Fray us with things that be not." [1]

" In our childhood," says Reginald Scot, " our
mothers' maids have so terrified us with an oughe
divell, having hornes on his head, fier in his mouth,
and a taile in his breech, eies like a bason, fanges like
a dog, clawes like a beare, a skin like a niger, and a
voice roaring like a lion, whereby we start, and are

---

[1] Epithalamium.

C

afraid when we heare one crie Bough! and they have
so fraied us with bull-beggers, spirits, witches, urchens,
elves, hags, fairies, satyrs, pans, sylens, Kit with the
cansticke, tritons, centaurs, dwarfes, giants, imps,
calcars, conjurors, nymphes, changling, *Incubus*, ROBIN
GOOD-FELLOW, the spoorne, the mare, the man in the
oke, the hell wain, the fier drake, the puckle,[1] Tom
Thombe, Hob gobblin,[2] Tom Tumbler, boneless, and
such other bugs, that we are afraid of our owne
shadowes."[3] "And know you this by the waie," he
says, "that heretofore Robin Good-fellow and Hob
goblin were as terrible, and also as credible, to the
people as hags and witches be now. . . . And, in
truth, they that mainteine walking spirits have no
reason to denie Robin Good-fellow, upon whom there
hath gone as manie, and as credible, tales, as upon
witches; saving that it hath not pleased the translators of the Bible to call spirits by the name of Robin
Good-fellow."[4]

"Your grandams' maides," he says, "were woont
to set a boll of milke before '*Incubus*,' and his
cousine Robin Good-fellow, for grinding of malt or
mustard, and sweeping the house at midnight; and
you have also heard that he would chafe exceedingly
if the maid or goodwife of the house, having compassion of his nakedness, laid anie clothes for him,
beesides his messe of white bread and milke, which
was his standing fee. For in that case he saith, What
have we here?

---

[1] Perhaps a typographical error for Pucke.
[2] Not, as Mr Tyrwhitt has supposed, *Hop goblin*, *Hob* being a
well-known diminutive of *Robin ;* and even this learned gentleman seems to have forgotten a still more notorious character of
his own time,—Hob *in the well.*
[3] Discoverie of Witchcraft, London, 1584, 4to, p. 153.
[4] P. 131.

" Hemton hamten,
Here will I never more tread nor stampen." [1]

Robin is thus characterised, in the " Midsummer-Night's Dream," by a female fairy—

" Either I mistake your shape and making quite,
Or else you are that shrewd and knavish sprite
Call'd Robin Good-fellow ; are you not he
That fright the maidens of the villagery,
Skim milk, and sometimes labour in the quern,
And bootless make the breathless housewife churn,
And sometime make the drink to bear ne barm,
Mislead night-wanderers, laughing at their harm?
Those that Hob-goblin call you and sweet Puck, [2]
You do their work, and they shall have good luck."

To these questions Robin thus replies—

" Thou speak'st aright,
I am that merry wanderer of the night.
I jest to Oberon, and make him smile,
When I a fat, and bean-fed horse beguile,
Neighing in likeness of a filly foal :
And sometimes lurk I in a gossip's bowl,
In very likeness of a roasted crab ;
And, when she drinks, against her lips I bob,
And on her wither'd dewlap pour the ale.
The wisest aunt, telling the saddest tale,
Sometime for three-foot stool mistaketh me,
Then slip I from her bum, down topples she,
And 'rails or ' cries, [3] and falls into a cough,
And then the whole quire hold their hips and lough,

---

[1] Discoverie of Witchcraft, p. 85.
[2] *Puck*, in fact.
[3] This is Warburton's reading, which has surely more sense than the apparently corrupted reading of the old and new editions, "*tailor* cries," which Doctor Johnson miserably attempts to defend by asserting that "the trick of the fairy is represented as producing rather merriment than anger." Had, however, the worthy doctor ever chanced to fall by the removal from under him of a three-foot stool, it is very doubtful whether he himself would have expressed much pleasure on feeling the

And 'yexen'[1] in their mirth, and neeze, and swear
A merrier hour was never wasted there."

His usual exclamation in this play is *Ho, ho, ho!*

" *Ho, ho, ho!* Coward, why com'st thou not ?"[2]

So in " Grim, the Collier of Croydon "—

" *Ho, ho, ho,* my masters! No good fellowship !"

In the song printed by Peck, he concludes every
stanza with *Ho, ho, ho!*
" If that the bowle of curds and creame were not
duly set out for Robin Good-fellow, the frier,[3] and
Sisse the dairy-maid, why then either the pottage was
burnt-to next day in the pot, or the cheeses would not
curdle, or the butter would not come, or the ale in
the fat never would have good head.   But if a Peter-
penny, or an housle-egge were behind, or a patch of
tythe unpaid, then 'ware of bull-beggars, spirits, &c."

This frolicsome spirit thus describes himself in
Jonson's masque of " Love Restored :" " Robin
Good-fellow, he that sweeps the hearth and the
house clean, riddles for the country-maids, and does

---

pain of the fall, and finding himself the laughing-stock of the
whole company. He would have been more ready, like the
frogs in the fable, to exclaim, " This may be *sport* to you, but it
is *death* to me."   The old woman had both reason to *rail* and
cry, as she would naturally suspect the stool had been plucked
from under her just as she was going to sit down ; than which
there cannot well be a more disagreeable accident, as the incredulous reader who doubts the fact may be easily convinced
of, by trying the experiment.
    [1] *Xexen* is to *hiccup*, a much better reading than *waxen*.   It
was originally suggested by Dr Farmer, but never adopted.
    [2] It is officiously altered, in the last edition, to *Ho, ho!
ho, ho!*
    [3] Friar Rush.

all their other drudgery while they are at hot cockles;
one that has conversed with your court-spirits ere
now." Having recounted several ineffectual attempts
he had made to gain admittance, he adds : " In this
despair, when all invention, and translation too, failed
me, I e'en went back, and stuck to this shape you see
me in of mine own, with my *broom* and my *canles*,
and came on confidently." The mention of his *broom*
reminds us of a passage in another play, "Midsummer-
Night's Dream," where he tells the audience—

> " I am sent with *broom* before,
> To sweep the dust behind the door."

He is likewise one of the *dramatis personæ* in the
old play of "Wily Beguiled," in which he says :
"Tush ! fear not the dodge : I'll rather put on my
flashing-red nose, and my flaming face, and come
wrap'd in a calf-skin, and cry *Bo, bo:* I'll pay the
scholar, I warrant thee." [1] His character, however,
in this piece is so diabolical, and so different from
anything one could expect in Robin Good-fellow,
that it is unworthy of further quotation.

He appears, likewise, in another, entitled "Grim,
the Collier of Croydon," in which he enters "in a suit
of leather close to his body, his face and hands
coloured russet-colour, with a 'flail.'"

He is here, too, in most respects the same strange
and diabolical personage that he is represented in
"Wily Beguiled," only there is a single passage which
reminds us of his old habits :—

> " When as I list in this transform'd disguise
> I'll fright the country people as I pass ;
> And sometimes turn me to some other form,

---

[1] Harsnet's Declaration, London, 1604, 4to.

> And so delude them with fantastic shews.
> But woe betide the silly dairymaids,
> For I shall fleet their cream-bowls night by night."

In another scene he enters while some of the other characters are at a bowl of cream, upon which he says—

> " I love a mess of cream as well as they,
> I think it were best I stept in and made one :
> Ho, ho, ho, my masters ! No good fellowship !
> Is Robin Good-fellow a bugbear grown,
> That he is not worthy to be bid sit down ? "

There is, indeed, something characteristic in this passage, but all the rest is totally foreign.

Dr Percy, Bishop of Dromore, has reprinted, in his " Reliques of Ancient English Poetry," a very curious and excellent old ballad, originally published by Peck—who attributes it, but with no similitude, to Ben Jonson—in which Robin Good-fellow relates his exploits with singular humour.   To one of these copies, he says, " were prefixed two wooden cuts which seem to represent the dresses in which this whimsical character was formerly exhibited upon the stage."   In this conjecture, however, the learned and ingenious editor was most egregiously mistaken, these cuts being manifestly printed from the identical blocks made use of by Bulwer in his " Artificial Changeling," printed in 1653, the first being intended for one of the black-and-white gallants of Seale-bay, adorned with the moon, stars, &c. ; the other a hairy savage. After this discovery, originally made by the present compiler, the right reverend prelate changes his tone, but cannot prevail upon himself to part entirely with the dear illusion.   Having mentioned that these two wooden cuts are " said to be taken from Bulwer's ' Artificial Changeling,' &c. [a book, by the way, of easy access, and probably enough in his lordship's own possession], which, as they seem to correspond ['Seems! I know not seems'] with the notions then entertained of the whimsical appearances of this fantastic spirit, and PERHAPS were copied in the dresses in which he was formerly exhibited on the stage, are, to gratify the CURIOUS [with an imposture] engraven below." Nothing, surely, was ever more ridiculous and contemptible ; we know by these extracts how "he was formerly exhibited upon the stage," and that it was not like a *Seale-bay gallant* or *hairy savage;* and moreover, that these blocks, manifestly engraved for Bulwer's work, in which are many others of the same kind, were calculated merely to give an idea of some barbarous nations in foreign parts, and could not possibly have the most slight or distant allusion to the English stage. How, therefore, durst this learned but pertinacious prelate (as, whatever he was when he first published his book, he is now, when he has given a new edition with alterations and additions) affirm that "ALL CONFIDENCE [had] BEEN DESTROYED" by the inadvertent transposition of *two syllables*, and the omission of *a note of interrogation*, and that only in the preface to a book, in which the passage occurs ACCURATELY PRINTED ; which passage, by the way, he himself, "being quoting," as he pretends, "from memory" (though he is not willing to allow a similar apology to any one else, in the same case), had already corrupted, "the better," in his own words, "to favour a position" that "Maggy Lawder" is an "old song."

Burton, speaking of fairies, says that "a bigger kind there is of them, called with Hobgoblins, and Robin Good-fellowes, that would in those superstitious times grinde corne for a messe of milke, cut wood, or do any kind of drudgery worke." Afterward, of the deemons that mislead men in the night, he says, " We commonly call them Pucks." [1]

Cartwright, in " The Ordinary," introduces Moth, repeating this curious charm—

> " Saint Francis, and Saint Benedight,
> Blesse this house from wicked wight ;
> From the night-mare, and the goblin
> That is hight GOOD-FELLOW ROBIN ;
> Keep it from all evil spirits,
> FAIRIES, weezels, rats, and ferrets :
> From curfew-time,
> To the next prime." [2]

This Puck, or Robin Good-fellow, seems likewise to be the illusory candle-holder so fatal to travellers, and who is more usually called *Jack-a-lantern*, or *Will-with-a-wisp;* and as it would seem from a passage elsewhere cited from Scot, " *Kit with the canstick.*" Thus a fairy, in a passage of Shakespeare already quoted, asks Robin—

> " Are you not he
> That fright the maidens of the villagery,
> Mislead night-wanderers, laughing at their harm ?"

Milton alludes to the deceptive gleam in the following lines—

> " A wandering fire,
> Compact of unctuous vapour, which the night
> Condenses and the cold environs round,
> Kindled through agitation to a flame,
> Which oft, they say, some EVIL SPIRIT attends,
> Hovering and blazing with delusive light,
> Misleads th' amaz'd night-wanderer from his way
> To bogs and mires, and oft through pond and pool." [3]

---

[1] Anatomy of Melancholie. [2] Act iii. sc. r.
[3] Paradise Lost, b. ix. This great poet is frequently content to pilfer a happy expression from Shakespeare : on this occasion " *night-wanderer,*" on a former " *the easterngate.*"

He elsewhere calls him "the frier's lantern."[1] This facetious spirit only misleads the benighted traveller (generally an honest farmer, in his way from the market in a state of intoxication) for the joke's sake, as one very seldom, if ever, hears any of his deluded followers (who take it to be the torch of Hero in some hospitable mansion, affording "provision for man and horse") perishing in these ponds or pools, through which they dance or plunge after him so merrily.

"There go as manie tales," says Reginald Scot, "upon Hudgin, in some parts of Germanie, as there did in England of Robin Good-fellow. . . . Frier Rush was for all the world such another fellow as this Hudgin, and brought up even in the same schoole—to wit, in a kitchen—insomuch as the selfsame tale is written of the one as of the other concerning the skullian, who is said to have beene slaine, &c., for the reading whereof I referre you to frier Rush his story, or else to John Wierus, *De præstigiis demonum.*"[2]

In the old play of "Gammer Gurton's Needle," printed in 1575, Hodge, describing a "great black devil" which had been raised by Diccon, the bedlam, and being asked by Gammer—

"But, Hodge, had he no horns to push?"

replies—

" As long as your two arms. Saw ye never FRYER RUSHE,
Painted on a cloth, with a side-long cowes tayle,
And crooked cloven feet, and many a hoked nayle?

---

[1] *L'Allegro—*
"And by the *frier's lantern* led."

[2] Discoverie of Witchcraft, p. 521. The Historie of Frier Rushe, a common stall or chap book in the time of Queen Elizabeth, and even down to the fire of London, since which event it has rarely been met with. The story of Hudgin will be found among the tales.

For al the world (if I schuld judg) chould reckon him his
   brother;
Loke even what face Frier Rush had, the devil had such
   another."

The fairies frequented many parts of the bishopric
of Durham. There is a hillock, or *tumulus*, near
Bishopton, and a large hill near Billingham, both
which used in former time to be "haunted by fairies."
Even *Ferry-hill*, a well-known stage between Dar-
lington and Durham, is evidently a corruption of
Fairy-hill. When seen, by accident or favour, they
are described as of the smallest size, and uniformly
habited in green. They could, however, occasionally
assume a different size and appearance ; as a woman,
who had been admitted into their society, challenged
one of the guests, whom she espied in the market
selling fairy-butter.[1] This freedom was deeply re-
sented, and cost her the eye she first saw him with.
Mr Brand mentions his having met with a *man* who
said he had seen *one* that had seen *fairies.* Truth, he
adds, is to come at in most cases ; none ever came
nearer to it, in this, than he has done. However that
may be, the present editor cannot pretend to have
been more fortunate. His informant related that an
acquaintance in Westmoreland, having a great desire,
and praying earnestly to see a fairy, was told by a
friend, if not a fairy in disguise, that on the side of
such a hill, at such a time of day, he should have a
sight of one ; and accordingly, at the time and place
appointed, "the hobgoblin," in his own words, "stood
before him in the likeness of a green-coat lad ;" but,
in the same instant, the spectator's eye glancing,

---

[1] This is well known, and frequently found on old trees,
gate-posts, &c.

vanished into the hill. This, he said, the man told him.

The streets of Newcastle, says Mr Brand, "were formerly (so vulgar tradition has it) haunted by a nightly *guest*, which appeared in the shape of a mastiff dog, &c., and terrified such as were afraid of shadows. I have heard," he adds, "when a boy, many stories concerning it." It is to be lamented that, as this gentleman was endeavouring to illustrate a very dull book, on this and similar subjects, he did not think it worth his while to make it a little more interesting, or at least amusing, by a few of these pleasant tales.

The no less famous *barguest*[1] of Durham, and the Picktree-*brag*, have been already alluded to. The former, beside its many other pranks, would sometimes, at the dead of night, in passing through the different streets, set up the most horrid and continuous shrieks, in order to scare the poor girls who might happen to be out of bed. The compiler of the present sheets remembers, when very young, to have heard a very respectable old woman, then a midwife at Stockton, relate that when in her youthful days she was a servant at Durham, being up late one Saturday night, cleaning the irons in the kitchen, she heard these *skrikes*, first at a great, and then at a less, distance, till at length the loudest and most horrible that can be conceived, just at the kitchen window, sent her up-stairs she did not know how, where she fell into the arms of a fellow-servant, who could scarcely prevent her fainting away.

" Pioners or diggers for metal," according to Lavater, " do affirme, that in many mines there appeare

---

[1] The etymology of this word is most probably from the Saxon buɲᴣ, a city, and ᴣaʃᴛ, a spirit; or possibly from a *bar*, or gate, in York, which was likewise once haunted by a goblin of this name.

straunge shapes and spirites, who are apparelled like
unto other laborers in the pit. These wander up and
down in caves and underminings, and seeme to be-
stuire themselves in alle kinde of labour, as to digge
after the veine, to carrie togither oare, to put it in
baskets, and to turne the winding-whele to drawe it
up, when, in very dede, they do nothing lesse. They
very seldome hurte the laborers (as they say) except
they provoke them by laughing and rayling at them ;
for then they threw gravel stones at them, or hurt
them by some other means. These are especially
haunting in pittes where mettall moste aboundeth."[1]
This is our great Milton's

" Swart faëry of the mine."[2]

"Simple foolish men imagine, I know not howe,
that there be certayne elves or fairies of the earth,
and tell many straunge and marvellous tales of them,
which they have heard of their grandmothers and
mothers, howe they have appeared unto those of the
house, have done service, have rocked the cradell,
and (which is a signe of good lucke) do continually
tary in the house."[3]

Mallet, though without citing any authority, says :

---

[1] Of Ghostes, &c. London, 1572, 4to, p. 73. He has this
from Sebastian Munster : see Olaus Magnus, lib. vi. c. x.
George Agricola, however, is the original author, whose words
are : " *Utut jocamur genus certè* dæmonum *in fodinis nonnullis
versari compertum est ;* quorum quidem nihil damni metallicis
inferunt, sed in puteis vagant, videntur se exercere : nunc
cavando venam, nunc ingerendo in modulos id quod effossum
est, nunc machinam versando tractoriam, nunc irritando opera-
rios, idque potissimum faciunt in his specubus è quibus multum
argenti effoditur, vel magna ejus inveniendi spes est."—Ber-
mannus, 432. He calls this *dæmon metallicus ;* in German,
" *Das bergmelin.*"

[2] Comus.   [3] Of Ghostes, &c., p. 49.

" After all, the notion is not everywhere exploded that there are in the bowels of the earth fairies, or a kind of dwarfish and tiny beings of human shape, and remarkable for their riches, their activity, and malevolence. In many countries of the north, the people are still firmly persuaded of their existence. In Ireland at this day the good folks show the very rocks and hills, in which they maintain that there are swarms of these small subterraneous men, of the most tiny size, but the most delicate figures." [1]

Sheringham, having mentioned the gods of the Germans, adds : " Among us, truly, this superstition and foolish credulity among the vulgar is not yet left off; for I know not what fables old women suggest to boys and girls about elves (with us by another word called fairies), by which their tender minds they so imbue, that they never depose these old-wifish ravings, but deliver them to others, and vulgarly affirm that groups of elves sometimes dance in bed-chambers, sometimes (that they may benefit the maids) scour and cleanse the pavement, and sometimes are wont to grind with a hand-mill." [2]

---

[1] Northern Antiquities, &c., ii. 47.

[2] De Anglorum Origine, p. 320. This is the observation of a gloomy and malignant mind, as the idea of a fairy could never inspire any but pleasing sensations, these little people being always distinguished for their innocent mirth and benevolent utility. It was far otherwise, indeed, with *superstition* and *witchcraft*, which, though equally false, were nevertheless as firmly believed, as they induced ignorance and bigotry to commit horrid crimes ; but nothing of this kind is imputable to the fairies. So strongly, according to Waldron, are the Manks possessed of the belief of fairies, and so frequently do they imagine to have seen and heard them, that they are not in the least terrified at them, but, on the contrary, rejoice whenever visited by them, as supposing them friends to mankind, and that they never come without bringing good fortune along with them.

There is not a more generally-received opinion throughout the principality of Wales than that of the existence of fairies ; amongst the commonality it is indeed universal, and by no means unfrequently credited by the second ranks.[1]

Fairies are said, at a distant period, "to have frequented Busser's Hill in St Mary's Island ; but their nightly pranks, aërial gambols, and cockle-shell abodes are now quite unknown."[2]

"Evil spirits, called fairies, are frequently seen in several of the isles [of Orkney], dancing, and making merry, and sometimes seen in armour."[3]

They call them *the good people*, all the houses are blessed where they visit. The Scots, likewise, call them *the good neighbours*.

[1] Pratt's Gleanings, &c., i. 137. He mentions a Welsh clergyman who not only believes in fairies, but is even so infatuated on the subject as to imagine they are continually in his presence, and has written a book about them.

[2] Heath's Account of the Islands of Scilly, p. 129.

[3] Brand's Description of Orkney, Edin. 1703, p. 61 : at p. 112 is some account of a *brouny*.

III.

Romance of Launfal.

———o———

ALTHOUGH there is little to be found of an earlier date than the sixteenth century that bears directly upon the popular notions of fairy mythology, as Shakespeare has embodied them in " A Midsummer - Night's Dream," yet it would not be easy to develop the gradual transitions which took place in public belief in those matters, without presenting the reader with the earliest documents on the subject that have descended to our times. Reserving more detailed observations for our Introduction, it will only be necessary to observe that there probably is no absolute connection between Tryamour, the daughter of Olyroun, and Titania. Tryamour is minutely described : we see in her a maiden of wonderful beauty, and possessed of superior powers ; but still there is not Shakespeare's idea of a fairy princess, and we might perhaps have failed to recognise the description, had the poet forgotten to inform us that her father was " Kyng of Fayrye." The romance of Launfal is one of the earliest pieces of the kind known to exist. It is translated from a French original written by the celebrated Marie de France, and is here given from MS. Cott. Calig. a. ii., the text adopted by Ritson ; and also in Way's " Fabliaux," ed.

1815, iii. 233-287. A later copy, written about 1508, is in MS. Rawl. c. lxxxvi., differing considerably from our text, but of course of less authority. See the extracts at the end of this article. It was printed in the sixteenth century, having been licensed to John Kynge in 1558, and mentioned in "Laneham's Letter," 1575, but I am not aware that any perfect copy has been preserved. Sir F. Madden mentions another copy in MS. Lambeth 305, which seems to be an error for the copy of Lybeaus Disconus in MS. No. 306 in the same collection. The author of the present translation was Thomas Chestre, as appears from the concluding lines. It is very seldom that the translators of the early metrical romances have recorded their names, and in more than one instance a mere transcriber has been handed down for years in the list of our early poets.

LAUNFALE MILES.

Be douȝty Artours dawes,
That held Engelond yn good lawes,
   There felle a wondyre cas
Of a ley that was y-sette,
That hyȝt Launval, and hatte ȝette ;
   Now herkeneth how hyt was.
Douȝty Artoure som whyle
Sojournede yn Kardevyle,[1]

---

[1] That is, Carlisle in Cumberland, according to Ritson. The old romance of Merlin calls it "la ville de Carduil en Galles ;" and the French MS. says "Kardoyl," apparently a corruption for Cairleon in Wales. At the commencement of the French romance ("Lai de Lanval, Poes. de Marie de France," ed. Roquefort, 8vo, 1820, tom. i. p. 202) we are told—

> "A Cardueill sejurna li reis
> Artus, li prex, e li curteis,
> Pur les Escos, e pur les Pis,
> Qu destruiseient mult le pais."

Wyth joye and greet solas ;
And kny3tes that were profitable,
With Artour, of the rounde table,
Never noon better ther nas.
Sere Persevalle, and syr Gawayn,
Syr Gyheryes, and syr Agrafrayn,
And Launcelet du Lake,
Syr Kay, and syr Ewayn,
That welle couthe fy3te yn playn,
Bateles for to take.
Kyng Ban-Boo3t, and kyng Bos,[1]
Of ham ther was a greet los,
Men sawe tho nowhere her make ;
Syr Galafre, and syr Launfale.
Wherof a noble tale
Among us schalle awake.
With Artoure ther was a bachelere,
And hadde y-be welle many a 3ere,
Launfal for soth he hy3t ;
He gaf gyftys largelyche,
Gold, and sylver, and clodes ryche,
To squyer and to kny3t.
For hys largesse and hys bounté,
The kynges stuward made was he
Ten yer, y you ply3t ;
Of alle the kny3tes of the table rounde
So large ther nas noon y-founde,
Be dayes ne be ny3t.
So hyt be-fylle, yn the tenthe 3ere,
Marlyn was Artours counsalere,
He radde hym fore to wende
To kyng Ryon of Irlond ry3t,
And fette hym ther a lady bry3t,

---

[1] This enumeration of Arthur's knights is not found in the French original.

D

Gwennere [1] hys douȝtyr hende.
So he dede, and hom her brouȝt,
But syr Launfal lykede her noȝt,
    Ne other knyȝtes that wer hende ;
For the lady bar los of swych word,
That sche hadde lemmannys unther her lord,
    So fele there nas noon ende.
They were y-wedded, as y you say,
Upon a Wytsonday,
    Before princes of moch pryde ;
No man ne may telle yn tale
What folk ther was at that bredale,
    Of countreys fer and wyde ;
No nother man was yn halle y-sette,
But he were prelat, other baronette,
    In herte ys naȝt to hyde :
Yf they satte noȝt alle y-lyke,
Hare servyse was good and ryche,
    Certeyne yn ech a syde.
And whan the lordes hadde ete yn the halle,
And the clothes wer drawen alle,
    As ye mowe her and lythe,
The botelers sentyn wyn
To alle the lordes that were theryn,
    With chere bothe glad and blythe.
The quene yaf y yftes for the nones,
Gold and selver, and precyous stonys,
    Her curtasye to kythe ;
Everych knyȝt sche ȝaf broche and ryng,
But syr Launfal sche yaf no thyng,

---

[1] According to Geoffrey of Monmouth, Guenever was descended from a noble Roman family, and in beauty surpassed all the women in the island. She is usually represented as the paramour of Sir Launcelot, and, according to Caradoc, was ravished by Melvas, King of Estiva, now Somersetshire.

That grevede hym many a syde.
And whan the bredale was at ende,
Launfal tok hys leve to wende
   At Artour the kyng,
And seyde a lettere was to hym come,
That deth hadde hys fadyr y-nome,
   He most to hys beryynge.
Tho seyde kyng Artour, that was hende,
Launfal, yf thou wylt fro me wende,
   Tak with the greet spendyng;[1]
And my suster sones two,
Bothe they schulle with the go,
   At hom the for to bryng.
Launfal tok leve, withoute fable,
With kny3tes of the rounde table,
   And wente forth yn hys journé
Tyl he com to Karlyoun,[2]
To the meyrys hous of the toune,
   Hys servaunt that hadde y-be.
The meyr stod, as ye may here,
And sawe hym come ryde up anblere
   With two kny3tes and other mayné;
Agayns hym he hath wey y-nome,
And seyde, "Syre, thou art welle-come,
   How faryth oure kyng tel me."
Launfal answerede and seyde than,
" He faryth as welle as any man,

---

[1] It is probably implied that Launfal refused this offer, as we find him shortly afterwards in great poverty at Caerleon. In the French original, Launfal is made to quit the king's court because he had impoverished himself by his extravagance and generosity.

[2] This shows that *Kardevyle* in the first stanza cannot be Caerleon, as has been conjectured. In the romance of Geraint the Son of Erbin, Arthur's court is held at Caerlleon upon Usk. See Lady C. Guest's edition of the Mabinogion, part iii.

And elles greet ruth hyt wore ;
But, syr meyr, without lesyng,
I am thepartyth fram the kyng,
   And that rewyth me sore :
Ne ther thare no man benethe ne above,
Fore the kyng Artours love,
   Onowre me never more :
But, syr meyr, y pray the par amour,
May y take with the sojour?
   Som tyme ye knewe us yore."
The meyr stod, and betho3te hym there
What my3t be hys answere,
   And to hym than gan he sayn,
" Syr, vij. kny3tes han here hare in y-nome,
And ever y wayte whan they wyl come,
   That arn of Lytylle-Bretayne."
Launfal turnede hymself and low3,
Therof he hadde scorn i-now3,
   And seyde to hys kny3tes tweyne,
" Now may ye se swych ys service, ·
Unther a lord of lytylle pryse,
   How ye may therof be fayn."
Launfal awayward gan to ryde,
The meyr bad he schuld abyde,
   And seyde yn thys manere,
" Syr, yn a chamber by my orchard syde,
Ther may ye dwelle with joye and pryde,
   3yf hy't your wylle were."
Launfal anoon-ry3tes,
He and hys two knytes
   Sojournede ther yn fere ;
So savagelych hys good he besette,
That he ward yn greet dette,
   Ry3t yn the ferst yere.
So hyt befelle at Pentecost,
Swych tyme as the Holy Gost

Among mankend gan ly3t,
That syr Huwe and syr Jon
Tok here leve for to gon
    At syr Launfal the kny3t.
They seyd, "Syr, our robes beth to-rent,
And your tresour [1] ys alle y-spent,
    And we goth ewylle y-dy3t."
Thanne seyde syr Launfal to the kny3tes fre,
"Tell ye no man of my poverté
    For the love of God almy3t."
The kny3tes answerede and seyde tho,
That they nolde hym wreye never mo,
    Alle thys world to wynne.
With that word they wente hym fro,
To Glastyngbery bothe two,
    Ther kyng Artour was inne.
The kyng saw the kny3tes hende,
The a3ens ham he gan wende,
    For they were of hys kenne :
Noon other robes they ne hadde
Than they out with ham ladde,
    And tho were to-tore and thynne.
Than seyde quene Gwenore, that was fel,
"How faryth the prowde kny3t Launfal?
    May he hys armes welde ?"
"3e, madame," sayde the knytes than,
"He faryth as welle as any man,
    And ellys God hyt schelde."
Moche worchyp and greet honour
To Gonore the quene and kyng Artour
    Of syr Launfal they telde ;
And seyde, "He lovede us so,
That he wold us evermo
    At wylle have y-helde.

---

[1] MS. has *tosour*.

But upon a rayny day hyt befel,
An huntynge wente syr Launfel,
   To chasy yn holtes hore ; [1]
In our old robes we yede that day,
And thus be beth y-went away,
   As we before hym wore."
Glad was Artour the kyng
That Launfal was yn good lykyng,
   The quene hyt rew welle sore ;
For sche wold, with alle her my3t,
That he hadde be, bothe day and ny3t,
   In paynys more and more.
Upon a day of the Trinité
A feste of greet solempnité
   In Carlyoun was holde ;
Erles and barones of that countré,
Ladyes and borjaes of that cité,
   Thyder come bothe yongh and old.
But Launfal for hys poverté
Was not bede to that semblé,
   Lyte men of hym tolde ;
The meyr to the feste was of sent,
The meyrys dou3ter to Launfal went,
   And axede yf he wolde
In halle dyne with her that day.
"Damesele," he sayde, "nay,
   To dyne have I no herte ;
Thre dayes ther ben agon,
Met ne drynke eet y noon,
   And alle was for poverte.
To-day to cherche y wolde have gon,
But me fawtede hosyn and schon,

---

[1] That is, hoary forests. Few expressions are more common in early English metrical romances. See Torrent of Portugal, p. 26.

Clenly brech and scherte ;
And for defawte of clodynge,
Ne myȝte y yn with the peple thrynge,
  No wonther douȝ me smerte !
But o thyng, damesele, y pray the,
Sadel and brydel lene thou me,
  A whyle for to ryde,
That y myȝte confortede be
By a launde unther thys cyté,
  Al yn thys undern-tyde."
Launfal dyȝte hys courser,
Withoute knave other squyer
  He rood with lytylle pryde ;
Hys hors slod and fel yn the fen,
Wherefore hym scornede many men,
  Abowte hym fer and wyde.
Poverly the knȝt to hors gan sprynge,
For to dryve away lokynge,
  He rood toward the west ;
The wether was hot the undern-tyde,
He lyȝte adoun, and gan abyde
  Under a fayr forest ;
And for hete of the wedere,
Hys mantelle he feld togydere,
  And sette hym doun to reste.
Thus sat the knyȝt yn symplyté
In the schadwe unther a tre,
  Ther that hym lykede best.
As he sat yn sorow and sore,
He sawe come out of holtes hore
  Gentylle maydenes two ;
Har kerteles wer of Inde sandel,
I-lased smalle, jolyf and welle,
  Ther myȝt noon gayer go.
Har manteles wer of grene felwet,
Y-bordured with gold ryȝt welle y-sette,

I-pelvred with grys and gro ;
Har heddys were dyȝt welle withalle,
Everych hadde oon a jolyf coronalle,
     Wyth syxty gemmys and mo.
Har faces wer whyt as snow on downe,
Har rode was red, her eyn wer browne,
     I sawe never non swyche ;
That oon bar of gold a basyn,
That other a towayle whyt and fyn,[1]
     Of selk that was good and ryche.
Har kercheves wer well schyre,
Arayd wyth ryche gold wyre.
     Launfal began to syche ;
They com to hym over the hoth,
He was curteys, and aȝens hem goth,
     And greette hem myldelyche,
" Damesels," he seyde, " God yow se ! "
" Syr knyȝt," they sede, " welle the be !
     Our lady, dame Tryamour,
Bad thou schuldest com speke with here,
ȝyf hyt wer thy wylle, sere,
     Wythoute more sojour."
Launfal hem grauntede curteyslyche,
And wente wyth hem myldelyche,
     They weryn whyt as flour ;
And when they come in the forest an hyȝ,
A pavyloun y-teld he syȝ
     With merthe and mochelle honour.
The pavyloun was wrouth for sothe, y-wys,
Alle of werk of Sarsynys,
     The pomelles of crystalle ;

---

[1] See an incident similar to this in the English versions of the
Gesta Romanorum, edited by Sir F. Madden, p. 100. Compare
also Warton, Introduction [Hazlitt's edit. i. 274].

Upon the toppe an ern ther stod,
Of bournede gold ryche and good.
   I-florysched with ryche amalle.
Hys eyn wer carbonkeles bryȝt,
As the mone the schon a nyȝt,
   That spreteth out ovyr alle ;
Alysaundre the conquerour,
Ne kyng Artour, yn hys most honour,
   Ne hadde noon scwych juelle.
He fond yn the pavyloun
The kynges douȝter of Olyroun,
   Dame Tryamour that hyȝte ;
Her fadyr was kyng of fayrye,
Of Occient fer and nyȝe,
   A man of mochelle myȝte.
In the pavyloun he fond a bed of prys,
I-heled with purpur bys,
   That semylé was of syȝte ;
Therinne lay that lady gent,
That after syr Launfal hedde y-sent,
   That lefsom lemede bryȝt.
For hete her clothes down sche dede
Almest to her gerdyl stede,
   Than lay sche uncovert ;
Sche was as whyt as lylye yn May,
Or snow that sneweth yn wynterys day,
   He seygh never non so pert.
The rede rose, whan sche ys newe,
Aȝens her rode nes naȝt of hewe,
   I dar welle say yn sert ;[1]

---

[1] The whole of this description of the fairy princess and her lover is superior to most other things of the kind composed in English at the same period, yet much inferior to the French original. Compare the extract given by Warton from Adam Davie's poem.

Her here schon as gold wyre,
May no man rede here atyre,
 Ne nauȝt welle thenke yn hert.
Sche seyde, " Launfal, my lemman swete,
Al my joye for the y lete,
 Swetyng paramour ;
Ther nys no man yn Cristenté,
That y love so moche as the,
 Kyng neyther emperoure."
Launfal beheld that swete wyȝth,
Alle hys love yn her was lyȝth,
 And keste that swete flour ;
And sat adoun her bysyde,
And seyde, " Swetyng, what so betyde,
 I am to thyn honoure."
She seyde, " Syr knyȝt, gentyl and hende,
I wot thy stat, ord, and ende,
 Be nauȝt aschamed of me ;
Yf thou wylt truly to me take,
And alle wemen for me forsake,
 Ryche I wylle make the :
I wylle the ȝeve an alner,
I-mad of sylk and of gold cler,
 With fayre ymages thre ;
As oft thou puttest the hond therinne,[1]
A mark of gold thou schalt wynne,
 In wat place that thou be."
Also sche seyde, " Syr Launfal,
I ȝeve the Blaunchard my stede lel,
 And Gyfre my owen knave :
And of my armes oo pensel,
Wyth thre ermyns y-peynted welle,
 Also thou schalt have.

---

[1] The multiplication of riches by invisible agency is a very
favourite fiction in Oriental romance.

In werre, ne yn turnement,
Ne schalle the greve no knyȝtes dent,
  So welle y schalle the save."
Than answerede the gantyl knyȝt,
And seyde, "Gramarcy, my swete wyȝt,
  No bettere kepte y have."
The dameselle gan her up sette,
And bad her maydenes her fette
  To hyr hondys watyr clere;
Hyt was y-do without lette,
The cloth was spred, the bord was sette,
  They wente to hare sopere.
Mete and drynk they hadde a-fyn,
Pyement, claré, and Reynysch wyn,
  And elles greet wondyr hyt wer :
Whan they had sowpeth and the day was gon,
They wente to bedde, and that anoon,
  Launfal and sche yn fere.
For play lytylle they sclepte that nyȝt,
Tylle on morn hyt was day-lyȝt,
  Sche badd hym aryse anoon;
Hy seyde to hym, "Syr, gantyl knyȝt,
And thou wylt speke with me any wyȝt,
  To a derne stede thou gon ;
Welle privyly I wolle come to the,
No man alyve ne schalle me se,
  As stylle as any ston."
Tho was Launfal glad and blythe,
He cowde no man hys joye kythe,
  And keste her welle good won.
"But of o thyng, syr knyȝt, I warne the,
That thou make no bost of me,
  For no kennes mede ;[1]

---

[1] The reader will find a similar injunction in the ballad of
Thomas of Ercildoun, hereafter printed.

And yf thou doost, y warn the before,
Alle my love thou hast forlore : "
    And thus to hym sche seyde.
Launfal tok hys leve to wende,
Gyfre kedde that he was hende,
    And brouȝt Launfal hys stede :
Launfal lepte ynto the arsoun,
And rood hom to Karlyoun
    In hys pover wede.
Tho was the knyȝt yn herte at wylle,
In hys chaunber he hyld hym stylle
    Alle that undern-tyde ;
Than come ther thorwgh the cyté ten
Welle y-harneysyth men,
    Upon ten somers ryde ;
Some wyth sylver, some wyth gold,
Alle to syr Launfal hyt schold,
    To presente hym wyth pryde ;
Wyth ryche clothes, and armure bryȝt,
They axede aftyr Launfal the knyȝt,
    Whar he gan abyde.
The yong men wer clodeth yn ynde,
Gyfre he rood alle behynde,
    Up Blaunchard whyt as flour ;
Tho seyde a boy that yn the market stod,
" How fere schalle alle thys good ?
    Telle us par amour."
Tho seyde Gyfre, " Hyt ys y-sent
To syr Launfal yn present,
    That hath leved yn greet dolour."
Than seyde the boy, "Nys he but a wrecche ? [1]
What thare any man of hym recche ?
    At the meyrys hous he taketh sojour."

---

[1] Ellis's mistake of printing these two words as a verb *awrecche* is rather violently handled by Ritson, Met. Rom. iii. 251.

At the meyrys hous they gon alyȝte,
And presented the noble knyȝte
   With swych good as hym was sent ;
And whan the meyr seyȝ that rychesse,
And syr Launfales noblenesse,
   He held hymself foule y-schent.
Tho seyde the meyr, " Syr, per charyté,
In halle to day that thou wylt ete with me,
   ȝesterday y hadde y-ment.
At the feste we wold han be yn same,
And y-hadde solas and game,
   And erst thou were y-went."
" Syr meyr, God for-ȝelde the,
Whyles y was yn my poverté,
   Thou bede me never dyne ;
Now y have more gold and fe,
That myne frendes han sent me,
   Than thou and alle dyne."
The meyr for schame away ȝede,
Launfal yn purpure gan hym schrede,
   I-pelvred with whyt ermyne ;
Alle that Launfal hadde borwyth before,
Gyfre be tayle and be score
   ȝald hyt welle and fyne.
Launfal helde ryche festes,
Fyfty fedde povere gestes,
   That yn myschef wer ;
Fyfty bouȝte stronge stedes,
Fyfty yaf ryche wedes
   To knyȝtes and squyere ;
Fyfty rewardede relygyous,
Fyfty delyverede povere prysouns,
   And made ham quyt and schere ;
Fyfty clodede gestours,
To many men he dede honours,
   In countreys fere and nere.

Alle the lordes of Karlyoun
Lette crye a turnement yn the toun,
 For love of syr Launfel,
And for Blaunchard, hys good stede,
To wyte how hym wold spede,
 That was y-made so welle ;
And whan the day was y-come,
That the justes were yn y-nome,
 They ryde out also snelle ;
Trompours gon hare bemes blowe,
The lordes ryden out a rowe,
 That were yn that castelle.
There began the turnement,
And ech kny3t leyd on other good dent
 Wyth mases and wyth swerdes bothe :
Me[n] my3te y-se some therefore
Stedes y-wonne, and some y-lore,
 And k[n]y3tes wonther wro3th.
Syth the rounde table was,
A bettere turnement ther nas,
 I dare welle say for sothe ;
Many a lord of Karlyoun,
That day were y-bore adoun,
 Certavn withouten othe.
Of Karlyoun the ryche constable
Rod to Launfalle, without fable,
 He nolde no lengere abyde :
He smot to Launfal, and he to hym,
Welle sterne strokes, and welle grym,
 Ther wer yn eche a syde.
Launfal was of hym y-ware,
Out of hys sadelle he hym bar
 To grounde that ylke tyde ;
And whan the constable was born adoun,
Gyfre lepte ynto the arsoun,
 And awey he gan to ryde

The erl of Chestere thereof segh,
For wreththe yn herte he was wod negh,
  And rood to syr Launfale,
And smot hym yn the helm on hegh,
That the crest adoun flegh,
  Thus seyd the Frenssch tale.[1]
Launfal was mochel of myȝt,
Of hys stede he dede hym lyȝt,
  And bare hym doun yn the dale ;
Than come they syr Launfal abowte
Of Walssche knyȝtes a greet rowte,
  The numbre y not how fale.
Than myȝte me[n] se scheldes ryve,
Speres to-breste and to-dryve,
  Behynde and ek before ;
Thoruȝ Launfal and hys stedes dent
Many a knyȝt, verement,
  To ground was i-bore.
So the prys of that turnay
Was delyvered to Launfal that day,
  Without oth y-swore :
Launfal rod to Karlyoun,
To the meyrys hous yn the toun,
  And many a lord hym before.
And then the noble knyȝt Launfal
Held a feste ryche and ryalle,
  That leste fourtenyȝt ;
Erles and barouns fale
Semely wer sette yn sale,
  And ryaly were adyȝt.
And every day dame Triamour,
Sche com to syr Launfale bour,

---

[1] Alluding, of course, to the original French text of Launfal, of which there are copies in MS. Harl. 978, and MS. Cott. Vespas. b. xiv. See p. 48.

A-day whan hyt was ny3t.
Of alle that ever wer ther tho,
Segh he[r] non but they two,
    Gyfre and Launfal the kny3t.

PART II.

A kny3t ther was yn Lumbardye,
To syr Launfal hadde he greet envye,
    Syr Valentyne he hy3te ;
He herde speke of syr Launfal.
That [1] he couth justy welle,
    And was a man of mochel my3te,
Syr Valentyne was wonther strong,
Fyftene feet he was longe ;
    Hym tho3te he brente bry3te,
But he my3te with Launfal pleye,
In the feld between ham tweye,
    To justy, other to fy3te.
Syr Valentyne sat yn hys halle,
Hys massengere he let y-calle,
    And seyde he moste wende
To syr Launfal the noble kny3t,
That was y-holde so mychel of my3t,
    To Bretayne he wolde hym sende,
And sey hym, for love of hys lemman,
Yf sche be any gantyle woman,
    Courteys, fre, other hende,
That he come with me to juste,
To kepe hys harneys from the ruste,
    And elles hys manhod schende.
The messengere ys forth y-went
To tho hys lordys commaundement,

---

[1] MS. repeats *that* erroneously.

He hadde wynde at wylle.
Whan he was over the water y-come,
The way to syr Launfal he hath y-nome,
  And grette hym with wordes stylle.
And seyd, " Syr, my lord, syr Valentyne,
A noble werrour, and queynte of gynne,
  Hath me sent the tylle,
And prayth the, for thy lemmanes sake,
Thou schuldest with hym justes take."
  Tho louȝ Launfal fulle stylle,
And seyde, as he was gentyl knyȝt,
Thylke day a fourtenyȝt
  He wold wyth hym play.
He yaf the messenger, for that tydyng,
A noble courser and a ryng,
  And a robe of ray.
Launfal tok leve at Triamour,
That was the bryȝt berde yn boure,
  And keste that swete may;
Thanne seyde that swete wyȝt,
" Dreed the nothyng, syr gentyl knyȝt,
  Thou schalt hym sle that day."
Launfal nolde nothyng with hym have
But Blaunchard hys stede, and Gyfre hys knave,
  Of alle hys fayr mayné ;
He schypede and hadde wynd welle good,
And wente over the salte flod,
  Into Lumbardye.
Whan he was over the water y-come,
There the justes schuld be nome,
  In the cyté of Atalye,
Syr Valentyn hadde a greet ost,
And syr Launfal abatede her bost,
  Wyth lytylle companye.
And whan syr Launfal was y-dyȝt,
Upon Blaunchard hys stede lyȝt,

E

With helm, and spere, and schelde,
Alle that sawe hym yn armes bryȝt,
Seyde they sawe never swych a knyȝt,
   That hym wyth eyen beheld.
Tho ryde togydere thes knyȝtes two,
That har schaftes to-broste bo,
   And to-scyverede yn the felde ;
Another cours togedere they rod,
That syr Launfale helm of glod,
   In tale as hyt ys telde.
Syr Valentyn logh, and hadde good game,
Hadde Launfal never so moche schame
   Beforhond yn no fyȝt ;
Gyfre kedde he was good at nede,
And lepte upon hys maystrys stede,
   No man ne segh with syȝt.
And er than thay togedere mette,
Hys lordes helm he on sette, ,
   Fayre and welle adyȝt ;
Tho was Launfal glad and blythe,
And donkede Gyfre many syde,
   For hys dede so mochel of myȝt.
Syr Valentyne smot Launfal soo,
That hys scheld fel hym fro,
   Anoon-ryȝt yn that stounde ;
And Gyfre the scheld up hente,
And broȝte hyt hys lord to presente,
   Ere hyt cam thoune to grounde.
Tho was Launfal glad and blythe,
And rode ayen the thrydde syde,
   As a knyȝt of mochelle mounde ;
Syr Valentyne he smot so there,
That hors and man bothe deed were,
   Gronyng wyth grysly wounde.
Alle the lordes of Atalye
To syr Launfal hadde greet envye,

That Valentyne was y-slawe,
And swore that he schold dye,
Ere he wente out of Lumbardye,
    And be hongede, and to-drawe.
Syr Launfal brayde out hys fachon,
And as ly3t as dew he leyde hem doune
    In a lytylle drawe.
And whan he hadde the lordes sclayn,
He wente ayen ynto Bretayn
    With solas and wyth plawe.
The tydyng com to Artour the kyng,
Anoon wythout lesyng,
    Of syr Launfales noblesse ;
Anoon a let[1] to hym sende,
That Launfalle schuld to hym wende
    At seynt Jonnys masse.
For kyng Artour wold a feste holde,
Of erles and of barouns bolde,
    Of lordynges more and lesse :
Sir Launfal schud be stward of halle,
For to agye hys gestes alle,
    For cowthe of largesse.
Launfal toke leve at Triamour,
For to wende to kyng Artour,
    Hys feste for to agye ;
Ther he fond merthe and moch honour,
Ladyes that wer welle bry3t yn boure,
    Of kny3tes greet companye.
Fourty dayes leste the feste,
Ryche, ryalle, and honeste,
    What help hyt for to lye ?
And at the fourty dayes ende,
The lordes toke har leve to wende,

---

[1] In the original MS. it is written "alet," which Ritson has corrected to " a letter."

Ever ych yn hys partye.
And aftyr mete syr Gaweyn,
Syr Gyeryes, and Agrafayn,
   And syr Launfal also,
Wente to daunce upon the grene,
Unther the tour ther lay the quene,
   With syxty ladyes and mo.
To lede the daunce Launfal was set,
For hys largesse he was lovede the bet
   Sertayn of alle tho;
The quene lay out and beheld hem alle,
" I se," sche seyde, " daunce large Launfalle,
   To hym than wylle y go.
Of alle the kny3tes that y se there,
He ys the fayreste bachelere,
   He ne hadde never no wyf:
Tyde me good, other ylle,
I wylle go and wyte hys wylle,
   Y love hym as my lyf."
Sche tok with her a companye,
The fayrest that sch[e] my3te aspye,
   Syxty ladyes and fyf;
And wente hem doun anoon-ry3tes,
Ham to pley among the kny3tes,
   Welle stylle wythouten stryf.
The quene yede to the formeste ende,
Betwene Launfal and Gauweyn the hende,
   And after her ladyes bry3t;
To daunce the wente alle yn same,
To se hem play hyt was fayr game,
   A lady and a kny3t.
They hadde menstrales of moch honours,
Fydelers, fytolyrs, and trompours,
   And elles hyt were unry3t:
Ther they playde, for sothe to say,
After mete the somerys day,

All what hyt was ney₃ ny₃t.
And whanne the daunce began to slake,
The quene gan Launfal to counselle take,
 And seyde yn thys manere :[1]
"Sertaynlyche, syr kny₃t,
I have the lovyd wyth alle my my₃t,
 More than thys seven ₃ere.[2]
But that thou lovye me,
Sertes y dye fore love of the,
 Launfal, my lemman dere."
Thanne answerede the gentylle kny₃t,
"I nelle be traytour thay ne ny₃t,
 Be God, that alle may stere."
Sche seyde, "Fy on the, thou coward,
An-hongeth worth thou hye and hard,
 That thou ever were y-bore !
That thou lyvest hyt ys pyté,
Thou lovyst no woman, ne no woman the,
 Thow wer worthy forlore."
The kny₃t was sore aschamed tho,
To speke ne my₃te he forgo,
 And seyde the quene before :
"I have loved a fayryr woman
Than thou ever leydest thy ney upon,
 Thys seven yer and more.
Hyr lothlokste mayde, wythoute wene,
My₃te bet be a quene,
 Than thou yn alle thy lyve."
Therfore the quene was swythe wroth,
Sche taketh hyr maydenes, and forthe hy goth

---

[1] MS. reads *marnere*.
[2] A slight stretch of imagination on the part of Queen Guenever who, as we have before seen, treated Launfal so indignantly
at her marriage, and wished him to be "in paynys more and
more."

Into her tour al so blyve.
And anon sche ley doun yn her bedde,
For wrethe syk sche hyr bredde,
　　And swore, so moste she thryve,
Sche wold of Launfal be so awreke,
That alle the lond schuld of hym speke,
　　Wythinne the dayes fyfe.
Kyng Artour com fro huntynge,
Blythe and glad yn alle thyng,
　　To hys chamber than wente he.
Anoon the quene on hym gan crye,
"But y be awreke, y schalle dye,
　　Myn herte wylle breke athre.
I spak to Launfal yn my game,
And he besoȝte me of schame,[1]
　　My lemman for to be;
And of a lemman hys yelp he made,
That the lodlokest mayde that sche hadde
　　Myȝt be a quene above me."
Kyng Artour was welle wroth,[2]
And be God he swor hys oth,
　　That Launfal schuld be sclawe.
He wente aftyr doȝty knyȝtes,
To brynge Launfal anoon-ryȝtes,
　　To be hongeth and to-drawe.
The knyȝtes soȝte hym anoon,
But Launfal was to hys chanber gon,
　　To han hadde solas and plawe;
He soȝte hys leef, but sche was lore,
As sche hadde warnede hym before,
　　Tho was Launfal un[scl]awe.

---

[1] Few incidents are more common in old romances than this; it may be traced to the history of Joseph and Potiphar's wife in Genesis.　　　[2] *Worth* in MS.

He lokede yn hys alner,
That fond hym spendyng alle plener,
  Whan that he hadde nede,
And ther nas noon, for soth to say,
And Gyfre was y-ryde away
  Up Blaunchard hys stede.
Alle that he hadde before y-wonne,
Hyt malt as snow aȝens the sunne,
  In romaunce as we rede ;
Hys armur, that was whyt as flour,
Hyt becom of blak colour,
  And thus than Launfal seyde :
"Alas," he seyde, "my creature,
How schalle I from the endure,
  Swetyng Tryamoure ?
Alle my joye I have forlore,
And the, that me ys worst fore,
  Thou blysfulle berde yn boure."
He bet hys body and hys hedde ek,
And cursede the mouth that he with spek,
  With care and greet doloure ;
And for sorow, yn that stounde,
Anoon he felle aswowe to grounde,
  With that com knyȝtes foure,
And bond hym, and ladde hym tho,
Tho was the knyȝte yn doble wo,
  Before Artour the kyng.
Than seyde kyng Artour,
"Fyle ataynte traytour !
  Why madest thou swyche yelpyng ?
That thy lemmannes lodlokest mayde
Was fayrer than my wyf, thou seyde,
  That was a fowlle lesynge !
And thou besoȝtest her befor than,
That sche schold be thy lemman,
  That was mysprowd lykynge !"

The knyȝt answerede with egre mode,
Before the kyng ther he stode,
　　The quene on hym gan lye;
"Sethe that y ever was y-born,
I besoȝte her here beforn
　　Never of no folye.
But sche seyde y nas no man,
Ne that me lovede no woman,
　　Ne no womannes companye;
And I answerede her and sayde,
That my lemmannes lodlekest mayde
　　To be a quene was better wordye.
Sertes, lorgynges, hyt ys so,
I am a-redy for to tho
　　Alle that the court wylle loke."
To say the soth, without les,
Alle togedere how hyt was,
　　xij. knyȝtes wer dryve to boke;
Alle they seyde ham betwene,
That knewe the maners of the quene,
　　And the queste toke;
The quene bar los of swych a word,
That sche lovede lemmannes wythout her lord,
　　Har never on hyt foresoke.
Therfor they seyden alle,
Hyt was long on the quene, and not on Laun-
　　Thereof they gonne hym skere;　　　[fal,
And yf he myȝte hys lemman brynge,
That he made of swych ȝelpynge,
　　Other the maydenes were
Bryȝtere than the quene of hewe,
Launfal schuld be holde trewe,
　　Of that yn alle manere;
And yf he myȝte not brynge hys lef,
He schud be hongede as a thef,
　　They seyden alle yn fere.

Alle yn fere they made proferynge,
That Launfal schuld hys lemman brynge :
  Hys heed he gan to laye.
Than seyde the quene, wythout lesynge,
ȝyf he bryngeth a fayrer thynge,
  Put out my eeyn gray.[1]
Whan that wajowr was take on honde,
Launfal therto two borwes fonde,
  Noble knyȝtes twayn ;
Syr Percevalle and syr Gawayn,
They wer hys borwes, soth to sayn,
  Tylle a certayn day.
The certayn day, I ȝow plyȝt,
Was xij. moneth and fourtenyȝt,
  That he schuld hys lemman brynge.
Syr Launfal, that noble knyȝt,
Greet sorow and care yn hym was lyȝt,
  Hys hondys he gan wrynge.
So greet sorowe hym was upon,
Gladlyche hys lyf he wold a forgon,
  In care and in marnynge ;
Gladlyche he wold hys hed forego,
Everych man therfor was wo,
  That wyst of that tydynge ;
The certayn day was nyȝyng,
Hys borowes hym broȝt befor the kyng,
  The kyng recordede tho,
And bad hym bryng hys lef yn syȝt,
Syr Launfal seyde that he ne myȝt,
  Therfore hym was welle wo.
The kyng commaundede the barouns alle
To yeve jugement on Launfal,

---

[1] Grey eyes were formerly considered a great mark of beauty.
Numerous instances might be quoted from the old romances.

And dampny hym to sclo.
Then sayde the erl of Cornewayle,
That was wyth ham at that counceyle,
  " We wylly naȝt do so ;
Greet schame hyt war[1] us alle upon
For to dampny that gantylman.
  That hath be hende and fre ;
Therfor, lordynges, doth be my reed,
Our kyng we wyllyth another wey lede,
  Out of lond Launfal schalle fle."
And as they stod thus spekynge,
The barouns sawe come rydynge
  Ten maydenes bryȝt of ble ;
Ham thoȝte they were so brȝt and schene,
That the lodlokest, wythout wene,
  Har quene than myȝte be.
Tho seyde Gawayn, that corteys knyȝt,
Launfal, brodyr, drede the no wyȝt,
  Her cometh thy lemman hende ;
Launfal answerede, and seyde, " y-wys
Non of ham my lemman nys,
  Gawayn, my lefly frende."
To that castelle they wente ryȝt,
At the gate they gonne alyȝt,
  Befor kyng Artour gonne they wende,
And bede hym make a-redy hastyly
A fayr chamber fore here lady,
  That was come of kynges kende.
" Ho ys your lady ? " Artour seyde,
" Ye schulle y-wyte," seyde the mayde,
  " For sche cometh ryde,"
The kyng commaundede, for her sake,
The fayryst chaunber for to take,

---

[1] Uncertain in MS.; perhaps *wor.*

In hys palys that tyde.
And anon to hys barouns he sente,
For to yeve jugemente
    Upon that traytour fulle of pryde :
The barouns answerede anoon-ry3t,
" Have we seyn the madenes bry3t,
    We [1] schulle not longe abyde."
A newe tale they gonne tho,
Some of wele and some of wo,
    Har lord the kyng to queme.
Some dampnede Launfal there,
And some made hym quyt and skere,
    Hare tales were welle breme.
Tho saw they other ten maydenes bry3t,
Fayryre than the other ten of sy3t,
    As they gonne hym deme ;
They ryd upon joly moyles of Spayne,
Wyth sadellĕ and brydelle of Champayne,
    Hare lorayns ly3t gonne leme.
They wer y-clodeth yn samyt tyre,
Ech man hadde greet desyre
    To se hare clodynge.
Tho seyde Gaweyn, that curtayse kny3t,
" Launfal, here cometh thy swete wy3t,
    That may thy bote brynge."
Launfal answerede, with drery do3t,
And seyde, " Alas, y knowe her [2] no3t,
    Ne non of alle the offsprynge."
Forth they wente to that palys,
And ly3te at the hye deys
    Before Artoure the kynge,
And grette the kyng and quene ek,
And oo mayde thys wordes spak

---

[1] *Whe* in MS.   [2] *Hem* in MS.

To the kyng Artour:
" Thyn halle agrayde, and hele the walles
With clodes and with ryche palles,
   Aȝens my Lady Tryamour."
The kyng answerede bedene,
" Welle-come, ye maydenes schene,
   Be our Lord the Savyoure."
He commaundede Launcelot du Lake to
    brynge hem yn fere
In the chamber ther har felawes were,
   With merthe and moche honour.
Anoon the quene suppose gyle,
That Launfal schulle yn a whyle
   Be'y-made quyt and skere,
Thoruȝ hys lemman that was commynge ;
Anon sche seyde to Artour the kyng :
   " Syre, curtays yf [thou] were,
Or yf thou lovedest thyn honoure,
I schuld be awreke of that traytoure,
   That doth me changy chere ;
To Launfal thou schuldest not spare,
Thy barouns dryveth the to bysmare,
   He ys hem lef and dere."
And as the quene spak to the kyng,
The barons seyȝ come rydynge
   A damesele alone,
Upoon a whyt comely palfrey,
They saw nevere non so gay
   Upon the grounde gone.
Gentylle, jolyf, as bryd on bowe,
In alle manere fayr i-nowe
   To wonye yn wodly wone ;
The lady was bryȝt as blosme on brere,
With eyen gray, with lovelych chere,
   Her leyre lyȝt schoone.

As rose on rys her rode was red,
The her schon upon here hed,
  As gold wyre that schynyth bry3t,
Sche hadde a crounne upon here molde,
Of ryche stones and of golde,
  That lofsom lemede ly3t.
The lady was clad yn purpere palle,
With gentylle body and myddle smalle,
  That semely was of sy3t;
Her mantylle was furryth with whyt ermyn,
I-reversyd jolyf and fyn,
  No rychere be ne my3t.
Her sadelle was semyly sett,
The sambus wer grene felvet,
  I-paynted with ymagerye;
The bordure was of belles,
Of ryche gold and nothyng elles,
  That any man my3te aspye.
In the arsouns, before and behynde,
Were twey stones of Ynde,
  Gay for the maystrye;
The paytrelle of her palfraye
Was worth an erldome stoute and gay,
  The best yn Lumbardye.
A gerfawcon sche bar on here hond,
A softe pas here palfray fond,
  That men here schuld beholde;
Thoru3 Karlyon rood that lady,
Twey whyte grehoundys ronne hyr by,
  Hare colers were of golde.
And whan Launfal sawe that lady,
To alle the folk he gon crye and hy,
  Bothe to younge and olde,
" Her," he seyde, " comyth my lemman swete,
Sche my3te me of my balys bete,
  3ef that lady wolde."

Forth sche wente ynto the halle,
Ther was the quene and the ladyes alle,
　　And also kyng Artoure;
Her maydenes come ayens her ry3t,
To take here styrop whan sche ly3t,
　　Of the lady dame Tryamoure.
Sche dede of her mantylle on the flet,
That men schuld her beholde the bet,
　　Wythoute a more sojour;
King Artoure gane here fayre grete,
And sche hym agayn with wordes swete,
　　That were of greet valoure.
Up stod the quene and ladyes stoute,
Her for to beholde alle aboute,
　　How even sche stod upry3t;
Than were they wyth her also donne,
As ys the mone ayen the sonne
　　A-day whan hyt ys ly3t.
Than seyde sche to Artour the kyng,
" Syr, hydyr I com for swych a thyng,
　　To skere Launfal the kny3t,
That he never, yn no folye,
Beso3te the quene of no drurye,
　　Be dayes ne be ny3t.
Therfor, syr kyng, good keep thou myne,
He bad na3t her, but sche bad hym,
　　Here lemman for to be;
And he answerede her and seyde,
That hys lemmannes lothlokest mayde
　　Was fayryr than was sche."
Kyng Artour seyde, withouten othe,
" Ech man may y-se that ys sothe,
　　Bry3tere that ye be."
With that dame Tryamour to the quene geth,
And blew on her swych a breth,
　　That never eft my3t sche se.

The lady lep an hyre palfray,
And bad hem alle have good day,
  Sche nolde no lengere abyde;
With that com Gyfre alle so prest,
With Launfalys stede out of the forest,
  And stod Launfal besyde.
The knyȝt to horse began to sprynge
Anoon wythout any lettynge, ·
  Wyth hys lemman away to ryde ;
The lady tok her maydenys achon,
And wente the way that sche hadde er gon,
  With solas and wyth pryde.
The lady rode dorth Cardevyle,
Fere ynto a jolyf ile,
  Olyroun that hyȝt ;
Every ȝer [1] upon a certayn day,
Me[n] may here Launfales stede nay,
  And hym se with syȝt.
Ho that wylle ther assay [2] justes,[3]
To kepe hys armes fro the rustes,
  In turnement other fyȝt,
Dare he never forther gon,
There he may find justes anoon,
  With syr Launfal the knyȝt.
Thus Launfal, withouten fable,
That noble knyȝt of the rounde table,
  Was take yn-to fayrye ;
Seththe saw hym yn this lond no man,
Ne no more of hym telle y ne can,
  For sothe, withoute lye.
Thomas Chestre made thys tale,
Of the noble knyȝt syr Launfale,
  Good of chyvalrye.

---

[1] *Er* in MS.   [2] *Axsy* in MS.   [3] *Justus* in MS.

Jhesus, that ys hevene kyng,
ʒeve us alle hys blessyng,
And hys modyr Marye !   Amen.
Explicit Launfal.

One leaf of Kynge's edition of Launfal is preserved in Douce's
collection, and the whole of it is reprinted in the catalogue of
that library, p. 311.   It is in couplets, and agrees very nearly
with the Rawlinson MS.   I am at a loss to understand why
the compiler of the Douce catalogue should conjecture this
fragment to be "part of a translation of Syr Perceval," with
which it has clearly nothing in common, or "a portion of an
earlier version of Launfal than that in Ritson," for the style of
Ritson's copy is decidedly more ancient than that in the Rawlinson
MS., or the printed fragment.   Percy mentions another copy in
his folio MS.   The Rawlinson MS. commences as follows :—

Sothly by Arthurys day
Was Bretayne yn grete nobyle,
For yn hys tyme a grete whyle
He sojourned at Carlile ;
He had with hyme a meyné there,
As he had ellys where,
Of the rounde table the kynghtes alle,
With myrth and joye yn hys halle.

The following extract from another part of the same MS. will
prove the identity of the version with that of the Douce fragment :—

Thise xij. wist, withouten wene,
Alle the maner of the quene
The kyng was good alle aboute,
And she was wyckyd oute and oute,
For she was of suche comforte,
She lovyd mene ondir her lorde ;
Therby wist thei it was alle
Longe one her, and not one Landewalle :

Herof they quyttene hyme as treue mene,
And sith spake they farder thenne,
That yf he myght hys lemane bryng
Of whome he maide knolishyng,
And yef her may devyse bryght and shyne
Werne fairer thane the quene,
In maykyng, semblaunt and hewe,
They wold quyte hyme gode and true ;
Yff he ne myght stound ther tille,
Thanne to be at the kynges wille.
This verdite thei yef tofore the kyng ;
The day was sett her for to bryng.
Borowys he founde to come ayene,
Sir Gawayne and Sir Ewyne.
" Alas," quod he, " now shalle I die,
My love shalle I never see with ee ! "
Ete ne drynke wold he never,
But wepyng and sorowyng evir :
Syres, sare sorrow hath he nome,
He wold hys endyng day wer come,
That he myght ought of lif goo !
Every mane was for hyme woo,
For larger kynght thane he
Was ther never in that countrey.
The day i-sett come one hynge,
His borowys hyme brought before the kyng ;
The kyng lett recorte tho
The sewt and the answer also,
And bad hyme bryng his borowis in syght,
Landevalle sayd that he ne myght.
Tho were commaundyd the barons alle
To gyve judgement one syr Landevalle.

These extracts will be sufficient to show that the text I have
adopted is superior both in language and antiquity to the version
in the Rawlinson manuscript.

F

Romance of King Orfeo.

———o———

THIS beautiful fairy romance-poem is founded on the classical tale of Orpheus and Eurydice, but metamorphosed in a manner that would lead us to believe that the compiler had either a very imperfect knowledge of his original, or that the variations were intentional. In the latter case, it is clear that much ingenuity and taste have been displayed ; and even if the other supposition be correct, the metamorphosis of hell into fairyland cannot but be an inprovement. Three copies of this romance, which has been conjectured with much probability to be a translation from the French, are known to exist ; one in MS. Harl. 3810, printed by Ritson, another in the Auchinleck MS., printed by Mr Laing, and a third in MS. Ashmole 61, lf. 151, the text we have here selected. According to the Auchinleck and Harleian MSS., Orpheo's father " was comen of King Pluto," and Chaucer speaks of Pluto and Proserpina as the king and queen of Faëry. The Edinburgh MS. reads Juno for Proserpina, but the variation is immaterial. The circumstance, however, seems to add one more proof to those adduced by Mr Wright, of the interchange between legends and popular fictions. The " Traitie of Orpheus kyng," by Robert Henryson, printed at Edinburgh in 1508, and reprinted in 1827, merely relates to the classical story, and it will be enough for us to refer to the extracts given by Mr Laing in his "Select Remains of the Ancient Popular Poetry of Scotland," 4to. Edinb. 1822. The Ashmolean MS. is a far better version than that printed by Ritson, and, although it agrees rather closely with the copy in the Auchinleck MS., it is more complete at the commencement, and in many respects superior to it, the MS. itself, however, being not more ancient than the time of Henry VI.

KING ORFEW,

MERY tyme is in Aperelle,[1]
That mekyll schewys of manys wylle ;
In feldys and medewys flow[r]ys spryng,
In grovys and wodes foules syng :
Than wex ʒong men jolyffe,
And than prevyth man and wyffe.
The Brytans, as the boke seys,
Off diverse thinges thei made ther leys ;
Som thei made of herpynges,
And some of other diverse thinges ;
Some of werre and some off wo,
Some of myrthys and joy also
Some of trechery and some off gyle,
Some of happys that felle some whyle,
And some be of rybawdry,
And many ther bene off fary :
Off all the venturys men here ore se,
Most off luffe fore-soth thei be,
That in the leys ben i-wrouʒht.
Fyrst fond and forth brouʒht.

---

[1] The introductory portion is not found in the Auchinleck MS., but it is given in Ritson's version, with some variation.

Off aventours that felle some deys,
The Bretonys [1] ther-of made ther leys,
Off kynges that be-fore us were,
When thei myȝt any woundres here,
They lete them wryte, as it were do,
And ther among is syr Orfewo.
He was fore-soth a nobulle kyng,
That most luffyd gle and herpyng ;
Wele sekyre was every gode herpere
To have off mekyll honour.
Hym-selve he lernyd forto herpe,
And leyd ther-on hys wytte so scherpe,
He lernyd so wele, with-outene les,
So gode herpere never non was ;
In all this werld was no man bore,
That had kyng Orfeo ben be-fore,
And he myȝht hys herpe here,
Bot he wold wene that it were
A blyssed full note of paradis,
Such melody ther-in is !
The Kyng jorneyd in Tracyens,[2]
That is a cyte off grete defence,
And with hym hys quene off price,
That was callyd dame Meroudys ;
A feyrere lady than sche was one,
Was never made off flessch ne bone ;
She was full off lufe and godnes,
Ne may no mañ telle hyre feyrnes.
It be-felle in the begyning of May,
When ffoules syng on every sprey,

---

[1] MS. *Brotonys.*
[2] Ritson's copy reads *Crassens.* The Edinburgh MS. very
ingeniously asserts that this was the ancient name for Win-
chester ; one way of transforming a Grecian tale into an English
one.

And blossom spryng on every bouʒhe,
Over all wexyth mery i-nowhe;
Than the quene dame Meroudys [1]
Toke with hyr ladés off grete price,
And went in an underon-tyde
To pley hyre in an horcherd syde.
Than the ladés all thre
Sett hem under an hympe tre.
Sche leyd hyre doūne that comly quene,
And fell on sclepe upoñ the grene;
The ladys durste hyr nouʒt wake,
Bot lete hyr lyʒe hyre rest to take.
Sche slepe welle fere after the none,
To the undryne-tyde wer gone;
And when that ladés gane hyr wake,
Sche cryed and grete noys gañ make,
And wrong their hondes with drery mode,
And crachyd hyr vysage all on blode;
Hyre ryche robys sche all-to rytte,
And was ravysed out of hyr wytte!
The ladés, that stod hyre be-syde,
Fled and durste not long a-byde,
Bot went un-to the palys a-ʒene,
And told both knyʒt and sueyne,
How that the quene awey wold,
And bad them come hyr to be-hold.
Sexty knyʒtes and ʒit mo,
And also fele ladys ther-to,
Hastely to the quene thei come,
And in ther armys thei hyr nome,
And brouʒt hyre to bed in haste,
And kepyd hyre both feyre and faste,

---

[1] In the Harl. MS. the Queen's name is spelt *Erodys* and
Erodysse; and in the Auchinleck MS. *Heurodis.*

And ever sche be-gañ to cryȝe,
As sche wold up and go hyre weye.
The kyng come to the chamber to the quene,
And be-fore hym knyȝtes tenne,
And wepte and seyd with grete pyté,
" My leffe wyffe, what ayles the ?
Thou that hast be so stylle,
Why cryest thou wonder schylle?
And ever thou hast be meke and myld,
Thou are be-come wode and wyld !
Thy flessch that was so whyte be-fo[r]ne,
With thi nayles thou hast torne !
Thy lyppes that were so bryȝt rede,
Semys as wañ as thou were dede,
And thi fyngyrs long and smale,
The be blody and all pale !
And thi luff-som eyne two
Loke on me, as I· wer thi fo !
God lemane, I cry the mersye,
Thou late be all this reufull crye,
And telle me, lady, fore thi prow,
What thing may thee helpe now."
Sche ley styll at the last,
And be-gañ to sey full fast,
And thus sche seyd the kyng unto :
" Alas ! my lord syr Orfeo,
Ever I have lovyd the all my lyfe,
Be-twene us was never stryfe,
Never seth we wedyd ¹ ware,
There-fore I make full mekyll care ;
Bot now we must per[t]e a-two,
Do thou the best, fore I must go ! "
" Alas ! " seyd the kyng, " lost I ame,
Whyder wyll thou go, and to whome ?

---

¹ MS. *dedyd.*

W[h]er thou arte, I would be with the,
And where I ame thou schall be with me ! "
" Do wey! " seyd the quene, "that schall not be,
Fore I schall never the more se !
I wyll the tell how it is,
And fore-soth I wyll not mysse.
As I went this undyre-tyde,
To pley me be myn orcherd syde,
I fell on slepe all be-dene,
Under an ympe upoñ the grene ;
My meydens durst me not wake,
Bot lete me lyȝe and slepe take,
Tyll that the time over-passyd so,
That the undryne was over-go.
Whe[n] I gan my-selve awake,
Ruly chere I gañ to make,
Fore I saw a sembly syȝt ;
To-werd me come a gentyll knyȝt,
Wele i-armyd at all ryȝht,
And bad I schuld upoñ hyȝeng,
Come speke with hys lord the kyng.
I ansuerd hym with wordes bold ;
I seyd, I durst not ne not I wold.
The knyȝht aȝen he rode full fast,
Than come ther kyng at the last,
With an hundreth knyȝtes also,
And an hundreth ladés and mo,
All thei ryden on whyte stedes,
Off mylke whyte was all ther wedes,
I saw never, seth I was borne,
So feyre creatours here be-forne.
The kyng had a crouñe on hys hede,
It was no sylver ne gold rede,
It was all off presyous stone,
Als bryȝt as any soñ it schone !
Also sone as he to me come,

Whether I wold ore not, up he me name,
And made me with hym forto ryde
Upoñ a stede by hys syde ;
He brovʒt me to a feyre palas,
Wele tyred and rychly in all case ;
He schewyd me hys castellus and toures,
And hys hey haules and boures,
Forestes, ryvers, frutes and floures ;
Hys grete stedes schewyd me ichone,
And sethyn he made me aʒene to gone
Into the sted where he me fette,
In that same sted ther he me sete,
And seyd, " Madame, loke that thou be
To-morrow here under this tre,
And than schall thou with us go,
And lyve with us ever-more so ;
Iff that thou make us any lete,
Where-ever thou be, thou schall be fete,
And to-torne thi lymys all,
No thyng helpe the ne schall !
And thoʒ thou be all to-torne,
ʒit shall thou a-wey with us to be borne ! "
When kyng Orfeo herd this case,
Than he seyd, " Alas ! Alas ! "
He askyd rede of many a mañ,
Bot no mañ helpe hym ne canne.
Alas ! " seyd the kyng, " that I ame wo !
What may I best fore my quene do ? "
On the morow when the ondryn cam,
Kyng Orfeo hys armys nam ;
Ten hundreth knyʒhtes he with hym toke,
Wele armyd, talle men and stoute.
With hys quene than went he
To the orchard under the ympe tre,
And seyd he wold ther abyde,
What aventour so be-tyde ;

Lyve and dyȝe thei wold ichone,
Or that the quene schuld fro them gone.
Than thei gon batell to make,
And sched blod fore hys quenys sake,
Bot among them all ryȝht
The quene was awey twȝht,
And with the feyry awey i-nome,
The ne wyst w[h]er sche was come.
There was cry, wepyng and wo!
The kyng unto hys chamber ȝede tho,
And oft he knelyd onne the stone,
And made gre[t] sorow fore sche was gone,
That ne hys lyve was i-spent;
Bot ther myȝt be none amendment.
He sent after his baro[u]ns,
Knyȝhtes, squyres off grete renowns:
When thei all come were,
He seyd, "Lo[r]dinges, be-fore ȝou here
I wold orden my hyȝe stuerd
To kepe my londes afterwerd,
And in my sted be he schalle
To kepe my landes over alle.
When that ȝe se my lyffe is spent,
Than make ȝou a perlament;
Chese ȝou than a new kyng,
And do ȝour best with all my thing.
Fore now I have my quene lorne,
The best woman that ever was borne,
To wylderne I wyll gone,
Fore I wyll never woman sene,
And lyve ther in holtys hore,
With wyld bestes ever-more!"
There was wepyng in the halle,
And grete sorow among them alle;
There was nother olde ne ȝong,
That myȝt speke a word with tong!

They felle on kneys all in fere,
Be-souȝt hym, iff hys wyll were,
That he schuld not fro them go.
" Do wey ! " he seyd, " it schall be so !
All this kyngdome I fore-sake."
A staff to hym he gañ take ;
He had neither gowne ne hode,
Schert ne noñ other gode,
Bot an harpe he toke algate,
Bare-fote he went furth at the ȝate !
There was weping and grete crye,
Grete dole fore the maysterye,
When the kyng with-outene crouñe
So porely went out off the touñe.
He went thorow wode and hethe,
And in-to wyldernes he gethe ;
So fere he went, I sey, i-wys,
That he wyst not where he was.
He that sate in boure and halle,
And on hym were the purpull palle,
Now in herd heth he lyȝet,
With levys and gresse his body hydyth.
He that had knyȝhtes off prise,
And be-fore hym knelyd ladés,
He sey not that hys herte lykyth,
Bot wyld bestes that by hym strykyth !
Also he had castellus and tourys,
Forestes, ryveres, frutys and flourys,
Now thoȝ it be store as frese,
He may not make hys bed in es.
The kyng that had grete plenté
Off mete and drinke with-outene le,
Long he may dyge and rote,
Or he have hys fyll of the rote.
In somour he lyvys be the frute,
And berys that were full suete ;

In wynter may he no-thing fynd,
Bot levys and grass and of the rynd.
Hys body is awey dwyned,
And fore grete cold al-to schend.
Hys berd was both blake and rowȝe,
And to hys gyrdell sted it drewȝe ;
He cañ telle off grete care
T[hat] he suffyre x. wynter and mo.
In a tre that was holow,
There was hys haule evyne and morow !
When the wether was feyre and bryȝht,
He toke his herpe anone-ryȝht,
In mydys the wodde he sett hym douñe,
And temperyd hys herpe with a mery souñe,
And harpyd after hys awne wylle,
Over all a-boute it was full schylle !
The wyld bestes that ther were,
They come a-boute hys herpe to here ;
The bestes of that forest wyld
Come a·boute hym meke and myld,
To here hys harpyng so fyne,
So much melody was ther·ine.
When he hys harpyng stynt wylle,
No lenger ther a-byde thei wylle,
And all the foulys that there were,
They come a-boute hym by bussch and brere.
Than myȝt he se hym beside,
In an hote undryne-tyde,
The king off fary and all hys route
Come ryding hym all a-boute,
With dynne, cry and with blowyng,
And with hundes berkyng,
Bot no dere ne best thei nome,
He wyst not w[h]er thei were become.
Other thinges he myȝht se,
A grete hoste come hym bye,

An hundreth knyȝhtes mo ȝit,
Wele armyd at all ryȝht,
With contynans stoute and fers,
And many spreding baners ;
Every man a draw suerd had in hond,
Bot he wyst not whether thei wold wend.
Also he myȝt se every-thing,
Knyȝhtes and ladés come daunsyng.
Anone he lokyd hym be-syde,
And say syxty ladés on palferays ryde,
Gentyll and gay as bryd on ryse,
Not a man among them i-wyse,
Bot every lady a faukon bere,
And rydene on huntyng be a ryvere.
Off game thei found well gode haunte,
Suannys, herons and courmerante,
And the faucons forth fleyng,
And the foulys fro the water rysing ;
Every fa[u]cone hys pray slowȝ,
Then sate the kyng Orfeo and lewȝ,
And seyd, " This is gode game,
Thyder I wyll be Godes name,
Sych game I was wont forto se."
Up he rose, and thether went he.
To a ladé he come tho,
He be-held hyre face and body also,
Hym thouȝt that it was in all wyse
Hys awne quene dame Meroudes.
He be-held hyr and sche hym eke,
And never a word to other thei speke,
Fore the poverte that sche on hym se.
That had bene so rych and hyȝe,
The terys rane doune be hyr eyȝe !
The ladés be-held and that they seyȝe,
And made hyr awey to ryde,
No lenger myȝht sche ther abyde.

"Alas!" seyd Orfeo, "that me is wo!
Why wold not myne hert breke a-two?
Now I may not speke with my wyffe.
Al to long lastes my lyffe!
Sche dare not a word with me speke,
Alas! why wold not my herte breke?
Alas!" seyd the kyng, "that I ne myȝht
Dyȝe after this same syȝht!
In-to what lond this lady ryde,
Folow [1] I wyll, what so be-tyde!
That same wey wyll I streche,
Off my lyve I do not reche!"
He toke a staff as he spake,
And threw an herpe at hys bake;
He sparyd nother stoke ne stone,
He had gode wyll forto gone.
In a roche off stone the ladés ryde,
Orpheo folowyd and not a-byde.
When he had ther-in go,
A myle or els two,
He come into a feyre cunturey,
Als bryȝt as soñ in somerys dey;
Hyll ne dale was ther none sene,
It was a welle feyre grene.
Orfeo full wele it seye,
A feyre castell ryall and hyȝe;
He be-held the werke full wele.
The [2] overyst werke a-bove the walle
Gañ schyne as doth the crystalle.
A hundreth tyretes he saw full stout,
So godly thei were bateyled a-boute.
The pylers that come oute off the dyche,
All thei wer of gold full ryche;

---

[1] *Forrow.*—MS.   [2] MS. *Tho.*

The frontys thei wer amelyd all
With all maner dyverse amell :
There-in he saw wyde wonys,
And all were full of presyos stonys.
Kyng Orfeo knokyd at the ȝate,
The pourter was redy ther-ate,
Freyned what he wold do.
He seyd, " I ame a mynstrell lo,
To glad thi lord with my gle,
And it hys suete wyll be."
The porter undyd the ȝate anone,
And as a mynstrell lete hym gone ;
Than lokyd he a-boute the walle,
And saw it stond over alle
With men that wer thyder brouȝht,
And semyd dede and wer nouȝht ;
Some ther stod with-outyne hede,
And some armys non hade,
And some ther bodés had wounde,
And some one hors ther armys sette,
And some wer strangyld at ther mete,
And men that wer nomene with them ete ;
So he saw them stonding ther.
Then saw he men and women in fere,
As thei slepyd ther undryne tyde,
He them saw [1] on every syde ;
Among them he saw hys wyve,
That he lovyd as his lyve,
That ley ther under that tre full trew,
Be hyre clothys he hyre knew.
In that castell he saw ȝit
A tabernakylle wele i-dyȝht,
And a ryall kyng ther-in sette,
And hys quene that was so swete ;

---

[1] *He saw he them saw.*—MS.

There crownys and clothys schyne so bryʒt,
That on them loke he ne myʒht !
A hundryth knyʒhtes in present
To do the kinges commandment.
When he had sene all this thing,
On kneys he fell be-fore the kyng,
And seyd, " Lord, and thi wyll were,
My mynstralsy thou woldyst here ? "
Than seyd the kyng, " What arte thou
That hether arte i-come now ?
I, no' none that is with me,
Never ʒit sent after the ;
Never seth that my reyne be-gan,
Fond I never none so herdy man,
That hyder durst to us wend,
Bot iff I wold after hym send.'
" Syre," he seyd, " I trow wele
I ame bot a pore mynstrelle,
And ʒit it ys the maner of us,
Forto seke to gret lordes hous ;
And thoʒ we not welcome be,
ʒit we be-hovy[t]h to profere oure gle."
Be-fore the kyng he sette hym done,
And toke hys herpe schyll of sowne,
And temperd yt as he wele cañ :
A blyssed-full note he be-gañ
The kyng sate wele styll,
To here hys herpe with ryʒt gode wyll ;
Wele hym lykyd to here his gle,
The ryche quene so deyd sche.
Men that in the castell wer
Come hys herpe for to here,
And felle dounne to hys fete,
They thouʒt hys herpe was so suete !
And when he stynt of hys herpying,
To hym than seyd the ryche kyng,

"Mynstrell, me lykes wele thi gle,
And what thou wyll aske of me,
Largely I wyll the pay:
Speke now, and thou may a-sey."
"Now, lord, I pray the
That thou wold ʒiff to me
The feyre lady bryʒt off ble,
That lyʒet under this impe tre."
"Nay," he seyd, "that thouʒt I never,
A foule coupull of ʒou it were,
Fore thou arte rowʒe and blake,
And sche is with-outyne lake;
A foule thing it wer fore-thy,
To se hyre go in thi company."
"Lord," he seyd, "thou ryche kyng,
ʒit it wer a foulere thing
To here a lesyng of thy mouthe,
That thou me seyst nowʒe,
That I schuld have what I wold,
Bot nedys a kyng word mot hold."
The ryche kyng spake wordes than,
And seyd, "Thou arte a trew mañ,
There-fore I grante that it be so,
Thou take hyre be the hond and go;
I wyll that thou be of hyre blyth."
He thankyd hym a hundreth sythe.
He toke hyre by the hond anone,
And fast went forth oute of that wone;
Fast thei hyed out of that palas,
And went ther wey thourow Godes grace;
To wyldernes both forth thei geth,
And passyth over holtys and heth.
So lo[ng] he hys wey ther nome,
To Trasyens thei wer i-come,
That some tyme was his awne cyté;
Bot no mane knew that it was he.

With a pore man he reste that ny3t,
There he thou3t to byde a-ply3t,
Unto hym and to hys wyffe,
As an herpere off pore lyffe,
And askyd tydinges of that lond,
Who that the kyngdome held in hond ;
In that same tyme that old mañ,
He told hym all that he cañ,
And how the quene was twy3t awey
Into ye lond of fayrey,
And how the kyng exiled 3ede,
Bot no mañ wyst into what stede ;
And how the stewerd the kyngdome hold,
And many other wonders hym told.
Amorow a3en the none-tyde,
He made hys quene ther-to a-byde ;
Fore-soth he toke hys herpe a-none,
In-to the syté he gañ gone.
And when [he] come into the syté,
Many a mañ com hym to se,
Men and wyves and maydnise bold,
Fast thei come hym to be-hold.
Also thei seyd every-chone,
How the mosse grew hym upone ;
" Hys berd is growyne to the kne,
His body is clong as a tree ! "
As the kyng went in the strete,
With hys stewerd he gañ mete,
And fell on kneys with grete pyté,
And seyd, " Lord, fore charyté,
I ame an herpere of hethynes,
Helpe me now, lord, yn this destres."
The stewerd said, " Cum with me home,
Off my gode thou schall have some ;
Fore my lordes love, syr Orfeo,
All herpers be welcum me to."

G

The stewerd and the lordes alle,
Anone thei went in-to the halle ;
The stewerd wessch and went to mete,
The lordes all be-gane to sytte ;
There wer he[r]pers and trumpers,
And mynst[r]ellus and grete renounys.
There was grete myrth in the halle,
Kyng Orfew sate among them alle,
And lystynd to thei wer styll,
And toke hys herpe and temperde schyll ;
The meryest note he made ther,
That every mañ my3t here with ere.
All thei lyked wele hys gle,
The rych stewerd so dyd he.
The stewerd the harpe knew full suyth,
And seyd, " Mynstrell, so mote thou thryve,
Where hades thou this herpe and how
Tell me now, fore thi prow."
" A ! lord, in a mournyng tyde,
Thorow a wyld forest I 3ede ;
A man with lyons was drawyne smale,
I fond hym ly3eng in a dale ;
Etyne he was with tethe so scherpe,
By hym I fond this ryall herpe
Ny3he x. wyntyre ago."
" Alas ! " seyd the stewerd, "me is wo,
That was my lord syr Orfeo ! "
Alas ! " he seyd, " what schall I do ?
And fore my lord that happyd so,
Alas ! " he seyd, " that me is wo,
That so evyll deth was merkyd,
And so herd grace hym be-happyd ! "
On swone he fell in the halle,
The lordes come be-fore hym alle,
And toke hym up sone a-none,
And comforth hym every-chone,

And told [1] hym how this werld geth,
" There is no bote of manys deth."
The kyng be-held the stewerd than,
And seyd he was a trew man,
And lovyd hym as he au3te to do,
And sterte up and seyd, " Lo !
Syre stuard, lystyns now this thing,
3iff I were Orfeo the kyng;
Therefore, stewerd, lystyns to me,
Now thou may the kyng here se ;
I have wonnyd x. winter and more
In wylderness with mekyll sore,
And have wonne my quene awey
Owte of the lond off fary,
And have brou3t that lady hend
Here unto the tounnes ende,
And over in was ther i-nome ;
And my-selve to the court come,
Thus in beger wede full styll,
Forto a-sey thi gode wyll ;
And fore I found the thus trewe,
Therefore thou schall never it rewe,
Fore be my lyve fore lufe on aye,
Thou shall be kyng after my dey ;
And if thou have of my deth blyth,
Thow schuld be hangyd also swyth ! "
All the lordes that there sette,
That was ther kyng thei under-3ete,
And with that word the stewerd hym knew,
And over that bord a-none he threw,
And fell anone douñe to hys fete,
And so did all that there sate ;
And all thi seyd with a cryeng,
" Welcum ever Orfew the kyng ! "

---

[1] Told told.—MS.

Off hys comyng thei wer blyth,
And broȝt hym to a chamber swyth,
And bathyd hym and schove his berd,
And tyred hym as a kyng in wede ;
And sethin with grete processyone,
The brouȝt the quene thorow the touñe ;
Fore ther was myrth and melody
Off yche maner mynstralsy.
There he was crouned—new i-wys,
So was the quene dame Meroudes,
And levyd long afterwerd,
And seth was kyng the trew stewerd.
Herpers of Bretayne[1] herd beforne
How this aventour was be-gone,
And made a ley of grete lykyng,
And callyd it after the kyng,
That Orfeo hyȝht, as mene wele wote,
Gode is the ley, suete is the note !
Thus endes here Orfeo the kyng,
God grante us all hys blyssing !
And all that this wyll here or rede,
God fore-gyff them ther mysded,
To the blysse of hevyn that thei may come,
And ever-more ther-in to wonne !
And that it may so be,
Prey we all for charyté !

Explicet Orfew.

---

[1] That is, Bretagne.   This passage seems to show that the
poem is a translation from the French.   See also p. 82.

V.

Thomas and the Fairy Queen.

———o———

THE connection between the purgatory and paradise of the
monks and the fairy lands of the people, observes Mr
Wright, is perhaps nowhere so fully exhibited as in the following ballad, which is besides no unfavourable specimen of early
poetry. There is something exceedingly graceful in the commencement of it, and a taste displayed which we vainly look for
in most contemporary pieces of the kind; and the wild and
fanciful tale on which the prophecies are engrafted impart interest
to the whole composition. Thomas of Erceldoune, whose adventures with the fairy queen are here narrated, was a legendary character, to whom were ascribed several prophecies, which passed for
a long time under his name, similar to those of Merlin. Sir W. Scott
and others have endeavoured to prove that the English romance of
Tristrem was written by Thomas of Erceldoune; but the translator merely alludes to him at the commencement in a fanciful
manner, and I think it, with Mr Wright, most probable that,
finding the name *Thomas* in the French original, and not understanding it, he was induced to take a character, then so famous,
to add some popularity to the subject. The language both of Sir
Tristrem and the following piece is certainly English; and,

indeed, the whole of the Auchinleck MS. was doubtlessly written in England.

Five early MS. copies of the following ballad 'exist in our public libraries, and there are probably others. We have taken the earliest and best of these for our text, a MS. in the Public Library at Cambridge, marked Ff. v. 48, which has been previously printed by Jamieson, but in so very incorrect a manner as to render its republication necessary, even did it not constitute a very material part in our series. This MS. was written in the early part of the fifteenth century. Mr Wright, however, has endeavoured to prove from internal evidence that it was written in the reign of Edward II., although the mention of Black Agnes clearly proves the contrary; and his evidence goes no farther than to show that some of the pieces were *composed* in that reign, the general character of the writing showing that the MS. itself belongs to a much more recent period. A copy is also in the Thornton MS. (ff. 149-153,) in the library of Lincoln cathedral, but, unfortunately, imperfect, only half of f. 152 and a small fragment of f. 153 being left of the latter part of the poem. This was printed by Mr Laing, in his Early Popular Poetry of Scotland, 4to, Edinb. 1822. The third transcript is in MS. Cott. Vitell. E x. ff. 231-234, partially burnt, the commencement of which is printed in Scott's Minstrelsy of the Scottish Border, ed. 1810, iii. 181-186. The fourth is contained in MS. Lansd. 762, ff. 24-31, which concludes abruptly with l. 445 of our text; and a fifth, a much later copy, is in MS. Sloane 2578, ff. 6-11, but unfortunately wanting the first fytte. The two last-mentioned copies do not appear to have been hitherto noticed, and the Sloane MS. is not well described in Ayscough's catalogue. A later version of it is also found in MS. Rawl. C. 258. The Lincoln MS. contains the following preface, which is peculiar to that copy:—

Lystyns, lordynges, bothe grete and smale,
  And takis gude tente what I wille saye,
I salle ʒow telle als trewe a tale
  Als ever was herde by nyghte or daye;

And the maste mervelle, for-owttyne naye,
   That ever was herde by-fore or syene,
And, therfore, pristly I ȝow praye
   That ȝe wille of ȝoure talking blyne.
It es an harde thyng for to saye
   Of doghety dedis that hase bene done,
Of felle feghtynges and batelles sere,
   And how that thir knyghtis hase wone thair
Bot Jhesu Crist, that syttis in trone,   [schone.
   Safe Ynglysche-mene bothe ferre and nere,
And I salle telle ȝow tyte and sone
   Of batelles donne sythene many a ȝere ;
And of batelles that done salle bee,
   In whate place, and howe and whare,
And wha salle hafe the heghere gree,
   And whethir pertye salle hafe the werre ;
Wha salle takk the flyghte and flee,
   And wha salle dye and by-leve thare.
Bat Jhesu Crist that dyed on tre,
   Save Inglysche-mene whare so thay fare !

The Cambridge MS. has been lamentably defaced by damp,
and more recently by an infusion of galls, so that in many places
it is extremely difficult to decipher.   I am sorry to add that the
greatest mischief appears to have been perpetrated by Jamieson,
who used the infusion with an unsparing hand ; and whatever
assistance it may have rendered him, the effect now is in some
places an entire obliteration.   It was only by placing the volume
in a peculiar position in a strong but not glaring light, that I
have been enabled to correct the errors which my predecessor
has committed ; and I am still doubtful in some very few cases.
My plan was to place the volume *when quite open* at right angles
to the surface, so that the back of the book was parallel, and
the writing at right angles to the ground ; a process which I have
often found to be of more efficient use than ordinary glasses.

𝔉𝔶𝔱𝔱𝔢 𝔈.

As I me went this andyrs day,[1]
  Fast on my way makyng my mone,
In a mery mornyng of May,
  Be Huntley bankes my-self alone,
I herde the jay and the throstelle,
  The mavys mevyd in hir song,
The wodewale farde as a belle,
  That the wode aboute me rong.
Alle in a longyng as I lay[2]
  Undurnethe a cumly[3] tre,
Saw I wher a lady gay
  Came ridand over a lovely[4] le;
ȝif I shuld sitte tille domusday,
  Alle with my tong to know and se,
Sertenly alle hir aray
  Shalle hit never be scryed for me.
Hir palfray was of dappulle gray,
  Sike on se I never non,
As dose the sune on somers day,
  The cumly lady hirselfe schone;
Hir sadille was of reuylle bone,
  Semely was that sight to se,
Stifly sette with precious stone,
  Compaste aboute with crapoté;[5]

---

[1] The Cott. MS. begins thus,—

> In a lande as I was lent,
> In the grykyng of the day,
> Me alone as I went,
> In Huntlé bankys me for to play.

[2] The Lincoln MS. reads, " Alloñe in longynge thus als laye."
[3] Cotton MS., " a dern tre."
[4] " Fayre."—Cott. MS.
[5] Jamieson reads *cramese*, confessing the difficulty of the MS., which clearly has *crapote*, agreeing with the Lincoln, Lansdowne, and Cotton MSS.

Stonys of oryons[1] gret plenté,
 Hir here aboute hir hed hit hong;
She rode out over that lovely le,
 A-while she blew, a-while she song.
Hir garthis of nobulle silke thei were,
 Hir boculs thei were of barys stone;[2]
Hir stiroppis thei were of cristalle clere,
 And alle with perry aboute be-gon;
Hir paytrelle was of a rialle fyne,[3]
 Hir cropur was of arafé,
Hir bridulle was of golde fyne,
 On every side hong bellis thre.
She led iij.[4] grehoundis in a leesshe,
 viij. rachis be hir fete ran,
To speke with hir wold I not seese,[5]
 Hir lire was white as any swan;
She bare a horne about hir halce,
 And undur hir gyrdille mony flonne;
For sothe, lordynges, as I yow telle,
 Thus was this lady fayre be-gon.
Thomas lay and saw that sight,
 Undurneth a semely tre;
He seid "yonde is Mary of myght,
 That bare the childe that died for me!
But I speke with that lady bright,
 I hope my hert will breke in thre;
But I wille go with alle my myght,
 Hir to mete at eldryn tre!"[6]

---

[1] "Oryente."—Lincoln MS.
[2] "Berelle stone."—Lincoln MS.
[3] "Of irale fyne."—Lincoln MS. In the next line, the Lincoln MS. reads *orpharé* for *araft*.
[4] The MS. originally read *foure*, which has been altered to *iij.* by an early hand.
[5] Not *presse*, as printed by Jamieson.
[6] "Eldoune tree."—Lincoln MS.

Thomas radly[1] up he rase,
    And ran over that mounteyne hye,
And certanly, as the story sayes,
    He hir mette at eldryne tre.
He knelid downe upon his kne,
    Undurneth the grenewode spray,
"Lovely lady, thou rew on me,
    Qwene of heven, as thou welle may!"
Than seid that lady bright,[2]
    "Thomas, let such wordis be,
For quen of heven am I noght,
    I toke never so hye degré!
But I am a lady of another cuntré,   .
    If I be parellid moost of price,
I ride aftur the wilde fee,
    My raches rannen at my devyse."
"If thou be pareld most of price,
    And ridis here in thi balye,[3]
Lufly lady, as thou art wyse,
    To gif me leve to lye the by!"
"Do way, Thomas, that were foly,
    I pray the hertely let me be,
For I say the securly
    That wolde for-do my bewté!"[4]
"Lufly lady, thou rew on me,
    And I shalle evermore with the dwelle,

---

[1] That is, *readily.* Not *sadly*, as printed by Jamieson.

[2] This line is plainly written in the MS. without any alteration, so that it is somewhat difficult to account for Jamieson's extraordinary variation from the original.

[3] "In thy folye."—Lincoln MS. Jamieson here substitutes the reading of the Lincoln MS., although the present text is far preferable. He reads *So* at the commencement of the next line but one, but I have thought it safer to follow the MS.

[4] This line is intelligible enough, yet Jamieson says it is wanting in the Cambridge MS., and supplies it from the other copies.

Here my trouth I plight to the,
  Whedur thou wilt to heven [1] or helle ! "
" Man of molde, thou wilt me marre,
  But ȝet thou shalt have [2] thy wille,
But trow thou welle thou thryvist the warre, [3]
  For alle my beauté thou wille spille."
Down then light that lady bright
  Underneth a grenewode spray,
And as the story tellus ful right,
  vii. tymes be hir he lay.
She seid, " Thomas, thou likes thi play,
  What byrde in boure may dwel with the ?
Thou marris me here this lefe-long day,
  I pray the, Thomas, let me be ! "
Thomas stondand [4] in that sted,
  And beheld that lady gay,
Hir here that hong upon hir hed,
  Hir een semyd out that were so gray ;
And alle hir clothis were away,
  That here before saw in that stede,
The to shanke was [5] blak, the tother gray,
  The body bloo as beton leed ! [6]
Thomas seid, " alas ! alas !
  In feith, this is a dolfulle sight !

---

[1] " In hevene."—Lincoln MS.
[2] The Lansdowne MS. here inserts *all*, which seems an improvement.
[3] " Thou chewys the werre."—Lincoln MS.
[4] " Stode up."—Lansd. MS.
[5] These two words are nearly scratched out in the MS., but are clearly necessary to the sense.
[6] This line was originally, " And alle hir body like the leede," the reading that Jamieson adopts. The Cotton MS. reads, " hyr body als blo as ony lede," but the Lansdowne MS. nearly agrees with our text.

That thou art so fadut in the face,
That before schone as sunne bright !"[1]
" Take thi leve, Thomas, at sune and mone,
And also at levys of eldryne tre ;
This twelmond shall thou with me gon,
That mydul-erth thou shalt not se."
He knelyd downe upone his kne,
To Mary mylde he made his mone,
" Lady, but thou rew on me,
Alle my games fro me ar gone !"
"Alas," he seyd, "woo is me !
I trow my dedis wil wyrk me woo !
Jhesu, my soule be-teche I the,
Wher so ever my bonys shalle goo !
She led hym to the eldryn hille [2]
Undernethe the grenewode lee,[3]
Wher hit was derk as any helle,[4]
And ever watur tille the knee ;

---

[1] The following additional lines are here inserted in the Lansdowne MS.—

> On every syde he lokyde abowete,
>   He sau he myght no whare fle,
> Sche woxe so grym and so stowte,
>   The dewyll he wende she had be !
> In the name of the Trynité
>   He conjuryde here anon-ryght,
> That she shulde not come hym nere,
>   But wende away of his syght !
> She said " Thomas, this is no nede,
>   For fende of hell am I none,
> For the now am I [in] grete desese,
>   And suffre paynis many one.
> This xij. mones thou shalt with me gang,
>   And se the maner of my lyffe,
> For thy trowthe thou hast me tane,
>   Ayene that may ye make no stryfe."

[2] Originally *tre* in the MS. Jamieson, for some reason, reads *birke*.

[3] " Undirnethe a derne lee."—Lincoln MS.

[4] " Als mydnyght myrke."—Lincoln MS. This was also originally the reading of our MS., but has been erased for the other.

Ther the space of dayes thre
    He herd but [1] the noyse of the flode ;
At the last he said, " Wo is me,
    Almost I dye for fowte of fode ! "
She led hym into a fayre herbere,
    Ther frute gro ande was gret plenté,
Peyres and appuls bothe ripe thei were,
    The darte [2] and also the damsyn tre ;
The fygge and also the white-bery,[3]
    The nyghtyngale biggyng hur nest,
The popynjay fast about can flye,
    The throstille song wolde have no rest.
He presed to pul the frute with his honde,
    As man for fode was nyhonde feynte ;
She seid, " Thomas, let them stand,
    Or elles the feend will the ateynte !
If thou pulle, the sothe to sey,
    Thi soule goeth to the fyre of helle,
Hit cummes never out til domus-day,
    But ther ever in payne to dwelle ! "
She seid, " Thomas, I the hight,
    Come lay thi hed on my kne,
And thou shalle se the feyrest sight
    That ever saw mon of the cuntré."
He leyd downe his hed as she hym badde,
    His hed upon hir kne he leide ;
Hir to pleese he was fulle gladde,
    And then that lady to hym she seide :
" Sees thou ȝondur [4] faire way,
    That lyes over ȝondur mownteyne ?

---

[1] The word *but* seems to be an early interpolation in the MS.

[2] " The date."—Lincoln MS.

[3] " Wyneberye."—Lincoln MS.

[4] A letter is apparently erased here, and Jamieson reads *is*, which makes nonsense.

ʒondur is the way to heaven for ay,
  Whan synful sowlis have duryd their
    peyne.
Seest thou now, Thomas, ʒondur way
  That lyse low undur ʒon rise?
Wide is the way, the sothe to say,
  Into the joyes of paradyse.
Sees thou ʒonder thrid way
  That lyes over ʒondur playne?
ʒonder is the way, the sothe to sey,[1]
  Ther sinfulle soules shalle drye ther payne.
Sees thou now ʒondur fourt way
  That lyes over ʒondur felle?
ʒonder is the way, the sothe to say,
  Unto the brennand fyre of helle!
Sees thou now ʒondur fayre castelle,
  That stondis upon ʒondur fayre hille?
Off towne and toure it berith the belle,
  In mydul-erth is non like ther-tille.
In faith, Thomas, ʒondur is myne owne,
  And the kyngus of this cuntré;
But me were better be hengud and drawyn,
  Then he wist that thou lay be me.
My lorde is served at ilke a messe[2]
  With xxx.ᵗⁱ knyʒtes fayre and fre,
And I shalle say, sittynd at the deese,
  I toke thi speche be-ʒonde the lee:
Whan thou comes to ʒondur castalle gay,
  I pray the curtes man to be,
And what-so-ever any man to the say,
  Loke thou onswer non but me."

---

[1] "With tene and traye."—Lincoln MS.
[2] This stanza and the next are transposed in the Lincoln and Landsdowne MSS.

Thomas stondyng in that stode,[1]
And behelde that lady gay.
She was as feyre and as gode
And as riche on hir palfray ;
Hir greyhoundis fillid with the dere blode,[2]
Hir rachis coupuld, be my fay ;
She blew hir horne on hir palfray gode,
And to the castelle she toke the way :
Into a halle sothly she went,
Thomas folud at hir hande,
Ladis comme bothe faire and gent
Ful curtesly to hir kneland;
Harpe and fidul both the fande,
The getorn and also the sautry,
The lute and the ribybe both gangand,
And alle maner of mynstralcy;
Knyȝtes dawnsyng be thre and thre,
Ther was revel, both game and play ;
Ther ware [3] ladys fayre and fre,
Dawnsyng one [4] riche aray.

---

[1] The Lincoln MS. reads, "Thomas stille als stane he
stude," which is substituted by Jamieson.

[2] Instead of this and the three next lines, the Lansdowne
MS. reads—

> Thomas said, "Lady, wele is me
>   That ever I baide this day ;
> Nowe ye bene so fayre and whyte,
>   By-fore ye war so blake and gray !
> I pray you that ye wyll me say,
>   Lady, yf thy wyll be,
> Why ye war so blake and gray,
>   Ye said it was because of me."
> "For sothe and I had not been so,
>   Sertayne sothe I shall the tell,
> Me had been as good to goo
>   To the brynnyng fyre of hell.
> My lorde is so fers and fell,
>   That is kyng of this contré.
> And full sone he wold have the smell
>   Of the defaute I did with the !"

[3] Jamieson reads, *the feart*, which is, I suppose, the
mistake alluded to by Mr Wright in Warton's Hist. Engl. Poet.
i. 71.   [4] Jamieson reads *with*.

The grettist ferlye that [1] Thomas thoʒt,
    When xxx^{ti}.[2] hartes lay upon flore,
And as mony dere in were broght,
    That was largely, long and store ;
Rachis lay lappand on the dere blode,
    The cokys thei stode with dressing knyves,
Brytnand the dere as thei were wode,
    Revelle was among them rife !
Ther was revelle, gamme, and play,
    More than I yow say perdye,[3]
Tille hit fel upon a day,
    My lufly lady seid to me,
" Buske the, Thomas, for thou most gon,
    For here no longur mayst thou be ;
Hye the fast with mode and mone,[4]
    I shalle the bryng to eldyn tre ! "
Thomas onswerid with heavy chere,
    " Lufly lady, thou let me be,
For certenly I have be here
    But the space of dayes thre."
" For sothe, Thomas, I the telle,
    Thou hast bene here seven ʒere and more ;[5]
For here no longur may thou dwelle,
    I shal tel the the skyl wherfore.
To-morou on of hel a fowle fend
    Among these folke shal chese his fee ;

---

[1] Jamieson reads *ther*. The Lansdowne MS. agrees with
our text.
[2] " Feftty."—Lincoln MS.
[3] The Lansdowne MS. reads—

> Thomas dwellyd in that place
> Longer than I sey perdé.

[4] " With myghte and mayne."—Lincoln MS.
[5] " Thre ʒere and more."—Lincoln MS., with which the
Lansdowne MS. agrees.

Thou art a fayre man and a hende,
Ful wel I wot he wil chese the :
For alle the golde that ever myght be,
Fro heven [1] unto the wordis ende,
Thou beys never trayed for me,
For with me I rede the wende."
She broght hym agayn to eldyn tre,
Undurneth the grenewode spray,
In Huntley bankes this [2] for to be,
Ther foulys syng bothe nyȝt and day.
" Fer out over ȝon mownten gray,
Thomas, a fowkyn [3] makes his nest,
A fowkyn is an yrons pray,[4]
For thei in place wille have no rest.
Fare wel, Thomas, I wende my way,
For me most ȝon bentes brown."
This is a fytte, twayn ar to sey
Off [5] Thomas of Erseltowne.

Fytte II.

" Fare wel, Thomas, I wend may, [6]
I may no lengur stand with the."
"Gif me sum tokyn, lady gay,
That I may say I spake with the."

---

[1] The Lincoln MS. reads, " fro hethyne," which seems more correct.
[2] So in the MS., which Jamieson properly corrects to *ther*.
[3] " My fawkone."—Lincoln MS.
[4] " An earlis praye."—Lincoln MS.
[5] " Alle of."—Lincoln MS.
[6] So in the MS. for " my waye," as in the Lincoln and Lansdowne MSS.

H

" To harpe or carpe, Thomas, wher so ever ʒe
   gon,
Thomas, take the chose with the." [1]
" Harpyng," he seid, " kepe [2] I non,
   For tong is chefe of mynstralsé."
" If thou wil spille or talys telle,
   Thomas, thou shal never make lye,
Wher so ever thou gos be frith or felle,
   I pray the speke never no ille of me.
Fare wel, Thomas, and wel thou be,
   I can no longer stand the by."
" Lovely lady, fayre and fre,
   Tel me ʒet of som farley."
" Thomas, truly I the say,
   Whan a tre rote is ded,
The levys fal and dwyne away,
   Frute hit berys nodur white nor red ;
So shalle thes folkys blode be falle,[3]
   That shal be like ʒon rotone tre ;
The Semewes and the Telys [4] alle,
   The Resulle [5] and the Frechel fre,
Alle shalle falle and dwyn away,
   No wondur thoʒ the rote dy,
And mekille bale shal aftur spray,
   Ther joy and blisse were wont to be !
Fare wel, Thomas, I wende my way,
   I may no longur stande the by."
" Lufly lady, gude and gay,
   Telle me ʒet of som ferly."

---

[1] Lincoln MS. reads, " Thomas, thou salle hafe the chose
sothely."
[2] So in MS.—not *ken*, as printed by Jamieson.
[3] The Lincoln MS. reads, " Of the Bayllioefe blod so salle it
falle."
[4] " Comyns " and " Barlays " in MS. Lincoln.
[5] " Russelles."—Lincoln MS.

" Whatkyns ferly, Thomas gode,
    Shuld I tel the, if thi wil be? "
" Telle me [1] of this gentil blode,
    Who shal thrife [2] and who shal the,
Who shal be kyng, who shall be non,
    And who shal weld the North cuntré;
Who shalle fle, and who shalbe tane,
    And wher thes battelles don shall be."
" Off a batelle I wil the telle,
    That shalle come sone at wille,
Barons shalle mete both fre [3] and felle,
    And fresshely feʒt at Ledyn [4] hille.
The Brutys [5] blode shalle undur falle,
    The Bretens blode shalle wyn the spray;
C. thowsand [6] men ther shalbe slayne
    Off Scottysshe men, that nyght and day.
Fare wel, Thomas, I wende my way,
    To stande with the me thynk fulle yrke;
Off the next batelle I wil the say,
    That shall be at Fawkyrke.
The Bretans blode shalle undur faile,
    The Brouttus blode shalle wyn the spray;
Vij. thousynd Englisshe-men, gret and smalle,
    Ther shalle be slayne that nyght and day!
Fare wel, Thomas, I pray the sees,
    No longur here thou tarry me;

---

[1] "Lady."—Lansdowne MS.
[2] "Unthrive."—Sloane MS.
[3] "Fers."—Lansdowne MS.
[4] "Eldone"—in the Lincoln and Sloane MSS. The Lansdowne MS. reads "Halydowne."
[5] "Brutys" and "Bretens" change places in the Lincoln MS., and the interchange is made in other places in the various copies of this ballad. The former means Scotch, the latter English.
[6] Six thousand English is the number in the Lincoln MS., and three thousand Scots in the Sloane MS.

Lo! wher my grayhounds breke ther leesshe,
   My raches breke their coupuls in thre :
Lo! qwer the dere goes be too and too,
   And holdis over ʒonde mowntene hye!"
Thomas seid, "God schilde thou goo,
   But telle me ʒet of sum ferly;
Holde thi greyhoundys in thi hande,
   And coupille thi raches to a tree,
And lat the dere reyke over the londe,
   Ther is a herde in holte ly."
"Off a batelle I wil the say,
   That shalle gar lagys mourne in mode;
At Barnokys-barne[1] is watur and clay,
   That shalbe myngyd with mannys blode,
And stedys shalle stumbulle for treson,
   Bothe bay and browne, griselle and gray,
And gentil knyʒtes shall tumbulle doune
   Thoro tokyn of that wyckud way;
The Bretans blode shall undur-falle,
   The Brutys blode shall wyn the spray,
Viij.[2] thousand Englisshemen grete and smalle,
   Ther shalbe slayne that nyght and day :
Then shall Scotland kyngles be seen.[3]
   Trow this wel, that I the say,
And thei shalle chese a kyng ful ʒong,
   That can no lawes lede perfay;
Robert with[4] care he shal begynne,
   And also he shalle wynde awey,

---

[1] That is, Bannockburn. See the Reliq. Antiq. i. 30.

[2] Six thousand, according to the Lincoln and Sloane MSS.

[3] Here is a long interpolation in the Lincoln and Sloane MSS. ; but all the copies differ so much in the account of the prophecies, that it will be scarcely neceesary to note them at length.

[4] "David withoute."—Lansdowne MS.

Lordys and ladys, bothe olde and yongg,
  Shalle draw to hym withoutyne nay,
And they with pryde to Englond ryde,
  Est and west that liggyest his way,
And take a toune of mych pryde,
  And sle alle the knyꝫtes veray.[1]
Betwene a parke and an abbay,
  A palys and a perissh kyrke,
Ther shalle the kyng mys of his way,[2]
  And of his life be fulle yrke ;
He shalbe teyryd ful wondur sore,
  So away he may not fle,
His neb shalle rife, or he then fare,
  The red blode triklond to his knee ;
Betwene a wycked way and a watur,[3]
  A perke and a stony way then,
Ther shal a cheften mete in fere,
  A ful dutey ther shalbe slayne ;[4]
The todur cheften shalbe tane,
  A pesans of blode hyme shal slee,
And lede hym away in won,
  And cloyse hym in a castelle hee !
Fare wel, Thomas I wende my way,
  For I most over ꝫond bentes browne."
Here ar twoo fyttes : on is to say
  Off Thomas of Erseldowne.

---

[1] " And let the men be slaine awaye."—Sloane MS.
[2] The Lincoln, Lansdowne, and Sloane MSS. read " praye."
[3] The Lincoln MS. is here very imperfect, but it is clear, from what still remains, that it had an insertion of about a column. The Sloane MS. is also more extended.
[4] The Sloane MS. reads, " The on shall doughtles be slayne ; " and the Lansdowne MS. reads, " And that o dowghty ther shall be slayne."

Fytte III.

" Thomas, truly I the say,
    This worlde is wondur wankille ;
Off the next batelle I wylle the say,
    That shalbe done at Spynard hille.
The Brutes blode shalle undur falle,
    The Brettens blode schalle wyne the spray ;
Xiij. thousand [1] ther shalbe slayne
    Off Scottishe men that nyght and day.
Off the next batelle I wil the telle,
    That shalbe done sone at wille,
Barons bothe flesshe [2] and felle,
    Shalle fresshely fyʒt at Pentland hylle ;
But when [3] Pentland and Edyn borow,
    And the hille that standes one the red clay,
Vij. thousande [4] ther shalbe slayne thore
    Off Scottisshe men that nyght and day.
Then shalle they met, bathe stiffe and strong,
    Betwene Seton and the see ;
The Englisshe shalle lyg the cragys among,
    The tother at the est banke falleth hye. [5]
The Florence forth shalle fare
    Upon a Sonday before the masse ;
V. thousande [6] ther shalbe slayne,
    Off bothe partyes more or lesse,

---

[1] Six thousand English is the number in the Lincoln MS.,
and seven thousand in the Sloane MS.
[2] " Fyers."—Sloane MS.
[3] So in the MS. for *between*.
[4] Eleven thousand is the number in the Lincoln MS., and
twelve thousand in the Sloane MS. The Landsowne MS. agrees
with our text.
[5] The Landsowne MS. reads, " That othere oste at Barklé."
[6] " Sevene thowsandes" is the reading of the Lincoln MS.
The Sloane and Landsowne MSS. agree with our text.

For that ther shalle no barrons presse,[1]
But fer asondur shalle they be,
Carfulle shalbe the furst masse
Betwene Setone and the see :
Then shall thei feʒt with helmy and shyld there,
    And woundyt men al Eneglych shall rone
    awey,
But on the morne ther shalbe care,
    For nedyr side shall have the gree ;
Then shalle thei take a truce and swere,
    Thre ʒere and more, I undurstonde,
Ther nouther side shall odir dere,
    Nouther be se, nor be londe,
Betwene the twoo Seynt Mary dayes,
    When the time waxis nere long,
Then shalle thei mete and baneres rese
    In Gleydes-more, that is so long ;
Gladys-more, that gladis us alle,
    This is begynyng of oure gle,
Gret sorrow then shalle falle,
    Wher rest and pees were wont to be.
Crowned kyngus ther shalbe slayne
    With dyntes sore, and wondur se ;
Out of a more a raven shal one,
    And of hym a schrew shalle flye,
And seke the more, withouten rest,
    Aftur a crosse is made of stone,
Hye and low, bothe est and west,
    But up he shall fynde non ;
He shalle liʒ ther the cross shuld be,
    And holde his neb up to the skye ;
And he shalle drynk of the see,
    Ladys shalle cry welawey !

---

[1] " Baneres presse."—Lincoln MS.

Then shal they f3ght with hem
   Unto the sun be set nere west,
There is no wy3t in that fylde
   That wottes qwylke side shalle have the best,
A bastarde shal cum fro a forest,[1]
   Not in Ynglond borne shall he be,
And he shalle wyn the gre for the best,
   Alle men leder of Bretan shal he be ;
And with pride to Ynglond ride,
   Est and west in certan,
And holde a perlement with pryde,
   Where never non before was seyne.
Alle [2] false lawes he shall laye doune,
   That ar begune in that cuntré ;
Truly to wyrke he shalbe boune,
   And alle leder of Bretans shal he be ;
The bastarde shal get hym power strong,
   And alle his foes he shalle doune dyng,
Off alle the v. kyngus landes,
   Ther shal no bodword home bryng ;
The bastarde shal dye in the holy land,
   Trow this wel, y the sey,
Take his sowle to his hond,
   Jhesu Christe that myculle may,
Thomas, truly, I the say,[3]
   This is trewith ylke a worde,
Off that laste battel I the say,
   It shalbe done at Sandeford.
Nere Sendyforth ther is a wroo,[4]

---

[1] " Out of the West."—Landsowne MS.
[2] " And "—Landsowne MS. The Cambridge MS. is very much defaced hereabouts.
[3] " Thomas, trowe that I the tell."—Sloane MS.
[4] The Sloane MS. reads *braye,* and the Landsowne MS. reads *bro.*

And nere that wro is a welle,
A ston ther is the wel even fro,
And nere the wel, truly to telle ;
On that grounde ther groeth okys thre,
And is called Sondyford,
There the last batel done shallbe,
Thomas, trow thou ilke a worde."
Then he seid with hevy chere—
The terys ran out of his een gray—
"Lady, or thou wepe so sore,
Take thi howndis and wend thi way."
" I wepe not for my way-walkyng,
Thomas, truly I the say,
But for ladys shall wed laddys ʒong,
When ther lordis ar dede awey ;
He shalle have a stede in stabul fed,
A hauk to beyre upon his hond,
A bright lady to his bed,
That before had none londe ! [1]
Farewel, Thomas, I wende my way,
Alle this day thou wil me mar."
" Lufly lady, tel thou me
Of Blak Agnes [2] of Donbar ;
And why she have gyvon me the warre,
And put me in hir prison depe,
For I walde dwel with hir,
And kepe hir plees and hir shepe."
" Off Blak Agnes cum never gode,
Wherfor, Thomas, she may not the,

---

[1] "His elders before him had no land."—Sloane MS.

[2] This was the celebrated Countess of Dunbar, who defended that castle against the English, in 1337. The connection which is here mentioned as existing between her and Thomas of Ercildoun may be compared with the curious prophecy in MS. Harl. 2253, which has been printed by Mr Laing.

For al hur welth and hir worldly gode,
　In Londone cloysed [1] shall she be :
Ther prevysse never gode of hir blode,
　In a dyke then shalle she dye,
Houndis of hir shalle have ther fode,
　Magrat of alle hir kyng of le."
Then Thomas a sory man was he,
　The terys ran out of his een gray ;
" Lufly lady, ʒet tell thou me
　If we shall perte for ever and ay."
" Nay, when thou sittes at Erseldown,
　To Hunteley bankes thou tak thi way,
And ther shal I be redy bowne
　To mete the, Thomas, if that I may."
She blew hir horne on hir palfray,
　And leffede Thomas at Eldyrn tre ;
Til Helmeseale she toke the way,
　Thus deperted that lady and he.
Off such a woman wold I here,
　That couth telle me of such ferly.
Jhesu crowned with thorne so clere,
　Bryng us to thy halle on hye !

Explicit.

---

[1] " Slayne."—Sloane MS.

VI.

The Adventures of Sir Gawen.

——*o*——

THE following tale is reprinted from an old chap-book in my possession, entitled, "The Singular Adventures of Sir Gawen, and the enchanted castle, a fairy tale," printed at Glasgow by J. and M. Robertson, and embellished with some hideous woodcuts, one of which represents the hero on horseback, dressed in the costume of the time of George I. Although this story is attributed to the period of Henry VIII., it is perhaps a ramification of one of the wonderful histories concerning Sir Gawayne, a celebrated knight of the Round Table, who is said to have flourished some centuries previously. The various romance-poems relating to this hero have been collected by Sir F. Madden, and published by the Bannatyne Club, 4to, Lond. 1839, where further particulars concerning him may be found.

Towards the latter end of the reign of Henry VIII., Sir Gawen, a man of some fortune and considerable curiosity, fond of enterprise, and insatiate of knowledge, travelled through the northern counties of England. The following singular adventure is

still extant among the family writings, and is still
recorded by his posterity.

It was towards sunset (saith the manuscript), when
Sir Gawen, after having traversed a very lone and
unfrequented path, arrived at the edge of a thick and
dark forest; the sky was suddenly overcast, and it
began to rain, the thunder rolled at a distance, and
sheets of livid lightening flashed across the heath.
Overcome with fatigue and hunger, he rode impati-
ently along the borders of the forest, in hopes of
discovering an entrance, but none was to be found.
At length, just as he was about to dismount, with an
intention of breaking the fence, he discerned, as he
thought, something moving upon the heath, and,
upon advancing towards it, it proved to be an old
woman gathering peat, and who, overtaken by the
storm, was hurrying home as fast as her infirm limbs
would carry her.   The sight of a human creature
filled the heart of Sir Gawen with joy, and hastily
riding up, he enquired how far he had deviated from
the right road, and where he could procure a night's
lodging.   The old woman now slowly lifted up her
palsied head, and discovered a set of features which
could scarcely be called human; her eyes were red,
piercing and distorted, and, rolling horribly, glancing
upon every object but the person by whom she was
addressed, and, at intervals, they emitted a fiery disagreeable light; her hair, of a dirty grey, hung matted
with filth in large masses upon her shoulders, and a
few thin portions rushed abrupt and horizontally from
the upper part of her forehead, which was much
wrinkled, and of a parchment hue; her cheeks were
hollow, withered and red, with a quantity of acrid
rheum; her nose was large, prominent, and sharp;
her lips thin, skinny, and livid; her few teeth black,
and her chin long and peaked, with a number of

bushy hairs depending from its extremity; her nails
also were acute, crooked, and bent over her fingers,
and her garments ragged, and fluttering in the wind,
displayed every possible variety of colour. The
Knight was a little daunted, but the old woman having mentioned a dwelling at some distance, and
offering to lead the way, the pleasure received from
this piece of news effaced the former impression, and
getting from his horse, he laid hold of the bridle, and
they slowly moved over the heath.

The storm had now ceased, and the moon rising,
gave presage of a fine night, just as the old woman,
taking a sudden turn, plunged into the wood by a
narrow path, and almost choaked up with a quantity
of brier and thorn. The trees were thick, and save a
few glimpses of the moon, which now and then
poured light on the uncouth features of his companion, all was dark and dismal; the heart of Sir
Gawen misgave him; neither spoke; and the knight
pursued his guide merely by the noise she made in
hurrying through the bushes, which was done with a
celerity totally inconsistent with her former decrepi-
tude.

At length the path grew wider, and a faint blue
light, which came from a building at some distance,
glimmered before them : they now left the wood, and
issued upon a rocky and uneven piece of ground ;
the moon, struggling through a cloud, cast a doubtful
and uncertain light, and the old woman with a leer,
which made the very hair of Sir Gawen stand an end,
told him that the dwelling was at hand. It was so ;
for a Gothic castle, placed on a considerable elevation,
now came in view; it was a large massy structure,
much decayed, and some parts of it in a totally ruin-
ous condition ; a portion, however, of the keep, or
great tower, was still entire, as was also the entrance

to the court or inclosure, preserved, probably, by the
ivy, whose fibres crept round with solicitous care.
Large fragments of the ruin were scattered about,
covered with moss, and half sunk in the ground, and
a number of old elm-trees, through whose foliage the
wind sighed with a sullen and melancholy sound,
dropped a deep and settled gloom, that scarce permitted the moon to stream by fits upon the building.
Sir Gawen drew near; ardent curiosity, mingled with
awe, dilated his bosom, and he inwardly congratulated
himself upon so singular an adventure, when turning
round to question his companion, a glimpse of the
moon poured full upon his eye so horrid a contexture
of feature, so wild and preternatural a combination,
that, smote with terror, and unable to move, a cold
sweat trickled from every pore, and immediately this
infernal being, seizing him by the arm, and hurrying
him over the drawbridge to the great entrance of the
keep, the portcullis fell with a tremendous sound, and
the knight, starting as it were from a trance, drew his
sword in [the] act to destroy his treacherous guide,
when instantly a horrible and infernal laugh burst
from her, and in a moment the whole castle was in
an uproar, peal after peal issuing from every quarter,
till at length, growing faint, they died away, and a
dead silence ensued.

Sir Gawen, who, during this strange tumult, had
collected all his scattered powers, now looked round
him with determined resolution; his terrible companion had disappeared, and the moon shining full
upon the portcullis, convinced him that any escape
that way was impracticable; the wind sighed through
the elms; the scared owl, uttering his discordant note,
broke from the rustling bough, and a dim twinkling
light beamed from a loop-hole near the summit of
the great tower.   Sir Gawen entered the keep, having

previously reasoned himself into a state of cool fortitude, and bent up every power to the appalling enterprise.   He extended his sword before him, for it was
dark, and proceeded carefully to search around, in
hopes either of discovering some aperture which might
lead to the vestibule or staircase, or of wreaking his
vengeance on the wretch who had thus decoyed him.
All was still as death ; but as he strode over the floor,
a dull, hollow sound issued from beneath, and
rendered him apprehensive of falling through into
some dismal vault, from which he might never be
able to extricate himself.   In this situation, dreading
the effect of each light footstep, a sound, as of many
people whispering, struck his ear ; he bent forward,
listening with eager attention, and as it seemed to
proceed from a little distance before him, he determined to follow it : he did so, and instantly fell
through the mouldering pavement, whilst at the same
time peals of horrid laughter again burst with reiter-
ated clamour from every chamber of the castle.   Sir
Gawen rose with considerable difficulty, and much
stunned with the fall, although, fortunately, the spot
he had dropped upon was covered with a quantity of
damp and soft earth, which gave way to his weight.

He now found himself in a large vault, arched in
the Gothic manner, and supported by eight massy
pillars, down whose sides the damp moisture ran in
cold and heavy drops, the moon shining with great
lustre through three iron-grated windows, which,
although rusty with age, were strong enough to resist
the efforts of Sir Gawen, who, after having in vain
tried to force them, looked around for his sword,
which, during the fall, had started from his grasp,
and in searching the ground with his fingers, he laid
hold of, and drew forth, the fresh bones of an enor-
mous skeleton, yet greasy and moist from the decay-

ing fibres. He trembled with horror. A cold wind brushed violently along the surface of the vault, and a ponderous iron door, slowly grating on its hinges, opened at one corner, and disclosed to the wandering eye of Sir Gawen a broken staircase, down whose steps a blue and faint light flashed by fits, like the lightning of a summer's eve.

Appalled by these dreadful prodigies, Sir Gawen felt, in spite of all his resolution, a cold and death-like chill pervade his frame, and kneeling down, he prayed fervently to that Power, without whose mandate no being is let loose upon another, and feeling himself more calm and resolved, he again began to search for his sword, when a moonbeam falling on the blade, at once restored it to its owner. Sir Gawen, having thus resumed his wonted fortitude and resolution, held a parley with himself, and perceiving no other way by which he could escape, boldly resolved to brave all the terrors of the staircase, and once more recommending himself to his Maker, began to ascend. The light still flashed, enabling him to climb those parts which were not broken or decayed.

He had proceeded in this manner a considerable way, mounting, as he supposed, to the summit of the keep, when suddenly a shrill and agonising shriek issued from the upper part of it, and something rudely brushing down, grasped him with tremendous strength; in a moment he became motionless, cold as ice, and felt himself hurried back by some irresistible being; but just as he had reached the vault, a spectre of so dreadful a shape stalked by within it, that straining every muscle he sprang from the deadly grasp; the iron door rushed in thunder upon its hinges, and a deep hollow groan resounded from beneath. No sooner had the door closed, than yelling screams, and sounds which almost suspended the very pulse of life, issued from the vault, as if a troop of hellish furies, with their chains untied, were dashing them in writhing frenzy, and howling to the uproar. Sir Gawen stood petrified with horror. A stony fear ran to his very heart, and dismayed every sense about him. He stared wide with his long locks upstanding stiffly, and the throbbing of his heart oppressed him.

The tumult at length subsiding, Sir Gawen recovered some portion of strength, which he immediately made use of to convey himself as far as possible from the iron door, and presently reaching his former elevation on the staircase, which, after ascending a few more steps, terminated in a winding gallery. The light, which had hitherto flashed incessantly, now disappeared, and he was left in almost total darkness, except that now and then the moon threw a few cool rays through some broken loopholes, heightening the horror of the scene. He dreaded going forward, and fearfully looked back, lest some yelling fiend should again plunge him into the vault. He stood suspended with apprehension. A mournful wind howled through the apartments of the castle, and listening, he thought he heard the iron door grate upon its hinges. He started with terror, the sweat stood in big drops upon his forehead, his knees smote each other, and he rushed forward with desperate despair, till having suddenly turned a corner of the gallery, a taper, burning with a faint light, gleamed through a narrow dark passage.

Sir Gawen approached the light; it came from an extensive room, the folding-doors of which were wide open. He entered. A small taper in a massy silver candlestick stood upon a table in the middle of the room, but gave so inconsiderable an illumination, that

I

the one end was wrapped in palpable darkness, and the other scarcely broken in upon by a dim light that streamed through a large ramified window, covered with thick ivy. An arm-chair, shattered and damp with age, was placed near the table, and the remains of a recent fire were still visible in the grate. The wainscot of black oak had formerly been hung with tapestry, and several portions still clung to those parts which were near the fire. They possessed some vivacity of tint, and with much gilding, yet apparent on the chimney-piece, and several moulding reliques of costly frames and paintings, gave indisputable evidence of the ancient grandeur of the place. Sir Gawen closed the folding-doors, and taking the taper, was about to survey the room, when a deep hollow groan from the dark end of it smote cold upon his heart. At the same time the sound, as of something falling with a dead weight, echoed through the room.

Sir Gawen replaced the taper, the flame of which was agitated, now quivering, sunk, now streaming, flamed aloft, and as the last pale portion died away, the scarce distinguished form of some terrific being floated slowly by, and again another dreadful groan ran deepening through the gloom. Sir Gawen stood for some time incapable of motion. At length, summoning all his fortitude, he advanced with his sword extended to the darkest part of the room : instantly burst forth in fierce irradiations a blue sulphureous splendor, and the mangled body of a man, distorted with the agony of death, his very fibre racked with convulsion, his beard and hair stiff and matted with blood, his mouth open, and his eyes protruding from their marble sockets, rushed on the fixed and maddening senses of Sir Gawen, whose heart had beat no more, had not a hiss, as of ten thousand fiends, loud, horrible, roused him from the dreadful scene; he started, uttering a wild shriek, his brain turned round, and running, he knew not whither, burst through the folding-doors.

Darkness again spread her sable pall over the unfortunate Sir Gawen, and he hurried along the narrow passage with a feeble and faltering step. His intellect shook, and overwhelmed with the late appalling objects, had not yet recovered any degree of recollection ; and as he wandered in a dream, a confused train of horrible ideas passing unconnected through his mind. At length, however, memory resumed her function, resumed it but to daunt him with harrowing suggestions. The direful horrors of the room behind, and of the vault below, were still present to his eyes, and as a man whom hellish fiends had frightened, he stood trembling, pale, and staring wild.

All was now silent and dark, and he determined to wait in this spot the dawn of day; but a few minutes had scarce elapsed, when the iron door, screaming on its hinges, bellowed through the murmuring ruin. Sir Gawen nearly fainted at the sound, which, pausing for some time, again swelled upon the wind, and at last died away in shrill melancholy shrieks. Again all was silent, and again the same fearful noise struck terror to his soul. Whilst he was thus agitated with horror and apprehension, a dim light streaming from behind, accompanied with a soft, quick, and hollow tread, convinced Sir Gawen that something was pursuing him, and struck with wildering fear, he rushed unconscious down the steps ; the vault received him, and its portal swinging to their close, sounded as the sentence of death. A dun fœtid smoke filled the place, in the centre of which arose a faint and bickering flame. Sir Gawen approached, and beheld a corse suspended over it by the neck, its fat dropped,

and the flame flashing through the vault, gleamed on
a throng of hideous and ghastly features, that now
came forward through the smoke.

Sir Gawen, with the desperate valour of a man who
sees destruction before him, ran furious forward. An
universal shriek burst forth. The corse dropped into
the fire, which, rising with tenfold brilliance, placed
full in view the dreadful form of his infernal guide,
dilated into horror itself. Her face was pale as death,
her eyes were wide open, dead, and fixed; a horrible
grin sat upon her features; her lips black, and half
putrid, were drawn back, disclosing a set of large blue
teeth, and her hair, standing stiffly erect, was of a
withered red.

Sir Gawen felt his blood freeze within him, his
limbs forgot to move, the face, enlarging as it came,
drew near, and swooning, he fell forward on the
ground. Slow passed the vital fluid through the
bosom of Sir Gawen, scarce did the heart vibrate to
its impulse; on his pallid forehead sat a chilly sweat,
and frequent spasms shook his limbs; but at length
returning warmth gave some vigour to his frame, the
energy of life became more suffused, a soothing lan-
guor stole upon him, and on opening his eyes, rushed
neither the images of death or the rites of witchcraft,
but the soft, the sweet and tranquil scenery of a summer's moonlight night.

Enraptured with this sudden and unexpected change
Sir Gawen rose gently from off the ground; over his
head towered a large and majestic oak, at whose foot,
by some kind and compassionate being, he concluded
he had been laid. Delight and gratitude dilated his
heart, and advancing from beneath the tree, whose
gigantic branches spread a large extent of shade, a
vale, beautiful and romantic, through which ran a
clear and deep stream, came full in view; he walked

to the edge of the water, the moon shone with mellow lustre on its surface, and its banks fringed with shrubs, breathed a perfume more delicate than the odours of the East. On one side, the ground, covered with a vivid, soft, and downy verdure, stretched for a considerable extent to the borders of a large forest, which, sweeping round, finally closed up the valley; on the other, it was broken into abrupt and rocky masses swarded with moss, and from whose clefts grew thick and spreading trees, the roots of which, washed by many a fall of water, hung bare and matted from their craggy beds. Sir Gawen forgot, in this delicious vale, all his former sufferings, and giving up his mind to the pleasing influence of curiosity and wonder, he determined to explore the place by tracing the windings of the stream. Scarce had he entered upon this plan when music of the most ravishing sweetness filled the air; sometimes it seemed to float along the valley, sometimes it stole along the surface of the water: now it died away among the woods, and now with deep and mellow symphony it swelled upon the gale.

Fixed in astonishment Sir Gawen scarce ventured to breathe; every sense, save that of hearing, seemed quite absorbed, and when the last faint warblings melted on his ear he started from the spot, solicitous to know from what being those more than human strains had parted, but nothing appeared in view. The moon, full and unclouded, shone with unusual lustre, the white rocks glittered in her beam, and filled with hope he again pursued the windings of the water, which conducting to the narrowest part of the valley, continued their course through the wood.

Sir Gawen entered by a path, smooth, but narrow and perplexed, where, although its branches were so numerous that no preference could be given, or any

direct route long persisted in, yet every turn presented
something to amuse, something to sharpen the edge
of research. The beauty of the trees through whose
interstices the moon gleamed in the most picturesque
manner ; the glimpses of the water, and the notes of
the nightingale, who now began to fill the valley with
her song, were more than sufficient to take off the
sense of fatigue, and he wandered on still eager to
explore, still panting for further discovery.

The wood now became more thick and obscure,
and at length almost dark, when the path taking
suddenly an oblique direction, Sir Gawen found himself on the edge of a circular lawn, whose tint and
softness were beyond compare, and which seemed to
have been lightly brushed by fairy feet. A number
of fine old trees, around whose boles crept the ivy and
the woodbine, rose at irregular distances ; here they
mingled into groves, and there separate, and emulous
of each other, they shook their airy summits in disdain.
The water, which had been for some time concealed,
now murmured through a thousand beds, and visiting
each little flower, added vigour to its vegetation, and
poignancy to its fragrance. Along the edges of the
wood and beneath the shadows of the trees, an innumerable host of glowworms lighted their inocuous
fires, lustrous as the gems of Golconda, and Sir Gawen,
desirous yet longer to enjoy the scene, went forward
with light footsteps on the lawn ; all was calm, and
except the breeze of night, that sighed soft and
sweetly through the world of leaves, a perfect silence
prevailed. Not many minutes, however, had elapsed
before the same enchanting music, to which he had
listened with so much rapture in the vale, again
arrested his ear, and presently he discovered on the
border of the lawn, just rising above the wood, and
floating on the bosom of the air, a being of the most

delicate form; from his shoulders streamed a tunic of the tenderest blue, his wings and feet were clothed in downy silver, and in his grasp he had a wand, white as the mountain snow. He rose swiftly in the air, his brilliance became excessive from the lunar rays, his song echoed through the vault of night, but having quickly diminished to the size and appearance of the evening star, it died away, and the next moment he was lost in æther.

Sir Gawen still fixed his eye on that part of the heavens where the vision had disappeared, and shortly had the pleasure of again seeing the star-like radiance, which in an instant unfolded itself into the full and fine dimensions of the beauteous being, who having collected dew from the cold vales of Saturn, now descended rapidly towards the earth, and waving his wand, as he passed athwart the woods, a number of like form and garb flew round him, and alighting on the lawn separating at equal distances on its circumference, and then shaking their wings which spread a perfume through the air, burst into one general song. Sir Gawen, who apprehensive of being discovered, had retreated within the shadow of some mossy oaks, now waited with eager expectation the event of so singular a scene. In a few moments a bevy of elegant nymphs, dancing two by two, issued from the wood on the right, and an equal number of warlike knights, accompanied by a band of minstrels, from that of the left. The knights were clothed in green; on their bosoms shone a plate of burnished steel, and in their hands they grasped a golden targe and lance of beamy lustre. The nymphs, whose form and symmetry were beyond whatever poets dream, were dressed in robes of white, their zones were azure, dropt with diamonds, and their light brown hair decked with roses hung in ample ringlets. So quick, so light and airy, was their

motion, that the turf, the flowers, shrunk not to the
gentle pressure, and each smiling on her favourite
knight, he flung his brilliant arms aside and mingled
in the dance.

Whilst thus they flew in rapid measures o'er the
lawn, Sir Gawen, forgetting his situation, and impatient
to salute the assembly, involuntarily stept forward, and
instantaneously a shrill and hollow gust of wind murmured through the woods, the moon dipt into a cloud,
and the knights, the dames and aërial spirits vanished
from the view, leaving the amazed Sir Gawen to repent
at leisure of his precipitate intrusion; scarce, however,
had he time to determine what he should pursue,
when a gleam of light flashed suddenly along the
horizon, and the beauteous being, whom he first
beheld in the air, stood before him; he waved his
snowy wand, and pointing to the wood, which now
appeared sparkling with a thousand fires, moved
gently on. Sir Gawen felt an irresistible impulse
which compelled him to follow, and having penetrated
the wood, he perceived many bright rays of light,
which, darting like the beams of the sun, through
every part of it, most beautifully illuminated the shafts
of the trees. As they advanced forwards, the radiance
became more intense and converged towards the
centre; and the fairy being turning quickly round,
commanded Sir Gawen to kneel down, and having
squeezed the juice of an herb into his eyes, bade him
now proceed, but that no mortal eye, unless it powers
of vision were increased, could endure the glory that
would shortly burst upon them.

Scarce had he uttered these words, when they
entered an amphitheatre. In its centre was a throne
of ivory inlaid with sapphires, on which sat a female
form of exquisite beauty; a plain coronet of gold
obliquely crossed her flowing hair, and her robe of

white sattin hung negligent in ample folds. Around
her stood five and twenty nymphs clothed in white
and gold, and holding lighted tapers; beyond
these were fifty of the aërial beings, their wings of
downy silver stretched for flight, and each a burning taper in his hand : and lastly, on the circumference of the amphitheatre shone one hundred knights
in mail of tempered steel; in one hand they shook
aloft a large targe of massy diamond, and in the other
flashed a taper. So excessive was the reflection, that
the targes had the lustre of an hundred suns, and
when shaken sent forth streams of vivid lightning;
from the gold, the silver, and the sapphires, rushed
a flood of tinted light, that, mingling, threw upon the
eye a series of revolving hues.

Sir Gawen impressed with awe, with wonder and
delight, fell prostrate on the ground, whilst the fairy
spirit advancing knelt and presented to the queen a
crystal vase. She rose, she waved her hand, and
smiling, bade Sir Gawen to approach. "Gentle
stranger," she exclaimed, "let not fear appal thine
heart; for to him whom courage, truth and piety
have distinguished, our friendship and our love is
given. Spirits of the blest we are, our sweet employment is to befriend the wretched and the weary, to
lull the torture of anguish, and the horror of despair.
Ah! never shall the tear of innocence or the plaint
of sorrow, the pang of injured merit or the sigh of
hopeless love, implore our aid in vain. Upon the
moonbeam do we float, and, light as air, pervade the
habitations of men ; and hearken, O favoured mortal!
I tell thee spirits pure from vice are present to thy
inmost thoughts; when terror and when madness, when
spectres and when death surrounded thee, our influence
put to flight the ministers of darkness; we placed
thee in the moonlight vale, and now upon thy head I

pour the planetary dew, from Hecate's dread agents, it will free thee from wildering fear and gloomy superstition."

She ended, and Sir Gawen, impatient to express his gratitude, was about to speak, when suddenly the light turned pale and died away, the spirits fled, and music soft and sweet was heard remotely in the air. Sir Gawen started, and in place of the refulgent scene of magic, he beheld a public road, his horse cropping the grass which grew upon its edge, and a village at a little distance, on whose spire the rising sun had shed his earliest beams.

VII.

Huon of Bourdeaux.

———o———

S HAKESPEARE probably took the name of Oberon from this
early French romance, which was translated into English
about 1540 by Lord Berners, at the request of the Earl of
Huntingdon. It is mentioned among Captain Cox's book's, Laneham's Letter, 1575, and in Markham's "health to the gentlemanly
profession of Serving-men," 1598; but the earliest edition of the
English translation now known to exist in a perfect state bears
date in 1601, "being now the third time imprinted, and the
rude English corrected and amended." From this edition the
following extracts are made, which are curious as being probably the work in which Shakespeare had read of Oberon and
fairy land, and reconciled him to transporting his native fairy
creed so far towards the magic regions of the East.

CHAP. 20.—*How Huon of Bourdeaux departed from
Brandis, and Garyn his uncle with him; and how
he came to Jerusalem, and from thence into the deserts,
whereas he found Gerames, and of their conference.*

When Huon and Garyn were entred into their

ship, they hoysed up their sailes, and sayled night and
daye, so that at last they arrived safely at the port of
Jaffe, where they tooke landing, and drew out their
horses, and road foorth so the same day, that they
came to Rames, and the next day to the citie of Jerusalem. That night they rested, and the next day they
did their pilgrimage to the Holy Sepulchre, and there
devoutly heard service, and offered according to their
devotion.

When Huon came before the Holy Sepulchre, he
kneeled downe upon his bare knees, and all weeping
made his prayers to our Lord God, requiring him to
ayd and comfort him in his voyage, so that he might
returne againe into Fraunce, and to have peace with
King Charlemaine. And when they all had made
their prayers and offered, Huon and Garyn went into
a little chapell upon the mount of Calverye, whereas
nowe lyeth the bodies of Godfrey of Bullen, and
Bauldwin his brother. There Huon called unto him
all those that came with him out of France, and said,
" Sirs, you that for the love of mee have left your
fathers and mothers, wives and children, lands and
signiories, for this courtesie that you have shewed mee
I thanke you. Now you may returne into Fraunce
againe, and humbly recommend mee to the kinges
good grace, and unto all the other barons : and when
you come to Bourdeaux, do my dutie to the Duchesse
my mother, and to Gerard my brother, and unto the
lords of my countrey." Then Guicard and all the
other knights answeared Huon and said, " Sir, as yet
we will not leave you, neither for death nor life, untill
we have brought you unto the Red Sea."—" Why
then," quoth Huon, " for the great service and curtesie
that you offer mee I thanke you." Then Garyn called
two of his servants, and commaunded them to returne
unto his wife, and to desire her to be of good cheere,

and that shortly he would returne; the which thing they did, and returned and did their messuage.

When Huon understood that his uncle Garyn was disposed to abide with him, he sayd, "Faire uncle, you shall not neede to travaile so much; I would councell you to returne unto your wife and children."—"Sir," quoth Garyn, "and God will I shall not leave you no day untill you returne yourselfe."—"Uncle," quoth Huon, "I thanke you of your courtesie."

Then they went to their lodging and dyned, and after dinner tooke their horses, and so road by hils and dales, so that if I should recount all the adventures that they found in their way, it should be too long a processe to shew it: but as the true historie witnesseth, they suffered much paine and travaile, for they passed such deserts, whereas they found but small sustenance, whereof Huon was right sorrowfull for the love of them that were with him, and began to weepe, and to remember his owne countrey, saying, "Alas, noble king of Fraunce, great wrong and great sinne you have done me, thus to drive me out of my countrey, and to send mee into a strange land, to the entent to shorten my dayes: I pray God to pardon you therefore." Then Garyn and the other knights comforted him, and said, "Alas, Sir, dismay you not for us; God is puissant ynough to ayd us; hee never fayleth them that loveth him."

Thus they road forth in the desert so long, untill at last they saw a little cottage, before the which sat an old ancient man with a long white beard, and his heare hanging over his shoulders. When Huon perceived him, he drew thether, and saluted the olde man in the name of God and of the blessed Virgin Marie. Then the ancient man lifted up his eyes and beheld Huon, and had great marvaile, for of a long season before, he had seene no man that spake of God. Then he beheld Huon in the face, and began sore to weepe, and stepping unto Huon, tooke him by the leg, and kissed it more than twentie times. " Freend," quoth Huon, " I desire you shew me why you make this sorrow." — " Sir," quoth he, " about thirtie yeares passed I came hether, and since that time, I never sawe man beleeving on the Christian faith, and now the regarding of your visage causeth me to remember a noble prince that I have seene in France, who was called Duke Sevin of Bourdeaux ; therefore I require you shew me if ever you saw him ; I pray you not hide it from me."—" Freend," quoth Huon, " I pray you shew me where you were borne, and of what line-age and countrey you be of."—" Nay, sir," quoth he, "that I will not doe; first you shal shew me what you be, and where you were borne, and why you come hether."—" Freend," quoth Huon, " seeing it pleaseth you to know, I shall shew you." Then Huon and all his companye alighted, and tyed theyr horses to trees.

When Huon was alighted, he sat downe by the old man, and said, " Freend, since you will needes know my businesse, I shall shew you : know for truth I was borne in the citie of Bourdeaux, and am son to Duke Sevin." And Huon shewed him all his whole case and enterprize, and of the death of Charlot, and how he discomfited Earle Amerie, and howe that Charlemaine hadde chaced him out of Fraunce, and of the messuage that he was charged to say unto the admirall Gaudise, affirming alle to be for certaintie. When the oulde man hadde well heard Huon, he began soore to weepe. "Sir," quoth Huon, " Since it pleaseth you to know of my sorrowe, Duke Sevin my father is dead seaven yeares past, my mother I trust be alive, and a brother of mine whome I have left with her. And nowe, sir, seeing you have heard of mine affaires, I require you give me your counsaile and advice, and also, if it

please you, to shew me what you be, and of what
countrey, and how you came into these parts." " Sir,"
quoth the old man, "know for troth I was borne in
Geronvill, and am brother to the good provost Guyer ;
and when I departed thence, I was a young knight
and haunted the justes and tourneys, so that on
a daie it fortuned at a tourney that was made at
Poytiers, I slew a knight of a noble bloud, wherefore
I was banished out of the realme of Fraunce. But
my brother the provost made such a request to Duke
Sevin your father, that by his meanes my peace was
made with the king, and my land saved, upon condition that I should goe to the Holy Sepulchre to punish
my bodie for the knight that I slew, and to forgive
my faults. Thus I departed out of my countrey, and
when I had done my voyage, I thought to have returned, but as I departed out of the citie of Jerusalem,
to take the way to Acres, passing by a wood between
Jerusalem and Naples, there came upon me ten
Sarazins, who tooke me and brought me to the citie of
Babilon, whereas I was in prison two yeares complet,
whereas I suffered much povertie and miserie ; but our
Lord God, who never fayleth them that serveth him, and
have in him full affiance, he sent me the grace, that
by the meanes of a right noble ladie, I was brought
out of prison in a night, and so I fled into this forrest,
whereas I have beene this thirtie yeares, and in all
this space I never saw nor heard man beleeving in Jesus
Christ : thus have I shewed you all mine affaires."

When Huon had heard the knight's tale, he had
great joy, and embraced him, and saide, " Howe
often times he had seene Guyer his brother the Provost weepe for him, and when I departed from Bourdeaux," quoth he, " I delivered unto him all my lands
to governe ; wherefore I require you shew mee your
name." " Sir," quoth he, " I am called Gerames, and

now I pray you, shew me your name." " Sir," quoth
he, " I am named Huon, and my younger brother is
called Gerard. But, sir, I pray you shew me how you
have so long lived heere, and what sustenance you
have had." " Sir," quoth Gerames, " I have eaten
none other thing but rootes and fruites that I have
found in the wood." Then Huon demaunded of him
if he could speake the language Sarazin. " Yes, sir,"
quoth he, " as well or better than any Sarazin in the
countrey, nor there is no way but that I know it."

When Huon had heard Gerames, then he demaunded further of him if he could goe to Babilon.
" Yes, sir," quoth Gerames, " I can goe thether by
two wayes; the most surest way is hence about fortie
days' journey, and the other is but fifteene dayes'
journey: but I councell you to take the longe way,
for if you take the shorter way, you must passe
thorow a wood about sixteene leagues of length, but
the way is so full of the fayryes and strang things,
that such as passe that way are lost, for in that wood
abideth a king of the fayryes named Oberon; he is
of height but of three foote, and crooked shouldered,
but yet he hath an angell-like visage, so that there is
no mortal man that seeth him, but that taketh great
pleasure to behold his face ; and you shall no sooner
be entred into that wood, if you go that way, but he
wil find the meanes to speake with you, and if you
speake unto him, you are lost for ever, and you shall
ever find him before you, so that it shall be in manner
impossible that you can scape from him without
speaking to him, for his words be so pleasant to
heare, that there is no mortall man that can well
scape without speaking unto him. And if he see
that you will not speake a word unto him, then he
will be sore displeased with you, and before you can
get out of the wood, he will cause raine and wind,

hayle and snowe, and will make marvelous tempests, with thunder and lightenings, so that it shall seeme unto you that all the world should perish, and he will make to seeme before you a great running river blacke and deepe, but you may passe it at your ease, and it shall not wet the feet of your horse, for all is but fantasie and enchauntments that the dwarfe shall make to the entent to have you with him, and if you can keepe yourselfe without speaking unto him, you may then well escape. But, sir, to eschew all perils, I councell you to take the longer way, for I thinke you cannot escape from him, and then you be lost for ever."

When Huon had well heard Gerames, he had great marvaile, and he had great desire in himselfe to see that dwarfe king of the fayryes, and the strang adventures that were in that wood. Then he said unto Gerames that for feare of any death hee would not leave to passe that way, seeinge hee might come to Babilon in fifteene dayes, for in taking the longer way, hee might perchaunce find more adventures, and since he was advertised that with keeping his tongue from speaking he might abridge his journey he sayd that surely he would take that way whatsoever chaunce befell. "Sir," quoth Gerames, you shall doe your own pleasure, for which way soever you take, it shall not be without me, I shall bring you to Babilon to the Admirall Gaudise: I knowe him right well, and when you bee come thether, you shall see there a damsell, as I have heard say, the most fairest creature in all Inde, and the onely and most sweetest and most courteous that ever was borne, and it is shee that you seeke, for shee is daughter to the admirall Gaudise."

K

CHAP. 21.—*How Gerames went with Huon and his companie, and so came into the wood, whereas they found King Oberon, who conjured them to speake unto him.*

When Huon had well heard Gerames, how he was minded to goe along with him, hee was thereof right joyfull, and thanked him of his courtesy and service, and gave him a goodly horse, whereon he mounted, and so road foorth together so long that they came into the wood whereas king Oberon haunted most. Then Huon, who was wearie of travaile, and what for famine and for heate, the which he and his companie had endured two dayes without bread or meat, so that he was so feeble that he could ride no further, and then he began pityously to weepe, and complayned of the great wronge that kinge Charlemaine had done unto him; and then Garyn and Gerames comforted him, and had great pitie of him, and they knew well by the reason of his youth, hunger oppressed him more than it did to them of greater age. Then they alighted under a great oake, to the entent to search for some fruit to eate. They glad thereof, let their horses goe to pasture.

When they were thus alighted, the dwarfe of the fayry kinge Oberon came ryding by, and had on a gowne so rich that it were marvaile to recount the riches and fashion thereof, and it was so garnished with precious stones, that the clearnesse of them shined like the sonne. Also he had a goodlie bow in his hand, so rich that it could not be esteemed, and his arrowes after the same sort; and they were of such a nature or qualitie, that any beast in the world that he would wish for, the arrowe would arrest him. Also he had about his necke a rich horne hanging by two

laces of gold. The horne was so rich and faire that
there never was seene any such. It was made by
foure ladies of the fayries in the isle of Chafalons; one
of them gave to the horne such a propertie, that whosoever heard the sound thereof, if he were in the
greatest sickenesse in the world, he should incontinent be whole and sound: the ladie that gave this gift
to the horne was named Glorianda. The second ladie
was named Translyna; she gave to this horne another
propertie, and that was, whosoever heard this horne,
if he were in the greatest famine of the worlde, he
should be satisfied as well as though he had eaten al
that he woulde wishe for, and so likewise for drinke as
well as though he had droonke his fil of the best wine
in al the world. The third ladie named Margala
gave to this horne yet a greater gift, and that was,
whosoever heard this horne, though he were never so
poore or feeble by sicknesse, he should have such joy
in his heart that he should singe and daunce. The
fourth ladie named Lempatrix gave to this horne
such a gift that whosoever heard it, if he were an
hundred dayes' journey of, he should come at the
pleasure of him that blew it farre or neare.

Then king Oberon, who knew well and had seene
the fourteene companions, he set his horne to his
mouth, and blew so melodious a blast that the fourteene companions, being under the tree, had so perfit
a joy at their hearts, that they al rose up and began
to sing and daunce. " Ah, good Lord," quoth Huon,
" what fortune is come unto us ? Me thinke we be in
Paradise; right now I could not sustaine myselfe for
lacke of meat and drinke, and nowe I feele myselfe
neither hungrie nor thirstie ! From whence may this
come ?" " Sir," quoth Gerames, " knowe for troth
this is done by the dwarfe of the fayrye, whome you
shall soone see passe by you. But, sir, I require you

on jeopardie of loosing of your life, that you speake
to him no word, without you purpose to abide ever
with him." "Sir," quoth Huon, "have no doubt of
me, seeing I know the jeopardie." Therewith the
dwarfe began to crie aloude, and saide, "Yee fourteene men that passe by my wood, God keepe you
all! and I desire you speake with mee, and I conjure
you thereto by God Almightie, and by the Christen-
dome that you have received, and by all that God
hath made, answeare mee!"

CHAP. 22.—*How king Oberon was right sorrowfull
and sore displeased, in that Huon would not
speake: and of the great feare that he put Huon
and his companie in.*

When that Huon and his companie heard the
dwarfe speake, they mounted on their horses, and road
away as fast as they might without speaking of any
word; and the dwarfe seeing how that they road
away and would not speake, hee was sorrowfull and
angrie. Then hee set one of his fingers on his horne,
out of the which yssued such a winde and tempest so
horrible to heare, that it bare downe trees, and therewith came such a raine and hayle, that it seemed that
heaven and the earth had fought together, and that
the world should have ended; the beasts in the woods
brayed and cryed, and the foules of the ayre fell down
dead for the feare that they were in; and there was
no creature but he would have been afrayd of that
tempest. Then suddainly appeared before them a
great river that ran swifter then the birds did flye, and
the water was so blacke and so perilous, and made
such a noyse that it might be heard ten leagues of.
"Alas!" quoth Huon, "I see well now we be all lost;
wee shall heere be oppressed without God have pitie

of us. I repent me that ever I entred into this wood. I had been better to have travailed a whole yeere then to have come hether." "Sir," quoth Gerames, "dismay you not, for all this is done by the dwarfe of the fayrye." "Well," quoth Huon, "I thinke it best to alight from our horses, for I thinke we shall never escape from hence, but that we shalbe all oppressed." Then Garyn and the other companions had great marvaile, and were in great feare. "Ah! Gerames," quoth Huon, "you showed mee well that it was great perill to passe this wood. I repent mee now that I had not beleeved you."

Then they sawe on the other side of the river a faire castell, envyroned with fourteene great towers, and on everie tower a clocher of fine gould by seeming, the which they long regarded, and by that time they had gone a little way by the river side, they lost the sight of the castle, it was cleane vanished away, whereof Huon and his companie were sore abashed. "Huon," quoth Gerames, "of all this that you see dismay you not, for all this is done by the crooked dwarfe of the fayrye, and all to beguile you, but he cannot greeve you, so you speake no word: howbeit, ere we depart from him, he will make us all abashed, for anone he will come after us like a mad man, bicause you will not speake unto him: but, sir, I require you as in God's name, be nothing afrayd, but ride foorth surely, and ever beware that you speake unto him no word." "Sir," quoth Huon, "have no doubt thereof, for I had rather he were destroyed then I should speake one word unto him." Then they road to passe the river, and they founde there nothing to let them, and so road about five leagues. "Sir," quoth Huon, "wee may well thanke God that wee bee thus escaped this dwarfe, who thought to have deceived us; I was never in such feare during my life, God confound him. Thus they road, devising of the little dwarfe, who had done them so much trouble.

CHAP. 23.—*How kinge Oberon, dwarfe of the fayry, pursued so much Huon that he constrained him to speake to him at last.*

When Gerames understood the companie, how they thought they were escaped from the dwarfe, he began to smile, and said, "Sirs, make no bragging that you be out of this danger, for I beleeve you shall soone see him againe." And as soone as Gerames had spoke the same words, they sawe before them a bridge the which they must passe, and they sawe the dwarfe on the other part. Huon saw him first and said, "I see that divell who hath done us so much trouble." Oberon heard him and saide, "Freend, thou doest me injurie without cause, for I was never divell nor ill creature : I am as other be ; but I conjure thee by the divine puissance, to speake unto me." Then Gerames said, "Sirs, for God's sake let him alone, nor speake no word to him, for by his faire language he may deceive us all, as he hath done many other; it is a pity that he hath lived so long." Then they road forth a good pace, and left the dwarfe alone, sore displeased in that they would not speake to him. Then he tooke his horne, and set it to his mouth, and blew it. When Huon and his companie heard it they had no power to ride any further, but they began all to sing. Then Oberon the dwarfe said, "Yonder company are fooles and proud, that for any salutation that I can give them, they disdaine to answeare mee : but by the God that made me, before they escape me, the refusall of my words shalbe deere bought." Then he tooke againe his horne, and strooke it three times on his bowe, and cryed out aloud, and

said, " Yee, my men, come and appeare before me."
Then there came to him aboute foure hundred men
of armes, and demaunded of Oberon what was his
pleasure, and who had displeased him. "Sirs," quoth
Oberon, " I shall shew you : howbeit I am greeved to
shewe it : heere in this woode there passed fourteene
knights, who disdaine to speak unto me ; but to the
entent that they shall not mocke me, they shall deerely
buy the refusing of their answeare ; wherefore I will
you goe after them, and slay them all : let none
escape." Then one of his knights said, " Sir, for
God's sake have pitie of them." " Certainly," quoth
Oberon, " mine honour saved, I cannot spare them,
since they disdaine to speak unto me." " Sir," quoth
Glorianda, " for God's sake doe not as you say ; but,
Sir, worke by my counsaile, and after doe as it
pleaseth you. Sir, I counsaile you yet once againe
goe after them : then, if they do not speake, we shall
slay them all ; for surely, sir, if they see you returne
again to them so shortly, they will be in great feare."
" Freend," quoth Oberon, " I shall do as you have
counsailed mee."

Thus Huon and his company road forth a great
pace, and Huon said, " Sirs, we are now from the
dwarfe about five leagues ; and I never sawe in my
life so faire a creature in the visage ; I have great
marvaile how he can speake of Almightie God, for I
thinke he be a devill of hell ; and since he speaketh
of God, meethinkes we ought to speake to him, for I
thinke such a creature can have no power to doe us
any evill ; I thinke hee be not past the age of five
yeares." " Sir," quoth Gerames, " as little as he seem-
eth, and that you take him for a child, he was borne
fortie yeares before the nativitie of our Lord Jesus
Crist." "Surely," quoth Huon, " I care not what
age he be of, but if he come againe, ill hap come to

me if I keepe my words and speach from him; I pray
you be not displeased.'

And thus as they rode devising fifteene dayes, suddainly Oberon appeared unto them, and said, "Sirs,
are you not yet advised to speake unto mee? Yet
againe I am come to salute you in the name of the
God that made and fourmed us, and I conjure you by
the puissance that he hath given me, that you speake
to me; for I repute you for fooles to thinke thus to
passe thorow my wood, and disdaine to speake to mee.
Ah! Huon, I know thee well ynough, and whether
thou wouldst goe.   I know all thy deedes, howe thou
slewest Charlot, and after discomfited Amerie, and I
knowe the messuage that Charlemaine hath charged
thee to say to the admirall Gaudise, the which thing
is impossible to be done without mine ayd, for without me thou shalt never accomplish this enterprize.
Speake to me, and I shall doe thee that courtesie that I
shall cause thee to atchive thine enterprize, the which
is else impossible without mee; and when thou hast
atchived thy messuage, I shall bring thee againe into
Fraunce in safegard.   I knowe the cause that thou wilt
not speake to mee; it is by reason of old Gerames,
who is there with thee.   Therefore, Huon, beware of
thyselfe, go no further, for I know well it is three dayes
passed since thou diddest eate any meate to profit thee.
If thou wilt beleeve me, thou shalt have ynough of
such sustenance as thou wilt wish for; and as soone
as thou hast dyned, I will give thee leave to depart,
if it be thy pleasure; of this have no doubt."   "Sir,"
quoth Huon, "you bee welcome."   "Ah!" quoth
Oberon, "thy salutation shalbe well rewarded; knowe
for truth thou never diddest salutation so profitable
for thyselfe.   Thou mayest thanke God that he hath
sent thee that grace."

CHAP. 24.—*Of the great marvailes that Oberon shewed unto Huon, and of the adventures that fell.*

When Huon had well heard Oberon, he had great marvaile, and demanded if it were true that hee had saide. "Yes, truly," quoth Oberon, "of that make no doubt."—"Sir," quoth Huon, "I have great marvaile for what cause you have alwayes pursued us."—"Huon," quoth Oberon, "know that I love thee well, bicause of the truth that is in thee, and therefore naturally I love thee, and if thou wilt knowe who I am, I shall shew thee. True it is Julius Cæsar engendred me on the Ladie of the secret Isle, who was sometime well beloved of the faire Florimont of Albania. But bicause that Florimont who as then was young, and he had a mother who did so much that she saw my mother and Florimont together in a solitary place on the sea side. When my mother perceived that she was espyed by Florimont's mother, she departed and left Florimont her lover in great weeping and lamentations, and never saw him after. And then shee returned into her owne countrey of the secret isle, the which now is named Chafalone, whereas she married after, and had a sonne who in his time after was king of Egipt, named Nactabanus. It was he, as it is said, that engendred Alexander the great, who after caused him to die. Then after a seaven yeares, Cæsar passed by the sea as he went unto the place whereas he fought with Pompey. In his way hee passed by Chafalone, where my mother fetched him, and hee fell in love with her, bicause she shewed him that he should discomfite Pompey, as he did.

Thus I have shewed you who was my father. At my birth there was many princes and barons of the

fairy, and many a noble ladie that came to see my
mother whiles she travailed of me, and amonge them
there was one was not content, bicause shee was not
sent for as well as the other; and when I was borne,
shee gave mee a gift, the which was, that when I
should passe three yeares of age, I should grow no
more, but thus as you see mee nowe: and when she
had thus done, and sawe that she had thus served me
by her words, she repented herselfe, and would recompence mee another way.   Then shee gave me another
gift, and that was that I should be the fairest creature
that ever nature fourmed, as thou mayest see mee
now; and another ladie of the fayry named Translyna
gave me another gift, and that was all that ever any
man can know or thinke good or ill I should knowe
it.   The third ladie, to doe more for me, and to
please my mother the better, she gave me that there
is not so farre a countrey but that if I wil wish myselfe
there, I shal be there incontinent with what number
of men as I list; and moreover, if I will have a castle
or a pallaice at mine own device, incontinent it shall
be made, and as soone gone againe when I list; and
what meat or wine that I would wish for, I should
have it incontinent; and also I am kinge of Momur,
the whiche is about foure hundred leagues from hence;
and if I list, incontinent I can be there.   Know for
troth that thou are arrived at a good port; I know
well thou hast great neede of meat, for this three dayes
thou hast had but small sustenance, but I shall cause
thee to have ynough.   I demaund of thee whether
thou wilt have meat and drinke heere in this meadow,
or in a pallaice, or in a hall; commaund whereas thou
wilt, and though shalt have it for thee and thy companie."—"Sir," quoth Huon, "I will follow your
pleasure, and never doe nor thinke the contrarie."—
"Huon," quoth he, "as yet I have not shewed all the

gifts that were given me at my birth. The fourth
ladie gave me that there is no bird nor beast, be they
never so cruell, but if I will have them, I may take them
with my hande; and also I shall never beseeme elder
then thou seest me now; and when I shal depart out
of this world; my place is appointed in Paradise, for I
knowe that all things created in this mortall world
must needs have an end."—"Sir," quoth Huon,
"such a gift ought to be well kept."—"Huon," quoth
Oberon, "well you were counsailed when you spake
to me, you had never before so faire adventure;
shew me by thy faith if thou wilt eate, and what meate
thou wilt have, and what wine thou wilt drinke."—
"Sir," quoth Huon, "so that I had meate and
drinke, I care not what it were, so that I and my
company were filled and rid from our famine." Then
Oberon laughed at him, and said, "Sirs, all you sit
down here in the meadowe, and have no doubt but all
that I will doe is done by the puissance of our Lord
God." Then Oberon began to wish, and said unto
Huon and his companie, "Sirs, arise up quickly," the
which they did. Then they looked before them, and
saw a faire and a rich pallaice garnished with chambers
and halles, hanged and bedded with rich cloathes of
silke beaten with gold, and tables ready set full of
meat. When Huon and his company sawe the rich
pallaice before them, they had great marvaile, and
Oberon took Huon by the hand, and with him mounted
up into the pallaice. When they came there, they
found servants there readie, bringing unto them
basons of gould garnished with precious stones.
They gave water to Huon, and he sat down at the
table, the which was furnished with all manner of
meate and drinke that man could wish.

Oberon sat the tables end upon a bench of ivorie,
richly garnished with gould and precious stones, the

which seat had such vertue given unto it by the fayrie, that whosoever by any subtil means would poyson him that should sit thereon, as soone as he should approach neere to the seat, he should fall downe starke dead. King Oberon sat thereon richly apparelled, and Huon, who sat neere unto him, began to eat a great pace; but Gerames had small appetite to eate, for he beleeved that they should never depart thence. When Oberon sawe him, he said, "Gerames, eate thy meat and drinke, for as soone as thou hast eaten, thou shalt have leave to goe when thou list." When Gerames heard that, he was joyfull; then he began to eate and drinke, for he knew well that Oberon would not doe against his assurance. All the companie did well eate and drinke; they were served with all thinges that they could wish for. When Huon sawe how they were all satisfied and repleat, and had well dyned, he saide to kinge Oberon, " Sir, when it shall be your pleasure, I would you should give us leave to depart." "Huon," quoth Oberon, "I am right well content so to doe, but first I will shewe you my jewels." Then he called Clariand, a knight of the fayrey, and said, " Freend, goe and fetch to me my cup." He did his commaundement, and when Oberon had the cup in his hand, he said unto Huon, " Sir, behold well, you see that this cup is nowe voyed and emptie." " That is true, sir," quoth Huon. Then Oberon set the cup on the table, and saide unto Huon, " Sir, behold the great power that God hath given mee, and that in the fayrie I may doe what is my pleasure." Then hee made over the cup the signe of a crosse three times, and incontinent the cup was full of wine; and then he said, " Behold, sirs, you may well see that this is done by the g[r]ace of God; yet I shall shewe you the great vertue that is in this cup, for if all the men in the world were heere assembled together, and

that the cup were in the handes of any man, being out
of deadly sinne, he might drinke thereof his fill: but
whosoever offers his hand to take it, being in deadly
sinne, the cuppe doth loose his vertue; and if thou
mayest drinke thereof, I offer to give thee the cup."
"Sir," quoth Huon, "I thanke you, but I am in doubt
that I am not worthy, nor of valour to drinke thereof,
nor to touch the cup; I never heard of such dignitie
as this cup is of: but, sir, knowe for truth I have been
confessed of all my sinnes, and I am repentant and
sorrowfull for that I have done, and I doe pardon and
forgive all the men in the world whatsoever injurie
hath beene done unto me, and I knowe not that I
have done wrong to any creature, nor I hate no man."
And so hee tooke the cup in both his handes and set
it to his mouth, and droonke of the good wine that
was therein at his pleasure.

CHAP. 25.—*Of the great gifts that Oberon gave unto
Huon, as his horne of ivorie, and his cup, the which
were of great vertues; and how Huon after thought to
proove the vertue of them, whereby he was in great
peril of death.*

When Oberon sawe that, hee was right glad, and
came and embraced Huon, saying that he was a
noble man, "and I give thee," quoth he, "this cup
as it is, in the manner I shall shewe, that in any wise
for anything for the dignitie of the cup, be thou ever
true and faithfull; for if thou wilt worke by my
counsaile, I shall aide thee, and give thee succour in
all thine affaires; but as soone as thou makest any
lye, the vertue of the cup will be lost, and loose his
bountie, and beside that, thou shalt loose my love
and aide." "Sir," quoth Huon, "I shall right well
beware thereof; and nowe, sir, I require you suffer

us to depart." "Abide yet," quoth he to Huon,
"yet I have another jewell, the which I will give
thee, bicause I thinke there bee truth and noblenes
in thee : I will give thee a rich horne of ivorie, the
which is full of great vertue, and which thou shalt
beare with thee ; it is of so great virtue, that if thou
be never so farre from me, as soone as thou blowest
the horne, I shall heare thee, and shalbe incontinent
with thee, with a hundred thousand men at armes for
to succour and ayd thee.   But one thinge I commaund thee on the payne of loosing of my love, and
on jeopardie of thy life, that thou be not so hardy
to sound the horne, without thou hast great neede
thereof, for if thou doe otherwise, I vow to God that
created mee, I shall leave thee in as great povertie
and miserie as ever man was, so that whosoever
should see thee in that case, should have pitie of
thee."   "Sir," quoth Huon, "I shall right well aware
thereof; now I desire you let me depart."   "I am
content," quoth Oberon, "and God be thy guide."
Then Huon tooke leave of the kinge Oberon, and
trussed up all his baggage, and did put his cup into his
bosome, and the horne about his necke.   Thus they
all tooke their leave of King Oberon, and all weeping
embraced Huon, who had marvaile why he wept, and
said, "Sir, why doe you weepe?"   "Freend," quoth
Oberon, "you may well know; you have with you
two things that I love dearely.   God ayd you !
More I cannot speak to you."

Thus the fourteene knightes departed, and so they
road foorth about fifteene leagues or more ; then they
sawe before them a great deepe river, and they could
finde no guide nor passage to passe over, and so they
wist not what to doe.   Then suddainly they sawe
passe by them a servant of king Oberon, bearing a
rod of gold in his hand ; and so without speaking of

any word, he entered into the river, and tooke his
rod, and stroke the water therewith three times;
then incontinent the water withdrew a both
sides in such wise that there was a path that three
men might ride afroont; and that done, he departed againe without speaking of any word. Then
Huon and his companie entred into the water, and
so passed thorowe without any danger; and when
they were past, they looked behind them, and sawe
the river close againe, and ran after his old course.
"By my faith," quoth Huon, "I thinke we be en-
chaunted, I beleeve surely king Oberon hath done
this; but seeing we be thus scaped out of perill, I
trust from henceforth we shall have no more doubt."
Thus they roade foorth together singing, and oftentimes spake of the great marvailes that they had seene
king Oberon doe; and as they road Huon beheld on
his right hand, and sawe a fair meadowe well garnished with hearbes and flowers, and in the middest
thereof a faire cleare fountaine. Then Huon roade
thether, and alighted, and let their horses goe to pasture; then they spread a cloath on the greene grasse,
and satereth on such meate as king Oberon had given
them at their departing; and there they did eat, and
drinke such drinke as they found in the cup. "By
my faith," quoth Huon, "it was a fair adventure for
us, when we met Oberon, and that I spake to him;
he hath shewed me great tokens of love, when he
gave me sech a cup; if I may return into Fraunce in
savegard, I shall give it to Charlemaine, who will
make great joy therwith; and if he cannot drinke
thereof, the barons of Fraunce will have great sport
thereof." Then againe he repented him of his owne
words, and said, "I am a foole to thinke or to say
thus, for as yet I cannot tell what end I shall come
to: the cup that I have is better worth then two

cities, but as yet I cannot beleeve the vertue to be in
the horne as Oberon hath shewed, nor that he may
heere it so farre off: but whatsoever fortune fall, I
will assay if it hath such vertue or not." "Alas!
sir," quoth Gerames, "Beware what you doe; you
knowe well when wee departed, what charge he gave
you; certainly you and we both are lost if you trespas
against his commaundement." "Surely," quoth
Huon, "whatsoever fortune fall, I will assay it;" and
so tooke the horne and set it to his mouth, and
blewe it so loud that the wood rang. Then Gerames
and all the other began to sing, and to make great
joy. Then Garyn said, "Faire Nephewe, blowe
still!" And so Huon blew still with such force, that
Oberon, who was in his wood about fifteene leagues
of, heard him clearely, and said:—"Alas! my
freends, I heare my freend blowe, whome I love best
of all the world! Alas! what man is so hardy as to
doe him any ill? I wish myselfe with him with a
hundred thousand men at armes." Incontinent he
was nere to Huon with a hundred thousand men at
armes.

When Huon and his companie heard the hoast
comming, and saw Oberon come ryding on before
them, they were affraid; and it was no marvaile,
seeing the commaundement that Oberon had given
them before. Then Huon saide, "Alas! sirs, I have
done ill! nowe I see well we cannot escape, but that
we are likely all to die." "Certainly," quoth Gerames,
"you have well deserved it." "Houlde your peace,"
quoth Huon, "dismay you not; let me speake to
him." Therewith Oberon came to them, and saide,
"Huon, what meaneth this? Where are they that
will doe thee any ill? Why hast thou broken my
commaundement?" "Alas! sir," quoth Huon, "I
shall shew you the truth. Wee were sitting right now

in this meadowe, and did eat of that you gave us. I
beleeve I tooke too much drinke out of the cup that
you gave me, the vertue of the which we well assayed.
Then I thought to trye also the vertue of the rich
horne, to the entent that if I shoulde have any neede
that I might be sure thereof. Now I know for troth
that all is true that you have shewed me. Wherefore, sir, in the honour of God, I require you to
pardon my trespas; else, sir, heere is my swoord,
strike off my head at your pleasure, for I know well,
without your ayd, I shall never come to atchieve
mine enterprise." "Huon," quoth Oberon, "the
bountie and great troth that is in thee constreyneth
me to give thee pardon; but beware from hencefoorth,
be not so hardy as to breake my commaundement."
"Sir," quod Huon, "I thanke you." "Well," quoth
Oberon, "I knowe surely that thou hast as yet much
to suffer, for thou must passe by a citie named Tor-
mont, wherein there is a tyrant called Macayr, and
yet he is thine owne uncle, brother to thy father Duke
Sevin. When he was in Fraunce he had thought to
have murdered King Charlemaine, but his treason
was knowne, and he had been slaine if thy father
Duke Sevin had not been; so he was sent to the
holy Sepulchre, to do his penaunce for the ill that he
had done, and so afterward there he renounced the
faith of our Lord God, and tooke upon him the Pay-
nim's Law, the which he hath kept ever since so
strongly, that if he heare any man speake of our Lord
God he will pursue him to death. And looke what
promise that hee maketh, he keepeth none. Therefore I advise thee trust not on him, for surely he will
put thee to death if he may, and thou canst not
escape if thou goest by that city; therefore I counsaile thee take not that way if thou be wise." "Sir,"
quoth Huon, "of your courtesie, love, and good

L

councell I thanke you ; but whatsoever fortune fall to
me I will go to mine uncle, and if he be such a one
as you say I shall make him to die an ill death, and
if neede be I shall sound my horne, and I am sure at
my neede you will ayd me." " Of that you may be
sure," quoth Oberon, " but of one thing I forbid thee,
be not so haidy to sound thy home without thou bee
hurt, for if thou doe the contrarie I shall so martir
thee, that thy bodie shall not endure it." "Sir,"
quoth Huon, "bee assured your commaundement I
will not breake." Then Huon tooke leave of King
Oberon, who was sorie when Huon departed. "Sir,"
quoth Huon, "I have marvaile why you weepe. I
pray you shew mee the cause why you doe it."
"Huon," quoth Oberon, "the great love that I have
to thee is that causeth me to doe it, for as yet hereafter thou shalt suffer so much ill and travaile that no
human tongue can tell it." "Sir," quoth Huon, "ye
shew me many things not greatly to my profite."
"Sure," quoth Oberon, "and yet thou shalt suffer
more than I have spoken of, and al by thine owne
folly."

CHAP. 75.—*How King Oberon caused to be hanged the
foure traytours, Gerard, Gybonars, and the two
monkes, for their false witnesse, and of the peace
made betweene Huon and Charlemaine: and how
King Oberon gave unto Huon his realme of the
fayrie.*

When king Oberon had heard Gerard confesse the
treason done to his brother, and heard howe Gerard
had offered to goe and fetch the beard and great
teeth, and how he had denied him to goe, then he
sayd, "I wish them here upon this table." He had
no sooner made his wish but they were set on the

table, whereof all such as were there hadde great
marvaile. "Sir," quoth Huon to King Oberon,
"humbly I require you that of your grace you will
pardon my brother Gerard all the ill that he hath
done against me, for he did it by Gybovars; and as
for me, heere, and before God, I pardon him; and,
sir, if you will doe thus I shalbe content therewith;
and to thentent that we may use our lives from henceforth in good peace and love, I will give him the
halfe part of my lands and signiories; and, sir, in the
honour of our Lord Jesus Christ have pity of him."
When the lords that were there present understood
Huon, they all for pity began to weepe, and sayd
among themselves that Huon was a noble knight, and
that it had been pity if the matter had framed otherwise. "Sir Huon," quoth Oberon, "it is not necessarie to request this, for all the gold that is in the
world shall not respit their deaths. I wish by the
puissance that I have in the fayrie, that here beneath
in the meadow there be a paire of gallows, and all
iiij. thereon hanged." Incontinent it was don, and all
iiij. hanged. Thus, as ye have hard, the traitors were
paid their deserts.

When king Charlemaine had seene the great marvailes that were done by King Oberon, he sayd to his
lords, "Sirs, I beleeve this man be some God himselfe, for there is no mortall man can doe this that he
hath done." When Oberon understood the emperour,
he sayd, "Sir, know for truth I am no God, but I am
a mortall man as you be, and was engendred on a
woman, as you were, and my father was Julius Cæsar,
who engendred me on the ladie of the secret isle,
who had beene before lover to Florymont, sonne to
the Duke of Albany. She bare me nine moneths in
her wombe, and I was begotten by Julius Cesar;
when he went into Thessaly after Pompey the great,

he was amorous of my mother because she prophesied that my father Julius Cesar should winne the battaile, as he did; and when I was borne, there were with my mother many ladies of the fairye, and by them I had many gifts, and among other there was one that gave mee the gift to be such a one as you see I am; whereof I am sory, but I cannot be none otherwise, for when I came to the age of three yeeres I grew no more. And when this ladie sawe that I was so little, to content againe my mother, shee gave me againe that I should be the fairest creature of the world; and other ladyes of the fairie gave me divers other gifts, the which I overpasse at this time; and therefore, sir, know for truth, that above all things God loveth faith and troth, when it is in men, as it is here in Huon; and because I know for certaine that he is true and faithfull, therefore I have alwaies loved him.

After that king Oberon had ended his words, and shewed the emperour Charlemaine of all his estate, he called Huon, and sayd, "Sir, arise up, and take the beard and the teeth, and beare them to King Charlemaine, and desire him to render you your landes as he promised." "Sir," quoth Huon, "I ought so to doe." Then Huon came to king Charlemaine, and sayd, "Sir, by your grace, and if it may please you, receive here the beard and teeth of the admirall Gaudis." "Huon," quoth the king, "I hold you quit, and I render to you all your lands and signiories, and pardon you of all mine ill will, and put all rancour from mee, and from hencefoorth I retaine you as one of my peeres." "Sir," quoth Huon, "of this I thanke God and your grace." Then the emperour Charlemaine clipped and kissed Huon, in token of peace and love.

When the lords saw that, they wept for joy, and

thanked God that the peace was made, and especially
Duke Naymes was joyfull : then within a while, divers
of the lords departed from the court. Then king
Oberon called Huon unto him, and sayd, "Sir, I
commaund you as dearely as you love mee that this
same day foure yeare to come, that you come into
my citie of Momur, for I will give you my realme and
all my dignitie, the which I may lawfully do, for at my
birth, it was given me that I might so doe, for it lyeth
in mee to give it whereas I thinke best, and bicause I
love you so entirely, I shall set the crowne upon your
head, and you shalbe king of my realme. And also I
will that you give unto Gerames all your landes and
signiories in these parts, for he hath well deserved it,
for with you and for your love, hee hath suffered many
great travailes." "Sir," quoth Huon, "seeing this is
your pleasure, I ought well to be pleased therewith,
and I shall accomplish all your commandements."
"Huon," quoth Oberon, "know for troth I shall not
abide longe in this world, for so is the pleasure of God,
it behoveth me to go into Paradice, whereas my place
is appointed in the fayrie, I shall bide no longer, but
beware as dearly as you love your life, that yee faile
not to be with me at the daie that I have appointed.
Beware that yee forget it not, for if yee faile, I shall
cause you to die an ill death ; and therefore remember
it well." When Huon heard king Oberon, he was
right joyfull, and stooped downe to have kissed his
feet ; but then Gloriant and Mallaborn tooke him up.
Then said Huon, "Sir, for this great guift I thanke
you."

CHAP. 146. *How the noble kinge Oberon crowned Huon
and Escleremond, and gave them all his realme and
dignitie that he hadde in the land of the fayrie, and
made the peace betweene Huon and king Arthur.*

When the people of the fayrie, both knightes and
ladies, had well heard and understood king Oberon,
they were right sorrowfull in that hee should leave
them, and sayd, "Sir, since it is your pleasure, and
that it is your will, of reason wee must bee content to
receive Huon of Bourdeaux for our kinge, and madame
Escleremond his wife for our quene." When the king
understood his lordes and people, then he caused to
be brought thether two crownes; the one was set
uppon Huon's head, and the other upon Escleremond's
head. Then Oberon sent for his horne, napkin, and
cup, and the good armour, and hee delivered them
unto Huon, to doe with them his pleasure; great joy
and feasting was made in the pallaice by the knights
and ladies of the fayrie. Then king Huon looked
out at a window, and sawe upon the mountaine that
he passed over at his comming thether, a great number
of tents and pavillions: and hee sayd unto king
Oberon, "Sir, uppon yonder mountaine I see a great
number of men asssembled, and many tentes and
pavillions pitcht up." "Huon," quoth king Oberon,
" know for troth that it is kinge Arthur, who weeneth
to have my realme and dignitie, but hee cometh too
late, for the promise you have made unto me you have
kept; therefore he fayleth and commeth too late; for
if you hadde not come, I had given him my realme
and dignity; I know well that hee will be heere soone
to see me, and hee will be sorrowfull and angrie of
your comming hether; but if I can, I shall doe so
much that you shall bee both in peace and rest, for
good reason it is that he doe obay you."

Therewith kinge Arthur and all his chivalrie entred into the citie of Momur, and came and alighted at the pallaice, and with him his sister, Queene Morgue le Fay, and Transeline their neece, they came and saluted king Oberon, who received them with great joye, and sayde,—"Great kinge Arthur, you are welcome, and Morgue your sister, and Transeline your neece ; and, sir, I pray you to shewe mee what faire childe is that I see there before your sister Morgue ?" "Sir," quoth Arthur, "hee is called Marlyn, and is sonne to Ogier the Dane, who hath wedded my sister Morgue, and I have left him in my countrey to rule it untill I returne." "Sir," quoth king Oberon, "the child shall have good fortune ; hee shall bee in his time feared and redoubted, for Ogier his father is a good and a valiant knight : and noble king Arthur, you are welcome, and of your comming I am right joyfull ; I have sent for you to shewe you the pleasure of our Lord God that I shall depart out of this world ; and to the entent that you should be content, in that I have given you heretofore in the fayrie so much dignitie and puissance, where- with I desire you to be contented, for behold here Duke Huon of Bourdeaux, and his wife the Duchesse Escleremond, unto whome I have given my realme and my dignity, to use it as I have done heeretofore : and therefore I pray and commaund you that you will obay him as kinge and soveraigne of all the fayrie, and you to live together with good love and peace."

When king Arthur heard king Oberon, he answeared fiercely and sayd, "Sir, I have well heard you, and you know well that your realme and dignity you gave me after your decease, and now I see well that you have given it to Duke Huon : Sir, lette him goe into his owne countrey, and unto his citie of Bourdeaux, whereas hee hath left his daughter Clariet, and let him goe and marrie her, for as heere he hath nothing to doe, I hadde rather to bee cleane exiled for ever and chaced out of my realme, then I should obay him or doe unto him any homage, for he shall have nothing to doe over mee, without hee winne it with the point of the sworde." When kinge Huon hadde well heard king Arthur of Brittaine, he answeared fiercely, and said, " King Arthur, knowe for troth, for all your wordes and threatninges I will not spare to say unto you that whether you will or not, it must behoove you to obay and to be under me, since it is the pleasure of my lord kinge Oberon heere present; or else you may depart, and go and dwell in the countrey of Brittaine." Then king Oberon seeing appearance of great war to bee mooved betweene these two kinges, hee spake and sayde that hee would have their evill will layd downe, and never to have war between them, and sayd unto king Arthur, " Sir, I will that you hould your peace, for if you speake one worde more against Huon the soveraigne king of the fayrie, that hee would condemne him perpetually to be a warre-wolfe in those parts, and there to end his dayes in paine and miserie; but if hee will beleeve him, hee woulde agree them together." Then kinge Arthur stood still, and would speake no word. Then Morgue and Transeline fell downe upon their knees, and desired king Oberon to have pitie of king Arthur, and to pardon him of all his ill will; and after that Morgue had spoken, then kinge Arthur kneeled downe, and sayd, " Right deere Sir, I pray you to pardon mee, in that I have spoken so much against your pleasure." " Arthur," quoth kinge Oberon, " I will that you well knowe, that if it were not for the love of your sister, who hath desired mee to pardon you, I would have shewed you the power that I have

in the fayrie, the which from hencefoorth I give unto
Duke Huon of Bourdeaux, and all the dignitie and
puissance that I have used in all my life." Then
Duke Huon thanked kinge Oberon right humbly of
his courtesie.

CHAP. 147.—*Of the ordinances that the noble king
Oberon made before he dyed.*

When king Oberon had deposed himselfe of his
realme and dignitie, and that he had put all his
puissance into the hands of Huon, then he sayd unto
king Arthur, " Sir, because I desire with all my heart
that after my decease Huon and you shoulde live
together in good peace and love, I give you all my
realme of Boulquant, and all the realme that Sibilla
holdeth of me, to do therewith at your pleasure ; and
of all the fayries that bee in the plaine of Tartary, I
will that you have so much puissance there, as Huon
hath heere ; provided that heere before me you make
homage unto him, and that good peace and love may
be betweene you." Then Arthur, Morgue, and Transeline, and all the other lordes and ladies that were
there, thanked king Oberon, and sayd how that they
never heard or saw so rich a guift given before as that
kinge Oberon had given unto kinge Arthur. Then
king Arthur, in the presence of king Oberon, came
and made homage, and kissed duke Huon. Then
kinge Oberon and all the other hadde thereof great
joy because of the peace made betweene those two
kinges, and great feasting and joy was made in the
pallaice ; for all the most noble lordes and ladies of
the fayrie were there assembled, there was great
solemnitie made.

Thus as they were in this great joy, kinge Oberon
feeling that his last end approached, for hee knewe

the day and houre ; then, seeing that in his life time
he had provided a king for his realme, he humbly
thanked our Lord God of the graces that he had
given him in this world. Then hee called before him
Huon of Bourdeaux, and kinge Arthur, Gloriand, and
Mallabron, and sayd, "Sirs, I advertise you that
longe I shall not abide among you ; therefore, Huon,
for your bountie and noblenesse wherewith you have
beene alwayes indued, I have chosen you among
other to have the keeping and signiorie, and the
ministration of all the fayrie, as well of the countrey of
warre-wolves, as of other things secret reserved, and
not to bee shewed to any mortall men ; and also I
have given you my dignitie and puissance, to doe
therewith as I have done in my time ; and because I
have thus chosen you, therefore I will that when I
depart out of this world that you doe make a newe
abbey of monkes, the which I will bee set in the
meadowe heere before this citie, because all my dayes
I have loved this citie, and I will that in the church
of the same abbey you doe burie my bodie as richly
as you shall thinke convenient ; and I recommend
unto you all such as have well served me, and I will
that you retaine them into your service." When king
Oberon had sayd as much as pleased him, Huon
answeared and sayd, "Deere sir, of the great good-
nesse and honour that you have done unto me, I
thanke you, and all that you have ordained or will do,
by the grace of God it shall be done in such wise that
my soule shall beare no charge for it at the day of
judgement." When the lordes and ladies that were
there assembled heard the words of king Oberon,
and saw well that his last end approached neere, the
cryes and clamours that were there made was great
marvaile to heare, and especially there was such
weepings and lamentations in the citie, that great

pittie it was to heare it, for they were advertized that
kinge Oberon drewe neere unto his last end, who lay
in his rich couch in the middest of his pallaice, making his prayers unto our Lord God, and holding
Huon by the hand, and at the last hee sayd, "My
right deere freend Huon, pray for mee." And then
hee made the signe of the crosse, and recommending
his soule unto God, the which incontinent was borne
into Paradice by a great multitude of angels sent from
God, who at their departing, made such shining and
clearnesse in the pallaice, that there was never none
such seene before, and therewith there was so sweet
a smell, that everie man thought that they had been
ravished into Paradice; whereby they knewe surely
that kinge Oberon's soule was saved.

When king Huon, and king Arthur, and Queene
Escleremond, Morgue le Fay, and Transeline, and
king Carahew, Gloriand, and Mallabron, and all
other knightes and ladies, knew that King Oberon
was dead, there is no humane tong can tell the cries,
weepings, and complaints that were made there for
the death of king Oberon: then his bodie was taken,
and borne to the place where his sepulcher was
devised, the which king Huon caused to be made
right richly, and founded there an abbey as Oberon
had devised. After the buriall, they returned to the
pallaice, whereas the tables were set, and there sat
three crowned kinges, and two excellent queens, full
of great beautie. At the upper end of the table sat
king Huon, and next unto him king Arthur, and
then king Carahew and the two queens; and the
other ladies departed, and went and dyned in their
chambers, and they were all served of everie thinge
that was necessarie. And after dinner and grace sayd,
king Arthur and king Carahew tooke their leave of
king Huon, and of queene Escleremond, and so

departed everie man into his owne countrey ; and Morgue and Transeline tarried a certaine space with queene Escleremond in great joy and solace. Now let us leave speaking of kinge Huon : and Queene Escleremond, who tarried still in the fayrie, and shall do untill the day of judgment, and let us returne unto our former matter, and speake of faire Clariet, daughter unto king Huon, who was at the noble citie of Bourdeaux.

VIII.

Life of Robin Goodfellow.

———o———

THIS most important, indeed the most valuable illustration we have of The Midsummer's Night's Dream, is reprinted from a black-letter tract of the utmost rarity, published at London in 1628, under the title of " Robin Goodfellow ; his mad prankes, and merry Jests, full of honest mirth, and is a fit medicine for melancholy." Mr Collier made an excellent reprint of this curious production for the Percy Society, but he has kindly permitted me to include it in this collection. Mr Collier's preface, and the bibliographical particulars there mentioned, are here omitted ; the latter purposely, that the members of the Percy Society might not have to complain that one of their publications had suffered in value. The earlier commentators on Shakespeare were unacquainted with it, and not more than four copies, and three of those with different dates, are known to exist. One copy is in the possession of Lord Ellesmere, another in the library of Mr Henry Heith. The earliest is dated 1628, but it is in all probability a much older production, and, although we have no proof of the fact, had most likely been seen by Shakespeare in some form or other.

The First Part.

Not omitting that antient forme of beginning tales,
Once upon a time, it was my chance to travaile into
that noble county of Kent.   The weather beeing wet,
and my two-leg'd horse being almost tyred (for indeede my owne leggs were all the supporters that my
body had), I went dropping into an alehouse : there
found I, first a kinde wellcome, next good lyquor,
then kinde strangers (which made good company),
then an honest hoast, whose love to good liquor was
written in red characters both in his nose, cheekes
and forehead : an hoastesse I found there too, a
woman of very good carriage; and though she had
not so much colour (for what she had done) as her
rich husband had, yet all beholders might perceive
by the roundness of her belly, that she was able to
draw a pot dry at a draught, and ne're unlace for the
matter.

Well, to the fire I went, where I dryed my outside
and wet my inside.   The ale being good, and I in
good company, I lapt in so much of this nappy liquor,
that it begot in mee a boldnesse to talke, and desire
of them to know what was the reason that the people
of that country were called Long-tayles.[1]   The hoast
sayd, all the reason that ever he could heare was,
because the people of that country formerly did use
to goe in side skirted coates.   There is (sayd an old
man that sat by) another reason that I have heard :
that is this.   In the time of the Saxon's conquest of
England there were divers of our countrymen slaine
by treachery, which made those that survived more

---

[1] An old nickname for Kentishmen.   Lambarde mentions it
in his " Perambulation," 4to, Lond. 1576.

carefull in dealing with their enemies, as you shall
heare.

After many overthrowes that our countrymen had
received by the Saxons, they dispersed themselves
into divers companies into the woods, and so did
much damage by their suddaine assaults to the Saxons,
that Hengist, their king, hearing the damage that they
did (and not knowing how to subdue them by force),
used this policy. Hee sent to a company of them,
and gave them his word for their liberty and safe
returne, if they would come unarmed and speake
with him. This they seemed to grant unto, but for
their more security (knowing how little hee esteemed
oathes or promises) they went every one of them
armed with a shorte sword, hanging just behind under
their garments, so that the Saxons thought not of any
weapons they had : but it proved otherwise ; for
when Hengist his men (that were placed to cut them
off) fell all upon them, they found such unlooked a
resistance, that most of the Saxons were slaine, and
they that escaped, wond'ring how they could doe that
hurt, having no weapons (as they saw), reported that
they strucke downe men like lyons with their tayles ;
and so they ever after were called Kentish Long-
tayles.

I told him this was strange, if true, and that their
countries honor bound them more to beleeve in this
then it did me.

Truly, sir, sayd my hoastesse, I thinke we are called
Long-tayles, by reason our tales are long, that we use
to passe the time withall, and make our selves merry.
Now, good hoastesse, sayd I, let me entreat from you
one of those tales. You shall (sayd shee), and that
shall not be a common one neither, for it is a long
tale, a merry tale, and a sweete tale ; and thus it
beginnes.

The Hoastesse tale of the birth of Robin Goodfellow.

Once upon a time, a great while agoe, when men
did eate more and drinke lesse,—then men were more
honest, that knew no knavery then some now are,
that confesse the knowledge and deny the practise,—
about that time (when so ere it was) there was wont
to walke many harmlesse spirits called fayries, dancing
in brave order in fayry rings on greene hills with
sweete musicke (sometime invisible) in divers shapes :
many mad prankes would they play, as pinching of
sluts black and blue, and misplacing things in ill-
ordered houses ; but lovingly would they use wenches
that cleanly were, giving them silver and other pretty
toyes, which they would leave for them, sometimes in
their shooes, other times in their pockets, sometimes
in bright basons and other cleane vessels.

Amongst these fayries was there a hee fayrie ;
whether he was their king or no I know not, but
surely he had great government and commaund in
that country, as you shall heare. This same hee
fayry did love a proper young wench, for every night
would hee with other fayries come to the house, and
there dance in her chamber ; and oftentimes shee was
forced to dance with him, and at his departure would
hee leave her silver and jewels, to expresse his love
unto her. At last this mayde was with childe, and
being asked who was the father of it, she answered a
man that nightly came to visit her, but earely in the
morning he would go his way, whither she knew not,
he went so suddainly.

Many old women, that then had more wit than
those that are now living and have lesse, sayd that a
fayry had gotten her with childe ; and they bid her
be of good comfort, for the childe must needes be
fortunate that had so noble a father as a fayry was,

and should worke many strange wonders. To be short, her time grew on, and she was delivered of a man childe, who (it should seeme) so rejoyced his father's heart, that every night his mother was supplied with necessary things that are befitting a woman in child-birth, so that in no meane manner neither ; for there had shee rich imbroidered cushions, stooles, carpits, coverlets, delicate linnen : then for meate shee had capons, chickins, mutton, lambe, phesant, snite, woodcocke, partridge, quaile. The gossips like this fare so well, that she never wanted company : wine had shee of all sorts, as muskadine, sacke, malmsie, clarret, white and bastard : this pleased her neighbours well so that few that came to see her, but they had home with them a medicine for the fleaes. Sweet meates too had they in such abundance, that some of their teeth are rotten to this day ; and for musicke shee wanted not, or any other thing she desired.

All praysed this honest fayry for his care, and the childe for his beauty, and the mother for a happy woman. In briefe, christened hee was, at the which all this good cheare was doubled, which made most of the women so wise, that they forgot to make themselves unready, and so lay in their cloathes ; and none of them next day could remember the child's name, but the clarke, and hee may thanke his booke for it, or else it had been utterly lost. So much for the birth of little Robin.

Of Robin's Good-fellowes behaviour when he was young.

When Robin was growne to six yeares of age, hee was so knavish that all the neighbours did complaine of him ; for no sooner was his mothers backe turned, but hee was in one knavish action or other, so that

M

his mother was constrayned (to avoyde the complaints) to take him with her to market, or wheresoever shee went or rid. But this helped little or nothing, for if hee rid before her, then would he make mouthes and ill-favoured faces at those hee met: if he rid behind her, then would hee clap his hand on his tayle; so that his mother was weary of the many complaints that came against him, yet knew she not how to beat him justly for it, because she never saw him doe that which was worthy blowes. The complaints were daily so renewed that his mother promised him a whipping. Robin did not like that cheere, and therefore, to avoyde it, hee ranne away, and left his mother a heavy woman for him.

How Robin Good-fellow dwelt with a taylor.

After that Robin Good-fellow had gone a great way from his mother's house hee began to be a-hungry, and going to a taylor's house, hee asked something for God's sake. The taylor gave him meate, and understanding that he was masterlesse, hee tooke him for his man, and Robin so plyed his worke that he got his master's love.

On a time his master had a gowne to make for a woman, and it was to bee done that night: they both sate up late so that they had done all but setting on the sleeves by twelve a clocke. This master then being sleepy sayd, "Robin, whip thou on the sleeves, and then come to bed: I will goe to bed before." "I will," sayd Robin. So soone as his master was gone, Robin hung up the gowne, and taking both sleeves in his handes, hee whipt and lashed them on the gowne. So stood he till the morning that his master came downe: his master seeing him stand in that fashion, asked him what he did. "Why," quoth hee, "as you bid mee, whip on the sleeves." "Thou rogue," sayd his master, "I did meane that thou shouldst have set them on quickly and slightly." "I would you had sayd so," sayd Robin, "for then had I not lost all this sleepe." To bee shorte, his master was faine to do the worke, but ere hee had made an end of it, the woman came for it, and with a loud voyce chafed for her gowne. The taylor, thinking to please her, bid Robin fetch the remnants that they left yesterday (meaning thereby meate that was left); but Robin, to crosse his master the more, brought downe the remnants of the cloath that was left of the gowne. At the sight of this, his master looked pale, but the woman was glad, saying, "I like this breakfast so well, that I will give you a pint of wine to it." She sent Robin for the wine, but he never returned againe to his master.

What hapned to Robin Good-fellow after he went from the taylor.

After Robin had travailed a good dayes journy from his master's house hee sate downe, and beeing weary hee fell a sleepe. No soon had slumber tooken full possession of him, and closed his long opened eye-lids, but he thought he saw many goodly proper per-sonages in anticke meassures tripping about him, and withall hee heard such musicke, as he thought that Orpheus, that famous Greeke fidler (had hee beene alive), compared to one of these had beene as infamous as a Welch-harper that playes for cheese and onions. As delights commonly last not long, so did those end sooner then hee would willingly they should have done; and for very griefe he awaked, and found by him lying a scroule, wherein was written these lines following in golden letters.

Robin, my only sonne and heire,
How to live take thou no care :
By nature thou hast cunning shifts,
Which Ile increase with other gifts.
Wish what thou wilt, thou shall it have ;
And for to fetch both foole and knave,
Thou hast the power to change thy shape,
To horse, to hog, to dog, to ape.
Transformed thus, by any meanes
Seen none thou harm'st but knaves and queanes ;
But love thou those that honest be,
And helpe them in necessity.
Doe thus, and all the world shall know
The prankes of Robin Good-fellow ;
For by that name thou cald shalt be
To ages last posterity.
If thou observe my just command.
One day thou shalt see Fayry Land !
This more I give : who tels thy prankes
From those that heare them shall have thankes.

Robin having read this, was very joyfull, yet longed
he to know whether he had the power or not, and to
try it hee wished for some meate : presently it was
before him.   Then wished hee for beere and wine :
he straightway had it.   This liked him well, and
because he was weary, he wished himselfe a horse :
no sooner was his wish ended, but he was transformed,
and seemed a horse of twenty pound price, and
leaped and curveted as nimble as if he had beene in
stable at racke and manger a full moneth.   Then
wished he himselfe a dog, and was so : then a tree,
and was so : so from one thing to another, till hee
was certaine and well assured that hee could change
himself to any thing whatsoever.

How Robin Good-fellow served a clownish fellow.

Robin Good-fellow going over a field met with a
clownish fellow, to whom he spake in this manner :

" Friend," quoth he, " what is a clocke?"   " A thing,"
answered the clowne, " that shewes the time of the
day."   " Why then," sayd Robin Good-fellow, " bee
thou a clocke, and tell me what time of the day it
is."   " I owe thee not so much service," answered
hee againe, " but because thou shalt thinke thyselfe
beholding to mee, know that it is the same time of
the day, as it was yesterday at this time."

These crosse answers vext Robin Good-fellow, so
that in himselfe hee vowed to be revenged of him,
which he did in this manner.

Robin Good-fellow turned himselfe into a bird,
and followed this fellow who was going into a field
a little from that place to catch a horse that was at
grasse.   The horse being wilde ran over dike and
hedge, and the fellow after, but to little purpose, for
the horse was too swift for him.   Robin was glad of
this occasion, for now or never was the time to put
his revenge in action.

Presently Robin shaped himselfe like to the horse
that the fellow followed, and so stood before the
fellow : presently the fellow tooke hold of him and
got on his backe, but long had he not rid, but with a
stumble he hurld this churlish clowne to the ground,
that he almost broke his necke ; yet tooke he not this
for a sufficient revenge for the crosse answers he had
received, but stood still and let the fellow mount him
once more.

In the way the fellow was to ride was a great
plash of water of a good depth ; thorow this must
he of necessity ride.   No sooner was hee in the
middest of it, but Robin Good-fellow left him with
nothing but a pack-saddle betwixt his leggs, and in
the shape of a fish swomme to the shore, and ran
away laughing, *ho, ho, hoh !* leaving the poore fellow
almost drowned.

How Robin Good-fellow helped two lovers, and deceived an old man.

Robin going by a woode heard two lovers make great lamentation, because they were hindred from injoying each other by a cruell old leacher, who would not suffer this loving couple to marry. Robin, pittying ·them, went to them and sayd : " I have heard your complaints, and do pitty you : be ruled by me, and I will see that you shall have both your hearts content, and that suddainly if you please." After some amazement the maiden sayd, " Alas ! sir, how can that be ? my uncle, because I will not grant to his lust, is so streight over me, and so oppresseth me with worke night and day, that I have not so much time as to drinke or speake with this young man, whom I love above all men living." " If your worke bee all that hindreth you," sayd Robin, " I will see that done : aske mee not how, nor make any doubt of the performance ; I will doe it. Go you with your love : for twenty-four houres I will free you. In that time marry or doe what you will. If you refuse my proffered kindnesse never looke to enjoy your wished for happinesse. I love true lovers, honest men, good fellowes, good huswives, good meate, good drinke, and all things that good is, but nothing that is ill; for my name is Robin Good-fellow, and that you shall see that I have power to performe what I have undertooke, see what I can do." Presently he turned himselfe into a horse, and away he ran : at the sight of which they were both amazed, but better considering with themselves, they both determined to make good use of their time, and presently they went to an old fryer, who presently married them. They payd him, and went their way.

Where they supped and lay I know not, but surely
they liked their lodging well the next day.

Robin, when that he came neare the old man's
house, turned himselfe into the shape of the young
maide, and entred the house, where, after much
chiding, he fell to the worke that the mayde had to
do, which hee did in halfe the time that another
could do it in. The old man, seeing the speede he
made, thought that she had some meeting that night,
for he tooke Robin Good-fellow for his neece : therfore he gave him order for other worke, that was too
much for any one to do in one night. Robin did
that in a trise, and playd many mad prankes beside
ere the day appeared.

In the morning hee went to the two lovers to their
bedside and bid God give them joy, and told them all
things went well, and that ere night he would bring
them ten pounds of her uncles to beginne the world
with. They both thanked him, which was all the
requital that he looked for, and beeing therewith well
contended, hee went his way laughing.

Home went he to the old man, who then was by,
and marveiled how the worke was done so soone.
Robin, seeing that, sayd : " Sir, I pray marvaile not,
for a greater wonder then that this night hath happened
to me." " Good neece, what is that ?" sayd the old
man. " This, Sir ; but I shame to speake it, yet I
will : weary with worke, I slept, and did dreame that
I consented to that which you have so often desired
of me, you know what it is I meane, and me thought
you gave me as a reward ten pounds, with your consent to marry that young man that I have loved so
long." " Diddest thou dreame so ? thy dreame I will
make good, for under my hand wrighting I give my
free consent to marry him, or whom thou doest please
to marry (and withall writ) and for the ten pounds,

goe but into the out barne, and I will bring it thee
presently.　How says thou (sayd the old leacher),
wilt thou?" Robin with silence did seeme to grant,
and went toward the barne.　The old made haste,
told out his money, and followed.

Being come thither, he hurled the money on the
grounde, saying, "This is the most pleasing bargaine
that ever I made;" and going to embrace Robin,
Robin tooke him up in his armes and carried him
foorth; first drew him thorow a pond to coole his
hot blood, then did he carry him where the young
married couple were, and said, " Here is your uncle's
consent under his hand; then, here is the ten pounds
he gave you, and there is your uncle; let him deny it
if hee can."

The old man, for feare of worse usage, said all was
true.　"Then am I as good as my word," said Robin,
and so went away laughing.　The old man knew
himselfe duly punished, and turned his hatred into
love, and thought afterward as well of them, as if shee
had beene his owne.　The second part shall shew
many incredible things done by Robin Good-fellow,
or otherwise called Hob-goblin, and his companions,
by turning himselfe into divers sundry shapes.

The Second Part.

How Robin Good-fellow helped a mayde to worke.

Robin Good-fellow oftentimes would in the night
visite farmers' houses, and helpe the maydes to breake
hempe, to bowlt, to dresse flaxe, and to spin and do
other workes, for hee was excellent in every thing.

One night hee comes to a farmer's house, where there was a goode handsome mayde. This mayde having much worke to do, Robin one night did helpe her, and in six houres did bowlt more than she could have done in twelve houres. The mayde wondred the next day how her worke came, and to know the doer, she watched the next night that did follow. About twelve of the clocke in came Robin, and fell to breaking of hempe, and for to delight himselfe he sung this mad song.

> And can the physitian make sicke men well,
> And can the magician a fortune devine,
> Without lilly, germander, and sops in wine?
>> With sweet-bryer
>> And bon-fire,
>> And straw-berry wyer,
>> And collumbine.

> Within and out, in and out, round as a ball,
> With hither and thither, as straight as a line,
> With lilly, germander, and sops in wine.
>> With sweet-bryer,
>> And bon-fire,
>> And straw-berry wyer,
>> And collumbine.

> When Saturne did live, there lived no poore,
> The king and the beggar with rootes did dine,
> With lilly, germander, and sops in wine.
>> With sweet-bryer,
>> And bon-fire,
>> And straw-berry wyer,
>> And collumbine.

The mayde seeing him bare in clothes, pittied him, and against the next night provided him a wast-coate. Robin comming the next night to worke, as he did before, espied the wast-coate, wherat he started and said :—

> Because thou lay'st me himpen, hampen,[1]
> I will neither bolt nor stampen :
> 'Tis not your garments new or old
> That Robin loves : I feele no cold.
> Had you left me milke or creame,
> You should have had a pleasing dreame :
> Because you left no drop or crum,
> Robin never more will come.

So went he away laughing *ho, ho, hoh !* The mayde was much grieved and discontented at his anger : for ever after she was faine to do her worke herselfe without the helpe of Robin Good-fellow.

How Robin Good-fellow led a company of fellowes out of their way.

A company of young men having beene making merry with their sweet hearts, were at their comming home to come over a heath. Robin Good-fellow, knowing of it, met them, and to make some pastime, hee led them up and downe the heath a whole night, so that they could not get out of it ; for hee went before them in the shape of a walking fire, which they all saw and followed till the day did appeare : then Robin left them, and at his departure spake these words :—

> Get you home, you merry lads :
> Tell your mammies and your dads,
> And all those that newes desire,
> How you saw a walking fire.
> Wenches, that doe smile and lispe
> Use to call me Willy Wispe.
> If that you but weary be,
> It is sport alone for me.

---

[1] These words, and two very similar lines, are given in Scot's Discoverie of Witchcraft, as what Robin Good-fellow said if any one gave him clothes instead of milk or cream. Reginald Scot says that he would in that case " chafe exceedingly."

Away : unto your houses goe,
And I'le goe laughing *ho, ho, hoh !*

The fellowes were glad that he was gone, for they were all in a great feare that hee would have done them some mischiefe.

How Robin Good-fellow served a leacherous gallant.

Robin alwayes did helpe those that suffered wrong, and never would hurt any but those that did wrong to others. It was his chance one day to goe thorow a field where he heard one call for helpe : hee, going neere where he heard the cry, saw a lusty gallant that would have forced a young maiden to his lust ; but the mayden in no wise would yeelde, which made her cry for helpe. Robin Good-fellow, seeing of this, turned himselfe into the shape of a hare, and so ranne betweene the lustful gallant's legges. This gallant, thinking to have taken him, hee presently turned himselfe into a horse, and so perforce carried away this gallant on his backe. The gentleman cryed out for helpe, for he thought that the devill had bin come to fetch him for his wickednesse ; but his crying was in vaine, for Robin did carry him into a thicke hedge, and there left him so prickt and scratched, that hee more desired a playster for his paine, then a wench for his pleasure. Thus the poore mayde was freed from this ruffin, and Robin Good-fellow, to see this gallant so tame, went away laughing, *ho, ho, hoh !*

How Robin Good-fellow turned a miserable usurer to a good house-keeper.

In this country of ours there was a rich man dwelled, who to get wealth together was so sparing that hee could not find in his heart to give his belly foode enough. In the winter hee never would make so

much fire as would roast a blacke-pudding, for hee
found it more profitable to sit by other means.   His
apparell was of the fashion that none did weare ; for
it was such as did hang at a broker's stall, till it was
as weather-beaten as an old signe.   This man for his
covetousnesse was so hated of all his neighbours, that
there was not one that gave him a good word.   Robin
Good-fellow grieved to see a man of such a wealth
doe so little good, and therefore practised to better
him in this manner.

One night the usurer being in bed, Robin in the
shape of a night-raven came to the window, and there
did beate with his wings, and croaked in such manner
that this old usurer thought hee should have presently
dyed for feare.   This was but a preparation to what
he did intend ; for presently after hee appeared before
him at his bed's feete, in the shape of a ghost, with a
torch in his hand.   At the sight of this the old usurer
would have risen out of his bed, and have leaped out
of the window; but he was stayed by Robin Good-
fellow, who spake to him thus :—

> If thou dost stirre out of thy bed,
> I doo vow to strike thee dead.
> I doe come to doe thee good ;
> Recall thy wits and starkled blood.
> The mony which thou up dost store
> In soule and body makes thee poore.
> Doe good with mony while you may ;
> Thou hast not long on earth to stay.
> Doe good, I say, or day and night
> I hourely thus will thee afright.
> Thinke on my words and so farewell,
> For being bad I live in hell.

Having said thus he vanished away and left this
usurer in great terror of mind ; and for feare of being
frighted againe with this ghost, hee turned very liberall,

and lived amongst his neighbours as an honest man should doe.

How Robin Good-fellow loved a weaver's wife, and how the weaver would have drowned him.

One day Robin Good-fellow walking thorow the streete found at a doore sitting a pretty woman : this woman was wife to the weaver, and was a winding of quils for her husband. Robin liked her so well, that for her sake he became servant to her husband, and did daily worke at the loome ; but all the kindnesse that hee shewed was but lost, for his mistres would shew him no favour, which made him many times to exclame against the whole sex in satyricall songs ; and one day being at worke he sung this, to the tune of *Rejoyce Bag-pipes.*

> Why should my love now waxe
>   Unconstant, wavering, fickle, unstayd ?
> With nought can she me taxe :
>   I ne'er recanted what I once said.
> I now doe see, as nature fades,
>   And all her workes decay,
> So women all, wives, widdowes, maydes,
>   From bad to worse doe stray.
>
> As hearbs, trees, rootes, and plants
>   In strength and growth are daily lesse,
> So all things have their wants :
>   The heavenly signes moove and digresse.
> And honesty in women's hearts
>   Hath not her former being :
> Their thoughts are ill, like other parts,
>   Nought else in them's agreeing,
>
> I sooner thought thunder
>   Had powers o're the laurell wreath,
> Then shee, women's wonder
>   Such perjurd thoughts should live to breathe.
> They all hyena-like will weepe,
>   When that they would deceive :

Deceit in them doth lurke and sleepe,
  Which makes me thus to grieve.

Young man's delight, farewell;
  Wine, women, game, pleasure, adieu :
Content with me shall dwell;
  I'le nothing trust but what is true.
Though she were false, for her I'le pray ;
  Her false-hood made me blest:
I will renew from this good day
  My life by sinne opprest.

Moved with this song and other complaints of his, shee at last did fancy him, so that the weaver did not like that Robin should bee so saucy with his wife, and therefore gave him warning to be gone, for hee would keepe him no longer.   This grieved this loving couple to parte one from the other, which made them to make use of the time that they had.   The weaver one day comming in, found them a-kissing : at this hee said [nothing], but vowed in himselfe to bee revenged of his man that night following.   Night being come, the weaver went to Robin's bed, and tooke him out of it (as hee then thought) and ran apace to the river side to hurle Robin in ; but the weaver was deceived, for Robin, instead of himselfe, had laid in his bed a sack full of yarne : it was that that the weaver carried to drowne.   The weaver standing by the river side said :—
"Now will I coole your hot blood, Master Robert, and if you cannot swimme the better, you shall sincke and drowne."   With that he hurled the sack in, thinking that it had bin Robin Good-fellow.   Robin, standing behind him, said :—

For this your kindnesse, master, I you thanke :
Go swimme yourselfe, I'le stay upon the banke !

With that Robin pushed him in, and went laughing away, *ho, ho, hoh !*

*How Robin Good-fellow went in the shape of a fidler
to a wedding, and of the sport that he had there.*

On a time there was a great wedding, to which
there went many young lusty lads and pretty lasses.
Robin Good-fellow, longing not to be out of action,
shaped himselfe like unto a fidler, and with his
crowd under his arme went amongst them, and was a
very welcome man. There played hee whilst they
danced, and tooke as much delight in seeing them as
they did in hearing him. At dinner he was desired
to sing a song, which hee did, to the tune of *Watton
Towne's End.*

The Song.

It was a country lad
   That fashions strange would see,
And he came to a valting schoole,
   Where tumblers use to be :
He lik't his sport so well,
   That from it he'd not part :
His doxey to him still did cry,
   Come, busse thine owne sweet heart.

They lik't his gold so well,
   That they were both content,
That he that night with his sweet heart
   Should passe in merry-ment.
To bed they then did goe,
   Full well he knew his part,
Where he with words, and eke with deedes,
   Did busse his owne sweet heart.

Long were they not in bed,
   But one knockt at the doore,
And said, Up, rise, and let me in :
   This vext both knave and whore.
He being sore perplext
   From bed did lightly start ;
No longer then could he indure
   To busse his owne sweet heart.

With tender steps he trod,
  To see if he could spye
The man that did him so molest ;
  Which he with heavy eye
Had soone beheld, and said,
  Alas ! my owne sweet heart,
I now doe doubt, if e're we busse,
  It must be in a cart.

At last the bawd arose,
  And opened the doore,
And saw Discretion cloth'd in rug,
  Whose office hates a whore.
He mounted up the stayres,
  Being cunning in his arte :
With little search at last he found
  My youth and his sweete heart.

He having wit at will,
  Unto them both did say,
I will not heare them speake one word ;
  Watchmen, with them away !
And cause they lov'd so well,
  'Tis pitty they should part.
Away with them to New Bride-well ;
  There busse your own sweet heart.

His will it was fulfil'd,
  And there they had the law ;
And whilst that they did nimbly spin,
  The hempe he needs must taw.
He grownd, he thump't, he grew,
  So cunning in his arte,
He learnt the trade of beating hempe
  By bussing his sweet heart.

But yet, he still would say,
  If I could get release,
To see strange fashions I'le give o're,
  And henceforth live in peace,
The towne where I was bred,
  And thinke by my desert,
To come no more into this place
  For bussing my sweet heart.

They all liked his song very well, and said that the young man had but ill lucke. Thus continued hee playing and singing songs till candle-light; then hee beganne to play his merry trickes in this manner. First, hee put out the candles, and then beeing darke, hee strucke the men good boxes on the eares: they, thinking it had beene those that did sit next them, fell a-fighting one with the other; so that there was not one of them but had either a broken head or a bloody nose. At this Robin laughed heartily. The women did not scape him, for the handsomest he kissed; the other he pinched, and made them scratch one the other, as if they had beene cats. Candles being lighted againe, they all were friends, and fell againe to dancing, and after to supper.

Supper beeing ended a great posset was brought forth: at this Robin Good-fellowes teeth did water, for it looked so lovely that hee could not keepe from it. To attaine to his wish he did turne himselfe into a beare: both men and women (seeing a beare amongst them) ranne away, and left the whole posset to Robin Good-fellow. He quickly made an end of it, and went away without his money, for the sport hee had was better to him than any money whatsoever. The feare that the guests were in did cause such a smell, that the bride-groome did call for perfumes, and instead of a posset, he was faine to make use of cold beere.

How Robin Good-fellow served a tapster for nicking his pots.

There was a tapster, that with his pots smalnesse, and with frothing of his drinke, had got a good summe of money together. This nicking of the pots he would never leave, yet divers times he had been

N

under the hand of authority, but what money soever hee had [to pay] for his abuses, hee would be sure (as they all doe) to get it out of the poore man's pot againe. Robin Good-fellow, hating such knavery, put a tricke upon him in this manner :—

Robin shaped himselfe like to the tapster's brewer, and came and demaunded twenty pounds which was due to him from the tapster. . The tapster, thinking it had beene his brewer, payd him the money, which money Robin gave to the poore of that parish before the tapster's face. The tapster praysed his charity very much, and sayd that God would blesse him the better for such good deedes ; so after they had drank one with the other, they parted.

Some foure days after the brewer himselfe came for his money : the tapster told him that it was payd, and that he had a quittance for him to shew. Hereat the brewer did wonder, and desired to see the quittance. The tapster fetched him a writing, which Robin Good-fellow had given him in stead of a quittance, wherein was written as followeth, which the brewer read to him.

I, Robin Good-fellow, true man and honest man, doe acknowledge to have received of Nicke and Froth, the cheating tapster, the summe of twenty pound, which money I have bestowed (to the tapster's content) amongst the poore of the parish, out of whose pockets this aforesayd tapster had picked the aforesaid summe, not after the manner of foisting, but after his excellent skill of bombasting, or a pint for a peny.

> If now thou wilt goe hang thy selfe,
> Then take thy apron-strings.
> It doth me good when such foule birds
> Upon the gallowes sings.
> *Per me* ROBIN GOOD-FELLOW.

At this the tapster swore Walsingham;[1] but for all his swearing, the brewer made him pay him his twenty pound.

How King Obreon called Robin Good-fellow to dance.

King Obreon, seeing Robin Good-fellow doe so many honest and merry trickes, called him one night out of his bed with these words, saying :

> Robin, my sonne, come quickly rise :
> First stretch, then yawne, and rub your eyes ;
> For thou must goe with me to night,
> To see and taste of my delight.
> Quickly come my wanton sonne ;
> Twere time our sports were now begunne.

Robin, hearing this, rose and went to him. There were with King Obreon a many fayries, all attyred in greene silke : all these, with King Obreon, did welcome Robin Good-fellow into their compay. Obreon tooke Robin by the hand and led him a dance : their musician was little Tom Thumb ; for hee had an excellent bag-pipe made of a wren's quill, and the skin of a Greenland louse : this pipe was so shrill, and so sweete, that a Scottish pipe compared to it, it would no more come neere it, than a Jewes-trump doth to an Irish harpe. After they had danced, King Obreon spake to his sonne, Robin Good-fellow, in this manner :

> When ere you heare my piper blow,
> From thy bed see that thou goe ;
> For nightly you must with us dance,
> When we in circles round doe prance.

---

[1] The Shrine of the Virgin of Walsingham was formerly much frequented, and our Lady of Walsingham was thought a proper person to swear by. See Nares, in v.

> I love thee, sonne, and by the hand
> I carry thee to Fairy Land,
> Where thou shalt see what no man knowes:
> Such love thee King Obreon owes.

So marched they in good manner, with their piper before, to the Fairy Land: there did King Obreon shew Robin Good-fellow many secrets, which hee never did open to the world.

How Robin Good-fellow was wont to walke in the night.

Robin Good-fellow would many times walke in the night with a broome on his shoulder, and cry chimney sweepe, but when any one did call him, then would he runne away laughing *ho, ho, hoh!* Somtime hee would counterfeit a beggar, begging very pitifully, but when they came to give him an almes, he would runne away, laughing as his manner was. Sometimes would hee knocke at men's doores, and when the servants came, he would blow out the candle, if they were men; but if they were women, hee would not onely put out their light, but kisse them full sweetly, and then go away as his fashion was, *ho, ho, hoh!* Oftentimes he would sing at a doore like a singing man, and wher they did come to give him his reward, he would turne his backe and laugh. In these humors of his hee had many pretty songs, which I will sing as perfect as I can. For his chimney-sweeper's humors he had these songs: the first is to the tune of, *I have beene a fiddler these fifteene yeeres.*

> Blacke I am from head to foote,
> And all doth come by chimney soote:
> Then, maydens, come and cherrish him
> That makes your chimnies neat and trim.

Hornes have I store, but all at my backe
My head no ornament doth lacke :
I give my hornes to other men,
And ne'er require them againe.

Then come away, you wanton wives,
That love your pleasures as your lives :
To each good woman Ile give two,
Or more, if she thinke them too few.

Then would he change his note and sing the following to the tune of *What care I how faire she be?*

Be she blacker than the stocke,
    If that thou wilt make her faire,
Put her in a cambricke smocke,
    Buy her painte and flaxen haire.

One your carrier brings to towne
    Will put downe your city bred ;
Put her on a broker's gowne,
    That will sell her mayden-head.

Comes your Spaniard, proud in minde,
    Heele have the first cut, or else none :
The meeke Italian comes behind,
    And your French-man pickes the bone.

Still she trades with Dutch and Scot,
    Irish, and the Germaine tall,
Till she get the thing you wot ;
    Then her ends an hospitall.

A song to the tune of the *The Spanish Pavin.*

When Vertue was a country maide,
And had no skill to set up trade,
She came up with a carrier's jade,
    And lay at racke and manger.
She whift her pipe, she drunke her can,
The pot was nere out of her span ;
She married a tobacco man,
    A stranger, a stranger.

They set up shop in Hunney lane,
And thither flies did swarme amaine,
Some from France, some from Spaine,
  Traind in by scurvy panders.
At last this hunney pot grew dry,
Then both were forced for to fly
  To Flanders, to Flanders.

Another to the tune of *The Coranto.*

I peeped in at the Wool-sacke,
O, what a goodly sight did I
Behold at mid-night chyme !
The wenches were drinking of muld sacke ;
Each youth on his knee, that then did want
A yeere and a halfe of his time.
    They leaped and skipped,
    They kissed and they clipped,
    And yet it was counted no crime.

The grocer's chiefe servant brought sugar,
And out of his leather pocket he puld,
And kuld some pound and a halfe ;
For which he was sufferd to smacke her
That was his sweet-heart, and would not depart,
But turn'd and lickt the calfe.
    He rung her, and he flung her,
    He kist her, and he swung her,
    And yet she did nothing but laugh.

Thus would he sing about cities and townes, and when any one called him, he would change his shape, and go laughing, *ho, ho, hoh!* For his humors of begging he used this song, to the tune of *The Jovial Tinker.*

Good people of this mansion,
  Unto the poore be pleased
To doe some good, and give some food,
  That hunger may be eased.
My limbes with fire are burned,
  My goods and lands defaced ;
Of wife and child I am beguild,
  So much am I debased.

Oh, give the poore some bread, cheese, or butter,
  Bacon, hempe, or flaxe ;
Some pudding bring or other thing
  My need doth make me aske.

I am no common begger,
  Nor am I skild in canting :
You nere shall see a wench with me,
  Such trickes in me are wanting.
I curse not if you give not,
  But still I pray and blesse you,
Still wishing joy, and that annoy
  May never more possesse you.
Oh, give the poore some bread, cheese or butter,
  Bacon, hempe or flaxe ;
Some pudding bring, or other thing,
  My neede doth make me aske.

When any came to releeve him, then would he change himselfe into some other shape, and runne laughing, *ho, ho, hoh !* Then would hee shape himselfe like to a singing man ; and at men's windowes and doores sing civil and vertuous songs, one of which I will sing to the tune of *Broome.*

If thou wilt lead a blest and happy life,
  I will describe the perfect way :
First must thou shun all cause of mortall strife,
  Against thy lusts continually to pray.
    Attend unto God's word :
    Great comfort 'twill afford ;
    'Twill keepe thee from discord.
    Then trust in God, the Lord,
      for ever,
      for ever ;
    And see in this thou persever.

So soone as day appeareth in the east
  Give thanks to him, and mercy crave ;
So in this life thou shalt be surely blest,
  And mercy shalt thou find in grave.
    The conscience that is cleere ,
    No horror doth it feare ;

'Tis voyd of mortall care,
And never doth despaire :
            but ever,
            but ever
Doth in the word of God persever.

Thus living, when thou drawest to thy end
    Thy joyes they shall much more encrease,
For then thy soule, thy true and loving friend,
    By death shall find a wisht release
        From all that caused sinne,
        In which it lived in ;
        For then it doth beginne
        Those blessed joyes to win,
            for ever,
            for ever,
    For there is nothing can them sever.

Those blessed joyes which then thou shalt possesse,
    No mortall tongue can them declare :
All earthly joyes, compar'd with this, are lesse
    Then smallest mote to the world so faire.
        Then is not that man blest
        That must injoy this rest ?
        Full happy is that guest
        Invited to this feast,
            that ever,
            that ever
    Indureth, and is ended never.

When they opened the window or doore, then
would he runne away laughing, *ho, ho, hoh !* Sometimes would he goe like a Belman in the night, and
with may pretty verses delight the eares of those that
waked at his bell ringing : his verses were these.

            Maydes in your smockes,
            Looke well to your lockes,
            And your tinder boxe,
            Your wheeles and your rockes,
            Your hens and your cockes,
            Your cowes and your oxe,
            And beware of the foxe.
            When the bell-man knockes,

Put out your fire and candle light,
So they shall not you affright :
May you dreame of your delights,
In your sleeps see pleasing sights.
Good rest to all, both old and young :
The bell-man now hath done his song.

Then would be goe laughing *ho, ho, hoh!* as his use
was. Thus would he continually practise himselfe in
honest mirth, never doing hurt to any that were
cleanly and honest minded.

*How the fairyes called Robin Good-fellow to dance with
them, and how they shewed him their severall con-
ditions.*

Robin Good-fellow being walking one night heard
the excellent musicke of Tom Thumb's brave bag-pipe :
he, remembering the sound (according to the command
of King Obreon) went toward them. They, for joy
that he was come, did circle him in, and in a ring did
dance round about him. Robin Good-fellow, seeing
their love to him, danced in the midst of them, and
sung them this song to the tune of *To him Bun.*

THE SONG.

Round about, little ones, quick and nimble,
In and out wheele about, run, hop, or amble.
Joyne your hands lovingly : well done, musition !
Mirth keepeth man in health like a phisition.
Elves, urchins, goblins all, and little fairyes
That doe fillch, blacke, and pinch mayds of the dairyes ;
Make a ring on the grass with your quicke measures,
Tom shall play, and Ile sing for all your pleasures.

Pinch and Patch, Gull and Grim,
   Goe you together,
For you can change your shapes
   Like to the weather.

Sib and Tib, Licke and Lull,
   You all have trickes, too ;
Little Tom Thumb that pipes
   Shall goe betwixt you.
Tom, tickle up thy pipes
   Till they be weary :
I will laugh, *ho, ho, hoh!*
   And make me merry.
Make a ring on this grasse
   With your quicke measures :
Tom shall play, I will sing
   For all your pleasures.

The moone shines faire and bright, [1]
   And the owle hollows,
Mortals now take their rests
   Upon their pillows :
The bats abroad likewise,
   And the night raven,
Which doth use for to call
   Men to Death's haven.
Now the mice peepe abroad,
   And the cats take them,
Now doe young wenches sleepe,
   Till their dreames wake them.
Make a ring on the grasse
   With your quicke measures :
Tom shall play, I will sing
   For all your pleasures.

Thus danced they a good space : as last they left and sat downe upon the grasse ; and to requite Robin Good-fellowes kindnesse, they promised to tell him all the exploits that they were accustomed to doe : Robin thanked them and listned to them, and one begun to tell his trickes in this manner.

---

[1] If this work is really anterior to the Midsummer Night's Dream, this perhaps suggested to Shakespeare the beautiful lines of Puck, commencing,

     "How the hungry lion roars."

See further observations on the similarity in my Introduction to that play, p. 39.—*Halliwell.*

The trickes of the fayry called Pinch.

After that wee have danced in this manner as you have beheld, I, that am called Pinch, do goe about from house to house : sometimes I find the dores of the house open ; that negligent servants had left them so, I doe so nip him or her, that with my pinches their bodyes are as many colors as a mackrels backe. Then take I them, and lay I them in the doore, naked or unnaked I care not whether : there they lye, many times till broad day, ere they waken ; and many times, against their wills, they shew some parts about them, that they would not have openly seene.

Sometimes I find a slut sleeping in the chimney corner, when she should be washing of her dishes, or doing something else which she hath left undone : her I pinch about the armes, for not laying her armes to her labor. Some I find in their bed snorting and sleeping, and their houses lying as cleane as a nasty doggs kennell ; in one corner bones, in another eg-shells, behind the doore a heap of dust, the dishes under feet, and the cat in the cubbord : all these sluttish trickes I doe reward with blue legges, and blue armes. I find some slovens too, as well as sluts : they pay for their beastlinesse too, as well as the women-kind ; for if they uncase a sloven and not unty their points, I so pay their armes that they cannot sometimes untye them, if they would. Those that leave foule shooes, or goe into their beds with their stockings on, I use them as I did the former, and never leave them till they have left their beastli-nesse.

But to the good I doe no harme,
But cover them, and keepe them warme :
Sluts and slovens I doe pinch,
And make them in their beds to winch.

> This is my practice and my trade
> Many have I cleanely made.

The trickes of the fayry called Pach.

About mid-night do I walke, and for the trickes 1 play they call me Pach.   When I find a slut asleepe, I smuch her face if it be cleane; but if it be durty, I wash it in the next pissepot that I can finde: the balls I use to wash such sluts withal is a sows pan-cake, or a pilgrimes salve.   Those that I find with their heads nitty and scabby, for want of combing, I am their barbers, and cut their hayre as close as an apes tayle; or else clap so much pitch on it, that they must cut it off themselves to their great shame. Slovens also that neglect their master's businesse, they doe not escape.   Some I find that spoyle their master's horses for want of currying: those I doe daube with grease and soote, and they are faine to curry themselves ere they can get cleane.   Others that for laysinesse will give the poor beasts no meate, I oftentimes so punish them with blowes, that they cannot feed themselves they are so sore.

> Thus many trickes, I, Pach, can doe,
> But to the good I ne'ere was foe :
> The bad I hate and will doe ever,
> Till they from ill themselves doe sever.
> To help the good Ile run and goe,
> The bad no good from me shall know.

The tricks of the fairy called Gull.

When mortals keep their beds I walke abroad, and for my prankes am called by the name of Gull. I with a fayned voyce doe often deceive many men, to their great amazement.   Many times I get on men and women, and so lye on their stomackes, that I cause their great paine, for which they call me by the name of Hagge, or Night-mare. Tis I that doe steale children, and in the place of them leave changelings. Sometime I also steale milke and creame, and then with my brothers, Patch, Pinch, and Grim, and sisters Sib, Tib, Licke and Lull, I feast with my stolne goods : our little piper hath his share in all our spoyles, but hee nor our women fayries doe ever put themselves in danger to doe any great exploit.

> What Gull can doe, I have you showne ;
> I am inferior unto none.
> Command me, Robin, thou shalt know,
> That I for thee will ride or goe :
> I can doe greater things than these
> Upon the land, and on the seas.

The trickes of the fairy cald Grim.

I walke with the owle, and make many to cry as loud as she doth hollow. Sometimes I doe affright many simple people, for which some have termed me the Blacke Dog of New-gate. At the meetings of young men and maydes I many times am, and when they are in the midst of all their good cheare, I come in, in some feareful shape, and affright them, and then carry away their good cheare, and eate it with my fellow fayries. Tis I that do, like a skritch-owle, cry at sicke men's windowes, which makes the hearers so fearefull, that they say, that the sicke person cannot live. Many other wayes have I to fright the simple, but the understanding man I cannot moove to feare, because he knowes I have no power to do hurt.

> My nightly businesse I have told,
> To play these trickes I use of old ;
> When candles burne both blue and dim,
> Old folkes will say, Here's fairy Grim.

More trickes than these I use to doe :
Hereat cry'd Robin, *Ho, ho, hoh !*

The trickes of the women fayries told by Sib.

To walke nightly, as do the men fayries, we use not ;
but now and then we goe together, and at good huswives fires we warme and dresse our fayry children.
If wee find cleane water and cleane towels, wee leave
them money, either in their basons or in their shooes ;
but if wee find no cleane water in their houses, we
wash our children in their pottage, milke or beere, or
what-ere we finde ; for the sluts that leave not such
things fitting, wee wash their faces and hands with a
gilded child's clout, or els carry them to some river,
and ducke them over head and eares.   We often use
to dwell in some great hill, and from thence we doe
lend money to any poore man or woman that hath
need ; but if they bring it not againe at the day appointed, we doe not only punish them with pinching,
but also in their goods, so that they never thrive till
they have payd us.

> Tib and I the chiefest are,
> And for all things doe take care.
> Licke is cooke and dresseth meate,
> And fetcheth all things that we eat :
> Lull is nurse and tends the cradle,
> And the babes doth dresse and swadle.
> This little fellow, cald Tom Thumb,
> That is no bigger then a plumb,
> He is the porter to our gate,
> For he doth let all in thereat,
> And makes us merry with his play,
> And merrily we spend the day.

Shee having spoken, Tom Thumb stood up on tip-
toe, and showed himselfe, saying—

> My actions all in volumes two are wrote,
> The least of which will never be forgot.

He had no sooner ended his two lines, but a shepheard, that was watching in the field all night, blew up
a bag-pipe, this so frighted Tom that he could not tell
what to do for the present time.   The fayries seeing
Tom Thumbe in such a feare, punisht the shepheard
with his pipes losse, so that the shepherds pipe presently brake in his hande, to his great amazement.
Hereat did Robin Good-fellow laugh *ho, ho, hoh !*
Morning beeing come, they all hasted to Fayry Land,
where I thinke they yet remaine.

My hostesse asked me how I liked this tale.   I said
it was long enough and good enough to passe time
that might be worser spent.   I, seeing her dry,
called for two pots : she emptied one of them
at a draught, and never breathed for
the matter.   I emptied the other
at leasure ; and being late
I went to bed, and did   .
dream of this which
I had heard.

IX.

The Merry Puck.

———o———

THIS ballad is printed from a copy in Mr Collier's possession, collated with a second belonging to Mr David Laing;
and it is evidently founded upon the preceding work. It is
illustrated by three cuts, of which one is a repetition; the title
will be found in Hazlitt, p. 512. As both the known copies are
more or less defective, a few *lacunæ* are supplied between
brackets by conjecture.

𝕿𝖍𝖊 𝖒𝖊𝖗𝖗𝖞 𝖕𝖗𝖆𝖓𝖐𝖘 𝖔𝖋 𝕽𝖔𝖇𝖎𝖓 𝕲𝖔𝖔𝖉=𝖋𝖊𝖑𝖑𝖔𝖜 : 𝖇𝖊𝖗𝖞 𝖕𝖑𝖊𝖆𝖘𝖆𝖓𝖙 𝖆𝖓𝖉 𝖜𝖎𝖙𝖙𝖞.

CHAPTER I.—*Shewing his birth, and whose sonne he
was.*

> Here doe begin the merry iests
> of Robin Good-fellow;
> I'de wish you for to reade this booke,
> if you his pranks would know.
> But first I will declare his birth,
> and what his mother was,
> And then how Robin merrily
> did bring his knacks to passe.

In time of old, when fayries us'd
   to wander in the night,
And through key-holes swiftly glide,
   now marke my story right,
Among these pretty fairy elves
   was Oberon, their king,
Who us'd to keepe them company
   still at their revelling.

And sundry houses they did use,
   but one, above the rest,
Wherein a comely lasse did dwell,
   that pleased King Oberon best.
This lovely damsell, neat and faire,
   so courteous, meek, and mild,
As sayes my booke, by Oberon
   she was begot with child.

She knew not who the father was,
   but thus to all would say—
In night time he to her still came,
   and went away ere day.
The midwife having better skill
   than had this new made mother,
Quoth she, " Surely some fairy 'twas,
   for it can be no other."

And so the old wife rightly judg'd,
   for it was so indeed.
This fairy shew'd himself most kind,
   and helpt his love at need ;
For store of linnen he provides,
   and brings her for her baby ;
With dainty cates and choised fare,
   he serv'd her like a lady.

The Christening time then being come,
   most merry they would be,

The Gossips drank good store of sack
    as then provided be.
And Robin was this infant call'd,
    so named then was he;
What pranks he did, and how he liv'd,
    I'll tell you certainly.

CHAPTER II.—*How Robin Good-fellow carried himselfe, and how he run away from his mother.*

When Robin was a pretty bud,
    some dozen years of age,
He us'd much waggish tricks to men,
    as they at him would rage.
Unto his mother they complain'd,
    which grieved her to heare,
And for these pranks she threatened him
    he should have whipping cheare,

If that he did not leave his tricks,
    his jeering mocks and mowes:
Quoth she, " Thou vile untutor'd youth,
    these prankes no breeding shewes :
I cannot to the market goe,
    but ere I backe returne,
Thou scofst my neighbours in such sort,
    which makes my heart to mourne.

" But I will make you to repent
    these things, ere I have done :
I will no favour have on thee,
    although thou beest my sonne."
Robin was griev'd to heare these words
    which she to him did say,
But to prevent his punishment,
    from her he run away.

And travelling long upon the way,
   his hunger being great,
Unto a taylor's house he came,
   and did entreat some meat:
The taylor tooke compassion then
   upon this pretty youth,
And tooke him for his prentice straight,
   as I have heard in truth.

CHAPTER III.—*How Robin Good-fellow left his master,
and also how Oberon told him he should be turned into
what shape he could wish or desire.*

Now Robin Good-fellow, being plac't
   with a taylor, as you heare,
He grew a workman in short space,
   so well he ply'd his geare.
He had a gowne which must be made,
   even with all haste and speed;
The maid must have't against next day
   to be her wedding weed.

The taylor he did labour hard
   till twelve a clock at night;
Betweene him and his servant then
   they finished aright
The gowne, but putting on the sleeves:
   quoth he unto his man,
"Ile goe to bed: whip on the sleeves
   As fast as ere you can."

So Robin straightway takes the gowne;
   and hangs it on a pin,
Then takes the sleeves and whips the gowne;
   till day he nere did lin.
His master rising in the morne,
   And seeing what he did,

Begun to chide ; quoth Robin then,
 " I doe as I was bid."

His Master then the gowne did take,
 and to his worke did fall :
By that time he had done the same,
 the maid for it did call.
Quoth he to Robin, " Goe thy wayes
 and fetch the remnants hither,
That yesterday we left," said he,
 " wee'l breake our fasts together."

Then Robin hies him up the staires
 and brings the remnants downe,
Which he did know his master sav'd
 out of the woman's gowne.
The taylor he was vext at this ;
 he meant remnants of meat,
That this good woman, ere she went,
 might there her breakfast eate.

Quoth she, " This is a breakfast good
 I tell you, friend, indeed ;
And to requite your love I will
 send for some drinke with speed."
And Robin he must goe for it
 with all the speed he may :
He takes the pot and money too,
 and runnes from thence away.

When he had wandred all the day,
 a good way from the towne,
Unto a forest then he came :
 to sleepe he laid him downe.
Then Oberon came with all his elves,
 and danced about his sonne,
With musick pleasing to the eare ;
 and, when that it was done,

King Oberon layes a scroule by him,
    that he might understand
Whose sonne he was, and how hee'd grant
    whate'er he did demand :
To any forme that he did please
    himselfe he would translate ;
And how one day hee'd send for him
    to see his fairy state.

Then Robin longs to know the truth
    of this mysterious skill,
And turnes himselfe into what shape
    he thinks upon or will.
Sometimes a neighing horse was he,
    sometimes a gruntling hog,
Sometimes a bird, sometimes a crow,
    sometimes a snarling dog.

CHAPTER IV.—*How Robin Good-fellow was merry
at the bridehouse.*

Now Robin having got this art,
    he oft would make good sport,[1]
And hearing of a wedding day,
    he makes him ready for't.
Most like a joviall fidler then
    he drest himselfe most gay,
And goes unto the wedding house,
    there on his crowd to play.

He welcome was unto this feast,
    and merry they were all ;
He play'd and sung sweet songs all day,
    at night to sports did fall.

---

[1] So in A Midsummer Night's Dream, act iii. sc. 2—
    " I with the morning's love have *oft made sport.*"

He first did put the candles out,
    and being in the dark,
Some would he strike, and some would pinch,
    And then sing like a lark.

The candles being light againe,
    and things well and quiet,
A goodly posset was brought in
    to mend their former diet.
Then Robin for to have the same
    did turne him to a beare :
Straight at that sight the people all
    did run away for feare.

Then Robin did the posset eate,
    and having served them so,
Away goes Robin with all haste,
    then laughing hoe, hoe, hoe !

CHAPTER V.—*Declaring how Robin Good-fellow serv'd
    an old lecherous man.*

There was an old man had a neece,
    a very beauteous maid ;
To wicked lust her unkle sought
    this faire one to perswade.

But she a young man lov'd too deare
    to give consent thereto ;
'Twas Robin's chance upon a time
    to heare their grievous woe.
" Content your selfe," then Robin saies,
    " and I will ease your griefe,
I have found out an excellent way
    that will yeeld you reliefe."

He sends them to be married straight,
    and he, in her disguise,

Hies home with all the speed he may
　to blind her uncle's eyes :
And there he plyes his work amaine,
　doing more in one houre,
Such was his skill and workmanship,
　than she could doe in foure.

The old man wondred for to see
　the worke goe on so fast,
And there withall more worke doth he
　unto good Robin cast.
Then Robin said to his old man,
　"good uncle, if you please
To grant me but one ten pound,
　I'le yeeld your love-suit ease."

"Ten pounds," quoth he, "I will give thee,
　sweet Neece, with all my heart,
So thou wilt grant to me thy love,
　to ease my troubled heart."
"Then let me a writing have," quoth he,
　"from your owne hand with speed,
That I may marry my sweet-heart
　when I have done this deed."

The old man he did give consent
　that he these things should have,
Thinking that it had bin his neece
　that did this bargain crave ;
And unto Robin then quoth he,
　"my gentle n[eece, behold,
Goe thou into [thy chamber soone,
　and I'le goe [bring the gold."

When he into [the chamber came,
　thinking in[deed to play,
Straight Robin [upon him doth fall,
　and carries h[im away

Into the chamb[er where the two
  faire lovers [did abide,
And gives to th[em their unkle old,
  I, and the g[old beside.

The old man [vainly Robin sought,
  so man[y shapes he tries ;
Someti[mes he was a hare or hound,
  someti[mes like bird he flies.
The [more he strove the less he sped,
  th[e lovers all did see ;
And [thus did Robin favour them
  full [kind and merrilie. .

[Thus Robin lived a merry life
  as any could enjoy,
'Mongst country farms he did resort,
  and oft would folks annoy :]
But if the maids doe call to him,
  he still away will goe
In knavish sort, and to himselfe
  he'd laugh out hoe, hoe, hoe !

He oft would beg and crave an almes,
  but take nought that they'd give :
In severall shapes he'd gull the world,
  thus madly did he live.
Sometimes a cripple he would seeme,
  sometimes a souldier brave :
Sometimes a fox, sometimes a hare ;
  brave pastimes would he have.

Sometimes an owle he'd seeme to be
  sometimes a skipping frog ;
Sometimes a kirne, in Irish shape,
  to leape ore mire or bog ;
Sometime he'd counterfeit a voyce,
  and travellers call astray,

Sometimes a walking fire he'd be,
  and lead them from their way.

Some call him Robin Good-fellow,
  Hob-goblin or mad Crisp,
And some againe doe tearme him oft
  by name of Will the Wispe ;
But call him by what name you list,
  I have studied on my pillow,
I think the best name he deserves
  is Robin the Good Fellow.

At last upon a summer's night
  King Oberon found him out,
And with his elves in dancing wise
  straight circled him about.
The fairies danc't, and little Tom Thumb
  on his bag-pipe did play,
And thus they danc't their fairy round
  till almost break of day.

Then Phebus he most gloriously
  begins to grace the aire,
When Oberon with his fairy traine
  begins to make repaire,
With speed unto the fairy land,
  they swiftly tooke their way,
And I out of my dreame awak't,
  And so 'twas perfect day.

Thus having told my dreame at full
  I'le bid you all farewell.
If you applaud mad Robin's prankes,
  may be ere long I'le tell
Some other stories to your eares,
  which shall contentment give :
To gaine your favours I will seeke
  the longest day I live.

X.

Rowlands on Goblins.

———o———

FROM a curious tract by Rowlands, called "More Knaves yet? The Knaves of Spades and Diamonds," 4to. Lond. n.d. It has been reprinted entire by the Percy Society, under the care of Dr Rimbault. The following is entitled, "Of Ghoasts and Goblins."

In old wives daies, that in old time did live
(To whose odde tales much credit men did give)
Great store of goblins, fairies, bugs, night-mares,
Urchins, and elves, to many a house repaires.
Yea far more sprites hid haunt in divers places,
Then there be women now weare devils faces.
Amongst the rest was a Good Fellow devill,
So cal'd in kindnes, cause he did no evill,
Knowne by the name of Robin (as we heare),
And that his eyes as broad as sawcers were,
Who came a-nights, and would make kitchins
 cleane,
And in the bed bepinch a lazie queane.
Was much in mils about the grinding meale,
(And sure, I take it, taught the miller steale) ;

Amongst the creame-bowles and milke-pans would
    be,
And with the country wenches, who but he
To wash their dishes for some fresh cheese hire,
Or set their pots and kettles 'bout the fire.
'Twas a mad Robin that did divers pranckes,
For which with some good cheare they gave him
    thankes,
And that was all the kindnes he expected,
With gaine (it seemes) he was not much infected.
But as that times is past, that Robin's gone,
He and his night-mates are to us unknowne,
And in the stede of such good-fellow sprites
We meet with Robin Bad-Fellow a-nights,
That enters houses secret in the darke,
And only comes to pilfer, steale, and sharke,
And as the one made dishes cleane (they say),
The other takes them quite and cleane away,
What'ere it be that is within his reach,
The filching tricke he doth his fingers teach.
But as Good-Fellow Robin had reward
With milke and creame that friends for him prepar'd,
For being busie all the night in vaine,
(Though in the morning all things safe remaine),
Robin Bad-Fellow wanting such a supper,
Shall have his breakfast with a rope and butter,
To which let all his fellowes be invited,
That with such deeds of darknesse are delighted.

XI

An Episode of Fairies.

—o—

[From the Maydes Metamorphosis, 4to, Lond. 1600, a Play
attributed by Kirkman to Lilly.]

Enter the Fairies, singing and dancing.

BY the moon we sport and play,
　　With the night begins our day :[1]
As we dance the dew doth fall;
Trip it, little urchins all,
Lightly as the little bee,
Two by two, and three by three,
And about go we, and about go we.[2]

Jo. What mawmets are these?

Fris. O, they be the fairies that haunt these woods.

---

[1] So Milton—

" Come, let us our rites begin ;
'Tis only daylight that makes sin."

[2] This song is set to music in an old collection by Ravenscroft and others, and is quoted in Douce's Illustrations, vol. i.
p. 11.

Mop. O, we shall be pinch'd most cruelly.

1 *Fay.* Will you have any music, sir?

2 *Fay.* Will you have any fine music?

3 *Fay.* Most dainty music?

Mop. (*aside.*) We must set a face on't now, there's no flying.   No, sir, we are very merry, I thank you.

1 *Fay.* O, but you shall, sir.

Fris. No, I pray you save your labour.

2 *Fay.* O, sir, it shall not cost you a penny.

Jo. Where be your fiddles?

3 *Fay.* You shall have most dainty instruments, sir.

Mop. I pray you, what might I call you?

1 *Fay.* My name is Penny.

Mop. I am sorry I cannot purse you.

Fris. I pray you, sir, what might I call you?

1 *Fay.* My name is Cricket.

Mop. I would I were a chimney for your sake.[1]

Jo. I pray you, you pretty little fellow, what's your name?

3 *Fay.* My name is Little-little Prick.

Jo. Little-little Prick! O, you are a dangerous fairy, and fright all the little wenches in the country out of their beds.   I care not whose hand I were in, so I were out of yours.

1 *Fay.* I do come about the cops,
Leaping upon flowers' tops.
Then I get upon a fly,
She carries me above the sky,
And trip and go.

2 *Fay.* When a dew-drop falleth down,
And doth light upon my crown,
Then I shake my head and skip,
And about I trip.

---

[1] All this is so similar to The Midsummer Night's Dream, iii. 1, that one must have been taken from the other.

3 *Fay.* When I feel a girl asleep,
Underneath her frock I peep,
There to sport, and there I play.
Then I bite her like a flea,
And about I skip.
    Jo. Ay, I thought where I should have you.
    1 *Fay.* Wilt please you dance, sir?
    Jo. Indeed, sir, I cannot handle my legs.
    2 *Fay.* O, you must needs dance and sing,
Which if you refuse to do,
We will pinch you black and blue,
And about we go.

    They all dance in a ring, and sing as followeth.

Round about, round about, in a fine ring-a;
Thus we dance, thus we dance, and thus we sing-a.
Trip and go, to and fro, over this green-a,
All about, in and out, for our brave queen-a.

Round about, round about, in a fine ring-a;
Thus we dance, thus we dance, and thus we sing-a.
Trip and go, to and fro, over this green-a,
All about, in and out, for our brave queen-a.

We have danc'd round about in a fine ring-a;
We have danc'd lustily, and thus we sing-a,—
All about, in and out, over this green-a,
To and fro, trip and go, to our brave queen-a.

XII.

The Cozenages of the Wests.

———o———

THE following is reprinted from a very scarce tract, published at London in 1613, with a rough but curious print on the title, illustrating one of the incidents here related. It is principally valuable for our purpose as showing the popular belief in the existence of fairies, and also for the mention of the Queen of Fairies falling in love with a mortal; but anything of the kind is so rarely met with, that its subject alone would sanction its introduction into this collection.

The severall notorious and lewd Cousonages of John West and Alice West, falsely called the King and Queene of Fayries, practised verie lately both in this citie and many places neere adjoyning: to the impoverishing of many simple people, as well men as women: who were arraigned and convicted for the same at the Sessions house in the Old Baily, the 14. of January, this present yeare, 1613.

CHAP. I.—*The lewd cousonages of* JOHN WEST *and* ALICE WEST, *falsely called the King and Queene of Fayries.*

The hot sunne after the overflow of Nilus, engen-

dred not more straunge and ugly imperfect monsters
in Egypt, then this age doth impostures in and about
the citie of London : no cousonage is left unpractised,
no cheat unattempted, no meanes to deceive unaf-
fected, insomuch that the suburbs in some places may
be compared to a schoole of cousonages, and a mart
of unheard of abuses, of which every succeeding month
begets sundrie of the newest and last edition, every
one striving to exceed another in craft and subtlety.

What straine of invention stretcht to the highest
key of subornation, what almost incredible forgerie,
without bound, limit, or dimension, what degree of
jugling, counterfetting, what fraud or fallacies have
not beene practised in that height of cunning, able,
as it were, to foole the simplicity of the former times,
to gull the present ages, and to give precedents to the
succeeding seasons, scarce to be equald or paraleld ?

The innocency of the first world strived to excell
in vertue, but the poyson of this infected age strives
to exceed in vice.   Happy was that man, that in the
nonage of the golden world could leave behinde him
any presedent worthy to imitate, but they hold themselves in this dotage of the iron age most remarkable,
that can put upon these times any imputation which
deservedly can undergoe the scandall of reproofe.
Why should else such new impostures be continually
hatcht, of which the first and most innocent seasons
were not so much guilty as to know how to entitle
them ?   To these new abuses we had therefore need
of Callepine to devise new names, for as there is no
Latine, Greeke, or Hebrew word for Tobacco, but
Tobacco, the reason is, it was an herbe not knowne by
our granfathers, nor that customary habit which the
world hath lately entertained it : so I may speake of
these cousonages now in use, which till now not
knowne, I know not how to stile them by any name

borrowed from antiquitie, since such new fraudulencies have but of late daies beene put in execution, but onely by the generall names of cousonages, which shall comprehend the roote and manifold branches. I will not stand now to distinguish their severall kindes, which for their commonnesse are not worthie my remembrance: neyther is my purpose to trouble you with any long discourse of practises in another kinde, as to kneele downe to prayers in Pauls, and leave a handbasket carelesly by, with capons legs hanging out, which when a cheater hath cunningly come behinde the Orisant and stolne away, when he hath ransackt for poultrie, he hath found a child to call him father? Neyther being myselfe no gamester, is it my purpose to lay open the cosonages at cards, and cheating at dice, in which hee is held no compleat gallant, that is not most dishonestly expert.

These and infinite others of the like nature I advisedly let passe, as connicatchings almost quite worne out of breath, and come to circumstances of riper, newer, and fresher invention, and, as I may truly say, now in fashion.

CHAP. 2.—*Alice West her first cousenage at Fulham.*

There were arraigned at Newgate this last Sessions, two notorious and infamous practisers of this new devised leger-demaine. One John West, and Alice his wife, who dwelt at Fulham, some foure miles from London; these understanding that one Thomas Moore of Hammersmith was well possest, sought by some strange fraudulent meanes to cheat him of such money and goods as they knew certainly hee had in his use and custodie: and because they knew common cousonages had for the most part common discovery, and so consequently a common and ordinary punishment

denounced against offenders in that kinde, they therefore devised a new forme, in which for the strangenesse
and varietie they could hardly be traced.

This woman takes upon her to bee familiarly acquainted with the king and queene of fairies, two that
had in their power the command of inestimable treasure ; and growing inward with a maid servant that
belonged to this Thomas Moore, communicates to
her a strange revelation, how that the fayrie king and
queeñe had appeard to her in a vision, saying they
had a purpose to bestow great summes of gold upon this
man and this woman, which by her meanes and direc-
tions, was undoubtedly to be compast : in which atchieve-
ment, there was nothing so necessary as secrecie, for
if it were revealed to any save them three whom it did
essentially concerne, they should not onely hazard
their good fortune, but incurre the danger of the fayries,
and so consequently be open to great mishapes, and
fearefull disasters.　This being by the maid acquainted
to the simple man and his wife, after conjuration of
secrecy, they were as greedily willing to receive the
benefit, as fearefull loath to entertaine the punishment,
and so their simplicitie begat an easier way to their
jugling ; which, she perceiving, prosecutes to her first
devised purpose, and first entreats for money to performe the due rites of sacrifice to his great patron, the
king of fayries.　After them, she sends for more to
furnish other ceremonies before forgot, still pretending
that somthing or other was eyther neglected, or wanting to the attayning of so inestimable a masse.　And
the first rites that must be performed, was a great
banquet, which must be prepared for the royall king
and queene of fayries ; then all the chamber must be
hung with the richest linnen that they had in their
possession, which according to their estate was very
sufficient.　The banker cost a prettie summe of money,

but all this was no charges in regard it should be returned tenfold; therefore the more they bestowed, the
more would be their gaines, in so much that their
covetous simplicity so overswayed their understanding,
that at several times this Circe had enchanted from
them the sum of 40 pounds : and to encourage them
the further, they brought him into a vault, where they
shewed him two attired like the king and queene of
fayries, and by them elves and goblings, and in the
same place an infinite company of bags, and upon
them written, " This is for Thomas Moore," " This is
for his wife," but would not let him touch anything,
which gave him some incouragement to his almost
despairing hope; but still he received no profit.

Yet at last beginning to looke into his estate, and
what impossibility there was, he began to doubt some
imposture, and thought to acquaint these proceedings
to some friend, to whom he might communicate the
busines. He was as some think, and as by the sequel
it appeared, stroke lame by her sorceries, after which
she presently repaired to him, told him his purpose
to blab the secrets of the fayries was come to the eares
of Oberon, for which he inraged, had inflicted this
punishment upon him, but at the intercession of the
fayrie queene, and in hope of his future secresie, she
had provided him an oile, with which being bathed,
he should instantly recover; which accordingly hapned,
and gave no greater strength to his limbs then it did
grouth to his opinion. She therfore upon disbursing
of more money, caused them to buy chests, trunks,
nay sacks, halfe tubs and barrels, which she promised
the faryies wold fill with treasure. But though they
were carefully provided, yet they stood empty, and he
almost as void of hope, as his vessels of mony, till at
length she drue the maid into a dark celler, and by
some strong illusion shewed two in strange habits,

whom she termed the K. and Q. of fayries, and by
them, so much imagined treasure, that the maid justi-
fied before the bench there could not be so litle as
seventeen hundred thousand pound, al which this
cheatresse affirmed was for her master, but she was
not suffred to beare any part of it away, because the
time was not come, and the ceremonies not yet ended,
after performance of which the treasure was to be
tendred. To compasse which, she demanded so much
money to provide her necessaries, as she imagined the
poore man had of his own, or upon his credit could
borow : which she received, to the summe of foure
score pound.

And having drawn him thus dry, she and her husband fled the town by night, and after lived privatly
in S. Katherens, where she practised many such
cosonages as shal be declared hereafter.

This was against her proved the 14. of January, at
the Sessions, for which she was convicted with her
husband, and judged to bee whipt through London,
and certain daies to stand on the pillory, which according to her judgement, hath to the example of all
such practisers beene performed, and she yet till
further evidence can be brought against her, kept
still a prisoner in Newgate.

CHAP. 3.—*Her second cosonage of a man and his wife,*
which of them should die first.

Many other of good reputation and quality hath
she brought within the compasse of these gulleries ;
some for their credit's sake I forbeare to name, others,
because they would not call their wits in publike
question, have forborne to justifie manifest truthes
against her. One gentleman amongst the rest, whom
by circumstance she gathered did not affect his wife,

she so farre perswaded with him, that hee constantly presumed to lay in her power to tell him which of them should die first. She humourd him so long, and with such cunning tricks and shifts deluded him, that at sundry times, upon his owne protestation, she had of him at least three score pound, putting him in hope that she should not outlive this day nor that: but he being urgent to know what to trust to, because he had alreadie bespoke his second wife, she assured him she should die as the last Christmas Eve, yet upon Christmas day she was able to sup as hote plumbe pottage, and eat as hard brawne as the youngest wife betweene East and West Cheap.

CHAP. 4.—*How she made a maid in the Strand sit all a cold night in a garden naked, with a pot of earth in her lap, promising her it should be turned to gold in the morning.*

Another simple maid, whom she knew had hourded the best part of seven yeares wages of her good hus-wivery togither upon promise of the greatest part she had, she perswaded to sit naked in a garden a whole cold frostie winters night, with a pot of earth in her lap, promising that ere morning the queene of fayries should turne it into gold: and in the meane time that this poore maid sate there, this cunning queane ranne away with he money and her cloathes; and others she had cousend in the like kinde.

CHAP. 5.—*How a young man came to her to know when his master should die.*

A young man came to this cunning woman to know when his master should die, for he had more than a monthes minde to marry with his mistresse. Shee

held him long in hand with trifles and delayes, and
stil fetcht him off from time to time, now with a
crowne, then with an angell, till shee had left his
purse as barren as his braine, and so giving him the
slip, left him as meere an asse as she found him.

Chap. 6.—*Of saylers wives that came to her, to know when their husbands should come home.*

And saylers wives came ordinarily to her whilest
shee lived in Saint Katherines, to know when their
husbands would come, that they might freely play
the good fellows with their friends :   and shee would
answere, not of long time, and yet many of them
returned, and tooke their wives napping with other
womens husbands, yet many of these shee deluded,
and got from them as much monie as they were able
to make or to borrow, and yet could she cunningly,
when they were most suspitious of her, put them off
with some evasion or other, shadowing all her craft
with a kind of simplicitie.

Poor farmers in the countrie have paid for her
subtletie. When monie was scarce, she would not
refuse pigges, capons, geese, or corne, but except of
any these countrie commodities, for which she would
promise that all the fayries, like so many court-pages,
should be at their service.

But to give the greater grace to these fraudulencies,
she hath the opinion to be halfe or the greatest part
of a witch : without which, it were impossible that by
any outward management, shee could goe through so
many things as shee hath done, but especially in and
so neere London, where the people for the most part
assume to understand most things, nay to know all :
nor hath she laid traines for prentises, maides, and
the simple sort of people, but she hath fetcht off usurers

and misers, as finely as they fetch off young heires
that are newly come to their lands. As for example.

CHAP. 7.—*How she cousened a gentlewoman of much
gold and silver.*

A gentlewoman ancient of great fortunes, and
therefore should be wise, but assuredly wealthy, and
therefore commonly covetous, to her shee brings a
smooth compacted tale from the queene of fayries,
who went to bestow on her a large quantity of coyne,
which to the gentlewoman appearing at first little
better then ridiculous, shee told her shee would for
her better satisfaction shew her apparently that there
was no impossibilitie in anything that she had before
suggested, and for instance, quoth she, lend me from
you a faire white diaper napkin, and two new shillings,
and you shall see what, by the help of the fayrie
queene, I can make of them. The gentlewoman did
so. She presently making her beleeve she had
tyed the two shillings in the corners of the napkin,
by a cunning jugling slight conveighed into their
places two twentie shilling peeces, unknowne to
the gentlewoman, who took them to be no other
then those shillings she had before delivered her:
she perswades her to locke them safe in a chest,
of which shee herselfe would keepe the key, con-
firming to her that within six dayes, or there abouts,
by the power of the fayrie queene, they should turn
to double soveraignes. The six dayes expired,
and according as shee had promised, when they
came to open the diaper napkin, they found instead
of two King James his shillings, two faire Elizabeth soveraignes.

This put the gentlewoman in some hope, and
three or foure times after the same fashion shee

had deluded her, till she had jugled from her some foure score pound in monie, intimating unto her, that within such a time every shilling in silver should be made twentie in gold. But when she could not extract more from her, without palpable discoverie of her notorious cheating, she took away the napkin and monie, and left her to a solitarie repentance of her late greedie avarice. Infinite cosonages of lesse nature she hath beene tainted with.

CHAP. 8.—*How the same Alice West used to tell prentises, maides, and such ignorant people, their fortunes.*

Shee had by the porch and doore to her house a little closet, where she might heare every word spoken at the doore. When a young fellow came to know what success hee should have, at what trade hee should best thrive, or when any maid came to know where any thing was lost, or when any woman came to know whether her husband should burie her, or shee him, or in the like kind, shee would send one to the doore by sundrie interrogatories to understand their businesse, as whether they had lost a spoone, or come to use her advise in physicke, or if a maid came to know who should be her husband, or a batcheler whether hee should have such a maid, or such a widdow. Which no sooner in her closset she heard, but she would straight come to the doore, give them entertainment, bid them welcome, and tell them that the queene of fayries had told her their businesse, and so recite to them particularly every thing that shee had evesedropt in her closset: which gave such credit to her profession that the simple people did simply beleeve that it should happen, which out of the invention of her braine she did extemporally devise for them, by which subtletie shee purchast to herselfe great opinion of her skill, and many large summes of monie.

CHAP. 9.—*How two men came to know where a spoone was lost, and how they spared their monie.*

It happened, that a silver spoone being lost in a gentleman's house of good worship, and the butler, because it was through his negligence, was enjoyned to pay for it, hee called to one of his fellowes, and early in the morning, came to this woman's house, purposing for his better satisfaction to know a private theefe, and for his owne better justification, to give her ten groats, but to shew him the fellow or to helpe him to his spoone againe. And comming betimes in the morning, they found her scolding and clamouring with her neighbours, because some rude fellow had in knaverie plaid the beast just upon the threshold of the doore ; and amongst other exclamations, quoth shee, "If I did but know, what man, woman, or child, had done me this wrong, I would bee severely revenged for so grosse an injurie." The butler, apprehending her wordes, "Come," saith he to his fellow, "wee will goe backe, and save this monie."—"Why?" quoth his fellow. "Because," saith hee, "if this wise woman cannot tell who hath plaid the beast upon the threshold of the doore, which is so neare her, how can shee tell who hath my spoone, which was stolne so far off?" and so returned the same way they came, without adding losse to losse, or shooting a second arrow after the first,[1] which they assuredly knew was lost.

---

[1] A kind of proverbial expression, which Shakespeare has amplified, and made so good use of in the "Merchant of Venice," act i. sc. 1.

CHAP. 10.—*How this woman changed with a grocer a bastard for a sugar-loafe.*

It was well knowne, in a populous place about the citie, and not farre from Smithfield, that this woman, attired like a maid-servant, came into a grocer's shop with a handbasket, to cheapen a sugar-loafe. The grocer, being a batcheler and without a wife, it was her purpose belike to helpe him to an heyre. Shee tels him that her mistresse, being a gentlewoman of good account that dwelt by, would bestow such a quantity in Barbarie sugar, and after some colourable circumstances, and long beating the price, they grew to a conclusion : when "Stay," quoth she, "Ile leave my handbasket, till I but step over the way to know whether my mistresse like the price and sugar, and returne instantly :" the grocer, suspecting nothing, lets her goe quite away with the sugar-loafe, and takes his lute, for hee much delighted in that instrument, and playes to a yong bastard that shee had left in her handbasket, which bastard the grocer was glad to keepe.

CHAP. 11.—*How one of her companions served a gentleman.*

A gentleman, a tearmer that came to the citie to receive monie, being a good companion and having good store of crownes, she grieving hee should spend any of his monie abroad, and not in her friend's house, thought to take a speedy order for it.

It happened the gentleman, being a little troubled with a corne upon his toe, she perswaded him to have it cut, and brought one of her owne devilish consorts, whom shee pretended to have extraordinarie skill in that art, who at the first cut, cut him to the bone, so that the gentleman was not able to goe or stand : shee then tooke upon her to play the surgeon, but she so ordered the matter, that in two tearmes hee was not able to pull on a boot, not stir from his lodging, till his monie was almost quite wasted.

CHAP. 12.—*How she cousoned another woman of many rings and jewels.*

There dwelt in one of the best parts of the citie a woman of no meane substance, if her wit had been answerable to her wealth, or her understanding to her yeares. This cousoner, meaning to lay a pit-fall to entrap her, inquires secretly what country woman shee was, how educated, what was the name of her first and second husband, where she had dwelt, how long in a place, how many children she had, how many were living, how many sonnes, how many daughters, with a particular of their names, and how they were bestowed ; how many suters she had then, and whom she best respected. All which she privatly learned of an old char-woman that frequented the house much, and whom she had corrupted to her purpose. This done, and many other instructions learned, she cunningly gets a letter to be drawne from a deere friend of this gentlewoman's in the country, whom she much respected, and attiring herselfe like a plaine countri-woman, inquires for such a gentlewoman, knocks at her dore, and with many a counterfeit courtesie, delivers it to her. Which when that gentlewoman had read, and understood the contents, she intreats her to sit downe, sends for wine, and desires her of fur-ther conference. For that letter contained a particular character of this counterfeit, that she was extra-ordinarily skilled in magick, could tell fortunes,

could tell where any treasure was hid, and obtaine
it; besides could advise her in many other things
that were for her future good, of which the letter
said the gentleman her friend had made perfect and
sound triall.   After some discourse afar off, shee
began to tell her shee was never in London till
then, yet could she discours of many things that
had privatly hapned to her, tel her what rooms she
had in her house, and how they were furnisht, what
chests, what rings, what stones in them and how
fashioned, for al these things and more she had
privatly learned before, which put the gentlewoman in
an undoubted belief of her cunning.   She next desired
to see her hand, and at sight of it smilingly said she
was born to many good fortunes, and much beloved
of the king of fayries.   Then she asked her if she
was not borne in such a place, had not had so many
husbandes, and had not so many children so bestowed.
To which the simple gentlewoman answered yea,
with great admiration how she that never saw her till
then, and was never in the citie before, could make
such a true relation.   And now she begins in her
heart to esteeme the care and love of her friend, and
so to give way to this woman's purpose.   Then she
told her what suters she had, and smilingly said, and
in sooth, and tell me true, doe you not love such a
man best?   She answered yes, still more and more
amazed at her cunning.   True saith she, your seller
is vauted thus and thus, and there is such a corner in
it, is there not?   To all which she answered yea.
Undoubtedly then, quoth she, but I must sweare you
to secrecie, there is much gold and silver hid in that
place, but unlesse you protest to keepe it close to yourselfe, and never to call my name in question, I will
not undertake the taking of it up.   Protestations past
on both sides, the one for the undertaking, the other

for concealing; she bad her then shew her two such rings of such a fashion, and a chaine which lay in such a casket, for with them she must present the king of fayries, whom she must of necessity use in this business.   The gentlewoman said she had such jewels indeed, and in such a place, and greatly admired at her skill that could know so much.   And to be briefe, after many cunning gloses and private wispering in her eare of such passages as had before hapned her, this cunning quean so far perswaded her, that for that time she only tooke survey of the place where the gold was hid.   The second time she cleanly carried away the chaine, ringes, and certaine money which was to provide things necessary to such ceremonies : but the third time till she was publikly arraigned for many other cosonages, she could never set eye of her. Many ridiculous and frivolus impositôs in this busines she put upon this gentlewoman, which for modesty sake I am willing to conceale, as to sit looking so many houres crosse legd towards the East, and so long another way : that her predecessor so famous for cheating the tripewife in Newgate market could never equall, much lesse exceed her in these new devised tricks of legerdemaine.

CHAP. 13.—*Another done by one of her companions.*

This companion comes to a young shopkeeper, a goldsmith's prentise, one that had the charge of more wealth then wit, and desires to speake with him, and in smooth language so insinuated, that she made him beleeve the queene of fayries did most ardently doat upon him;[1] the fellow liking the motion, askt how

---

[1] This may be considered an illustration of the love between Titania and Bottom the Weaver.

he might see or speak with her. Why thus, quoth
she, bring foure of the fairest silver and guilt peeces
of plate in thy master's shop into such a close by S.
Giles, and place them at the foure corners of the
close, and they shal not onely be turned to perfect
gold, but there thou shalt confer with the amorous
queen of fayries.   The young man the next morning
got up early according to his houre, went to the close,
and placed the plate at the foure corners, still expecting the queen of fayries, and then this Alice West had
plast in a ditch foure of her consorts, who came forth,
and with stones and brickbats so beat the poore prentise that he ran home, and forgot to take his plate
with him.   His corage was cold for meeting the Q.
of fayries.

There remains many other that are not yet revealed,
but at their next arainment, when they come to light,
we will acquaint you with the projects which appeare
to me as things necessary to be divulged, because
that such as have not falne in these pitfals, may by
this means avoid them, seeing such daily presidents
before their eyes of lamentable repentance, wishing
withall, that the ancient proverbe in the accedence,
may in such hereafter be verifyed.   *Happy are they
whom other men's harmes do make to beware.*

XIII.

Drayton's Nymphidia.

---o---

THIS beautiful poem, without which our collection could not be complete, is not so popularly known as to preclude its insertion. The text is taken from the original edition of 1627, containing the *Battle of Agincourt*, and other poems. There is no doubt that it was a posterior production to the "Midsummer Night's Dream," as Drayton himself calls it one of his "latest poems."—See Malone's "Shakespeare," ed. 1821, v. 206.

Old Chaucer doth of Topas tell,
Mad Rabelais of Pantagruel,
A latter third of Dowsabel,
   With such poor trifles playing:
Others the like have labour'd at,
Some of this thing, and some of that,
And many of they know not what,
   But that they must be saying.

Another sort there be, that will
Be talking of the Fairies still,
Nor never[1] can they have their fill,
   As they were wedded to them :
No tales of them their thirst can slake,
So much delight in them they take,
And some strange thing they fain would make,
   Knew they the way to do them !

Then since no muse hath been so bold,
Or of the later, or the old,
Those elvish secrets to unfold,
   Which lie from others' reading ;
My active muse to light shall bring
The court of that proud Fairy King,
And tell there of the revelling :
   Jove prosper my proceeding !

And thou, Nymphidia, gentle fay,
Which meeting me upon the way,
These secrets didst to me bewray,
   Which now I am in telling :
My pretty, light, fantastic maid,
I here invoke thee to my aid,
That I may speak what thou hast said,
   In numbers smoothly swelling.

This palace standeth in the air,
By necromancy placed there,
That it no tempests needs to fear,
   Which way soe'er it blow it :
And somewhat southward tow'rd the noon,

---

[1] Ritson alters this to *ever.* I prefer the ancient duplication of the negative, although of course not grammatically correct. Other instances occur in the course of the poem.

Whence lies a way up to the moon,
And thence the Faëry can as soon
  Pass to the earth below it.

The walls of spiders' legs are made,
Well morticed and finely laid ;
He was the master of his trade
  It curiously that builded :
The windows of the eyes of cats,
And for the roof, instead of slats,
Is cover'd with the skins of bats,
  With moonshine that are gilded.

Hence Oberon, him sport to make,
(Their rest when weary mortals take,
And none but only fairies wake)
  Descendeth for his pleasure :
And Mab, his merry queen, by night
Bestrides young folks that lie upright,
(In elder times the mare that hight)
  Which plagues them out of measure.

Hence shadows, seeming idle shapes
Of little frisking elves and apes,
To earth do make their wanton scapes,
  As hope of pastime hastes them :
Which maids think on the hearth they see
When fires well-near consumed be,
There dancing hays [1] by two and three,
  Just as their fancy casts them.

These make our girls their slutt'ry rue,
By pinching them both black and blue,
And put a penny in their shoe,

---

      [1] [A kind of dance.]

The house for cleanly sweeping :
And in their courses make that round,
In meadows and in marshes found,
Of them so call'd the fairy-ground,
   Of which they have the keeping.

These, when a child haps to be got,
Which after proves an idiot,
When folks perceive it thriveth not,
   The fault therein to smother,
Some silly doating brainless calf,
That understands things by the half,
Says that the Faëry left this aulf,[1]
   And took away the other.

But listen, and I shall you tell,
A chance in Faëry that befell,
Which, certainly, may please you well,
   In love and arms delighting,
Of Oberon, that jealous grew
Of one of his own fairy crew :
Too well (he fear'd) his queen that knew,
   His love but ill requiting.

Pigwiggen was this fairy knight :
One wond'rous gracious in the sight
Of fair queen Mab, which day and night
   He amorously observed :
Which made king Oberon suspect
His service took too good effect,
His sauciness and often check'd,
   And could have wish'd him starved.

Pigwiggen gladly would commend
Some token to queen Mab to send,

                   .   [1] [Elf.]

If sea or land him aught could lend
　Were worthy of her wearing.
At length this lover doth devise
A bracelet made of emmets' eyes,
A thing he thought that she would prize,
　No whit her state impairing.

And to the queen a letter writes,
Which he most curiously indites,
Conjuring her by all the rites
　Of love, she would be pleased
To meet him, her true servant, where
They might without suspect or fear
Themselves to one another clear,
　And have their poor hearts eased.

At midnight, the appointed hour,
And for the queen a fitting bow'r
(Quoth he) is that fair cowslip-flow'r,
　On Hipcut Hill that groweth;
In all your train there's not a fay,
That ever went to gather may,
But she hath made it in her way,
　The tallest there that groweth.

When by Tom Thumb, a fairy page,
He sent it, and doth him engage,
By promise of a mighty wage,
　It secretly to carry.
Which done the queen her maids doth call,
And bids them to be ready all,
She would go see her summer-hall,
　She could no longer tarry.

Her chariot ready straight is made;
Each thing therein is fitting laid,
That she by nothing might be stay'd,

For nought must her be letting :
Four nimble gnats the horses were,
Their harnesses of gossamer,
Fly Cranion, her charioteer,
   Upon the coach-box getting.

Her chariot of a snail's fine shell,
Which for the colours did excel ;
The fair queen Mab becoming well,
   So lively was the limning :
The seat the soft wool of the bee,
The cover (gallantly to see)
The wing of a py'd butterfly :
   I trow 'twas simple trimming.

The wheels compos'd of crickets' bones,
And daintily made for the nonce ;
For fear of rattling on the stones,
   With thistle-down they shod it :
For all her maidens much did fear,
If Oberon had chanc'd to hear,
That Mab his queen should have been there,
   He would not have abode it.

She mounts her chariot with a trice,
Nor would she stay for no advice,
Until her maids, that were so nice,
   To wait on her were fitted,
But ran herself away alone ;
Which when they heard, there was not one,
But hasted after to be gone,
   As she had been diswitted.

Hop, and Mop, and Drop so clear,
Pip, and Trip, and Skip, that were
To Mab their sovereign ever dear,

Her special maids of honour ;
Fib and Tib, and Pinck, and Pin,
Tick and Quick, and Jil, and Jin,
Tit and Nit, and Wap, and Win :
   The train that wait upon her.

Upon a grasshopper they got,
And, what with amble and with trot,
For hedge nor ditch they spared not,
   But after her they hie them.
A cobweb over them they throw,
To shield the wind if it should blow,
Themselves they wisely could bestow,
   Lest any should espy them.

But let us leave queen Mab a while,
Through many a gate, o'er many a stile,
That now had gotten by this while, .
   Here dear Pigwiggen kissing ;
And tell how Oberon doth fare,
Who grew as mad as any hare,
When he had sought each place with care,
   And found his queen was missing.

By grisly Pluto he doth swear :
He rent his clothes and tore his hair :
And as he runneth here and there,
   An acorn cup he greeteth ;
Which soon he taketh by the stalk,
About his head he lets it walk,
Nor doth he any creature baulk,
   But lays on all he meeteth.

The Tuscan poet doth advance
The frantic Paladine of France,
And those more ancient do enhance

Alcides in his fury;
And others Ajax Telamon;
But to this time there hath been none
So bedlam as our Oberon,
    Of which I dare assure ye.

And first encount'ring with a wasp,
He in his arms the fly doth clasp,
As tho' his breath he forth would grasp,
    Him for Pigwiggen taking.
" Where is my wife, thou rogue ? " (quoth he),
" Pigwiggen, she is come to thee ;
Restore her, or thou dy'st by me ! "
    Whereat the poor wasp quaking,

Cries, " Oberon, great fairy king,
Content thee, I am no such thing ;
I am a wasp, behold my sting ! "
    At which the fairy started.
When soon away the wasp doth go,
Poor wretch was never frighted so,
He thought his wings were much too slow,
    O'erjoy'd they were so parted.

He next upon a glow-worm light,
(You must suppose it now was night)
Which for her hinder part was bright,
    He took to be a devil ;
And furiously doth her assail
For carrying fire in her tail ;
He thrash'd her rough coat with his flail,
    The mad king fear'd no evil.

" O ! " quoth the glow-worm, "hold thy hand,
Thou puissant king of Fairy-land,
Thy mighty strokes who may withstand ?

Hold, or of life despair I."
Together then herself doth roll,
And tumbling down into a hole,
She seem'd as black as any coal,
    Which vext away the fairy.

From thence he ran into a hive,
Amongst the bees he letteth drive,
And down their combs begins to rive,
    All likely to have spoiled :
Which with their wax his face besmear'd,
And with their honey daub'd his beard ;
It would have made a man afeard,
    To see how he was moiled.

A new adventure him betides :
He met an ant, which he bestrides,
And post thereon away he rides,
    Which with his haste doth stumble,
And came full over on her snout ;
Her heels so threw the dirt about,
For she by no means could get out,
    But over him doth tumble.

And being in this piteous case,
And all beslurried head and face,
On runs he in this wild-goose chase,
    As here and there he rambles,
Half blind, against a mole-hill hit.
And for a mountain taking it,
For all he was out of his wit,
    Yet to the top he scrambles.

And being gotten to the top,
Yet there himself he could not stop.
But down on th'other side doth chop,

And to the foot came rumbling :
So that the grubs therein that bred,
Hearing such turmoil over head,
Thought surely they had all been dead,
 So fearful was the jumbling.

And falling down into a lake,
Which him up to the neck doth take,
His fury somewhat it doth slake,
 He calleth for a ferry :
Where you may some recovery note,
What was his club he made his boat,
And in his oaken cup doth float,
 As safe as in a wherry.

Men talk of the adventures strange
Of Don Quishot, and of their change,
Through which he armed oft did change,
 Of Sancha Pancha's travel :
But should a man tell every thing
Done by this frantic fairy king,
And then in lofty numbers sing,
 It well his wits might gravel.

Scarce set on shore, but therewithal
He meeteth Puck, which most men call
Hob-goblin, and on him doth fall
 With words from frenzy spoken :
" Ho, ho," quoth Hob, " God save thy grace !
Who dress'd thee in this piteous case?
He thus that spoil'd my sov'reign's face,
 I would his neck were broken."

This Puck seems but a dreaming dolt,
Still walking like a ragged colt,
And oft out of a bush doth bolt,

Of purpose to deceive us ;
And, leading us, make us to stray,
Long winter's nights out of the way,
And when we stick in mire and clay,
    He doth with laughter leave us.

" Dear Puck," quoth he, " my wife is gone.
As e'er thou lov'st king Oberon,
Let every thing but this alone,
    With vengeance and pursue her :
Bring her to me, alive or dead,
Or that vile thief Pigwiggen's head !
That villain hath defil'd my bed :
    He to this folly drew her."

Quoth Puck, " My liege, I'll never lin,
But I will thorough thick and thin,
Until at length I bring her in ;
    My dearest lord, ne'er doubt it.
Thorough brake, thorough briar,
Thorough muck, thorough mire,
Thorough water, thorough fire ! " [1]
    And thus goes Puck about it.

This thing Nymphidia overheard,
That on this mad king had a guard,
Not doubting of a great reward,
    For first this bus'ness broaching :
And through the air away doth go,
Swift as an arrow from the bow,[2]

---

[1] Compare A Midsummer Night's Dream, act ii. sc. 2—

    Over hill, over dale,
      Thorough bush, thorough briar ;
    Over park, over pale,
      Thorough flood, thorough fire.

[2] So in A Midsummer Night's Dream, act iii. sc. 2—

    I go, I go ; look how I go !
    Swifter than arrow from the Tartar's bow.

To let her sovereign Mab to know
   What peril was approaching.

The queen, bound with loves pow'rful'st charm,
Sat with Pigwiggen arm in arm ;
Her merry maids, that thought no harm,
   About the room were skipping :
A humble-bee, their minstrel, play'd
Upon his hobby ; ev'ry maid
Fit for this revel was array'd,
   The hornpipe neatly tripping.

In comes Nymphidia, and doth cry,
" My sovereign, for your safety fly,
For there is danger but too nigh,
   I posted to forewarn you :
The king hath sent Hob-goblin out,
To seek you all the fields about,
And of your safety you may doubt,
   If he but once discern you."

When, like an uproar in the town,
Before them every thing went down ;
Some tore a ruff, and some a gown,
   'Gainst one another justling.
They flew about like chaff i' th' wind ;
For haste some left their masks behind,
Some could not stay their gloves to find ;
   There never was such bustling !

Forth ran they, by a secret way,
Into a brake, that near them lay,
Yet much they doubted there to stay,
   Lest Hob should hap to find them :
He had a sharp and piercing sight,

All one to him the day and night,
And therefore were resolv'd by flight
　　To leave this place behind them.

At length one chanc'd to find a nut,
In th'end of which a hole was cut,
Which lay upon a hazel root,
　　There scatter'd by a squirrel,
Which out the kernel gotten had :
When quoth this fay, " Dear queen, be glad,
Let Oberon be ne'er so mad,
　　I'll set you safe from peril."

" Come all into this nut," quoth she,
" Come closely in, be rul'd by me ;
Each one may here a chooser be,
　　For room ye need not wrestle,
Nor need ye be together heapt."
So one by one therein they creept,
And (lying down) they soundly slept,
　　As safe as in a castle.

Nymphidia, that this while doth watch,
Perceiv'd, if Puck the queen should catch,
That he would be her over-match,
　　Of which she well bethought her ;
Found it must be some pow'rful charm,
The queen against him that must arm,
Or surely he would do her harm,
　　For throughly he had sought her.

And list'ning if she aught could hear,
What her might hinder or might fear ;
But finding still the coast was clear,
　　Nor creature had descri'd her :

Each circumstance and having scann'd,
She came thereby to understand,
Puck would be with them out of hand,
 When to her arms she hi'd her.

And first her fern-seed doth bestow,
The kernel of the mistletoe ;
And here and there as Puck should go,
 With terror to affright him,
She night-shade straws to work him ill,
Therewith her vervain and her dill,
That hind'reth witches of their will,
 Of purpose to despite him.

Then sprinkles she the juice of rue,
That groweth underneath the yew,
With nine drops of the midnight dew
 From lunary distilling ;
The molewarp's brain mixt therewithal,
And with the same the pismire's gall :
For she in nothing short would fall,
 The fairy was so willing.

Then thrice under a briar doth creep,
Which at both ends was rooted deep,
And over it three times she leap,
 Her magic much availing :
Then on Proserpina doth call,
And so upon her spell doth fall,
Which here to you repeat I shall,
 Not in one tittle failing.

" By the croaking of the frog,
By the howling of the dog,
By the crying of the hog

Against the storm arising ;
By the evening curfew-bell,
By the doleful dying knell,
O ! let this my direfull spell,
   Hob, hinder thy surprising !

" By the mandrake's dreadful groans,
By the lubrican's sad moans,
By the noise of dead men's bones
   In charnel-houses rattling ;
By the hissing of the snake,
The rustling of the fire-drake,
I charge thee this place forsake,
   Nor of Queen Mab be prattling!

" By the whirlwind's hollow sound,
By the thunder's dreadful stound,
Yells of spirits under ground,
   I charge thee not to fear us :
By the screech-owl's dismal note,
By the black night-raven's throat,
I charge thee, Hob, to tear thy coat
   With thorns, if thou come near us ! "

Her spell thus spoke, she stept aside,
And in a chink herself doth hide,
To see thereof what would betide,
   For she doth only mind him :
When presently she Puck espies,
And well she markt his gloating eyes,
How under every leaf he prys,
   In seeking still to find them.

But once the circle got within,
The charms to work do straight begin,
And he was caught as in a gin :

For as he thus was busy,
A pain he in his head-piece feels,
Against a stubbed tree he reels,
And up went poor Hob-goblin's heels :
　　Alas ! his brain was dizzy !

At length upon his feet he gets,
Hob-goblin fumes, Hob-goblin frets,
And as again he forward sets,
　　And through the bushes scrambles,
A stump doth trip him in his pace,
Down comes poor Hob upon his face,
And lamentably tore his case,
　　Amongst the briars and brambles.

" A plague upon queen Mab," quoth he,
" And all her maids, where'er they be ;
I think the devil guided me,
　　To seek her, so provoked ! "
When stumbling at a piece of wood,
He fell into a ditch of mud,
Where to the very chin he stood,
　　In danger to be choked.

Now worse than e'er he was before,
Poor Puck doth yell, poor Puck doth roar,
That wak'd queen Mab, who [1] doubted sore
　　Some treason had been wrought her :
Until Nymphidia told the queen,
What she had done, what she had seen,
Who then had well-near crack'd her spleen
　　With very extreme laughter.

But leave we Hob to clamber out,
Queen Mab, and all her fairy rout,
And come again to have a bout

---

[1] [Old copy, *what.*]

With Oberon yet madding :
And with Pigwiggen now distraught,
Who was much troubled in his thought,
That he so long the queen had sought,
    And through the fields was gadding.

And, as he runs, he still doth cry,
"King Oberon, I thee defy,
And dare thee here in arms to try,
    For my dear lady's honour :
For that she is a queen right good,
In whose defence I'll shed my blood,
And that thou in this jealous mood
    Hast laid this slander on her."

And quickly arms him for the field;
A little cockle-shell his shield,
Which he could very bravely wield,
    Yet could it not be pierced ;
His spear a bent both stiff and strong,
And well near of two inches long :
The pile was of a horse-fly's tongue,
    Whose sharpness nought reversed.

And puts him on a coat of mail,
Which was of a fish's scale,
That, when his foe should him assail,
    No point should be prevailing :
His rapier was a hornet's sting ;
It was a very dangerous thing,
For if he chanced to hurt the king,
    It would be long in healing.

His helmet was a beetle's head,
Most horrible and full of dread,
That able was to strike one dead,

Yet did it well become him :
And, for a plume, a horse's hair
Which, being tossed with the air,
Had force to strike his foe with fear,
    And turn his weapon from him.

Himself he on an ear-wig set,
Yet scarce he on his back could get,
So oft and high he did curvet,
    Ere he himself could settle :
He made him turn, and stop, and bound,
To gallop, and to trot the round,
He scarce could stand on any ground,
    He was so full of mettle.

When soon he met with Tomalin,
One that a valiant knight had been,
And to King Oberon of kin :
    Quoth he, " You manly fairy,
Tell Oberon I come prepar'd,
Then bid him stand upon his guard ;
This hand his baseness shall reward,
    Let him be ne'er so wary.

" Say to him thus : that I defy
His slanders and his infamy,
And as a mortal enemy
    Do publicly proclaim him :
Withal, that if I had mine own,
He should not wear the fairy crown,
But with a vengeance should come down ;
    Nor we a king should name him ! "

This Tomalin could not abide,
To hear his sovereign vilifi'd,
But to the fairy court him hi'd :

Full furiously he posted,
With everything Pigwiggen said,
How title to the crown he laid,
And in what arms he was array'd
   As how himself he boasted.

'Twixt head and foot, from point to point,
He told the arming of each joint,
In every piece how neat and quaint;
   For Tomalin could do it:
How fair he sat, how sure he rid,
As of the courser he bestrid,
How manag'd, and how well he did.
   The king, which listen'd to it,

Quoth he, "Go, Tomalin, with speed,
Provide me arms, provide my steed,
And every thing that I shall need,
   By thee I will be guided:
To straight account call thou thy wit,
See there be wanting not a whit,
In every thing see thou me fit,
   Just as my foe's provided."

Soon flew this news through fairy-land,
Which gave queen Mab to understand
The combat that was then at hand
   Betwixt those men so mighty:
Which greatly she began to rue,
Perceiving that all Faëry knew
The first occasion from her grew
   Of these affairs so weighty.

Wherefore, attended with her maids,
Through fogs and mists, and damps, she wades,
To Proserpine the queen of shades,

                           R

To treat, that it would please her
The cause into her hands to take,
For ancient love and friendship's sake,
And soon thereof an end to make,
    Which of much care would ease her.

A while there let we Mab alone,
And come we to King Oberon
Who, arm'd to meet his foe is gone,
    For proud Pigwiggen crying!
Who sought the fairy king as fast,
And had so well his journies cast,
That he arrived at the last,
    His puissant foe espying.

Stout Tomalin came with the king,
Tom Thumb doth on Pigwiggen bring,
That perfect were in every thing
    To single fights belonging:
And therefore they themselves engage,
To see them exercise their rage
With fair and comely equipage,
    Not one the other wronging.

So like in arms these champions were,
As they had been a very pair,
So that a man would almost swear
    That either had been either:
Their furious steeds began to neigh,
That they were heard a mighty way:
Their staves upon their rests they lay;
    Yet, ere they flew together,

Their seconds minister an oath,
Which was indifferent to them both,
That on their knightly faith and troth

No magic them supplied ;
And sought them that they had no charms,
Wherewith to work each others' harms,
But came with simple open arms
    To have their causes tried.

Together furiously they ran,
That to the ground came horse and man ;
The blood out of their helmets span,
    So sharp were their encounters.
And though they to the earth were thrown,
Yet quickly they regain'd their own ;
Such nimbleness was never shown,
    They were two gallant mounters.

When in a second course again,
They forward came with might and main,
Yet which had better of the twain,
    The seconds could not judge yet :
Their shields were into pieces cleft,
Their helmets from their heads were reft,
And to defend them nothing left,
    These champions would not budge yet.

Away from them their staves they threw,
Their cruel swords they quickly drew,
And freshly they the fight renew,
    That every stroke redoubled ;
Which made Proserpina take heed,
And make to them the greater speed,
For fear lest they too much should bleed,
    Which wond'rously her troubled.

When to th' infernal Styx she goes,
She takes the fogs from thence that rose,
And in a bag doth them enclose,

When well she had them blended :
She hies her then to Lethe spring,
A bottle and thereof doth bring,
Wherewith she meant to work the thing
    Which only she intended.

Now Proserpine with Mab is gone
Unto the place, where Oberon
And proud Pigwiggen, one to one
    Both to be slain were likely :
And there themselves they closely hide,
Because they would not be espi'd ;
For Proserpine meant to decide
    The matter very quickly.

And suddenly unties the poke,
Which out of it sent such a smoke,[1]
As ready was them all to choke.
    So grievous was the pother :
So that the knights each other lost,
And stood as still as any post,
Tom Thumb nor Tomalin could boast
    Themselves of any other.

But, when the mist 'gan somewhat cease,
Proserpina commandeth peace,
And that a while they should release
    Each other of their peril :
"Which here," quoth she, "I do proclaim
To all, in dreadful Pluto's name,

---

[1] With this may be compared the artifice of Oberon to hinder
Lysander and Demetrius from fighting—

    Thou seest these lovers seek a place to fight ;
    Hie, therefore, Robin ! overcast the night ;
    The starry welkin cover thou anon
    With drooping fog as black as Acheron ;
    And lead these testy rivals so astray,
    As one come not within another's way.

That, as ye will eschew his blame,
　You let me hear the quarrel.

" But here yourselves you must engage
Somewhat to cool your spleenish rage,
Your grievous thirst and to asswage,
　That first you drink this liquor ;
Which shall your understandings clear,
As plainly shall to you appear,
Those things from me that you shall hear,
　Conceiving much the quicker.

" This Lethe water, you must know,
The memory destroyeth so,
That of our weal, or of our woe,
　It all remembrance blotted."[1]
Of it nor can you ever think :
For they no sooner took this drink,
But nought into their brains could sink,
　Of what had them besotted.

King Oberon forgotten had
That he for jealousy ran mad ;
But of his queen was wond'rous glad,
　And ask'd how they came thither.[2]
Pigwiggen, likewise, doth forget
That he Queen Mab had ever met,
Or that they were so hard beset,
　When they were found together.

---

[1] A similar artifice, though not so fully explained, occurs in
A Midsummer Night's Dream—

> And think no more of this night's accidents,
> But as the fierce vexation of a dream.

[2] So Lysander, after his fairy adventures—

> I cannot truly say how I came here.

Nor neither of them both had thought,
That e'er they had each other sought,
Much less that they a combat fought,
   But such a dream were loathing;
Tom Thumb had got a little sup,
And Tomalin scarce kiss'd the cup,
Yet had their brains so sure lock'd up,
   That they remember'd nothing.

Queen Mab and her light maids the while
Amongst themselves do closely smile,
To see the king caught with this wile,
   With one another jesting:
And to the fairy-court they went,
With mickle joy and merriment,
Which thing was done with good intent,
   And thus I left them feasting.

XIV.

A Fairy Wedding.

———o———

THIS is another piece by the same author, and is not so generally known as the "Nymphidia." It is the eighth nymphal of "The Muses Elizium, lately discovered by a new way over Parnassus, &c., by Michael Drayton, Esquire," 1630, pp. 67-74. The speakers are Mertilla, Claia, and Cloris.

> " A nymph is married to a Fay
> Great preparations for the day ;
> All rites of nuptials they recite you,
> To the bridal and invite you."

Mert. But will our Tita wed this fay?
Claia. Yea, and to-morrow is the day.
Mert. But why should she bestow herself
Upon this dwarfish fairy elf?
Claia. Why, by her smallness you may find
That she is of the fairy kind,

And therefore apt to choose her make
Whence she did her beginning take.
Besides, he's deft and wondrous airy,
And of the noblest of the fairy!
Chiefe of the Crickets of much fame,
In fairy a most ancient name:
But to be brief, 'tis clearly done,
The pretty wench is woo'd and won.

    Cloris. If this be so, let us provide
The ornaments to fit our bride,
For they knowing she doth come
From us in Elizium,
Queen Mab will look she should be drest
In those attires we think our best;
Therefore some curious things let's give her,
Ere to her spouse we her deliver.

    Mert. I'll have a jewel for her ear,
Which for my sake I'll have her wear;
'T shall be a dewdrop, and therein
Of Cupids I will have a twin,
Which struggling with their wings shall break
The bubble, out of which shall leak
So sweet a liquor, as shall move
Each thing that smells to be in love.

    Claia. Believe me, girl, this will be fine,
And to this pendant then take mine;
A cup in fashion of a fly,
Of the lynx's piercing eye,
Wherein there sticks a sunny ray,
Shot in through the clearest day;
Whose brightness Venus' self did move
Therein to put her drink of love,
Which for more strength she did distill,
The limbeck was a phœnix quill!
At this cup's delicious brink,
A fly approaching but to drink,

Like amber or some precious gum
It transparent doth become.
 Cloris. For jewels for her ears she's sped,
But for a dressing for her head
I think for her I have a tire
That all fairies shall admire;
The yellows in the full-blown rose,
Which in the top it doth enclose,
Like drops of gold ore shall be hung
Upon her tresses, and among
Those scattered seeds, the eye to please,
The wings of the cantharides;
With some o' th' rainbow, that doth rail
Those moons in, in the peacock's tail;
Whose dainty colours, being mixt
With th'other beauties, and so fixt,
Her lovely tresses shall appear,
As though upon a flame they were!
And to be sure she shall be gay,
We'll take those feathers from the jay,
About her eyes in circlets set,
To be our Tita's coronet.
 Mert. Then, dainty girls, I make no doubt,
But we shall neatly send her out;
But let's amongst ourselves agree
Of what her wedding gown shall be.
 Claia. Of pansy, pink, and primrose leaves,
Most curiously laid on in threaves,
And all embroidery to supply,
Powder'd with flowers of rosemary:
A trail about the skirt shall run,
The silk-worm's finest, newly spun,
And every seam the nymphs shall sew
With th' smallest of the spinner's clue,
And having done their work, again
These to the church shall bear her train,

Which for our Tita we will make
Of the cast slough of a snake,
Which quivering as the wind doth blow,
The sun shall it like tinsel show.

 Cloris. And being led to meet her mate,
To make sure that she want no state,
Moons from the peacock's tail we'll shred,
With feathers from the pheasant's head,
Mix'd with the plume of (so high price)
The precious bird of Paradise;
Which to make up, our nymphs shall ply
Into a curious canopy
Borne o'er her head, by our enquiry,
By elves, the fittest of the faery.

 Mert. But all this while, we have forgot
Her buskins, neighbours: have we not?

 Claia. We had: for those I'll fit her now;
They shall be of the lady-cow,
The dainty shell upon her back
Of crimson, strew'd with spots of black,
Which, as she holds a stately pace,
Her leg will wonderfully grace.

 Cloris. But then for music of the best,
This must be thought on for the feast.

 Mert. The nightingale, of birds most choice,
To do her best shall strain her voice;
And to this bird, to make a set,
The mavis, merle, and robinet,
The lark, the linnet, and the thrush,
That make a quoir of every bush!
But for still music, we will keep
The wren and titmouse, which to sleep
Shall sing the bride, when she's alone,
The rest into their chambers gone;
And like those upon ropes that walk
On gossamer, from stalk to stalk,

The tripping fairy tricks shall play
The evening of the wedding day.
 Claia. But for the bride-bed what were fit ?
That hath not been talk'd of yet.
 Cloris. Of leaves of roses white and red
Shall be the covering of her bed ;
The curtains, valance, tester, all
Shall be the flower imperial ;
And for the fringe, it all along
With asure harebells shall be hung ;
Of lillies shall the pillows be,
With down stuft of the butterflee.
 Mert. Thus far we handsomely have gone,
Now for our prothalamion
Or marriage song, of all the rest
A thing that much must grace our feast.
Let us practice then to sing it,
Ere we before th'assembly bring it :
We in dialogues must do it,
Then, my dainty girls, set to it !
 Claia. *This day must Tita married be*
Come, nymphs, this nuptial let us see !
 Mert. *But is it certain that ye say :*
Will she wed the noble fay ?
 Cloris. *Sprinkle the dainty flowers with dews,*
Such as the Gods at banquets use :
Let herbs and weeds turn all to roses,
And make proud the posts with posies.
Shoot your sweets into the air,
Charge the morning to be fair !
 Claia. } *For our Tita is this day*
 Mert. } *To be married to a fay.*
 Claia. *By whom then shall our bride be led*
To the temple to be wed ?
 Mert. *Only by yourself and I ;*
Who that room should else supply ?

Cloris. Come, bright girls, come all together,[1]
And bring all your offering hither;
Ye most brave and buxom bevy,
All your goodly graces levy;
Come in majesty and state,
Our bridal here to celebrate.

 Mert. } *For our Tita is this day*
 Claia. } *Married to a noble fay.*

 Claia. *Whose lot will't be the way to strew*
On which to church our bride must go?

 Mert. *That (I think) as fitt'st of all,*
To lively Lelipa will fall.

 Cloris. *Summon all the sweets that are,*
To this nuptial to repair,
Till with their throngs themselves they smother,
Strongly stifling one another,
And at last they all consume,
And vanish in one rich perfume.

 Mert. } *For our Tita is this day*
 Claia. } *Married to a noble fay.*

 Mert. *By whom must Tita married be?*
'Tis fit to that we all should see.

 Claia. *The priest he purposely doth come,*
Th' arch-Flamen of Elizium.

 Cloris. *With tapers let the temples shine,*
Sing to Hymen hymns divine!
Load the altars, till there rise
Clouds from the burnt sacrifice;
With your censors sling aloof
Their smells, till they ascend the roof.

 Mert. } *For our Tita is this day*
 Claia. } *Married to a noble fay.*

---

[1] *Altogether* in the original, a common way of printing the phrase in old works.

Mert. *But coming back when she is wed,*
Who breaks the cake above her head ? [1]

Claia. *That shall Mertilla, for she's tallest,*
And our Tita is the smallest.

Cloris. *Violins, strike up aloud,*
Ply the gittern, scour the crowd !
Let the nimble hand belabour
The whistling pipe and drumbling tabor :
To the full the bagpipe rack,
Till the swelling leather crack.

Mert. ⎱ *For our Tita is this day*
Claia. ⎰ *Married to a noble fay.*

Claia. *But when to dine she takes her seat,*
What shall be our Tita's meat ?

Mert. *The gods this feast as to begin,*
Have sent of their ambrosia in.

Cloris. *Then serve we up the straw's rich berry,*
The respas, and Elizian cherry ;
The virgin honey from the flowers
In Hibla, wrought in Flora's bowers :
Full bowls of nectar, and no girl
Carouse but in dissolved pearl.

Mert. ⎱ *For our Tita is this day*
Claia. ⎰ *Married to a noble fay.*

Claia. *But when night comes and she must go*
To bed, dear nymphs, what must we do ?

Mert. *In the posset must be brought,*
And points [2] *be from the bridegroom caught.*

Cloris. *In masques, in dances, and delight,*
And rear-banquets, pass the night ;
Then about the room we ramble,
Scatter nuts, and for them scramble,

---

[1] This curious custom is alluded to in Brand's Popular Antiquities.

[2] The points or tags that were used to hold the dress.

Over stools and tables tumble,
Never think of noise nor rumble.

Mert. } *For our Tita is this day*
Claia. } *Married to a noble fay.*

XV.

The Land of Faerie.

———o———

[From Lane's "Triton's Trumpet," a MS. in the British Museum, Bib. Reg. 17 B. xv.]

FROM Faerie Lande, I com, quoth Danus now,
    Ha! that, quoth June, mee never chauncd to
    knowe,
Ne could or nould thigh poet Spencer tell,
(So farr as mote my witt this ridle spell)
Though none that breatheth livinge aier doth knowe,
Wheare is that happie land of Faerie,
Which I so oft doe vaunt yet no wheare showe,
But vouch antequities which no bodie maie knowe.

No marveile that, quoth Danus mirrelie,
For it is movable of Mercurie,
Which Faeries with a trice doe snatch up hence,
Fro sight and heering of the common sense;

Yet coms on sodaines to the thoughtlesse eye
And eare (favored to heere theire minstrelsy),
Ne bootes climbe promontories yt to spie,
For then the Faeries dowt the seeinge eye.

Onlie right seld it to some fewe doth chaunce,
That (ravishd) they behold it in a traunse,
Wheare yt a furor calls, rage, extacie,
Shedd but on the poetick misterie,
Which they with serious apprehension tend,
Ells from them also yt doth quicklie wend :
But caught ! with it they deale most secretly,
As deignes the Muse instruct them waerely.

The glorie wheaerof doth but this arive,
They farr more honord dead are then alive.
But now folke vaunt by use, to call yt prittie,
Them selves theareby comparinge (vâh) more wittie ;
Nathlesse kinges, captaines, clercks, astrologers,
And everie learnd th'ideal spirit admires.
But ah ! well fare his lines alive not dead,
Yf of his readers his reward bee bread.

Which proves, while poets thoughts up sore divine,
These fleshe-flies, earth wormes, welter but in slyme.
Ha ! yet near known was, but meere poetrie,
Came to ann ancor at sadd povertie.

XVI.

Sports of the Fairies.

—o—

[From MS. Ashmole 36, 37.]

I SPIED kinge Oberon and his beuteous queene
   Attended by a nimble footed trayne
Of fayeryes trippinge ore the medows greene,
  And to meewards (methought) they came amayne.
   I coucht myselfe behinde a bushe to spye,
   What would betide the noble company.

It gann to rayne, the kinge and queene they runne
   Under a mushroom fretted over head,
With glowormes artificially donne,
   Resemblinge much the canopy of a bedd
     Of cloth of silver : and such glimmeringe light
     It gave, as stars doe in a frosty night.

The kinge perceivinge it grew night apace,
   And that faint light was but for show alone,
Out of a box made of a fayre topace,
   Hee toke a blasinge carbuncle that showne
     Like to a flameinge barre of iron, and
     Stuck it among the glowormes with his hand.

                         S

Like as the sunne darts forth his ruddy beames,
  Unable longer to hold up his head,
Glaunceinge his gloateinge eye upon the streames,
  Such was the lustre that this mixture bredd,
    So light it was that one might plainely see,
    What was donne under that rich canopy.

The floore whereon they trode, it was of jett
  And mother of pearle, pollished and cutt,
Chequerd, and in most decent order sett,
  A table dyamond was theire table, butt
    To see th'reflection from the roofe to the table,
    'Twas choyce, meethought, and showed admir-
      able.

Like to a heaven directly was that table,
  And these bright wormes they doe resemble starres,
That precious carbunckle soe invaluable,
  Lookt like a meteor with his ominous barres
    Hung out in heaven by th' allseeinge eye,
    Bidd us expect to heare a tragedye.

Soe this great light appeard amongst the rest.
  But now it grew towards suppertyme apace,
And for to furnish out this suddaine feast,
  The servitours, who knew each one his place,
    Disperse themselves immediately, and
    Some find the choycest daynes on the land.

Others dive downe to th'bottome of the deepe,
  Another mounts up to the lofty skye,
To fetch downe hony dew of mowntaynes steepe—
  In every corner doe they serch and pry,
    Who can the best accepted present bringe,
    To please theire soe much honoured queene and
      kinge.

One gathers grapes ripe from the lusty vine,
  And with his little hands hee squeazeth out
The juice, and then presents it up for wine ;
  And straight theire presses in among the rowt
    Another loaden with an eare of wheate,
    The whitest and the fairest hee cann gett.

XVII.

Conjurations for Fairies.

—o—

FROM MS. Ashmole 1406, written about the year 1600.
    One of these has been printed by Dr Percy. The impiety
        of the originals has been omitted ; but it runs through all
the old charms and conjurations, and affords a curious picture of
the times. The three last are given from a MS. in my own
possession.

*An excellent way to gett a fayrie, but for myselfe I call
    Margarett Barrance, but this will obteine any one
    that is not allready bownd.*

First, gett a broad square cristall or Venus glasse,
in length and breadth three inches. Than lay that
glasse or christall in the bloud of a white henne three
Wednesdayes, or three Fridayes ; then take it out
and wash it with holy *aqua*, and fumigate it. Then
take three hazle stickes or wands of an yeare groth,
pill them fayre and white, and make soe longe as
you write the spiritts name, or fayries name, which
you call three times, on every sticke being made flatt

one one side. Then bury them under some hill,
whereas you suppose fayries haunt, the Wednesday
before you call her, and the Friday followinge take
them uppe, and call her at eight or three or ten of
the clocke, which be good plannetts and howres for
that turne.   But when you call, be in cleane life, and
turne thy face towardes the East ; and when you
have her, bind her to that stone ore glasse.

*An unguent to annoynt under the eyelids, and upon the
    eylidds, ev[e]ninge and morninge ; but especially when
    you call, or finde your sight not perfect.*

Take one pint [of] sallet oyle, and put it into a
viall glasse, but first wash it with rose-water, and
marygold flower water, the flowers be gathered
towards the East.   Wash it till the oyle come white ;
then put it into the glasse, *ut supra*, and then put
thereto   the   budds   of   holyocke,   the   flowers   of
marygold, the flowers or toppes of wilde time, the
budds of younge hazle, and the time must be gathered
neare the side of a hill where fayries use to be, and
the grasse of a fayrie throne there.   All these put into
the oyle into the glasse, and sett it to dissolve three
dayes in the sonne, and then keepe it for thy use, *ut
supra*.

To call Elabigathan, a fayrie.

I, E. A., call the Elaby-Gathen, in the name &c.,
And I adjure the, Elaby-Gathen, conjure, and
straightly charge and command thee by Tetragrammaton, Emanuell, Messias, Sether, Panton, Cratons,
Alpha et Omega, and by all other high and reverent
names &c., I adjure and commande thee, Elaby, by
all the powers and grace and vertues of all the holy
meritorious virginnes and patriarckes, and I conjure

thee, Elaby-Gathen, by these holy names, Saday,
Eloy, Iskyros, Adonay, Sabaoth, that thou appeare
presently meekely and myldly in this glasse without
doing hurt or daunger unto me, or any other livinge
creature, and to this I binde thee by the whole power
and vertue &c. of Adonay, Adonatos, Eloy, Elohim,
Suda, Ege, Jeth, and Heban, that is to say, Lord of
vertue and king of Israell, dwellinge upon the whole
face of the earth, whose seate is in heaven, and his
power in earth, and by Him, and by these glorious
and powerfull names, I binde thee to give and doe
thy true, humble, and obedient servise unto me,
E. A., and never to depart without my consent and
lawfull authoritie, in the name &c.   And I command
thee, Elaby-Gathen, by all &c., that thou doest come
and appeare presently to me, E. A., in this cristall or
glasse meekely and myldlye, to my true and perfect
sight, and truly without fraud, dissymilation, or deceite,
resolve and satisfie me in and of all manner of such
questions and commands, and demandes, as I shall either
aske, require, desire, or demande of thee; and that thou,
Elaby-Gathen, be true and obedient unto me, both
now and ever hereafter, at all time and times, howers,
dayes, nightes, mynittes, and in and at all places
wheresoever, either in field, howse, or in any other
place whatsoever and wheresoever I shall call upon
thee; and that thou, Elaby-Gathen, doe not start,
depart, or desire to goe or departe from me, neyther
by arte or call of any other artist of any degree or
learninge whatsoever, but that thou in the humblyest
manner that thou mayest be commaunded to attend
and give thy true obedience unto me, E. A., and that
even as thou wilt, answer it as thou wilt, answer it
unto and before &c.   And to this, I, E. A., sweare
thee, Elaby-Gathen, and binde thee by the whole
power &c., to be true and faithfull unto thee in all

reverente humility. Let be done quickly! quickly!
quickly! come! come! come! fiat! fiat! fiat!
amen! amen! amen! &c.

A call to call any fayrie.

In nomine &c., Amen, I, E. A., with a true and
stedfast faith &c., call thee &c. by the power &c.,
and commaund thee &c., that thou doest come and
appeare before me in the christall stone or glasse,
humblye, meekly, and mildly, and that in the lowliest,
humbliest shape and manner that thou canst, to the
true and perfecte sight of me, the said E. A., without
prejudice, feare, harme, or danger of me, my body or
soule, or any other member unto my body belonginge.
I, E. A., doe therefore call thee, &c., by all the strength,
power, and vertue &c., I commaund thee &c., and I
conjure thee &c., I call thee &c., to appeare in this
christall stone or glasse, by all the most high, excellent
and reverent names, &c., and by these most holy
names, Tetragrammaton, Sother, Panton, Craton,
Alpha et Omega, and by the whole powers, dominion,
rule, and command of, &c., I adjure, conjure, and
straightly commaund thee, &c., to attend me, and
come and appeare unto me as aforesayed in this
cristall, and with all thy power, skill, and best
experience that thou hast, or by thy superiors and
rulers thou canst or may any kinde of way get and
obtayne, that thou doest presently, and at all time
and times, both now and ever hereafter, reveale unto
me the same, and fully resolve, absolve, and fulfill all
and every one of my questions, requestes, com-
maundes, and desires, truly, sensibly, and faithfully,
without any manner of deceipt, delution, dissimulation
or fraude, and that as thou doest feare the heavy
wrath and judgment &c. Therefore and to this end
I adjure thee by the power of all thy superiors who

hath any power over thee, and whome thou art subject unto, that thou doest by the power &c., and by these holy names, Tagla, Agla, Tetragrammaton, Sabaoth, Adonay, Athanatos, Ely, Eloy; and also I adjure, conjure, and command the to appeare mildely and firmely to my sight in this christall as aforesaid, at all times, dayes, nights and houres when and wheresoever I shall call upon the, by the power &c., I commaund the, &c., to come quickly as aforesayed at all times, dayes, nightes, and houres and in all places either one land or water, howse or field, sittinge or lying, standinge or walkinge, in valleyes, dales, woods or pastures, where and whensoever by the vertues &c. I binde thee, &c., and compell thee truly and reverently to attend and obey me from this time forth and evermore, and to this end by the power, strength, and vertue of all these, I sweare thee, &c., to give thy true allegeance, attendance onely one me, and one noe other person livinge, And sweare, adjure, conjure, commaund, compell, constrayne, and charge thee, &c., by the high name Horlon, by the greate name Gorthenthion, by the excellent name Jebar, by the fearefull name Gosgamer, and by the holy name Heloy, marvelous and honorable, and by the seale wherewith you or many of you were sealed, and by the ball and glasse wherein you or many of you were included, and by all other vertues and powers of heaven whatsoever, that thou never be dissloyall, but ever true and faithfull unto me. To this I bind thee, &c., and sweare thee by the whole power &c., make noe delay nor tarriance, but come by the power of all the celestiall company, quickly! quickly! quickly! fiat! fiat! fiat! Amen.

To goe invisible.

Take water, and powre it upon an antt-hill, and

looke imediatly after, and you shall finde a stone of divers colours sente from the faerie. This beare in thy righte hande, and you shall goe invisible.

A conjuration for a fairy.

I conjure thee, I exsorsize thee, I compell, command, constraine and bind thee, spirit N., by the power of Tetragrammaton and Athanatos and Aglay, and by the vertue of the great Tetragrammaton, that thou appeare to mine owne person visible to the sight of mine owne eyes, so that I may see and deserne thee, and that thou shew me the truth of all thinges that I shall demand of thee, without decept, fraud, or guile; nether shalt thou hurt or crack this stone, nor mee, nor any other creatur, in mind, soule or body; nether shalt thou by cavell or deceat leave mee, nor depart from my presence or commandment, untill thou have made me true answere; and to shew mee true signes to all questions and demands. This I abjure, conjure, and command thee &c. Amen.

A discharge of the fairies, or other spirits or elphes, from ony place or ground wher treasher is hid or laid.

First shall the master say in the name &c., Amen! and then say as followeth :—I conjure you, speritts or elphes, which bee seven sisters, and have these names, Lilia, Restila, Tetar, Afryta, Julia, Nevula, I conjure and charge you &c., and by all the apostles, marters, confessors, and all virgins, and all the elect, that from henceforth nether you nor any other for you have power or rule upon this ground, nether within nor without, nor upon this servant, nether by day nor night, but the &c. be allwayes upon him or her. Amen! Amen!

XVIII.

Randolph's Amyntas.

———o———

THE following scenes are taken from a play by Randolph, entitled "Amyntas, or the Impossible Dowry," 4ᵘ, Oxford, 1638. They are extremely amusing, and detail a laughable imposition, which will probably remind the reader of Mistress Quickly and her elves in the "Merry Wives of Windsor." Here we have for the first time fairy Latin, and it does no discredit whatever to the order.

Thestylis, Mopsus, Jocastus.

Mop. Jocastus, I love Thestylis abominably! The mouth of my affection waters at her.

Joc. Be wary, Mopsus, learne of me to scorn the mortalls. Choose a better match : Go, love some fairy lady ! Princely Oberon shall stand thy friend, and beauteous Mab, his queen, give thee a Maid of Honour.

Mop. How, Jocastus? Marry a puppet? Wed a mote i' th' sunne? Go looke a wife in nutshells?

Wooe a gnat that's nothing but a voice? No, no,
Jocastus, I must have flesh and bloud, and will have
Thestylis. A fig for fairies!

Thes. 'Tis my sweet-heart Mopsus and his wise
brother. O, the twins of folly! These doe I entertaine only to season the poore Amyntas madnesse.

Mop. Sacred red and white, how fares thy reverend
beauty?

Thes. Very ill, since you were absent, Mopsus!
Where have you been all this live-long houre?

Mop. I have been discoursing with the birds.

Thes. Why, can birds speak?

Joc. In Fairy Land they can: I have heard 'em
chirp very good Greek and Latin.

Mop. And our birds talk better farre than they:
A new-laid egge of Sicily shall out-talk the bravest
parrot in Oberon's Utopia.

Thes. But what languages doe they speak, servant?

Mop. Severall languages, as Cawation, Chirpation,
Hootation, Whistleation, Crowation, Cackleation,
Shreekation, Hissation.

Thes. And Foolation?

Mop. No, that's our language. We ourselves
speak that, that are the learned augurs.

Thes. What successe does your art promise?

Mop. Very good.

Thes. What birds met you then first?

Mop. A woodcock and a goose.

Thes. Well met.

Mop. I told'm so.

Thes. And what might this portend?

Mop. Why thus—and first the Woodcock. Wood
and Cock—both very good signes. For first the
wood doth signify the fire of our love shall never goe
out, because it has more fuell: wood doth signifie
more fuell.

Thes. What the Cock?

Mop. Better then the t'other: 'that I shall crow o're those that are my rivals, and roost myselfe with thee.

Thes. But now the goose?

Mop. I, I, the goose! That likes me best of all. Th'ast heard our gray-beard sheapheards talke of Rome, and what the geese did there. The goose doth signifie that I shall keep thy Capitoll.

Thes. Good gander!

Joc. It cannot choose but strangely please his high-nesse.

Thes. What are you studying of, Jocastus, ha?

Joc. A rare device, a masque to entertaine his grace of Fairy with.

Thes. A masque? what is't?

Joc. An anti-masque of fleas, which I have taught to dance currantos on a spider's thread.

Mop. An anti-masque of fleas! Brother, methinks a masque of birds were better, that could dance the morice in the ayre, wrens and robbin-red brests, lin-nets, and titmice.

Joc. So! and why not rather your geese and wood-cocks? Mortall, hold thy tongue; thou dost not know the mystery.

Thes. Tis true, he tells you. Mopsus, leave your augury: follow his counsell, and be wise.

Mop. Be wise! I skorn the motion! Follow his counsell and be wise! That's a fine trick, i'faith! Is this an age for to be wise in?

Thes. Then you mean, I see, t'expound the oracle.

Mop. I doe mean to be th' interpreter.

Joc. And then a jig of pismires is excellent.

Mop. What, to interpret oracles? A foole must be th' interpreter.

Thes. Then no doubt but you will have honour.

Mop. Nay I hope I am as faire for't as another man, if I should now grow wise against my will, and catch this wisdome!

Thes. Never feare it, Mopsus.

Mop. Twere dangerous vent'ring. Now I think on't too, pray Heaven this ayre be wholesome! Is there not an antidote against it? What doe you think of garlick every morning?

Thes. Fye upon't, 'twill spoyle our kissing! and besides I tell you garlick's a dangerous dish; eating of garlick may breed the sicknesse, for as I remember 'tis the philosophers' diet.

Mop. Certainly I am infected, now the fit's upon me! Tis some thing like an ague; sure I caught it with talking with a schollar next my heart.

Thes. How sad a life live I bewixt your folly and Amyntas madnesse! For Mopsus, Ile prescribe you such a diet as shall secure you.

Mop. Excellent she-doctor! Your women are the best physitians, and have the better practice.

Thes. First, my Mopsus, take heed of fasting, for your hungry meales nurse wisdome.

Mop. True! O, what a stomack have I to be her patient!

Thes. Besides, take speciall care you weare not thredbare clothes: 'twill breed at least suspition you are wise.

Joc. I, marry will it.

Thes. And walk not much alone; or if you walk with company, be sure you walke with fooles, none of the wise.

Mop. No, no, I warrant you, Ile walk with nobody but my brother here, or you, or mad Amyntas.

Thes. By all meanes take heed of travell; your beyond-sea wit is to be fear'd.

Mop. If ere I travell, hang me!

Joc. Not to the Fairy Land?

Thes. Thither he may.   But above all things weare
no beard ; long beards are signes the brains are full,
because the excrements[1] come out so plentifully.

Joc. Rather emptie ; because they have sent so much
out, as if their brains were sunk into their beards.
King Oberon has ne're a beard, yet for his wit I am
sure he might have beene a gyant.   Who comes here?

Enter Dorylas.

Dor. All haile unto the fam'd interpreter of fowles
and Oracles !

Mop. Thankes, good Dorylas.

Dor. How fares the winged cattell?   Are the
woodcocks, the jayes, the dawes, the cuckoes, and
the owles in health?

Mop. I thanke the gratious starres they are.

Dor. Like health unto the president of the jigs ! I
hope King Oberon and his royall Mab are well.

Joc. They are ; I never saw their Graces eate such
a meale before.

Dor. E'ne much good do 't 'em !

Joc. They're rid a hunting.

Dor. Hare or deere, my Lord?

Joc. Neither ; a brace of snailes of the first head.

Thes. But, Dorylas, ther's a mighty quarrell here,
and you are chosen umpire.

Dor. About what?

Thes. The exposition of the Oracle.   Which of
these two you think the verier foole?

Dor. It is a difficult cause.   First, let me pose'em ;
you, Mopsus, cause you are a learned augur, how
many are the seven liberall sciences?

---

[1] The same phrase is used by Shakespeare in Love's Labour's
Lost, act v. sc. 1, and Merchant of Venice, act. iii. sc. 2.

Mop. Why, much about a dozen.

Dor. You, Jocastus—when Oberon shav'd himselfe, who was his barber?

Joc. I knew him well, a little dapper youth : they call him Perriwinckle.

Dor. Thestilis, a weighty cause, and askes a longer time.

Thes. Wee'l in the while to comfort sad Amyntas.

[*Exeunt.*

.   .   .   .

Dorylas, Mopsus, Jocastus, Thestylis, Amyntas.

Joc. Ist not a brave sight, Dorylas? Can the mortalls caper so nimbly?

Dor. Verily they cannot!

Joc. Does not King Oberon beare a stately presence? Mab is a beauteous empresse.

Dor. Yet you kissed her with admirable courtship.

Joc. I doe think there will be of Jocastus brood in Fairy.

Mop. You cuckold-maker, I will tell King Oberon you lye with Mab his wife.

Joc. Doe not, good brother, and I'le wooe Thestylis for thee.

Mop. Doe so then.

Joc. Canst thou love Mopsus, mortall?

Thes. Why suppose I can, sir, what of that?

Joc. Why then be wise, and love him quickly.

Mop. Wise! then I'le have none of her. That's the way to get wise children! Troth, and I had rather they should be bastards.

Amy. No, the children may be like the father.

Joc. True, distracted mortall. Thestylis, I say, love him, he's a fool.

Dor. But we will make him rich, then 'tis no matter.

Thes. But what estate shall he assure upon me?

Joc. A royall joynture, all in Fairy land.

Amy. Such will I make Urania.

Joc. Dorylas knowes it, a curious parke.

Dor. Pal'd round about with pick-teeth.

Joc. Besides a house made all of mother of pearle; an ivory tenis-court.

Dor. A nut-meg parlour.

Joc. A saphyre dairy-roome.

Dor. A ginger-hall.

Joc. Chambers of agate.

Dor. Kitchins all of cristall.

Amy. O admirable! This is it for certain.

Joc. The jacks are gold.

Dor. The spits are Spanish needles.

Joc. Then there be walks—

Dor. Of amber.

Joc. Curious orchards—

Dor. That beare as well in winter as in summer.

Joc. 'Bove all the fish-ponds! Every pond is full—

Dor. Of Nectar! Will this please you? Every grove stor'd with delightfull birds!

Mop. But be there any lady-birds there?

Joc. Abundance.

Mop. And cuckoes too, to presage constancy?

Dor. Yes.

Thes. Nay then, let's in to seale the writings.

Amy. There boy, so ho, ho, ho!　　　　*[Exeunt.*

Dor. What pretty things are these both, to be born to lands and livings! We poore witty knaves have no inheritance but brains. Who's this?

.　　　　.　　　　.　　　　.　　　　.　　　　.

Dor. So, so, this hony with the very thought
Has made my mouth so liquorish, that I must
Have something to appease the appetite.
Have at Jocastus orchard! Dainty apples,

How lovely they look! Why, these are Dorylas
    sweet-hearts.
Now must I be the princely Oberon,
And in a royall humour with the rest
Of royall fairies attendant goe in state
To rob an orchard. I have hid my robes
On purpose in a hollow tree. Heaven blesse me !

   .   .   .   .   .   .

Dorylas with a bevy of Fairies.

  Dor. How like you my Grace? Is not my coun-
    tenance
Royall and full of majesty? Walk I not
Like the young Prince of Pigmies? Ha! my knaves,
Wee'l fill our pockets. Look, look yonder, elves !
Would not yon apples tempt a better conscience
Then any we have, to rob an orchard? ha!
Fairies, like nymphs with child, must have the things
They long for. You sing here a fairy catch
In that strange tongue I taught you, while yourselfe
Doe climbe the trees. Thus princely Oberon
Ascends his throne of state.

      Elves. Nos beati fauni proles,
          Quibus non est magna moles,
          Quamvis lunam incolamus,
          Hortos sæpe frequentamus.

          Furto cuncta magis bella,
          Furto dulcior puella.
          Furto omnia decora ;
          Furto poma dulciora.

          Cum mortales lecto jacent,
          Nobis poma noctu placent !
          Illa tamen sunt ingrata,
          Nisi furto sint parata.j

          [We the fairies blithe and antic,
          Of dimensions not gigantic ; ,

                      T

Though the moonshine mostly keep us,
Oft in orchards frisk and peep us.

Stolen sweets are always sweeter ;
Stolen kisses much completer :
Stolen looks are nice in chapels ;
Stolen, stolen be your apples !

When to bed the world are bobbing,
Then's the time for orchard robbing !
Yet the fruit were scarce worth pealing,
Were it not for stealing, stealing.]

Jocastus, Bromius.

Joc. What divine noyse fraught with immortall harmony salutes mine eare?

Bro. Why, this immortall harmony rather salutes your orchard ! These young rascalls, these pescodshelers do so cheat my master ; we cannot have an apple in the orchard, but streight some fairy longs for't. Well, if I might have my will, a whip again should jerk 'hem into their old mortality.

Joc. Dar'st thou, screetch-owle, with thy rude croaking interrupt their musique, whose melody hath made the spheares to lay their heavenly lutes aside, only to listen to their more charming notes?

Bro. Say what you will. I say a cudgell now were excellent musique !

Elves. Oberon, descende citus,
         Ne cogaris hinc invitus ;
         Canes audio latrantes,
         Et mortales vigilantes.

[Fairy king, from that tree skip,
Ere angry mortals make thee trip ;
Busy men surround and mark,
Watchful dogs and mastiffs bark.]

Joc. Prince Oberon? I heard his Grace's name.

Bro. O ho : I spye his Grace ! Most noble Prince, come down, or I will pelt your Grace with stones, that I believe your Grace was ne're so pelted since 'twas a Grace.

Dor. Bold mortall, hold thy hand !

Bro. Immortall thiefe, come downe, or I will fetch you ! Methinks it should impaire his Grace's honour to steale poore mortalls apples. Now, have at you !

Dor. Jocastus, ·we are Oberon, and we thought that one so neare to us as you in favour, would not have suffered this prophane rude groome thus to impaire our royalty.

Joc. Gracious Prince, the fellow is a foole, and not yet purged from his mortality.

Dor. Did we out of love
And our entire affection, of all orchards
Choose yours to make it happy by our dances,
Light ayry measures, and fantasticke rings,
And you, ingratefull mortall, thus requite us
All for one apple?

Joc. Villaine, th'ast undone me ! His Grace is much incens'd.

Dor. You know, Jocastus, our Grace have orchards of our own more precious then mortals can have any, and we sent you a present of them t'other day.

Joc. Tis right ; your Grace's humble servant must acknowledge it.

Bro. Some of his owne I am sure.

Dor. I must confesse, their out-side look'd something like yours indeed, but then the taste more relish'd of eternity, the same with nectar.

Joc. Your good Grace is welcome to any things I have. Nay, gentlemen, pray doe not you spare neither.

Elves. Ti-ti-ta-ti.

Joc. What say these mightly peeres, great Oberon ?

Dor. They cannot speak this language, but in ours they thank you, and they say they will have none.

Elves. Ti-ti-ta-ti, 'Tititatie.

Joc. What say they now?

Dor. They doe request you now to grant them leave to dance a fairy-ring about your servant, and for his offence pinch him : doe you the while command the traitour not dare to stirre, not once presume to mutter.

Joc. Traitour, for so Prince Oberon deignes to call thee, stirre not, nor mutter.

Bro. To be thus abus'd!

Joc. Ha! mutter'st thou?

Bro. I have deserved better.

Joc. Still mutter'st thou?

Bro. I see I must endure it.

Joc. Yet mutter'st thou? Now, noble lords, begin when it shall please your honours.

Dor. Ti-ti-ta-tie.

Joc. Our noble friend permits. Tititatie. Doe you not, sir?

Joc. How shall I say I doe?

Dor. Ti-ti-ta-tie.

Joc. Ti-ti-ta-tie, my noble lords.

> *Elves.* Quoniam per te violamur,
> Ungues hic experiamur!
> Statim dices tibi datam
> Cutem valde variatam!
>
> [Since by thee comes violation,
> We'll treat thee with excoriation !
> We'll tatto o'er thy vulgar skin,
> Until thou art an Indian king.]

[They dance.

Joc. Titiatie to your Lordship for this excellent musick.

Bro. This 'tis to have a coxcombe to on's master.
Joc. Still mutter'st thou ?

[*Exit Bromius.*

Dorylas from the tree. Jocastus falls on his knees.

Dor. And rise up, Sir Jocastus, our deare knight.
Now hang the hallowed bell about his neck,
We call it a mellisonant Tingle-Tangle—
(Indeed a sheep-bell stol'n from's own fat weather)—

[*Aside.*

The ensigne of his knight-hood.   Sir Jocastus,
We call to minde we promis'd you long since
The president of our dances place ; we are now
Pleas'd to confirme it on you.   Give him there
His staffe of dignitie.
Joc. Your grace is pleas'd to honour your poore
liegeman.
Dor. Now begone.
Joc. Farewell unto your Grace, and eke to you,
Tititatie.   My noble lords, farewell.
Dor. Tititatie, my noble foole, farewell !   Now, my
nobilitie and honoured Lords, our Grace is pleas'd
for to part stakes.   Here, Jocalo, these are your
share ; these his, and these our graces.   Have we not
gull'd him bravely?   See, you rascalls, these are the
fruits of witty knaverie.

Mopsus enters barking.

Dor. Heaven shield Prince Oberon and his hon-
oured lords !   We are betraid.
Mop. Bow, wow, wow.   Nay, nay, since you have
made a sheep of my brother, Ile be a dogge to keep
him.
Dor. O good Mopsus !
Mop. Does not your grace, most low and mighty
Dorylas, feare whipping now?

Dor. Good Mopsus, bnt conceale us, and I will
promise by tomorrow night to get thee Thestylis.

Mop. I will aske leave
Of the birds first. An owle? the bird of night:
That plainly shewes that by to morrow night (*an owle
shreekes*)
He may performe his promise.

Dor. And I will.

Mop. Why then I will conceale you. But your
Grace must think your Grace beholding to me.

Dor. Well, we doe.

Mop. And thank the owle she stood your friend,
And for this time, my witty Grace, farewell.

Dor. Nay, be not so discourteous. Stay and take
an apple first. You, Jocalo, give him one, and you
another, and our Grace a third.

Mop. Your Grace is liberall, but now I feare I am
not he that must interpret th' oracle. My brother
will prevent me, to my griefe I much suspect it, for
this Dorylas, a scarre-crow cozend him most shame-
fully, which makes me feare hee's a more foole then I.
[*Exit Mopsus.*

Dor. So, we are clean got off! Come, noble peeres
Of Fairy, come attend our royall Grace.
Let's goe and share our fruit with our Queen Mab
And th' other dary-maids: whereof this theam
We will discourse amidst our cakes and cream.

Elves. Cum tot poma habeamus,
Triumphos læti jam canamus ;
Faunos ego credam ortos,
Tantum ut frequentent hortos.

I domum, Oberon, ad illas,
Quæ nos manent nunc ancillas,
Quarum osculemur sinum
Inter poma, lac et vinum.

[Now for such a stock of apples,
Laud us with the voice of chapels ;
Fays, methinks, were gotten solely
To keep orchard-robbing holy !

Hence then, hence, and let's delight us
With the maids whose creams invite us,
Kissing them, like proper fairies,
All amidst their fruits and dairies.]

.　.　.　.　.　.

Jocastus with a morrice, himselfe Maid Marrian,
Bromius the clowne.

Dor. See, Mopsus, see, here comes your fairy
　　brother ;
Hark you, for one good turne deserves another.
　　　　　　　　　　　[*Exeunt Dor. Mop.*
Joc. I did not think there had been such delight
in any mortall morrice.   They doe caper, like quarter
fairies at the least.   By my knighthood, and by this
sweet mellisonant tingle-tangle, the ensigne of my
glory, you shall be of Oberon's Revels.
Bro. What to doe, I pray? to dance away our
apples ?
Joc. Surely, mortall, thou art not fit for any office
there.

Enter Dorylas like the King of Fairies. Mopsus.

Joc. See, blind mortall, see, with what a port, what
grace, what majesty this princely Oberon comes.
Your grace is welcome.
Dor. A beauteous lady, bright and rare ;
Queen Mab herselfe is not so faire.
Joc. Does your grace take me for a woman then ?
Dor. Yes, beauteous Virgin ; thy each part
Has shot an arrow through my heart !
Thy blazing eye, thy lip so thin,

Thy azure cheek and christall chin,
Thy rainbow brow, with many a rose,
Thy saphyre eares, and rubie nose,
All wound my soule! O, gentle be,
Or, lady, you will ruin me!

Joc. Bromius, what shall I doe? I am no
woman! If gelding of me will preserve your grace,
with all my heart.

Bro. No, master, let him rather steale away all your
orchard apples.

Joc. I, and shall! Beauteous Queen Mab may lose
her longing else.

Dor. How's this? are you no woman then?
Can such bright beauty live with men?

Joc. An't please your grace, I am your knight
Jocastus.

Dor. Indeed, I thought no man but he
Could of such perfect beauty be.

Joc. Cannot your Grace distill me to a woman.

Dor. I have an hearb they moly call,
Can change thy shape, my sweet, and shall.
To taste this moly but agree,
And thou shalt perfect woman be.

Joc. With all my heart, ne'er let me move
But I am up to the eares in love.
But what if I doe marry thee?

Dor. My Queen Jocasta thou shalt be.

Joc. Sweet Moly! pray let Bromius have some Moly
too,
Hee'l make a very pretty waiting maid.

Brom. No, indeed, forsooth, you have ladies enough
already.

Dor. Halfe your estate then give to me,
Else, you being gon, there none will be
Whose orchard I dare here frequent.

Joc. Sweet Oberon, I am content.

Dor. The other halfe let Mopsus take.

Joc. And Thestylis a joynture make.

Bro. Why, master, are you mad?

Joc. Your mistresse, sirrah.
Our Grace has said it, and it shall be so.

Bro. What, will you give away all your estate?

Joc. We have enough beside in Fairy Land. You,
Thestylis, shall be our maid of honour.

Thes. I humbly thank your Grace.

Joc. Come, princely Oberon, I long to tast this
Moly. Pray bestow the Knighthood of the Mellisonant Tingle Tangle upon our brother Mopsus; we
will raise all of our house to honours.

Mop. Gracious sister!

Joc. I alwayes thought I was borne to be a queene.

Dor. Come let us walke, majestique queene,
Of fairy mortalls to be seen.
In chaires of pearle thou plac't shalt be,
And empresses shall envie thee,
When they behold upon our throne
Jocasta with her Dorylas.

All. Ha, ha, ha!

Joc. Am I deceiv'd and cheated, guld and foold?

Mop. Alas, sir, you were borne to be a queene.

Joc. My lands, my livings, and my orchard gone?

Dor. Your grace hath said it, and it must be so.

Bro. You have enough beside in Fairy-land.

Thes. What would your Grace command your maid
of honour?

Dor. Well, I restore your lands: only the orchard
I will reserve for feare queen Mab should long.

Mop. Part I'le restore unto my liberall sister in liew
of my great knighthood.

Thes. Part give I.

Joc. I am beholding to your liberality.

Bro. I'le something give as well as doe the rest ;
Take my fooles coat, for you deserve it best.

Joc. I shall grow wiser.

Dor. Oberon will be glad on't.

Thes. I must goe call Urania that she may come
vow virginity.

XIX.

Herrick's Fairy Poetry.

———o———

FROM the "Hesperides, or the Works both humane and divine of Robert Herrick," 8vo, Lond. 1648. Several of these pieces are very common in contemporary manuscripts, and are also inserted in a few printed collections.

Oberon's Feast.

A little mushroome table spred,
After short prayers they set on bread,
A moon-parcht grain of purest wheat,
With some small glit'ring gritt, to eate
His choice bitts with ; then in a trice
They make a feast lesse great then nice,
But all this while his eye is serv'd,
We must not thinke his eare was sterv'd ;
But that there was in place to stir
His spleen, the chirring grashopper,
The merry cricket, puling flie,
The piping gnat for minstralcy.[1]

---

[1] The following two lines are here inserted in a copy in Poole's

And now, we must imagine first,
The elves present to quench his thirst,
A pure seed-pearle of infant dew,
Brought and besweetned in a blew
And pregnant violet ; which done,
His kitling eyes begin to runne
Quite through the table, where he spies
The hornes of paperie butterflies,
Of which he eates ; and tastes a little
Of what we call the cuckoes spittle ;
A little fuz-ball pudding stands
By, yet not blessed by his hands,
That was too coorse ; but then forthwith
He ventures boldly on the pith
Of sugred rush, and eates the sagge
And well bestrutted bees sweet bagge ;
Gladding his pallat with some store
Of emits eggs ; what wo'd he more ?
But beards of mice, a newt's stew'd thigh,
A bloated earewig, and a flie ;
With the red-capt worme, that's shut
With the concave of a nut,
Browne as his tooth.   A little moth,
Late fatned in a piece of cloth ;
With withered cherries, mandrakes eares,
Moles eyes ; to these the slain stag's teares ;
The unctuous dewlaps of a snaile,
The broke-heart of a nightingale
Ore-come in musicke ; with a wine
Ne're ravisht from the flattering vine,
But gently prest from the soft side
Of the most sweet and dainty bride,

Parnassus, which contains many variations, generally for the
worse :—

> The humming dor, the dying swan,
> And each a chief musician.

Brought in a dainty daizie, which
He fully quaffs up to bewitch
His blood to height ; this done, commended
Grace by his priest ; the feast is ended !

Oberon's Palace.

Full as a bee with thyme, and red
As cherry harvest, now high fed
For lust and action ; on he'l go
To lye with Mab, though all say no.
Lust has no eares ; he's sharpe as thorn,
And fretfull, carries hay in's horne,
And lightning in his eyes ; and flings
Among the elves, if mov'd, the stings
Of peltish wasps ; we'l know his guard ;
Kings, though th'are hated, will be fear'd.
Wine lead[s] him on.   Thus to a grove,
Sometimes devoted unto love,
Tinseld with twilight, he and they
Lead by the shine of snails, a way
Beat with their num'rous feet, which by
Many a neat perplexity,
Many a turn and man' a crosse-
Track, they redeem a bank of mosse
Spungie and swelling, and farre more
Soft then the finest Lemster ore ;
Mildly disparkling, like those fiers
Which break from the injeweld tyres
Of curious brides ; or like those mites
Of candi'd dew in moony nights.
Upon this convex, all the flowers
Nature begets by th'sun and showers,
Are to a wilde digestion brought,
As if loves sampler here was wrought,
Or Citherea's ceston, which
All with temptation doth bewitch.

Sweet aires move here, and more divine
Made by the breath of great ey'd kine,
Who, as they lowe, empearl with milk
The foure-leav'd grasse, or mosse-like silk.
The breath of munkies, met to mix
With musk-flies, are th'aromaticks
Which cense this arch ; and here and there,
And farther off, and every where
Throughout that brave Mosaick yard,
Those picks or diamonds in the card :
With peeps of harts, of club and spade,
Are here most neatly interlaid.
Many a counter, many a die,
Half-rotten, and without an eye,
Lies here abouts ; and for to pave
The excellency of this cave,
Squirrils and children's teeth late shed,
Are neatly here enchequered
With brownest toadstones and the gum
That shines upon the blewer plum.
The nails faln off by whit-flawes; Art's
Wise hand enchasing here those warts,
Which we to others (from our selves)
Sell, and brought hither by the elves.
The tempting mole, stoln from the neck
Of the shie virgin, seems to deck
The holy entrance ; where within
The roome is hung with the blew skin
Of shifted snake ; enfreez'd throughout
With eyes of peacocks' trains, and trout-
Flies curious wings ; and these among
Those silver-pence, that cut the tongue
Of the red infant, neatly hung.
The glow-wormes eyes the shining scales
Of silv'rie fish, wheat-strawes, the snailes

Soft candle-light, the kitling's eyne,
Corrupted wood, serve here for shine
No glaring light of bold-fac't day,
Or other over-radiant ray,
Ransacks this roome ! but what weak beams
Can make reflected from these jems,
And multiply ; such is the light,
But ever doubtfull, day or night.
By this quaint taper-light, he winds
His errours up ; and now he finds
His moon-tann'd Mab, as somewhat sick,
And, love knowes, tender as a chick,
Upon six plump dandillions, high
Rear'd, lies her elvish majestie,
Whose woollie-bubbles seem to drown
Hir Mab-ship in obedient downe ;
For either sheet was spread the caule
That doth the infant's face enthrall,
When it is born, by some enstyl'd
The luckie omen of the child ;
And next to these, two blankets ore-
Cast of the finest gossamore ;
And then a rug of carded wooll,
Which, sponge-like, drinking in the dull
Light of the moon, seem'd to comply,
Cloud-like, the daintie deitie.
Thus soft she lies ; and over-head
A spinner's circle is bespread
With cob-web curtains ; from the roof
So neatly sunck, as that no proof
Of any tackling can declare
What gives it hanging in the aire.
The fringe about this, are those threds
Broke at the losse of maiden-heads ;
And all behung with these pure pearls,
Dropt from the eyes of ravisht girles,

Or writhing brides, when, panting, they
Give unto love the straiter way.
For musick now, he has the cries
Of fained lost virginities;
The which the elves make to excite
A more unconquer'd appetite.
The king's undrest; and now upon
The gnat's watch-word the elves are gone.
And now the bed, and Mab possest
Of this great little kingly guest;
We'll nobly think, what's to be done
He'll do no doubt: this flax is spun.

The Fairie Temple.

A way enchac't with glasse and beads
There is, that to the chappel leads;
Whose structure, for his holy rest,
Is here the halcion's curious nest;
Into the which who looks, shall see
His temple of idolatry;
Where he of god-heads has such store,
As Rome's Pantheon had not more.
His house of Rimmon this he calls,
Girt with small bones, instead of walls.
First, in a neech, more black than jet,
His idol-cricket there is set;
Then in a polisht ovall by,
There stands his idol beetle flie;
Next, in an arch, akin to this,
His idol canker seated is;
Then in a round, is plac't by these
His golden god, Cantharides.
So that where ere ye look, ye see
No capitoll, no cornish free,
Or freeze from this fine fripperie.

Now, this the fairies wo'd have known,
Their's is a mixt religion :
And some have heard the elves it call
Part pagan, part papisticall.
If unto me all tongues were granted,
I co'd not speak the saints here painted.
Saint Tit, Saint Nit, Saint Is, Saint Itis,
Who 'gainst Mab's state plac't here right is.
Saint Will o'th' Wispe, of no great bignes.
But alias call'd here *fatuus ignis.*
Saint Frip, Saint Trip, Saint Fill, S. Fillie,
Neither those other saint-ships will I
Here goe about for to recite
Their number, almost infinite ;
Which, one by one, here set downe are
In this most curious calendar.
First, at the entrance of the gate,
A little puppet-priest doth wait,
Who squeaks to all the commers there,
" Favour your tongues, who enter here.
Pure hands bring hither, without staine."
A second pules, " Hence, hence, profane."
Hard by, i'th'shell of halfe a nut,
The holy-water there is put ;
A little brush of squirrills haires,
Compos'd of odde, not even paires,
Stands in the platter, or close by,
To purge the fairy family.
Neere to the altar stands the priest,
There off'ring up the holy-grist ;
Ducking in mood and perfect tense,
With (much-good-do't-him) reverence.
The altar is not here foure-square,
Nor in a forme triangular ;
Nor made of glasse, or wood, or stone,
But of a little transverce bone,

Which boys and bruckel'd children call
(Playing for points and pins) cockall.
Whose linnen-drapery is a thin,
Subtile, and ductile codlin's skin ;
Which o're the board is smoothly spred
With little seale-work damasked.
The fringe that circumbinds it, too,
Is spangle-work of trembling dew,
Which, gently gleaming, makes a show,
Like frost-work glitt'ring on the snow ;
Upon this fetuous board doth stand
Something for shew-bread, and at hand
(Just in the middle of the altar)
Upon an end, the fairie-psalter,
Grac't with the trout-flies curious wings,
Which serve for watched ribbanings.
Now, we must know, the elves are led
Right by the rubrick, which they read :
And if report of them be true,
They have their text for what they doo,
I, and their book of canons too.
And, as Sir Thomas Parson tells,
They have their book of articles ;
And if that fairie knight not lies,
They have their book of homilies ;
And other scriptures, that designe
A short, but righteous discipline.
The bason stands the board upon
To take the free oblation :
A little pin-dust, which they hold
More precious then we prize our gold
Which charity they give to many
Poore of the parish, if there's any.
Upon the ends of these neat railes,
Hatcht with the silver-light of snails,
The elves, in formall manner, fix
Two pure and holy candlesticks,

In either which a small tall bent
Burns for the altar's ornament.
For sanctity, they have to these
Their curious copes and surplices
Of cleanest cob-web, hanging by
In their religious vesterie.
They have their ash-pans and their brooms
To purge the chappel and the rooms ;
Their many mumbling masse-priests here,
And many a dapper chorister.
Their ush'ring vergers here likewise ;
Their canons and their chaunteries ;
Of cloyster-monks they have enow,
I, and their abby-lubbers too.
And if their legend doe not lye,
They much affect the papacie ;
And since the last is dead, there's hope
Elve Boniface shall next be pope.
They have their cups and chalices,
Their pardons and indulgences,
Their beads of nits, bels, books, and wax
Candles, forsooth, and other knacks;
Their holy oyle, their fasting spittle,
Their sacred salt here, not a little.
Dry chips, old shooes, rags, grease, and bones,
Beside their fumigations,
To drive the devill from the cod-piece
Of the fryar, of work an odde-piece.
Many a trifle, too, and trinket,
And for what use, scarce man wo'd think it.
Next then, upon the chanter's side
An apples-core is hung up dry'd,
With ratling kirnils, which is rung
To call to morn and even-song.
The saint, to which the most he prayes,
And offers incense nights and dayes,

The lady of the lobster is,
Whose foot-pace he doth stroak and kisse,
And humbly chives of saffron brings,
For his most cheerfull offerings.
When after these h'as paid his vows,
He lowly to the altar bows ;
And then he dons the silk-worms shed,
Like a Turks turbant on his head,
And reverently departeth thence,
Hid in a cloud of frankincense ;
And by the glow-worms light wel guided,
Goes to the feast that's now provided.

The Beggar to Mab, the Fairie Queen.

Please your grace, from out your store
Give an almes to one that's poore,
That your mickle may have more.
Black I'm grown for want of meat,
Give me then an ant to eate,
Or the cleft eare of a mouse
Over-sowr'd in drinke of souce ;
Or, sweet lady, reach to me
The abdomen of a bee ;
Or commend a cricket's hip,
Or his huckson, to my scrip,
Give for bread a little bit
Of a pease that 'gins to chit,
And my full thanks take for it.
Floure of fuz-balls, that's too good
For a man in needy-hood ;
But the meal of mill-dust can
Well content a craving man ;
Any orts the elves refuse
Well will serve the beggar's use.
But if this may seem too much
For an almes, then give me such

Little bits that nestle there
In the pris'ner's panier.
So a blessing light upon
You and mighty Oberon ;
That your plenty last till when
I return your almes agen.

The night-piece, to Julia.

Her eyes the glow-worme lend thee,
The shooting-starres attend thee ;
    And the elves also,
    Whose little eyes glow,
Like the sparks of fire, befriend thee.

No Will-o'th'-Wispe mis-light thee,
Nor snake or slow-worme bite thee ;
    But on, on thy way,
    Not making a stay,
Since ghost ther's none to affright thee.

The Fairies.

If ye will with Mab find grace,
Set each platter in his place :
Rake the fier up, and get
Water in, ere sun be set.
Wash your pailes, and clense your dairies,
Sluts are loathsome to the fairies !
Sweep your house ; Who doth not so,
Mab will pinch her by the toe.

XX

The Holy Bush.

————o————

F ROM "Men-Miracles with other Poemes," 12mo, Lond. 1646, where it is entitled the "Song at the Holly-Bush Guard." The chorus is here omitted. It is also found in some editions of the "Academy of Complements."

> Cleare the eyes of the watch,
> Lazy sleepe we dispatch
>   From hence as farre as Dedford ;
> For the flocke-bed and feather
> We expose to the weather,
>   And hang all sheetes in the bed-cord.
>
> The goblins and the jigge
> We regard not a figge ;
>   Our phansies they cannot vary :
> We nere pity girles that doe
> Finde no treasure in their shooe,
>   But are nipt by the tyrannous fairy.
>
> List ! the noise of the chaires
> Wakes the wench to her pray'rs,

Queene Mab comes worse then a witch in,
Backe and sides she entailes
To the print of her nailes,
Shee'le teach her to snort in the kitchen.

Some the night-mare hath prest,
With that weight on their breast,
No returnes of their breath can passe ;
But to us the tale is addle,
We can take off her saddle,
And turne out the night-mare to grasse.

Now no more will we harke
To the charmes of the larke,
Or the tunes of the early thrush ;
All the woods shall retire,
And submit to the quire
Of the birds in the holly-bush.

While the country lasse
With her dairy doth passe,
Our joys no tongue can utter ;
For we centinells stand,
And exact by command
The excise of her lips and butter.

XXI.

King Oberon's Apparel.

——o——

A POEM by Sir Simon Steward,[1] from the "Musarum Deli-
ciæ, or the Muses Recreation," 12mo, Lond. 1656. Other
copies of it are in MS. Ashmole 38, f. 99, MS. Rawl.
Poet. 147, and MS. Malone 17. A great part of it, with some
variations, is inserted in Poole's "English Parnassus."

> When the monthly horned Queen
> Grew jealous, that the stars had seen
> Her rising from Endimions armes,
> In rage, she throws her misty charmes
> Into the bosome of the night,
> To dim their curious prying light.
> Then did the dwarfish faery elves
> (Having first attir'd themselves)
> Prepare to dresse their Oberon king
> In highest robes for revelling.
> In a cobweb shirt, more thin
> Then ever spider since could spin,

---

[1] [But see what is said in Hazlitt's edition of Herrick, 1869,
p. 475-7.]

Bleach'd by the whitenesse of the snow,
As the stormy windes did blow
It in the vast and freezing aire ;
No shirt halfe so fine, so faire.
    A rich wastcoat they did bring,
Made of the trout-flies gilded wing ;
At that his elveship 'gan to fret,
Swearing it would make him sweat,
Even with its weight, and needs would wear
His wastcoat wove of downy haire,
New shaven from an eunuch's chin ;
That pleas'd him well, 'twas wondrous thin.
    The outside of his doubtlet was
Made of the four leav'd true-love grasse,
On which was set so fine a glosse,
By the oyle of crispy mosse ;
That through a mist, and starry light,
It made a rainbow every night.
On every seam, there was a lace
Drawn by the unctuous snailes slow trace ;
To it, the purest silver thread
Compar'd, did look like dull pale lead.
    Each button was a sparkling eye
Ta'ne from the speckled adders frye,
Which in a gloomy night, and dark,
Twinckled like a fiery spark :
And, for coolnesse, next his skin,
'Twas with white poppy lin'd within.
    His breeches of that fleece were wrought,
Which from Colchos Jason brought ;
Spun into so fine a yarne,
That mortals might it not discerne ;
Wove by Arachne, in her loom,
Just before she had her doom ;
Dy'd crimson with a maiden's blush,
And lyn'd with dandelyon push.

A rich mantle he did wear
Made of tinsel gossamere,
Be-starred over with a few
Dyamond drops of morning dew.
　His cap was all of ladies love,
So passing light that it did move,
If any humming gnat or fly
But buzz'd the ayre, in passing by;
About it was a wreath of pearle,
Drop'd from the eyes of some poor girle
Pinch'd because she had forgot
To leave faire water in the pot.
And for feather, he did weare
Old Nisus fatall purple haire.
　The sword they girded on his thigh
Was smallest blade of finest rye.
　A paire of buskins they did bring
Of the cow-ladyes corall wing;
Power'd o'er with spots of jet,
And lin'd with purple-violet.
　His belt was made of mirtle leaves,
Plaited in small curious threaves,
Beset with amber cowslip studds,
And fring'd about with daizy budds;
In which bugle horne was hung,
Made of the babbling eccho's tongue;
Which set unto his moon-burn'd lip,
He windes and then his faeries skip;
At that, the lazy dawn 'gan sound,
And each did trip a faery round.

The remainder of the tract is occupied with extracts from Herrick, the beautiful little ballad of " Robin Goodfellow," printed by Percy, and the poem on Melancholy, prefixed to the early editions of Burton's " Anatomy of Melancholy." From this last-mentioned poem Milton is supposed to have derived the hint of " Il Pensoroso."

XXIII

Queen Mab's Invitation.

———o———

PERCY having inserted this song in his "Reliques," it is well known to most readers. Several copies of it are found in the poetical collections of the seventeenth century. One, hitherto unnoticed, is in MS. Ashmole 37, and another in a MS. in the Rawlinson collection. It was sung to the tune of the "Spanish Gipsy." See Thorpe's Catalogue of Manuscripts for 1831, p. 114.

> Come follow, follow me,
> Ye fairy elves that be
> Light tripping o'er the green,
> Come follow Mab, your queen :
> Hand in hand we dance around,
> For this place is fairy-ground.
>
> When mortals are at rest,
> And snoring in their nest,
> Unheard and unespied,
> Through key-holes we do glide ;

Over tables, stools, and shelves,
We trip it with our fairy elves.

And if the house be foul,
Or platter, dish, or bowl,
Up stairs we nimbly creep,
And find the sluts asleep ;
Then we pinch their arms and thighs ;
None us hears, and none us spies.

But if the house be swept,
And from uncleanness kept,
We praise the household maid,
And duly she is paid :
Every night before we go,
We drop a tester in her shoe.

Upon a mushroom's head
Our table-cloth we spread ;
A grain of rye or wheat
Is the diet that we eat ;
Pearly drops of dew we drink,
In acorn cups fill'd to the brink.[1]

The grasshopper, gnat, and fly,
Serve for our minstrelsy ;
Grace said, we dance awhile,
And so the time beguile ;
And when the moon doth hide her head,
The glow-worm lights us home to bed.

---

[1] In some copies is inserted the following stanza :—
The tongues of nightingales,
The unctuous fat of snails,
Between two muscles stew'd,
Is meat that's easily chew'd :
The brains of wrens, the beards of mice
Do make a feast of wondrous prize !

O'er tops of dewy grass
So nimbly we do pass,
The young and tender stalk
Ne'er bends as we do walk;
Yet in the morning may be seen
Where we the night before have been.

XXIV.

Heywood's Hierarchy.

———o———

[From Heywood's "Hierarchie of the blessed Angels," fol. Lond. 1635, p. 574.]

OF Faustus and Agrippa it is told,
    That in their travels they bare seeming gold
    Which would abide the touch; and by the way,
In all their hostries they would freely pay.
But parted thence, mine host thinking to find
Those glorious pieces they had left behind
Safe in his bag, sees nothing save together
Round scutes of horn and pieces of old leather.
Of such I could cite many, but I'll hie
From them, to those we call *Lucifugi.*
    These in obscurest vaults themselves invest,
And above all things light and day detest.
In John Milesius any man may read
Of devils in Sarmatia honored,
Call'd *Kottri,* or *Kibaldi ;* such as we
Pugs and hob-goblins call. Their dwellings be

In corners of old houses least frequented,
Or beneath stacks of wood : and these convented,
Make fearful noise in butteries and in dairies ;
Robin Good-fellowes some, some call them fairies.
In solitary rooms these uproars keep
And beat at doors to keep men from their sleep.
Seeming to force locks, be they ne're so strong
And keeping Christmas gambols all night long.
Pots, glasses, trenchers, dishes, pans and kettles
They will make dance about the shelves and settles,
As if about the kitchen tost and cast,
Yet in the morning nothing found misplas't.
Others such houses to their use have fitted
In which base murthers have been once committed :
Some have fearful habitations taken
In desolate houses, ruin'd and forsaken.

XXV.

The Midnight's Watch.

-—o—-

THE following curious tract, which is reprinted from a copy preserved in the British Museum, is of a political nature, but, at the same time, affords some illustration of the popular character of Robin Goodfellow, and is in many respects curious and interesting. The tract itself is printed on four leaves, in very small quarto.

The Midnights Watch, or Robin Good-Fellow His Serious Observation; wherein is discovered the true state and strength of the Kingdome as at this day it stands, without either Faction or Affaction. London, Printed for George Lindsey, 1643.

The harmlesse spirit and the merry, commonly knowne to the world by the name of Robin Good-fellow, having told his fairy mistresse of fleering upon strangers elves, and the tickling of her nose with her petulant finger, and receaving but frownes for his favours and checks for his counsailes, he grew weary

of her service, and being as light of love as he was
of care he resolved to visit her no more. The
troubles and commotions in the upper world had
wrought his thoughts another way, and in a serious
humour one night he resolved to goe abroad, to
observe the new courses and alterations of the
world.

The first place he came at was Windsor, where he
found a good part of the army newly come from
Redding, he heard them talke as confident of victory
as if they had killed the Cavaliers already, he much
admired the understanding and resolution of their
Generall, and daring not to stay there any longer for
feare he should be taken for a malignant and be whipt,
he made a swift dispatch for Oxford ; yet not farre
from Windsor he met at the townes end many sentinells and incountered some Courts of Guard, though
they were men of warre he heard them much to
desire peace, and freezing in the cold, Robin could
not chuse but laugh, to hear them comfort one
another by boasting in what hot service they had
been.

When he came to Oxford, the first place he ventured into was St. Maries Church, where indeed he
found a convocation of many reverend heads, some
whereof had lately departed from London for their
consciences sake, and esteemed the freedome of their
minds of a greater consequence then their revenues :
they much lamented the iniquity of the times, and
wisht indeed (if he could be found) that abler and
more learned men might supply their deserted places.
Robbin wondred at the gravity of the men, who
with great wisdome and moderation were discoursing
amongst themselves from whence the first cause of
these distempers did arise, and some imputing it to
this, and some to that, Robin departed from them

three times, sneezed out aloud, *Bishop, Bishop, Bishop.*

From thence he come to Christchurch where he found a pack of cunning heads assembled together ; these were men of another temper, and indeed they were the ottachousticons of the King's, who whispered into his sacred eares all the ill counsells that they had contrived. Those were they that possessed him with impossible things, and induced him to believe them. They would tell him of great battels which were never fought, wherein he had the victory, and some conquests were told him to be atchieved by the Parliament wherein he received no losse at all. A band or two of men have passed for a whole army, and a liter on the Thames for a whole fleet at sea. Robbin much wondred that they being so neare unto him the influence of so sacred a Majesty could work no better impression in their soules ; and drawing neare unto the bed chamber he found his Majesty though in these distracted times yet full of native constancy, and tranquillity of mind, and secured better by his innocence then his guard. With much joy and renowne he departed thence, and observing as he went (for it was past midnight) many a loose wench in the armes of many of the Cavaliers, he gave every wench as he passed by a blue and a secret nip on the arm without awakening her. He heard among the sentinells, as he was departing from Oxford, of a great victory obtained by one Sir Ralph Hopton against a part of the Parliament's forces, wherein the earle of Stamford's regiments were said to be quite routed, many of his souldiers slaine, many taken prisoners and great store of armes, and ammunition with them, amongst which a great brasse piece, on which the Crown and the Rose were stampt, was most remarkable. Robbin had a great desire to

thither himself, and to justifie the truth of so absolute
a victory.   He had not gone as far as Ensham, but
he espied the nine muses in a vintener's porch
crouching close together, and defending themselves
as well as they could from the cold visitation of the
winter's night.   They were extream poore, and
(which is most strange) in so short an absence and
distance from Oxford they were grown extreamly
ignorant, for they took him for their Apollo, and
craved his power and protection to support
them.   Robbin told them they were much mistaken in him, for though he was not mortal he
was but of middle birth no more than they, they
being the daughters of Memorie, and he the son
of Mirth, but he bade them take comfort for that
now in Oxford there was sure news of peace and a
speedy hope of their return to their discontinued
habitations: at this they seemed with much joy to
rouse up themselves, and did assure him that if what
he reported did prove true, they would sing his
praises throughout all generations.   The elf, proud
proud of such a favour, in the name of Oberon did
thank them, and did conjure them to perform it, and
in the twinkling of an eye he conveyed himself to
Salt-ash in Cornwall, where Sir R. Hopton's forces
were quartered.   He found the defeat given to the
earl of Stanford nothing so great as fame in Oxford
confirmed it to be.   Collonell Ruthen's regiment
indeed was sorely shaken, and some of his men slain,
and many taken prisoners.   With a curious eye he
observed what arms and ammunition were taken,
and above all he had a labouring desire to see the
brasse piece with the Crowne and the Rose on it,
which so much dignified his conquest ; he searched
up and down the army, and in and about the magazine, but he could not find it.   At length despairing

of what he looked for, the venterous elf came into Sir Ralph's chamber, and finding him asleepe, and safe as wine and innocence, he dived into his pocket, and the first thing he took out, hee found to beare the impression of the Rose and Crowne, and it was a brave piece indeed, for it was a farthing token which was all peradventure that was in it. Robbin ashamed to see himself so deluded could not at the first but smile at the conceit, and putting it into its magazine repenting himself of his journey, he did sweare that he would never trust fame, nor pamphlet more, though printed in a thousand universities.

From thence with much indignation, and more speed he flung away, and in a moment placed himselfe at Bristoll, where he found the face of things just like the aire of an April morning, it smiled and it rained both at once, some were greedy of peace, and some againe were as eager of war; here some stood for the King, there others for the Parliament, the greater number was for the one side, but the better for the other. The husband was divided against the wife, the sister against the brother, and the son lifting forbidden hands against the father. Robin beholding so strange a division amongst people so neer in blood, wished himselfe againe in Fairy Land; for, said he, we have no such dinne, no such tumults, nor unnaturall quarrels, but all silence and oblivion and a perpetuall peace. And quickly abandoning the place, he in an instant came into Glocestershire, to a towne called Tedbury, where the more to increase his misery he met with the spirit of faction and distempered zeale. This was the spirit that was accustomed to make a great hubbub in the churches, to teare off the surplice from the minister's shoulders, and when the children were to be signed with the signe of the Crosse (like a divell dispossessed) to teare himself for fury, and with great noyse and foaming to runne out of the Temple. This spirit would faine have persuaded Robin to turne Roundhead, and told him that they were the best sort of Christians : I, replyed Robin, that is even as true as God is in Glocestershire. As he was proceeding in his discourse, he was intercepted by a great noyse and tumult of people, who cried out flye, flye, flye. Amazed at the suddennesse of the cry, and the multitudes of the people that came thronging by ; he looked about him to understand what the businesse was, he found it a company of people, whom flying from Cirencester, the ignorant fury of the sword had spared. Prince Rupert had newly entred the towne, and having thrice summoned it, and they refused to yeeld it into his hands, he seized on it by violence, and on his first entrance he burned a great part of the towne, the shot from the windowes by the muskets of the towne did wonderfully among his men, and he found no better meanes to prevent that mischiefe but by setting fire on the houses, there was a great overthrow, and Colonell Carre, and Colonell Massey, two chiefe commanders for the Parliament, were either slaine, or desperately wounded. Robin found this Prince to be a gentleman of himselfe of a civill and serious disposition, a man few in words, and very little beholding to fame for the many strange reports he had delivered of him ; affrighted at the thunder of his armes, Robin dispatched himselfe from him with as much speed as the bullets flew from the mouth of his angry canons, and on the first summons of the cocke he came to Newarke, where either through feare of some new designe upon them, or through some great cold they had taken, he found every man of the earl of Newcastle's garrison souldiers to be sicke of a palsey : loath to continue amongst those crasie people, with an invitive dispatch hee came to Pontefract, where he found the earle of Newcastle, with the greatest part of his armie gone towards Yorke, not so much through feare as it was suggested, but for complement rather, and to entertaine the Queene of England, who was expected to be either at Newcastle or Yorke. He found the army of the recusants, though in many combats shaken and scattered, yet not to receive so great an overthrow as many tongues too credulously have voiced it.

Neither did he find in York masse to be said in every Church, it being crosse to the method of the close and subtill generation of the Papists to make a publick profession of their religion before they had fully perfected their intentions and by the strength of authority made both the ends of their designes to meet together. Howsoever it being discovered that the warre which was pretended for the maintaining of the King's prerogative, tended now indeed to the innovation of Religion, and to make the Papists appeare the King's best subjects, it hath turned many hearts and armed many hands against them. The newes of the Queen's landing made Robbin so brisk, and so overcharged him with newes, that being as unable to contain it, as he was so greedy to receive it, he could not take a full survay of Yorke, nor had the leisure to go unto Newcastle to discover what good service those foure ships have done to hinder any malignant vessells that come either from Holland or from Denmark, from landing at Newcastle ; a mad vagary tooke him to come up to London, which the vagabond elfe performed with such a suddennesse that could he be discovered in his way, he would have proved rather the object of the memory then of the eye. The first place hee came into, it was a conventicle of the family of love, it was then much about two of the clock in the morning, and the candles being put out, they were going from one exercise unto another. Robbin presented himself before them all, and seemed lusty as the spirit of youth when it is newly awakened from the morning's sleep : the women were well contented to stay, but the men cryed out a Satyre, a Satyre, a Satyre, and thrusting them before them all tumbling headlong, down the staires together, they left him laughing to himself alone.

XXVI.

Bovet on Fairies.

——o——

THE following narratives are taken from a curious little volume by Richard Bovet, entitled, " Pandæmonium, or the Devil's Cloyster, being a further blow to modern Sadduceism, proving the existence of witches and spirits," 12mo. London, 1684.

A remarkable passage of one named the Fairy-boy of Leith in Scotland, given me by my worthy friend Captain George Burton, and attested under his own hand.

About fifteen years since, having business that detained me for some time at Leith, which is near Edenborough in the kingdom of Scotland, I often met some of my acquaintance at a certain house there, where we used to drink a glass of wine for our refection. The woman which kept the house was of honest reputation among the neighbours, which made me give the more attention to what she told me one day about a fairy-boy, as they called him, who lived about

that town. She had given me so strange an account
of him, that I desired her I might see him the first
opportunity, which she promised ; and not long after,
passing that way, she told me there was the fairy-boy.
But a little before I came by, and casting her eye into
the street, said, "Look you, sir, yonder he is at play
with those other boys ;" and designing him to me, I
went, and by smooth words and a piece of money got
him to come into the house with me ; where, in the
presence of divers people, I demanded of him several
astrological questions, which he answered with great
subtility ; and through all his discourse carryed it with
a cunning much above his years, which seemed not
to exceed ten or eleven.

He seemed to make a motion like drumming upon
the table with his fingers, upon which I ask'd him
whether he could beat a drum.   To which he replied,
"Yes, sir, as well as any man in Scotland, for every
Thursday night I beat all points to a sort of people
that use to meet under yonder hill," pointing to the
great hill between Edenborough and Leith.   "How,
boy," quoth I, "what company have you there ?"
"There are, sir," said he, "a great company both of
men and women, and they are entertained with many
sorts of musick besides my drum ; they have, besides,
plenty of variety of meats and wine, and many times
we are carried into France or Holland in a night, and
return again ; and whilst we are there, we enjoy all
the pleasures the country doth afford."   I demanded
of him how they got under that hill.   To which he
replied that there were a great pair of gates that opened
to them, though they were invisible to others, and
that within there were brave large rooms as well
accommodated as most in Scotland.   I then asked
him how I should know what he said to be true.
Upon which he told me he would read my fortune,

saying I should have two wives, and that he saw the forms of them sitting on my shoulders, that both would be very handsom women. As he was thus speaking, a woman of the neighbourhood, coming into the room, demanded of him what her fortune should be? He told her that she had had two bastards before she was married ; which put her in such a rage, that she desired not to hear the rest.

The woman of the house told me that all the people in Scotland could not keep him from the rendesvous on Thursday night ; upon which, by promising him some more money, I got a promise of him to meet me at the same place in the afternoon the Thursday following, and so dismist him at that time. The boy came again at the place and time appointed, and I had prevailed with some friends to continue with me, if possible, to prevent his moving that night. He was placed between us, and answered many questions without offering to go from us, until about eleven of the clock he was got away unperceived of the company, but I suddenly missing him hasted to the door, and took hold of him, and so returned him into the same room. We all watched him, and on a sudden he was again got out of the doors ; I follow'd him close, and he made a noise in the street as if he had been set upon ; but from that time I could never see him.

GEORGE BURTON.

Advertisement. This gentleman is so well known to many worthy persons, merchants and others, upon the exchange in London, that there can be no need of my justifying for the integrity of the relation. I will only say thus much, that 1 have heard him very solemnly affirm the truth of what is here related ; neither do I find anything in it more then hath been reported by very unquestionable pens to the same

purpose.   What this manner of transvection was,
which the boy spoke of, whether it were corporal or
in a dream only, I shall not dispute, but I think there
be some relations of this kind that prove it may be
either way, and therefore that I leave to the reader to
determine.   But the Captain hath told me that at that
time he had a virtuous and a handsome wife, who
being dead, he thinks himself in election of another
such.   That too of the womans having had two
children happened to be very true, though hardly
any of the neighbours knew it in that place.   His
getting away in that manner was somewhat strange,
considering how they had planted him, and that
besides he had the temptation of wine and mony to
have detained him, arguments very powerful with lads
of his age and fortune.

*A relation of the apparition of fayries, their seeming to
    keep a fair, and what happened to a certain man that
    endeavoured to put himself in amongst them.*

Reading once the eighteenth of Mr Glanvil's
Relations, p. 203, concerning an Irshman that had
like to have been carried away by spirits, and of the
banquet they had spread before them in the fields &c.,
it called to mind a passage I had often heard of fairies
or spirits, so called by the country people, which
shewed themselves in great companies at divers
times ; at sometimes they would seem to dance, at
other times to keep a great fair or market.   I made
it my business to inquire amongst the neighbours
what credit might be given to that which was reported
of them ; and by many of the neighbouring inhabitants,
I had this account confirmed.

The place near which they most ordinarily shewed
themselves was on the side of a hill named Blackdown,
between the parishes of Pittminster and Chestonford,

not many miles from Tanton. Those that have had occasion to travel that way, have frequently seen them there, appearing like men and women of a stature generally near the smaller size of men ; their habits used to be of red, blew, or green, according to the old way of country garb, with high-crown'd hats. One time about fifty years since, a person living at Comb St. Nicholas, a parish lying on one side of that hill, near Chard, was riding towards his home that way, and saw just before him, on the side of the hill, a great company of people, that seemed to him like country folks, assembled, as at a fair ; there was all sorts of commodities to his appearance, as at our ordinary fairs, pewterers, shoe-makers, pedlars, with all kind of trinkets, fruit, and drinking booths ; he could not remember any thing which he had usually seen at fairs, but what he saw there. It was once in his thought that it might be some fair for Chestonford, there being a considerable one at some time of the year ; but then again he considered that was not the season for it. He was under very great surprize, and admired what the meaning of what he saw should be. At length it came into his mind what he heard con- cerning the fairies on the side of that hill ; and it being near the road he was to take, he resolved to ride in amongst them, and see what they were. Accordingly, he put on his horse that way, and though he saw them perfectly all along as he came, yet when he was upon the place where all this had appeared to him, he could discern nothing at all, only seemed to be crouded and thrust, as when one passes through a throng of people. All the rest became invisible to him, until he came at a little distance, and then it appeared to him again as at first. He found him- self in pain, and so hastened home ; where being arrived, a lameness seized him all on one side, which

continued on him as long as he lived, which was
many years; for he was living in Comb, and gave an
account to any that inquired of this accident for
more than twenty years afterward : and this relation I
had from a person of known honour, who had it
from the man himself.

There were some, whose names I have now forgot,
but they then lived at a gentleman's house named
Comb Farm, near the place before specified. Both
the man, his wife, and divers of the neighbours assured
me that they had at many times seen this fair-keeping
in the summer time, as they came from Tanton
market; but that they durst not venture in amongst
them, for that every one that had done so had received great damage by it.

Any person that is incredulous of what is here
related, may, upon inquiry of the neighbour inhabitants, receive ample satisfaction, not only as to what
is here related, but abundantly more, which I have
heard solemnly confirmed by many of them.

XXVII.

Puck's Pranks on Twelfth Day.

———o———

[From "Mercurius Fumigosus, or the Smoking Nocturnall," No. 32, Jan. 3-10, 1655.]

LAST Twelfth Day, a mad merry company being mett together to chuse King and Queen, the Cake being no sooner cutt, but Robbin Good-fellow came amongst them, and pulling one of them by the nose, he imagining it had been his fellow that sate next him, gave him a good cuff on the ear, and so falling to boxes, a woman catching up a great pot of apples and ale, thinking to save it from spilling, the merry Puck, that could not be seen, giving her a good nipp by the buttocks, made her so madd, that she flung all her pott of lambs-wooll in the faces of the combatants, which so blinded them with the roasted apples that came in their eyes, that without fear or witt they laid about them like two mad men, striking any that came neer them ; in which scuffle, there was given two black-eyes, one crack'd crown, and a bloody nose.

Y

XXVIII.

The Irish Fairies.

———o———

THE following curious narrative is printed entire from a copy of the pamphlet in the British Museum. It is a very interesting document in the history of Fairy Mythology.

Strange and Wonderful News from the county of Wicklow in Ireland, or a Full and True Relation of what happened to one Dr Moore (late Schoolmaster in London). How he was taken invisibly from his Friends, what happened to him in his absence, and how and by what means he was found, and brought back to the same Place. (With Allowance) London, printed for T. K., 1678.

Dr Moore having lately purchased an estate in the County of Wicklow, did (together with Mr Richard Uniack, and one Mr Laughlin Moore) about three weeks since go down to view his concerns there: And being come to their Inne, at a place called Dromgreagh, near Baltinglass, where they intended to lodge

that night, the Doctor began a discourse of several
things that happened to him in his childhood near
that place, and that it was about thirty-four years
since he had been in that country : That he had been
often told by his mother, and several others of his
relations, of spirits which they call'd Fairies, who used
frequently to carry him away, and continue him with
them for some time, without doing him the least prejudice : but his mother being very much frighted and
concern'd thereat, did, as often as he was missing,
send to a certain old woman, her neighbour in the
country, who by repeating some spells or exorcisms,
would suddenly cause his return. Mr Uniack used
several arguments to disswade the doctor from the
belief of so idle and improbable a story, but notwithstanding what was said to the contrary the Doctor
did positively affirm the truth thereof. And during
the dispute, the Doctor on a sudden starting up, told
them he must leave their company, for he was called
away. Mr Uniack perceiving him to be raised off
from the ground, catches fast hold of his arm with one
hand, and intwined his arm within the doctor's arm,
and with his other hand grasped the Doctor's shoulder;
Laughlin Moore likewise held him on the other side ;
but the Doctor (maugre their strength) was lifted off
the ground. Laughlin Moore's fear caused him presently to let go, but Mr Uniack continued his hold,
and was carried above a yard from the ground, and
then by some extraordinary unperceived force was
compelled to quit. The Doctor was hurried immediately out of the room, but whether conveyed
through the window, or out at the door, they being
so affrighted, none of them could declare.

The two gentlemen being greatly surprised at the
strangeness of the accident, and troubled for the loss
of their friend, call'd for the innkeeper, to whom they

related what had befallen their companion. He seem'd not to be much terrified thereat, as if such disasters were common thereabouts, but told them that within a quarter of a mile there lived a woman, who by the neighbourhood was call'd a wise woman, and who did usually give intelligence of several things that had been lost, and of cattel that were gone astray, and he doubted not but if the woman were sent for she could resolve them where their friend was, and by what means conveyed away. They forthwith sent a messenger for the woman, who being come, Mr Uniack demanded if she could give them any account of a gentleman, one Dr Moore, that had been spirited out of their company about an hour before. The woman told him she could, and that he was then in a wood about a mile distant preparing to take horse; that in one hand he had a glass of wine, in the other a piece of bread; that he was very much courted to eat and drink, but if he did either he should never be free from a consumption, and pine away to death. Mr Uniack gave the woman a cobb, and desired her to use some means for preventing his eating and drinking. She answered, He should neither eat nor drink with them: and then struck down her hand as if she were snatching at something. When she had thus done she often repeated a spell or charm in Irish, the substance whereof was : First she runs his pedigree back four generations, and calls his ancestors by their several names : then summons him from the East, the West, the North, and the South, from troops and regiments, especially from the governour mounted on the sorrel horse, &c. And after having repeated the charm she gave them an account of the several places the doctor should be carried unto that night.

At first from the wood to a Danes Fort about seven miles distant, where there should be great revelling

and dancing, together with a variety of meats and
liquors, to the eating and drinking whereof he should
be very much importuned, but promised she would
prevent his doing either. And from that fort he was
to be carried twenty miles farther, where there would
likewise be great merriment, and then to the *Seven
Churches;* and towards daybreak should be returned
safe to the company of his friends, without any damage
or mischief whatsoever: and so took leave of Mr
Uniack and Mr Moore.

About six o'clock the next morning Dr Moore
knocked at the door, and being let in desired meat
and drink might be provided for him, for that he
was both hungry and thirsty, having been hurried
from place to place all that night : and after having
refreshed himself discours'd of the manner of his
being taken away ; that it seem'd to him there came
into the room about twenty men, some mounted on
horseback, others on foot, and laid hold on him :
that he was sensible of Mr Uniack's and Mr Moore's
endeavours to have kept him, and of the force they
used, but it was all to no purpose, for had there been
fourty more they would have signified nothing ; that
from the house he was carried to a wood about a mile
distant, where was a fine horse prepared, and as he
was about to mount a glass of wine was given him
and a crust of bread, but when he offered to eat and
drink they were both struck out of his hand. That
from thence he went in the same company that had
taken him away to a Danes Fort, about seven miles
from the wood ; that he imagined himself to be
mounted on a white horse, whose motion was exceeding swift, and when they came to the fort their company multiplied to about three hundred large and
well-proportioned men and women ; he who seem'd
to be chief was mounted on a sorrel horse ; that they

all dismounted and fell to dancing, and that it came to the doctor's turn to lead a dance, which he did remember the tune he danced unto.

That after the dancing there appear'd a most sumptuous banquet, and the governour took him by the hand and desired him to eat; which he several times attempted, but was prevented by something that still struck the meat out of his hand: and so gives an account how from thence he was carried to the several places the old woman had mentioned the night before; and that about break of day, he found himself alone within sight of the inne.

Mr Uniack was so curious as to go seven miles out of his way to see the Danes Fort, and the doctor was his guide; who traced the path he had travelled the night before so exactly, that if his horse went but a yard out of the track, he would presently turn him into it again; and that upon view of the fort, he found the grass so trodden down, and the ground beaten, as if five hundred men had been there.

This was related by Mr Uniack in the presence of one Dr Murphy, a civilian, Dr Moore himself, and Mr Ludlow, one of the six clerks of the High Court of Chancery, November 18, 1678.

For satisfaction of the licenser, I certifie this following relation was sent to me from Dublin, by a person whom I credit, and recommended in a letter bearing date the 23d of November last, as true news much spoken of there.

JOHN COTHER.

XXIX.

The Cornish Fairies.

———o———

[From Morgan's " Phœnix Britannicus," 4to, Lond. 1732, p. 546, as abridged in Ritson's " Fairy Tales."]

ANNE JEFFERIES (for that was her maiden name) of whom the following strange things are related, was born in the parish of St Teath, in the county of Cornwall, in December 1626, and she is still living, 1696, being now in the 70th year of her age. She is married to one William Warren, formerly hind to the late eminent physician Dr Richard Lower deceased, and now lives as hind to Sir Andrew Slanning of Devon, Bart.

It is the custom in our county of Cornwall for the most substantial people of each parish to take apprentices the poor's children, and to breed them up till they attain to twenty-one years of age, and, for their service, to give them meat, drink, and clothes. This Anne Jefferies, being a poor man's child of the parish, by Providence fell into our family,[1] where she lived several years; being a girl of a bold, daring spirit, she would venture at those difficulties and dangers that no boy would attempt.

In the year 1645 (she then being nineteen years old), she being, one day, knitting in an arbour in our garden, there came over the garden-hedge to her (as she affirmed) six persons, of a small stature, all clothed in green, which she called fairies; upon which she was so frighted, that she fell into a kind of a convulsion-fit. But, when we found her in this condition, we brought her into the house, and put her to bed, and took great care of her. As soon as she recovered out of her fit, she cries out, "They are just gone out of the window; they are just gone out of the window; do you not see them?" And thus, in the height of her sickness, she would often cry out, and that with eagerness; which expressions were attributed to her distemper, supposing her light-headed.

[On her recovery she becomes very religious, goes constantly to church, and takes mighty delight in devotion, although she could not herself read. She even begins to work miracles, and, by the blessing of God, cures her old mistress's leg, which had been hurt by a fall, as she was coming from the mill, with continued stroking of the part affected; when our author thus proceeds:]

On this, my mother demanded of her, how she came to the knowledge of her fall? She [who had been walking at the time in the gardens and orchard till the old woman came from the mill] made answer, *That half a dozen persons told her of it.* That, replied

---

[1] The author's name is Moses Pitt, who communicates these particulars to the right reverend father in God Edward Fowler lord bishop of Gloucester, printed in 1696.

my mother, could not be, for there was none came
by at that time but my neighbour, who brought me
me home. Anne answers again, That *that* was truth,
and it was also true *that half a dozen persons told her
so:* For, said she, you know I went out of the house
into the gardens and orchard, very unwillingly, and
now I will tell you the truth of all matters and things
which have befallen me.

"You know, that this my sickness and fits came
very suddenly upon me, which brought me very low
and weak, and have made me very simple. Now the
cause of my weakness was this: I was, one day, knitting of stockings in the arbour in the garden, and
there came over the garden-hedge, of a sudden, six
small people, all in green clothes, which put me into
such a great fright, that was the cause of my great
sickness: and they continue their appearance to me,
never less than two at a time, nor never more than
eight: they always appear in even numbers, two, four,
six, eight. When I said, often, in my sickness, *They
were just gone out of the window;* it was really so,
although you thought me light-headed. At this time,
when I came out into the garden, they came to me,
and asked me, If you had put me out of the house
against my will? I told them, I was unwilling to
come out of the house. Upon this, they said,—You
should not fare the better for it; and thereupon, in
that place, and at that time, in a fair path-way, you
fell, and hurt your leg. I would not have you send
for a surgeon, nor trouble yourself, for I will cure
your leg:" the which she did in a little time.

This cure of my mother's leg, and the stories she
told of these fairies, made such a noise over all the
county of Cornwall, as that people of all distempers
came not only so far off as the Land's-end, but also
from London, and were cured by her. She took no

monies of them, nor any reward, that ever I knew or
heard of; yet had she monies, at all times, sufficient
to supply her wants.   She neither made, nor bought
any medicines, or salves, that ever I saw or heard of,
yet wanted them not, as she had occasion.   She for-
sook eating our victuals, and was fed by these fairies
from that harvest-time to the next Christmas-day;
upon which day she came to our table, and said,
Because it was that day, she would eat some roast
beef with us : the which she did, I myself being then
at table.

One time (I remember it perfectly well) I had a
mind to speak with her, and not knowing better where
to find her than in her chamber, I went thither, and
fell a knocking very earnestly, at her chamber-door,
with my foot, and calling to her earnestly, Anne, Anne,
open the door, and let me in.   She answered me,
Have a little patience, and I will let you in immediately.   Upon which, I looked through the key-hole
of the door, and I saw her eating; and when she had
done eating, she stood still by her bed-side, as long
as thanks to God might be given, and then she made
a courtesy (or bow), and opened the chamber-door,
and gave me a piece of her bread, which I did eat :
and, I think, it was the most delicious bread that ever
I did eat, either before or since.

[She could also render herself invisible, of which he
relates an instance ; and then proceeds :]

One day, these fairies gave my sister Mary (the now
wife of Mr Humphry Martyn) then about four years
of age, a silver cup, which held about a quart, bid-
ding her give it my mother, and she did bring it my
mother ; but my mother would not accept of it, but
bid her carry it to them again, which she did.   I presume this was the time my sister owns she saw the
fairies.

I have seen Anne in the orchard dancing among the trees, and she told me she was then dancing with the fairies.

The great noise of the many strange cures Anne did, and also her living without eating our victuals (she being fed, as she said, by these fairies) caused both the neighbour magistrates and ministers to resort to my father's house, and talk with her, and strictly examine her, about the matters here related ; and she gave them very rational answers to all those questions they then asked her (for by this time she was well recovered out of her sickness and fits, and her natural parts, and understanding much improved); my father, and all his family, affirming the truth of all we saw. The ministers endeavoured to persuade her they were evil spirits which resorted to her, and that it was the delusion of the devil, and advised her not to go to them, when they called her. Upon these admonitions of the ministers and magistrates, our Anne was not a little troubled. However, that night, my father, with his family, sitting at a great fire in his hall, Anne being also present, she spake to my father, and said, Now they call (meaning the fairies). We all of us urged her not to go. In less than half a quarter of an hour, she said, Now they call a second time. We incouraged her again, not to go to them, By-and-by she said, Now they call a third time : upon which, away to her chamber she went to them (of all these three calls of the fairies none heard them but Anne). After she had been in her chamber some time, she came to us again with a bible in her hand, and tells us, that, when she came to the fairies, they said to her, What ! has there been some magistrates and ministers with you, and dissuaded you from coming any more to us, saying, we are evil spirits, and that it was all the delusion of the devil? Pray desire them to read that place of scripture in the 1st epistle of St John, chap. 4, ver. 1, " Dearly beloved, believe not every spirit, but try the spirits, whether they are of God, &c." This place of scripture was turned down to in the said Bible.

After this, one John Tregeagle, esq. (who was steward to the late John earl of Radnor) being then a justice of peace in Cornwall, sent his warrant for Anne, and sent her to Bodmin jayl, and there kept her a long time. That day the constable came to execute his warrant, Anne milking the cows, the fairies appeared to her, and told her, that a constable would come that day, with a warrant, for to carry her before a justice of peace, and she would be sent to jayl. She asked them, if she should hide herself? They answered her, No: she should fear nothing, but go with the constable. So she went with the constable to the justice, and he sent her to Bodmin jayl, and ordered the prison-keeper that she should be kept without victuals; and she was so kept, and yet she lived, and that without complaining. . . . But poor Anne lay in jayl for a considerable time after; and also justice Tregeagle, who was her great persecutor, kept her in his house some time, as a prisoner, and that without victuals; and, at last, when Anne was discharged out of prison, the justices made an order, that Anne should not live any more with my father. Whereupon, my father's only sister, Mrs Frances Tom, a widow, near Padstow, took Anne into her family, and there she lived a considerable time, and did many great cures; and from thence she went to live with her own brother, and, in process of time, married, as aforesaid.

XXX

The Wiltshire Fairies.

———o———

THE following curious particulars are extracted from the miscellaneous Wiltshire collections of Aubrey, preserved in the library of the Ashmolean Museum, Oxford. Part of them are also to be found in his "Naturall History of Wiltshire," a MS. in the library of the Royal Society, p. 77, &c.

In the yeare 1633-4, soone after I had entered into my grammar at the Latin Schoole at Yatton Keynel, our curate Mr Hart was annoy'd one night by these elves or fayries. Comming over the downes, it being neere darke, and approaching one of the faiery dances, as the common people call them in these parts, viz. the greene circles made by those sprites on the grasse, he all at once sawe an innumerable quantitie of pigmies or very small people dancing rounde and rounde, and singing, and making all maner of small odd noyses. He, being very greatly amaz'd, and yet not being able, as he sayes, to run away from them, being, as he supposes, kept there in a kinde of enchantment, they no sooner perceave him but they surround him on all sides, and what betwixt feare and amazement, he fell down scarcely knowing what he did; and thereupon these little creatures pinch'd him all over, and made a sorte of quick humming noyse all the time; but at length they left him, and when the sun rose, he found himself exactly in the midst of one of these faiery dances. This relation I had from him myselfe, a few days after he was so tormented; but when I and my bedfellow Stump (?) wente soon afterwards at night time to the dances on the downes, we sawe none of the elves or fairies. But indeede it is saide they seldom appeare to any persons who go to seeke for them.

As to these circles, I presume they are generated from the breathing out of a fertile subteraneous vapour, which comes from a kinde of conical concave, and endeavours to get out at a narrow passage at the top, which forces it to make another cone inversely situated to the other, the top of which is the green circle. Every tobacco-taker knowes that 'tis no strange thing for a circle of smoake to be whifft out of the bowle of the pipe, but 'tis donne by chance. If you digge under the turfe of this circle, you will find at the rootes of the grasse a hoare or mouldinesse. But as there are fertile streames, so contrary-wise there are noxious ones which proceed from some mineralls, iron, &c., which also, as the others, *cæteris paribus*, appear in a circular forme. *Mem.* that pidgeon's dung and nitre, steeped in water, will make the fayry circles; it draws to it the nitre of the aire, and will never weare out.

Let me not omitt a tradition which I had many yeares since, when I was a boy, from my great uncles and my father's bayly, who were then old men; that in the harvest time, in one of the great fields at

Warminster, at the very time of the fight at Bosworth field in Leicestershire between King Richard III. and Henry VII., there was one of the parish (I have forgott whether he was not a naturall fool) who took two wheat-sheaves, one in one hand, and the other in the other hand, and sayed that the two armies were ingag'd. He play'd with the sheaves, crying with some intervalls, "Now for Richard!" "Now for Henry!" At last lets fall Richard, and cried, "Now for King Henry, Richard is slain!" And this action of his did agree with the very time, day, and houre. Query, might not this boy have been one changed by the fairies? The vulgar call them changlings.

XXXI.

Fairy Tales.

---*o*---

TALE I.

ELIDOR, OR THE GOLDEN BALL.

THERE befell in the parts of Gower and Swansey, in Wales, a thing not unworthy to be remembered, which Elidor, the priest, most firmly related to have happened to him. For when he already reckoned the twelfth year of puerile innocence, (because, as Solomon saith, the root of learning is bitter and the fruit sweet,) the boy, addicted to letters, that he might avoid discipline, and the frequent stripes of his preceptor, hid himself, a fugitive in the hollow bank of a certain river: and, when he had now lurked there two days, continually fasting, there appeared to him two little men, as it were of pygmy stature, saying: If thou wilt come with us, we will lead thee into a land full of sports and delights: he assenting, and rising up followed them, leading the way, through a road at first subterraneous and dark, into a most beautiful country, very much embellished with rivers and meads, woods and plains, nevertheless obscure, and not brightened with the open light of the sun. All the days there were as if cloudy, and the nights most hideous by the absence of moon and stars. The boy was brought to the king and presented to him before the court of the realm, and when he had a long time beheld him, with the admiration of all, he, at length, recommending, assigned him to his son, a boy he had. Now the men were of very small stature, but, for their size, very well shaped : all yellow-haired, and with luxuriant locks flowing down their shoulders in the manner of a woman. They had horses fit for their own height, with greyhounds conformable in size. They ate neither flesh nor fish, using, for the most part milky food, and things made with saffron in the manner of a pudding. There were no oaths among them ; for they detested nothing so much as lies. As often as they returned from the upper hemisphere, they reproached our ambitions, infidelities, and inconstancies. There was no religious worship among them openly ; being only, it seemed, chief lovers and worshippers of truth. Now the boy was wont frequently to ascend to our hemisphere, sometimes by the way in which he had come, sometimes by another ; at first with others, and afterward by himself. He only committed himself to his mother, declaring to her the mode of the country, and the nature and condition of the people. Admonished therefore, by his mother, that he would sometimes bring to her a present of the gold with which that country abounded, the golden ball with which the king's son had been accustomed to play, snatching it from him in the game, he, speedily hastening, carried to his mother, by the usual way ; and when he had now come to his father's house, yet not without a train

z

of that people, he hastened to enter, his foot stuck in
the threshold, and so, falling within the house, where
his mother was sitting, two pygmies following his footstep, seized the ball which had fallen out of his hand,
and, in going out, threw spit, contempt and derision
upon the boy.   He, verily, rising, and come to himself, was confounded with the wonderful shame of the
deed, and, when, very much cursing and detesting the
counsels of his mother, he prepared to return by the
road he had been accustomed to, he came to the
descent of the river, and subterraneous passage, no
entrance appeared to him.[1]

***

TALE II.

THE SILVER CUP.

THERE is a village a few miles distant from the eastern
sea, near which those famous waters, they vulgarly call
Gipse, burst out of the earth with a numerous sprink-
ling.   From this village a certain rustic, having gone
to salute a friend dwelling in a neighbouring place,
returned, late at night, not perfectly sober : and,
behold! from the next hill, which I have very often
seen, and is two or three furlongs from the village,
he heard the voices of persons singing, and, as it were,
festively banqueting.   Wondering who, in that place,
should break the silence of the unseasonable night,
he was willing to inspect this matter more curiously,
and seeing, in the side of the hill, a gate open, he
approached and looked within, and saw a house,
spacious and lightsome, and filled with people sitting,
as well men as women, as it were at a solemn feast.

---

[1] Girald Barry, *Itinerarium Cambriæ, à Pouelo, Londini,*
1585, 8vo, p. 129.

Now one of those ministering beholding a man standing at the door, offered to him the cup: which he,
having accepted, would not, discreetly, drink of; but,
pouring out the contents, and retaining the cup, hastily
departed; and a tumult being made in the feast, for
the taking away of the vessel, and the guests pursuing
him, he escaped by the fleetness of the horse on which
he was carried, and betook himself into his village
with his notable booty.   Finally, this vessel, of unknown material, and unusual form, was offered to
Henry king of the English for a great reward, and,
afterward being delivered to the queen's brother,
David, that is, king of the Scots, was preserved for a
great many years in the treasury of Scotland; and
before some years (as we know from veracious
relation) was resigned by William king of the Scots to
Henry the second, who desired to see it.[1]

TALE III.

THE ANTIPODES.

In Great Britain is a castle situate among certain
mountains to which the people have given the name
of *Bech.*   Its wall is hardly assailable, and in the
mountain the cavern of a hole, which as a pipe of
the winds, most powerfully belches for the time.
Whence so great a wind proceeds, people are astonished; and among a great many things, which
are carried about there with admiration, I received
from the most religious man, Robert prior of Renil-
dewlt, thence sprung, that when a certain noble
man William Peverell, possessed the aforesaid castle,

---

[1] W. of Newbury, *Historia rerum Anglicarum*, edit. Hearne,
p. 95.   See *Tam o' Shanter*, in Burns's *Poems.*

with the adjacent barony, a man, truly, brave and powerful, and abounding in divers animals : upon a certain day his swineherd, as he was negligent about the service committed to him, lost a pregnant sow, of the kind of those which bring forth pigs, rather fruitful. Fearing, therefore, by reason of the loss the bitter words of the lord's vicar, he thought within himself, if, perchance, by any accident that sow had entered the famous hole of Bech, but until those times inscrutable. He questioned, in his mind, how he should make himself the thorough-searcher of the secret place. He entered the cavern in a time then tranquil from all wind, and when he had proceeded a long way, at length he came by chance from darkness into a lucid place, opening into a spacious plain of fields. Having entered the land widely cultivated, he found persons collecting mature fruits, and, among the standing corn, he recognized the sow, which had multiplied from herself sucking pigs. Then the swineherd, being astonished, and rejoicing at his "recovered" loss, received the sow, and dismissed with joy, led her to the herd of swine.[1]

TALE IV.

THE CUP-BEARER.

THERE was in the county of Gloucester a hunting forest plentiful in boars, harts, and all venison according to the manner of the English. In this woody forest was a hillock, rising into a top to the stature of a man, into which knights and other hun-

---

[1] Gervase of Tilbury, *Otia imperialia, apud Scriptores rerum Brunsvicensium, à* Leibnitz, I. 975.

ters were accustomed to ascend, when, fatigued with
heat and thirst they sought some remedy of their
urgency. But some one, alone, his companions,
from the condition of the place and business, being
left at a distance, ascended : and when alone, as
if speaking to another, he said, I thirst ; immediately, on the sudden, by his side, stood a cup-
bearer, with a cheerful countenance, and a stretched-
out hand, bearing a great horn, adorned with gold
and precious stones, as the manner is among the
most ancient English, instead of a cup, wherein
was presented nectar of an unknown but most
sweet taste : which being drunk, all the heat and
lassitude of his "parched" body fled, so that he
would not believe that he was fatigued, but willed
to take fatigue. But, also, the nectar being taken,
the attendant held out a very clean towel in order
to dry his lips : and, his service being accomplished
he disappeared, nor waited a reward for his kind-
ness, or conversation for enquiry. This, in many
revolutions of ancient time, was talked of among
the oldest, as a thing famous and familiar. Finally,
a certain hunter, a knight, for the sake of hunting
came to the said place, and drink being requested,
and the horn taken, he did not (as it was of custom and urbanity) restore it to the cup-bearer, but
retained it to his own use. But the illustrious lord,
and earl of Gloucester,[1] the truth of the matter
being discovered, condemned the robber, and gave
the horn to the elder Henry king of the English,
that he might not be reputed to have been the
favourer of so great a crime, if he had deposited,
in his treasury, another's rapine of domestic pro-
perty.[2]

---

[1] Robert, that is, the natural son of Henry I.
[2] Gervase of Tilbury, D. 3.

TALE V.

HUTGIN.

IN these times, a certain malignant spirit, in the diocese of Hildesheim, for a long time, appeared visibly to many, in a rustic habit, his head covered with a hood, whence, also, vulgarly the peasants called him hooded, that is, *ein Hedeckin*, in the Saxon tongue. This spirit, Hutgin, did many marvels, and delighted to be with men, speaking, questioning, and answering familiarly to all, appearing, sometimes visibly, sometimes invisibly. He hurt no man, not being before hurt; but mindful of injury or derision, he bestowed, in his turn, shame to those bestowing it on himself. When Burcard count of Luc had been killed by count Herman of Winsenburg, and the county of Winsenburg seemed exposed to robbery, the aforesaid spirit, coming to Bernard bishop of Hildesheim, sleeping in his bed, waked him, saying: " Rise, o thou bald fellow, convoke thy army, because the county of Winsenburg, being vacant and desolate on account of homicide, thou wilt easily obtain the government." The bishop, rising, warned his knights, invaded, and obtained, the county, which to the church of Hildesheim, with the consent of the emperor, united in perpetuity. The same spirit, likewise, without being asked, oftentimes used to advise him in many dangers. Frequently appearing in the court of the same bishop, he used to serve the cooks for the most part with sufficient diligence, and to mingle frequent discourses with them : whence, when now, from custom, made familiar, he was feared by no man, a certain boy serving in the kitchen, began to despise, laugh to scorn, and "assail" him with bitter taunts, and, as often as he could, poured upon him the filth of the kitchen. He had often requested the master of the kitchen, that the boy should abstain from his injuries; threatening, at length, to avenge them; he was scoffed at by him, saying, "Thou art a spirit, and dost thou fear a boy?" To whom the dæmon replied: "Because thou art a boy thou despisest to amend at my petition, I, how much I fear that, will, after a few days, shew thee." These things said, the spirit departed in a passion. Not long after, when, on a certain day, after vespers, the boy, alone in the kitchen, being fatigued, slept, the spirit came, and "having" him suffocated, cut in pieces, and, being put into the pot, began to cook him at the fire: which when the master of the kitchen had perceived, he began to curse the spirit; who, being irritated, the roast meat puts on spits at the fire for the next day's dinner of the bishops and courtiers, two horrible toads being thereupon squeezed, besprinkled with the poison and blood of those animals: and being again affected with bitter taunts, he precipitated him from on high, by the bridge, into a deep hole. Upon the walls of the city and castle diligently going round, in the night-time, he forced all the guards to watch. A certain man, about to go a long way, when he had an unchaste wife, as if by way of joke, said to the spirit Hutgin: "Good fellow, I commend to thee my wife till I shall return, see thou guard her," and when, the husband being absent, the woman would employ her portion in adultery, and tempted, successfully, many lovers, so that this spirit, invisibly, always interposed in the midst, and the men being thrown from the bed upon the ground, permitted no one to arrive even at the touch of that woman. So the woman, every night, and almost every hour, in the whole time, always introduced new lovers: whom, nevertheless, the spirit, as soon as they attempted to touch her, cast far off upon the ground. At length, the husband returning, and being yet a long way from the house, the commissary spirit, joyful, met him, saying : " Thy arrival is very pleasing to me, by which I may be freed from the so unquiet labour, which thou hast imposed upon me." The husband said : "What, therefore, art thou ? " " I," he said, "am Hutgin, to whom, some time ago, about to depart, thou committedst thy wife to be kept. Behold, I have guarded her for thee, although with very great and continual labour, safe from adultery. But I pray thee, that thou wilt not henceforth deliver her to me to be guarded. For I had rather guard the hogs of all Saxony, than thy one very wife, she has tried, with so great frauds to circumvent me, and in so many ways, to abuse her body." This spirit did, likewise, innumerable other miracles, as well serious, as ridiculous, all which cannot be easily written, nor if they were written, would they find the belief of many. A certain idiot and simple man, a clerk, being cited to the synod, by a ring made of laurel-leaves, certain others being added, they report him, in a short time, to have rendered the most learned. At length, by the aforesaid bishop Bernard being turned out of doors by ecclesiastical censures, he was compelled to depart from the province.[1]

TALE VI.

THE PIED PIPER.

THERE came into the town of Hamel, in the countrey of Brunswyc [in Saxony], an od kynd of compagnion,

---

[1] Trithemius, *apud Wierum, De præstigiis dæmonum, Basilea,* 1583, 4to, p. 114.

who, for the fantastical cote which hee wore, beeing wrought with sundry colours, was called the pyed pyper; for a pyper hee was, besydes his other qualities. This fellow forsooth, offred the townsmen, for a certain somme of mony, to rid the town of all the rattes that were in it (for, at that time, the burgers were with that vermin greatly annoyed). The accord, in fyne, beeing made, the pyed pyper, with a shril pype, went pyping through the streets, and foorthwith the rattes came all running out of the howses in great numbers after him; all which hee led unto the river of Weaser, and therein drowned them. This donne, and no one rat more perceaved to bee left in the town, he afterward came to demaund his reward, according to his bargain: but beeing told that the bargain was not made with him in good earnest, to wit, with an opinion that ever hee could bee able to do such a feat, they cared not what they accorded unto, when they imagyned it could never be deserved, and so never to bee demaunded: but, neverthelesse, seeing he had donne such an unlykely thing in deed, they were content to give him a good reward, and so offred him far lesse than he lookt for; but hee, therewith discontented, said he would have his ful recompence, according to his bargain; but they utterly denying to give it him, hee threatened them with revenge; they bad him do his wurst: whereupon he betakes him again to his pype, and, going through the streets as before, was followed of a number of boyes out at one of the gates of the citie; and, coming to a litle hil, there opened in the syde thereof a wyde hole, into the which himself and all the children, beeing in number one hundredth and thirty, did enter; and beeing entred, the hil closed up again, and became as before. A boy, that, beeing lame, and came somwhat lagging behynd the rest, seeing this that

hapned, returned presently back, and told what hee
had seen. Foorthwith began great lamentation
among the parents for their children, and men were
sent out with all dilligence, both by land and by
water, to enquyre yf ought could bee heard of them :
but with all the enquyrie they could possibly use,
nothing more then is aforesaid could of them bee
understood. In memorie whereof it was then or-
dayned, That from thence-foorth no drum, pype, or
other instrument should bee sounded in the street
leading to the gate through which they had passed ;
nor no osterie to bee there holden : and it was also
established, that, from that tyme forward, in all
publyke wrytings that should bee made in that town,
after the date therein set down of the yeare of our
lord, the date of the yeare of the going foorth of their
children should bee added ; the which they have
accordingly eversince continued : and thisgreatwonder
hapned on the 22. day of July, in the year of our lord
one thowsand three hundreth, seaventie and six.[1]

TALE VII.

THE SHEPHERD'S DREAM.

A SHEPHEARD, whilst his flock did feede,
    him in his cloke did wrap,
Bids Patch his dog stand sentenell,
    both to secure a nap,
And, lest his bagpipe, sheephooke, skrip,
    and bottell (most his wealth)
By vagrants (more then, many now)
    might suffer of their stealth.

---

[1] Verstègan's *Restitution of decayed intelligence :* Antwerp,
1605, 4to, p. 85.

As he twixt sleepe and waking lay,
    against a greene bank's side,
A round of Fairie-elves, and Larrs
    of other kind, he spide :
Who, in their dancing, him so charm'd,
    that though he wakt he slept,
Now pincht they him, antickt about,
    and on, and off him lept.
Mongst them, of bigger bulke and voyce,
    a bare-breecht goblin was,
That at their gamboles laughed, like
    the braying of an asse.
At once of shepherd's bagpipe (for
    they also used it)
Was husht, and round about him they,
    as if in councell, sit.
Upon whose face the breechlesse Larr
    Did set his buttocks bare,
Bespeaking thus his beau-compeers,
    Like Caiphas in his chaire.
Poore Robin Good-fellow, sweet elfs,
    much thanks you for this glee,
Since last I came into this land,
    a raritie to see :
When nunnes, monks, friers, and votaries,
    were here of every sort,
We were accustomed, ye wot,
    to this and merrier sport.
Wo worth (may our great Pan, and we
    his puples say) that frier,
That by revealing Christ obscur'd
    to Christ did soules retire.
For since great Pan's great vicar on
    the earth was disobaid
In England, I, beyond the seas,
    A mal-content have staid.

Whence, by a brute of pouder that
    should blow to heaven or hell
The protestants, I hither came
    where all I found too well :
And in the catholick maine cause,
    small hope or rather none ;
No sooner, therefore was I come,
    but that I wisht me gone,
Was then a merry world with us,
    when Mary wore the crowne,
And holy-water-sprinkle was
    beleevd to put us downe.
Ho, ho, ho, ho, needs must I laugh,
    such fooleries to name :
And at my crummed mess of milke,
    each night, from maid or dame
To do their chares, as they supposd,
    when in their deadest sleepe
I puld them out their beds, and made
    themselves their houses sweepe.
How clatterd I amongst their pots
    and pans, as dreamed they !
My *hempen hampen* sentence,[1] when
    some tender foole would lay
Me shirt or slop, them greeved, for
    I then would go away.

---

[1] " Indeed," says Reginald Scott, " your grandam's maides were
woont to set a boll of milke before him [*Incubus*] and his
cousine Robin Good-fellow, for grinding of malt or mustard,
and sweeping the house at midnight : and you have also heard
that he would chafe exceedingly, if the maid or the good-wife
of the house, having compassion on his nakednes, laid anie
clothes for him beesides his messe of white bread and milke,
which was his standing fee. For in that case he saith, what
have we here?

Hemton hamten,
Here will I never more tread nor stampen."
Discoverie of witchcraf !] . 8.

Yee fairies too made mothers, if
    weake faith, to sweare that ye
Into their beds did foist your babes,
    and theirs exchang'd to be.
When yee (that elvish manners did
    from elvish shapes observe)
By pinching her, that beat that child,
    made child and mother swerve,
This in that erd beliefe, That, not
    corrected, bad that grew.
Thus yee, I, pope, and cloysterers,
    all in one teame then drew.
But all things have gone crosse with us
    since here the gospell shind,
Nor helps it aught that she that it
    unclowded is inshrind.[1]
Well, though our Romish exorcists
    and regulars be outed,
No lesse hypocrisie mongst some
    their contraries is doubted :
And may they so persever and
    so perish Robin prayes :
But too too zealous people are
    too many cloy my wayes.
For that this realme is in the right,
    Rome in the wrong for loore,
I must confesse, though much is else
    as faultie as before.
To farmers came I, that, at least,
    their lofe and cheese once freed,
For all would eate, but found themselves
    the parings now to need :
So do their landlords rack their rents :
    though in the mannor-place

Queen Elizabeth.

Scarce smoakt a chimney : yet did smoke
    perplex me in strange cace.
I saw the chimneys cleerd of fire,
    where neverthelesse it smokt
So bitterly, as one not used
    to like, it might have chokt.
But when I saw it did proceed
    from nostrels,[1] and from throtes
Of ladies, lords, and sillie groomes,
    not burning skins nor cotes,
Great Belsabub, thought I, can all
    spit fier as well as thine ?
Or where am I ? it cannot be
    under the torred line.
My fellow *Incubus* (who heere
    still residence did keepe,
Witnes so many dadlesse babes
    begot on girles asleepe [2])
Did put me by that feare, and said
    it was an Indian weede,
That feum'd away more wealth than would
    a many thousands feed.
Freed of that feare, the novelty
    of cooches scath'd me so,
As from their drifts and cluttering[3]
    I knew not where to go.

---

[1] A somewhat amusing satire on the use of tobacco, which had only been recently introduced, and was received with much prejudice.

[2] Gervase of Tilbury says, " *Vidimus quosdam dæmones tanto zelo mulieres amare, quod ad inaudita prorumpunt ludibria, et eum ad concubitum earum accedunt mirâ mole eas opprimunt, nec ab aliis videntur.*"—Otia imperialia, D. i. c. 17.

[3] In 1601 a bill was introduced into Parliament "to restrain the excessive use of coaches."

These also worke, quoth *Incubus*,
   to our availe, for why?
They tend to idle pride, and to
   inhospitalitie.
With that I, comforted, did then
   peepe into every one,
And of mine old acquaintances
   spide many a country Jone,
Whose fathers drove the dung-cart, though
   the daughters now will none.
I knew when prelates, and the peeres
   had faire attendance on,
By gentlemen and yeomandrie,
   but that faire world is gone :
For most, like Jehu, hurrie with
   pedanties two or three,
Yet all go downe the winde, save those
   that hospitalious bee.
Great'st ladies with their women, on
   their palfries mounted faire
Rode through the streets, well waited on,
   Their artless faces bare,
Which now in coches scorne to be,
   salued of the aire.
I knew when men-judicial rode
   on sober mules, whereby
They might of suters, these, and they,
   aske, answere, and replie.
I knew when more was thriv'd abroad
   by war than now by peace,
And English feared were they be frumpt,
   since hostile tearmes did cease ;
But by occasion, all things are
   produced, be, decrease.
Times were when practize also preacht,
   and well-said was well-done,
When courtiers cleerd the old before
   they on the new would run.

When no judiciall place was bought,
   lest justice might be sould,
When quirts, nor quillets, overthrew,
   or long did causes hold,
When lawyers more deservd their fees,
   and fatted lesse with gold.
When to the fifteenth psalme, sometimes
   had citizens recourse,
When lords of farmers, farmers of
   the poore had more remorse.
When Povertie had Patience more;
   when none, as some of late,
Illiterate, ridiculous,
   might on the altar wate.
When canons, rubrick, liturgie,
   and discipline throughout
One shiftlesse practice had, not to
   indifferencie a flout.
More than be convocations now,
   Diocessors were stout.
Although in clarks pluralities
   were tolerated then
Of lemmens (livings should I say)
   are now of clargie-men.
Pluralitie that huddle, have
   also their brace of wives;
But all the better, all that while
   hell's heer-employment thrives.
That thus and worse hold, and increase,
   sith Rome may not returne,
Pray, fairies, graunt, infernals, that
   in fire of envie burne.
I have, faire fairie-elves, besides
   large catalogue of sinne,
Observed in this land, in this
   short time I heere have bin,
The which at my departure, when
   Elizabeth first raign'd,

Were not in beeing, or were then
    religiously refraind.
Howbeit, hence for Ireland at
    the least I must transfreat ;
Where Rome hath roome there riot I ;
    somes faith is heere too great.
Yet largelier than most statesmen know,
    heere could I sport long while,
Insociable is not, ywis,
    for catholics this ile.
Suppose the shepheard all this while
    to have a troubled sleepe :
Well might he heare the preachment, by
    the pulpit could not peepe :
Till merrie Robin, gerding out
    a scape or twaine, did rise,
And, with the wind therof, might seeme,
    were cleered the shepherd's eyes ;
Who glad he was delivered so
    of them, then vanisht cleene,
Told some, I know not whom, what ye
    have heard was said and seene.[1]

TALE VIII.

THE FAIRY-PRINCE.

THERE lived in Spain a notable and beautiful
virgin, but far more famous for excellence at her
needle, insomuch that happy did the courtier think
himself, who could wear the smallest piece of her
work, though at a price almost invaluable. It happened one day, as this admirable seamstress sate

---

[1] Warner's *Albions England*, London, 1612, 4to, chap. 91.

working in her garden, that, casting aside her eyes
on some fair flower or tree, she saw, as she thought,
a little gentleman, yet one that shewed great nobility by his clothing, come riding toward her from
behind a bed of flowers; thus surprised how any
body should come into her garden, but much more
at the stature of the person, who, as he was on
horseback, exceeded not a foot's length in height,
she had reason to suspect that her eyes deceived
her.　But the gallant, spurring his horse up the
garden made it not long, though his horse was
little, before he came to see her : then greeting the
lady in a most decent manner, after some compliments passed, he acquaints her with the cause of
his bold arrival ; that, forasmuch as he was a prince
amongst the fairies, and did intend to celebrate his
marriage on such a day, he desired she would work
points for him and his princess against the time he
appointed.　The lady consented to his demands, and
he took his leave ; but whether the multitude of
business caused the lady to forget her promise, or the
strangeness of the thing made her neglect the work,
thinking her sight to have been deceived, I know
not ; yet so it fell out, that, when the appointed time
came, the work was not ready.　The hour wherein
she had promised the fairy-prince some fruits of her
needle, happened to be one day as she was at dinner
with many noble persons, having quite forgot her
promise ; when on a sudden, casting her eye to the
door, she saw an infinite train of fairies come in : so
that fixing her eyes on them, and remembering how
she [had] neglected her promise, she sate as one
amazed, and astonished the whole company.　But
at last, the train had mounted upon the table, and,
as they were prancing on their horses round the brims
of a large dish of white-broth, an officer that seemed

too busy in making way before them, fell into the dish,
which caused the lady to burst into a sudden fit of
laughter, and thereby to recover her senses.   When
the whole fairy company was come upon the table,
that the brims of every dish seemed filled with little
horsemen, she saw the prince coming toward her,
[who] hearing she had not done what she promised,
seemed to go away displeased.   The lady presently
fell into a fit of melancholy, and, being asked by her
friends the cause of these alterations and astonishments, related the whole matter ; but, notwithstanding all their consolations, pined away, and died not
long after.[1]

TALE IX.

THE SOW AND PIGS.

'TIS reported of a country girl, being sent out daily
by her mother to look to a sow that was then big
with pigs, that the sow always strayed out of the girl's
sight, and yet always came safe home at night ; this
the maid often observing, resolved to watch her more
narrowly, and followed her one day closely, till they
both came to a fair green valley, where was laid a
large bason full of milk and white bread.   The sow,
having eaten her mess, returned home, and that night
pigged eleven pigs.   The good wife, rising early the
next morning to look to her beast, found on the
threshold of the sty ten half-crowns, and, entering in,
saw but one pig ; judging by these things, that the
fairies had fed her sow, and bought her pigs.[2]

---

[1] *Pleasant treatise of witches, &c.*   London, 1673, p. 64.
[2] *Ibid.* p. 62.

TALE X.

THE CHANGELING.

A CERTAIN woman having put out her child to nurse
in the country, found, when she came to take it home,
that its form was so much altered that she scarce
knew it; nevertheless not knowing what time might
do, took it home for her own.   But, when, after some
years, it could neither speak nor go, the poor woman
was "fain" to carry it, with much trouble, in her
arms ; and, one day, a poor man coming to the door,
[said] God bless you, mistress, and your poor child,
be pleased to bestow something on a poor man.   Ah !
this child, replied she, is the cause of all my sorrow ;
and related what had happened; adding, moreover,
that she thought it was changed, and none of her
child.   The old man, whom years had rendered more
prudent in such matters, told her that to find out the
truth, she should make a clear fire, sweep the hearth
very clean, and place the child fast in his chair, that
he might not fall before it ; then break a dozen eggs,
and place the four and twenty half-shells before it ;
then go out, and listen at the door, for if the child
spoke, it was certainly a changeling ; and then she
should carry it out, and leave it on the dunghill to
cry, and not to pity it, till she heard its voice no
more.   The woman, having done all things according to these words, heard the child say, Seven years
old was I, before I came to the nurse, and four
years have I lived since, and never saw so many
milk-pans before.   So the woman took it up, and
left it upon the dunghill to cry, and not to be
pitied, till at last she thought the voice went up

into the air ; and, coming out, found, there in the
stead, her own natural and well-favoured child.[1]

TALE XI.

THE WHITE POWDER.

THERE was a poor illiterate man in Germany, who,
being apprehended for suspicion of witchcraft, and
examined by a judge, told him, That one night,
before day was gone, as he was going home from
his labour, being very sad and full of heavy thoughts,
not knowing how to get meat and drink for his wife
and children, he met a fair woman, in fine clothes,
who asked him why he was so sad, and he told her
that it was by reason of his poverty, to which she said,
that, if he would follow her counsel, she would help
him to that which would serve to get him a good
living ; to which he said he would consent with all
his heart, so it were not by unlawful ways : she told
him that it should not be by any such ways, but by
doing of good, and curing of sick people ; and so,
warning him, strictly, to meet her there, the next
night, at the same time, she departed from him, and
he went home.   The next night, at the time appointed,
he duly waited, and she (according to promise) came
and told him it was well that he came so duly, otherwise he had missed of that benefit that she intended
to do unto him, and so bade him follow her, and not
be afraid.   Thereupon she led him to a little hill, and
came to a fair hall, wherein was a queen sitting in
great state, and many people about her, and the
gentlewoman that brought him presented him to the

---

[1] *Ibid.* p. 62.

queen, and she said, he was welcome, and bid the gentlewoman give him some of the white powder, and teach him how to use it; which she did, and gave him a little wood-box full of the white powder, and bad him give two or three grains of it to any that were sick, and it would heal them, and so she brought him forth of the hill, and so they parted. Being asked by the judge, whether the place within the hill, which he called a hall, were light or dark, he answered, "Indifferent, as it is with us in the twilight;" and, being asked how he got more powder, he said, "When he wanted he went to that hill and knocked three times, and said every time, I am coming, I am coming;" whereupon it opened, and he, going in, was conducted by the aforesaid woman to the queen, and so had more powder given him.[1]

TALE XII.

THE MAUTHE DOOG.

THE Manks say, that an apparition, called in their language, the *Mauthe doog*, in the shape of a large spaniel, with curled shaggy hair, was used to haunt Peel-castle; and has been frequently seen in every room, but particularly in the guard-chamber, where, as soon as candles were lighted, it came and lay down before the fire, in the presence of all the soldiers, who, at length, by being so much accustomed to the sight of it, lost great part of the terror they were seized with at its first appearance. They still, however, retained a certain awe, as believing it was an evil spirit, which

---

[1] Hotham's epistle to the *Mysterium magnum* of Jacob Behmen, upon *Genesis*, as quoted in Webster's *Displaying of supposed witchcraft*: London, 1677, fo. p. 300.

only awaited permission to do them hurt, and, for
that reason, forbore swearing and all prophane discourse while in its company. But though they
endured the shock of such a guest when al together
in a body, none cared to be left alone with it; it
being the custom, therefore, for one of the soldiers to
lock the gates of the castle, at a certain hour, and
carry them to the captain, to whose apartment the
way led through a church; they agreed among themselves, that whoever was to succeed the ensuing night,
his fellow in this errand should accompany him that
went first, and, by this means, no man would be
exposed singly to the danger: for the *Mauthe Doog*,
was always seen to come from that passage at the
close of the day, and return to it again as soon as the
morning dawned, which made them look to this place
as its peculiar residence.

One night a fellow, being drunk, and by the
strength of the liquor, rendered more daring than
ordinary, laughed at the simplicity of his companions,
and though it was not his turn to go with the keys,
would needs take that office upon him to testify his
courage. All the soldiers endeavoured to dissuade
him, but the more they said, the more resolute he
seemed, and swore that he desired nothing more than
that [the] *Mauthe doog* would follow him as it
had done the others, for he would try if it were dog
or devil. After having talked in a very reprobate
manner for some time, he snatched up the keys, and
went out of the guard-room. In some time after his
departure a great noise was heard, but nobody had
the boldness to see what occasioned it, till the adven-
turer returning, they demanded the knowledge of
him; but as loud and noisy as he had been at leaving
them, he was now become sober and silent enough;
and though all the time he lived, which was three

days, he was entreated by all who came near him, either to speak, or, if he could not do that, to make some signs, by which they might understand what had happened to him, yet nothing intelligible could be got from him, only, that, by the distortion of his limbs and features, it might be guessed that he died in agonies more than is common to a natural death.

The *Mauthe Doog* was, however, never seen after in the castle, nor would any one attempt to go through that passage, for which reason it was closed up, and another way made. This accident happened about threescore years since, and I HEARD IT ATTESTED by several, but especially, BY AN OLD SOLDIER, who assured me, HE HAD SEEN IT OFTENER THAN HE HAD THEN HAIRS ON HIS HEAD.[1]

TALE XIII.

A FAIRY FEAST.

A MANKS-MAN, who had been led by invisible musicians for several miles together; and, not being able to resist the harmony, followed till it conducted him to a large common, where was a great number of little people sitting round a table, and eating and drinking in a very jovial manner. Among them were some faces which he thought he had formerly seen, but forbore taking any notice [of them] or they of him, till the little people offered him drink, one of them, whose features seemed not unknown to him, plucked him by the coat, and forbad him, whatever he did, to taste anything he saw before him; for, if

---

[1] Waldron's *History of the Isle of Man.* 2d edition: London, 1744, 8vo, p. 23.

you do, added he, you will be as I am, and return no
more to your family. The poor man was much
affrighted, but resolved to obey the injunction :
accordingly a large silver cup, filled with some sort of
liquor, being put into his hand, he found an opportunity to throw what it contained on the ground.
Soon after, the music ceasing, all the company disappeared, leaving the cup in his hand ; and he returned
home, though much wearied and fatigued. He went
the next day, and communicated to the minister of
the parish all that had happened, and asked his advice
how he should dispose of the cup ; to which the
parson replied he could not do better than to devote
it to the service of the church ; and this very cup,
they say, is that which is now used for the consecrated
wine in Kirk-Merlugh.[1]

TALE XIV.

THE UNFORTUNATE FIDDLER.

A FIDDLER, in the Isle of Man, having agreed with a
person, who was a stranger, for so much money, to
play to some company he should bring him to, all
the twelve days of Christmas, and received earnest
for it, saw his new master vanish into the earth the
moment he had made the bargain. Nothing could
be more terrified than was the poor fiddler ; he found
he had entered into the devil's service, and looked on
himself as already damned ; but, having recourse to a
clergyman, he received some hope : he ordered him,
however, as he had taken earnest, to go when he
should be called ; but that, whatever tunes should be

---

[1] Waldron, *as before*, p. 54. This tale, however, seems no
other than a slight alteration of *The silver cup*, already inserted.

called for, to play none but psalms. On the day
appointed, the same person appeared, with whom he
went, though with what inward reluctance 'tis easy to
guess; but, punctually obeying the minister's direc-
tions, the company to whom he played were so angry,
that they all vanished at once, leaving him at the top
of a high hill, and so bruised and hurt, though he was
not sensible when, or from what hand, he received
the blows, that he got not home without the utmost
difficulty.[1]

TALE XV.

THE FAIRY-ELF.

I was prevailed upon, says Waldron, to go and see a
child, who, they told me, was one of these changelings,
and, indeed, must own, was not a little surprised, as
well as shocked, at the sight: nothing under heaven
could have a more beautiful face; but, though between
five and six years old, and seeming healthy, he was so
far from being able to walk or stand, that he could not
so much as move one joint; his limbs were vastly long
for his age, but smaller than an infant's of six months;
his complexion was perfectly delicate, and he had the
finest hair in the world; he never spoke or cried; eat
scarce any thing; and was very seldom seen to smile;
but, if any one called him *a fairy-elf,* he would frown,
and fix his eyes so earnestly on those who said it, as
if he would look them through. His mother, or, at
least, his supposed mother, being very poor, frequently
went out a charing, and left him a whole day together:
the neighbours, out of curiosity, have often looked in
at the window, to see how he behaved when alone;

---

[1] Waldron *as before,* p. 56.

which whenever they did, they were sure to find him
laughing, and in the utmost delight. This made
them judge that he was not without company more
pleasing to him than any mortals could be ; and what
made this conjecture seem the more reasonable, was,
that, if he were left ever so dirty, the woman, at her
return, saw him with a clean face, and his hair combed
with the utmost exactness and nicety.[1]

TALE XVI.

THE KIDNAPPERS.

A SECOND account of this nature, he says, I had from
a woman to whose offspring the fairies seemed to have
taken a particular fancy. The fourth or fifth night
after she was delivered of her first child, the family
was alarmed with a most terrible cry of fire ; on which,
every body ran out of the house to see whence it proceeded, not excepting the nurse, who, being as much
frighted as the others, made one of the number. The
poor woman lay trembling in her bed, alone, unable
to help herself, and her back being turned to the infant,
saw not that it was taken away by an invisible hand.
Those who had left her, having inquired in the neighbourhood, and finding there was no cause for the out-
cry they had heard, laughed at each other for the
mistake ; but, as they were going to reenter the house,
the poor babe lay on the threshold, and by its cries
preserved itself from being trod upon. This exceedingly amazed all that saw it ; and, the mother being
still in bed, they could ascribe no reason for finding
it there ; but having been removed by fairies, who by

---

[1] Idem, *ut supra*, p. 57.

their sudden return, had been prevented from carrying it any farther.[1]

About a year after, he says, the same woman was brought to bed of a second child, which had not been born many nights, before a great noise was heard in the house where they kept their cattle. Every body that was stirring ran to see what was the matter, believing that the cows had got loose : the nurse was as ready as the rest ; but finding all safe, and the barn-door close, immediately returned, but not so suddenly but that the new-born babe was taken out of the bed, as the former had been, and dropped, on their coming, in the middle of the entry. This was enough to prove the fairies had made a second attempt ; and the parents, sending for a minister, joined with him in thanksgiving to god, who had twice delivered their children from being taken from them.[2]

But, in the time of her third delivery, every body seemed to have forgot what had happened in the first and second, and on a noise in the cattle-house, ran out to know what had occasioned it. The nurse was the only person, excepting the woman in the straw, who stayed in the house, nor was she detained through care, or want of curiosity, but by the bonds of sleep, having drunk a little too plentifully the preceding day. The mother, who was broad awake, saw her child lifted out of the bed, and carried out of the chamber, though she could not see any person touch it ; on which she cried out as loud as she could, Nurse! nurse! my child! my child is taken away! but the old woman was too fast [asleep] to be awakened by the noise she made, and the infant was irretrievably gone. When her husband, and those who had accompanied him, returned, they found her wringing

---

[1] Idem. u. s. p. 58.   [2] Idem, u. s. p. 59.

her hands, and uttering the most piteous lamentations for the loss of her child; on which, said the husband, looking into the bed, The woman is mad; do not you see the child lies by you? On which she turned, and saw, indeed, something like a child, but far different from her own, which was a very beautiful, fat, well-featured babe; whereas, what was now in the room of it was a poor, lean, withered, deformed creature. It lay quite naked, but the clothes belonging to the child that was exchanged for it lay wrapt up altogether on the bed.

This creature lived with them near the space of nine years, in all which time it eat nothing except a few herbs, nor was ever seen to void any other excrement than water: it neither spoke, nor could stand or go, but seemed enervate in every joint; and in all its actions showed itself to be of the same nature.[1]

TALE XVII.

THE LUCK OF EDEN-HALL.

In Eden-hall, in Cumberland, the mansion of the knightly family of Musgrave for many generations, is carefully preserved, in a leathern case, an old painted drinking-glass, which, according to the tradition of the neighbourhood, was long ago left by fairies near a well not far from the house, with an inscription along with it to this effect :

> If this glass do break or fall,
> Farewell the luck of Eden-hall.

From this friendly caution the glass obtained the

----

[1] Idem, *u. s.* p. 60.

name recorded in a humorous and excellent ballad, usually, but erroneously attributed to the duke of Wharton, of a famous drinking match at this place, which begins thus :

> God prosper long from being broke,
> *The luck of Eden-hall.*

The good-fortune, however, of this ancient house was never so much endangered as by the duke himself, who, having drunk its contents, to the success and perpetuity, no doubt, of the worthy owner and his race, inadvertently dropped it, and here, most certainly, would have terminated *The luck of Eden-hall*, if the butler, who had brought the draught, and stood at his elbow, to receive the empty cup, had not happily caught it in his napkin.

TALE XVIII.

THE MOTHER, THE NURSE, AND THE FAIRY.

GIVE me a son.   The blessing sent,
Were ever parents more content ?
How partial are their doating eyes !
No child is half so fair and wise.
   Wak'd to the morning's pleasing care,
The mother rose, and sought her heir.
She saw the nurse, like one possess'd,
With wringing hands, and sobbing breast.
   Sure some disaster has befel :
Speak, nurse ; I hope the boy is well.
   Dear madam, think me not to blame ;
Invisible the fairy came :
Your precious babe is hence convey'd
And in the place a changeling laid.

Where are the father's mouth and nose?
The mother's eyes, as black as sloes?
See here, a shocking awkward creature,
That speaks a fool in every feature.
  The woman's blind, the mother cries;
I see wit sparkle in his eyes.
Lord! madam, what a squinting leer!
No doubt the fairy hath been here.
  Just as she spoke, a pigmy sprite
Pops through the key-hole swift as light;
Perch'd on the cradle's top he stands,
And thus her folly reprimands.
  Whence sprung the vain, conceited lie,
That we the world with fools supply?
What! give our sprightly race away,
For the dull helpless sons of clay!
Besides, by partial fondness shown,
Like you we doat upon our own.
Where yet was ever found a mother,
Who'd give her booby for another?
And should we change with human breed,
Well might we pass for fools indeed.[1]

TALE XIX.

THE WHIPPING OF THE LITTLE GIRL.

A GIRL, about ten years old, daughter of a woman
who lived about two miles from Ballasalli, in the Isle
of Man, being sent over the fields to the town, for a
pennyworth of tobacco for her father, was, on the top
of a mountain, surrounded by a great number of little
men, who would not suffer her to pass any farther.

---

[1] Gay's *Fables*.

Some of them said she should go with them, and accordingly laid hold of her ; but one, seeming more pitiful, desired they would let her alone ; which they refusing, there ensued a quarrel, and the person who took her part fought bravely in her defence.   This so incensed the others, that, to be revenged on her, for being the cause, two or three of them seized her, and, pulling up her clothes, whipped her heartily ; after which, it seems, they had no further power over her, and she ran home directly, telling what had befallen her, and showing prints of several small hands. Several of the towns-people went with her to the mountain, and, she conducting them to the spot, the little antagonists had gone, but had left behind them proofs (as the good woman said) that what the girl had informed them was true ; for there was a great deal of blood to be seen on the stones.[1]

TALE XX.

THE CHRISTENING.

ANOTHER woman, equally superstitious and fanciful as the former, told the author that, being great with child, and expecting every moment the good hour, as she lay awake one night in her bed, she saw seven or eight little women come into her chamber, one of whom had an infant in her arms : they were followed by a man of the same size with themselves, but in the habit of a minister.   One of them went to the pail, and, finding no water in it, cried out to the others, What must they do to christen the child ?   On which they replied, it should be done in beer.   With that,

------

[1] Waldron, *u.s.* p. 62.

the seeming parson took the child in his arms and performed the ceremony of baptism, dipping his hand in a great tub of strong-beer, which the woman had brewed the day before, to be ready for her lying-in. She told me, that they baptized the infant by the name of Joan, which made her know she was pregnant of a girl, as it proved a few days after, when she was delivered. She added also, that it was common for the fairies to make a mock-christening when any person was near her time, and that, according to what child, male or female, they brought, such should the woman bring into the world.[1]

TALE XXI.

THE HORN.

A YOUNG sailor, coming off a long voyage, though it was late at night, chose to land rather than lie another night in the vessel : being permitted to do so, he was set on shore at Duglas. It happened to be a fine moon-light night, and very dry, being a small frost ; he, therefore, forebore going into any house to refresh himself, but made the best of his way to the house of a sister he had at Kirk-Merlugh. As he was going over a pretty high mountain, he heard the noise of horses, the halloo of a huntsman, and the finest horn in the world. He was a little surprised that any body pursued those kind of sports in the night, but he had not time for much reflection before they all passed by him, so near, that he was able to count what number there was of them, which, he said, was thirteen, and that they were all dressed in green, and

---

[1] Idem, *u. s.* p. 63.

2 B

gallantly mounted. He was so well pleased with the sight, that he would gladly have followed, could he have kept pace with them; he crossed the foot-way, however, that he might see them again, which he did more than once, and lost not the sound of the horn for some miles. At length, being arrived at his sister's, he tells her the story, who, presently, clapped her hands for joy that he was come home safe; For, said she, those you saw were fairies, and 'tis well they did not take you away with them.[1]

TALE XXII.

THE SCHOOL-BOYS.

At my first coming into the island of Man, says Waldron, and hearing this sort of stories, I imputed the giving credit to them merely to the simplicity of the poor creatures who related them; but was strangely surprised, when I heard other narratives of this kind, and altogether as absurd, attested by men who passed for persons of sound judgement. Among this number, was a gentleman, my near neighbour, who affirmed, with the most solemn asseverations, that, being of my opinion, and entirely averse to the belief that any such beings were permitted to wander for the purposes related of them, he had been at last convinced by the appearance of several little figures, playing and leaping over some stones in a field, whom, a few yards distance, he imagined were school-boys, and intended when he came near enough; to reprimand, for being absent from their exercises at that time of the day; it being then, he said, between three

---

[1] Idem. *n. s.* p. 64.

and four of the clock : but, when he approached as
near as he could guess, within twenty paces, they all
immediately disappeared, though he had never taken
his eye off them from the first moment he beheld
them ; nor was there any place they could so suddenly
retreat, it being an open field, without hedge or
bush, and, as is said before, broad day.[1]

TALE XXIII.

THE BARGAIN.

ANOTHER instance, which might serve to strengthen
the credit of the last, was told to Waldron by a person
who had the reputation of the utmost integrity.   This
man being desirous of disposing of a horse he had at
that time no great occasion for, and riding him to
market for that purpose, was accosted in passing over
the mountains by a little man in a plain dress, who
asked him if he would sell his horse.   'Tis the design
I am going on, replied the person who told the story:
on which the other desired to know the price.   Eight
pounds, said he.   No, resumed the purchaser, I will
give no more than seven, which, if you will take, here
is your money.   The owner, thinking he had bid
pretty fair, agreed with him, and the money being
told out, the one dismounted, and the other got on
the back of the horse, which he had no sooner done
than both beast and rider sunk into the earth, immediately leaving the person who had made the bargain
in the utmost terror and confusion.   As soon as he
had a little recovered himself he went directly to the
parson of the parish, and related what had passed,

---

[1] Idem. *u. s.* p. 66.

desiring he would give his opinion whether he ought to make use of the money he had received or not : To which he replied that as he had made a fair bargain, and no way circumvented, nor endeavoured to circumvent the buyer, he saw no reason to believe, in case it was an evil spirit, it could have any power over him. On this assurance he went home well satisfied, and nothing afterward happened to give him any disquiet concerning this affair.[1]

TALE XXIV.

FAIRY-MUSIC.

An English gentleman, the particular friend of our author, to whom he told the story, was about passing over Duglas-bridge before it was broken down, but the tide being high he was obliged to take the river, having an excellent horse under him, and one accustomed to swim. As he was in the middle of it he heard, or imagined he heard, the finest symphony, he would not say in the world, for nothing human ever came up to it. The horse was no less sensible of the harmony than himself, and kept in an immoveable posture all the time it lasted ; which, he said, could not be less than three quarters of an hour, according to the most exact calculation he could make when he arrived at the end of his little journey, and found how long he had been coming. He who before laughed at all the stories told of fairies now became a convert, and believed as much as ever a Manks-man of them all.[2]

---

[1] Idem, *u. s.* p. 67.
[2] Waldron, as before, p. 72. A little beyond a hole in the

TALE XXV.

THE PORRIDGE-POT.

IN the vestry of Frensham church in Surrey, on the north side of the chancel, is an extraordinary great kettle or caldron, which the inhabitants say, by tradition, was brought hither by the fairies, time out of mind, from Borough-hill, about a mile hence. To this place, if any one went to borrow a yoke of oxen, money, &c., he might have it for a year or longer, so he kept his word to return it. There is a cave where some have fancied to hear music. On this Borough-hill (in the same parish) is a great stone lying along, of the length of about six feet. They went to this stone, and knocked at it, and declared what they would borrow, and when they would repay, and a voice would answer when they should come, and that they should find what they desired to borrow at that stone. This caldron, with the trivet, was borrowed here after the manner aforesaid, but not returned according to promise; and though the caldron was afterward carried to the stone it could not be received, and ever since that time, no borrowing there.[1]

---

earth, just at the foot of a mountain, about a league and a half from Barool, which they call *The Devil's den*, "is a small lake, in the midst of which is a large stone, on which formerly stood a cross : round this lake the fairies are said to celebrate the obsequies of any good person ; and I have heard many people, and those of a considerable share of understanding too, protest, that in passing that way, they have been saluted with the sound of such musick as could proceed from no earthly instruments."
—P. 137.

[1] Aubrey's Natural History of Surrey, iii. 366.

TALE XXVI.

THE WELSH FAIRIES.

ONE D. Harding, about twenty years ago, in Lan-bistan parish, saw a circle upon the snow, and in it as it were the track of hundreds of children in little pump-shoes. It was near a way said to be haunted, or where people were usually disturbed in going to and coming from Knighton-market, or at other times at night.[1]

TALE XXVII.

KENSINGTON GARDENS.

Campos, ubi Troja fuit.—VIRG.

WHERE Kensington high o'er the neighb'ring lands,
'Midst greens and sweets, a regal fabrick stands,
And sees each spring, luxuriant in her bowers,
A snow of blossoms, and a wild of flowers,
The dames of Britain oft in crowds repair
To groves and lawns, and unpolluted air.
Here, while the town in damps and darkness lies,
They breathe in sunshine, and see azure skies,
Each walk, with robes of various dies bespread,
Sees from afar a moving tulip-bed,
Where rich brocades and glossy damasks glow,
And chints, the rival of the showery bow.
Here England's daughter, darling of the land,
Sometimes, surrounded with her virgin band,
Gleams through the shades. She, towering o'er the
    rest,
Stands fairest of the fairer kind confess'd,

---

[1] From a Welsh MS.

Form'd to gain hearts, that Brunswick's cause deny'd,
And charms a people to her father's side.
Long have these groves to royal guests been known,
Nor Nassau first preferr'd them to a throne.
Ere Norman banners waved in British air,
Ere lordly Hubba with the golden hair
Pour'd in his Danes; ere elder Julius came;
Or Dardan Brutus gave our isle a name;
A prince of Albion's lineage graced the wood,
The scene of wars, and stain'd with lovers' blood.
 You, who through gazing crowds, your captive
  throng,
Throw pangs and passions, as you move along,
Turn on the left, ye fair, your radiant eyes,
Where all unlevel'd the gay garden lies:
If generous anguish for another's pains
Ere heaved your hearts, or shiver'd through your veins,
Look down attentive on the pleasing dale,
And listen to my melancholy tale.
 That hollow space, where, now, in living rows,
Line above line the yew's sad verdure grows,
Was, ere the planter's hand its beauty gave,
A common pit, a rude, unfashion'd cave;
The landscape, now so sweet, we well may praise,
But far, far sweeter in its ancient days,
Far sweeter was it, when its peopled ground
With fairy domes and dazzling towers were crown'd.
Where, in the midst, those verdant pillars spring,
Rose the proud palace of the elfin king.
For every hedge of vegetable green,
In happier years, a crowded street was seen,
Not all those leaves, that now the prospect grace,
Could match the numbers of its pigmy race.
What urged this mighty empire to its fate,
A tale of woe and wonder, I relate.

When Albion ruled the land, whose lineage came
From Neptune mingling with a mortal dame,
Their midnight pranks the sprightly fairies play'd
On every hill, and danced in every shade.
But, foes to sun-shine, most they took delight
In dells and dales, conceal'd from human sight :
There hew'd their houses in the arching rock ;
Or scoop'd the bosom of the blasted oak ;
Or heard, o'ershadow'd by some shelving hill,
The distant murmurs of the falling rill.
They, rich in pilfer'd spoils, indulged their mirth,
And pitied the huge wretched sons of earth.
Even now, 'tis said, the hinds o'erheard their strain,
And strive to view their airy forms in vain ;
They to their cells at man's approach repair,
Like the shy leveret, or the mother-hare,
The whilst poor mortals startle at the sound
Of unseen footsteps on the haunted ground.
Amid this garden, then with woods o'ergrown,
Stood the loved seat of royal Oberon.
From every region to his palace-gate
Came peers and princes of the fairy state,
Who, rank'd in council round the sacred shade,
Their monarchs will and great behests obey'd.
From Thames' fair banks, by lofty towers adorn'd,
With loads of plunder oft his chiefs return'd :[1]
Hence in proud robes, and colours bright and gay,
Shone every knight, and every lovely fay.
Whoe'er on Powell's dazzling stage display'd
Hath famed king Pepin and his court survey'd,
May guess, if old by modern things we trace,
The pomp and splendour of the fairy race.

---

[1] This is calumny ; the fairies were always liberal, never un-
just : the only thing they ever stole were *children*, as represented
below.

By magick fenced, by spells encompass'd round,
No mortal touch'd this interdicted ground ;
No mortal entered, those alone who came
Stol'n from the couch of some terrestrial dame :
For oft of babes they robb'd the matron's bed,
And left some sickly changling in their stead.
   It chanced a youth of Albion's royal blood
Was foster'd here, the wonder of the wood.
Milkah for wiles above her peers renown'd,
Deep-skill'd in charms, and many a mystick sound,
As through the regal dome she sought for prey,
Observed the infant Albion where he lay.
In mantles broider'd o'er with gorgeous pride,
And stole him from his sleeping mother's side.
   Who now but Milkah triumphs in her mind !
Ah wretched nymph ! to future evils blind.
The time shall come when thou shalt dearly pay
The theft, hard-hearted ! of that guilty day :
Thou in thy turn shall like the queen repine,
And all her sorrows doubled shall be thine :
He who adorns thy house, the lovely boy,
Who now adorns it, shall at length destroy.
   Two hundred moons in their pale course had seen
The gay-robed fairies glimmer on the green,
And Albion now had reach'd in youthful prime
To nineteen years, as mortals measure time.
Flush'd with resistless charms he fired to love
Each nymph and little dryad of the grove ;
For skilful Milkah spared not to employ
Her utmost art to rear the princely boy ;
Each supple limb she swath'd, and tender bone,
And to the elfin standard kept him down ;
She robb'd dwarf-elders of their fragrant fruit,
And fed him early with the daisy's root,
Whence through his veins the powerful juices ran,
And form'd in beauteous miniature the man.

Yet still, two inches taller than the rest,
His lofty port his human birth confess'd
A foot in height, how stately did he show !
How look superior on the crowd below !
What knight like him could toss the rushy lance?
Who move so graceful in the mazy dance?
A shape so nice, or features half so fair,
What elf could boast ? or such a flow of hair?
Bright Kenna saw, a princess born to reign,
And felt the charmer burn in every vein,
She, heiress to this empire's potent lord,
Praised like the stars, and like the moon adored,
She, whom at distance thrones and princedoms view'd,
To whom proud Oriel and Azuriel sued,
In her high palace languish'd, void of joy,
And pined in secret for a mortal boy.
     He too was smitten, and discreetly strove
By courtly deeds to gain the virgin's love ;
For her he cull'd the fairest flowers that grew,
Ere morning suns had drain'd their fragrant dew ;
He chased the hornet in its mid-day flight
And brought her glow-worms in the noon of night ;
When on ripe fruits she cast a wishing eye,
Did ever Albion think the tree too high !
He showed her where the pregnant goldfinch hung,
And the wren-mother brooding o'er her young ;
To her th' inscription on their eggs he read :
(Admire, ye clerks, the youth whom Milkah bred !)
To her he show'd each herb of virtuous juice,
Their powers distinguish'd, and described their use ;
All vain their powers, alas ! to Kenna prove,
And well sung Ovid, *There's no herb for love.*
     As when a ghost, enlarged from realms below,
Seeks its old friend to tell some secret woe,
The poor shade shivering stands, and must not break
His painful silence, till the mortal speak ;

So fared it with the little love-sick maid,
Forbid to utter what her eyes betray'd,
He saw her anguish, and reveal'd his flame,
And spared the blushes of the tongue-tyed dame.
The day would fail me, should I reckon o'er
The sighs they lavish'd and the oaths they swore ;
In words so melting, that compared with those,
The nicest courtship of terrestrial beaus
Would sound like compliments from country clowns,
To red-cheek'd sweethearts in their home-spun gowns.
 All in a lawn of many a various hue,
A bed of flowers (a fairy forest) grew ;
'Twas here, one noon, the gaudiest of the May,
The still, the secret, silent, hour of day,
Beneath a lofty tulip's ample shade
Sate the young lover, and th' immortal maid.
They thought all fairies slept, ah luckless pair !
Hid, but in vain, in the sun's noon-tide glare !
When Albion, leaning on his Kenna's breast,
Thus all the softness of his soul express'd :
" All things are hush'd.   The sun's meridian rays
Veil the horizon in one mighty blaze ;
Nor moon nor star in heaven's blue arch is seen,
With kindly rays to silver o'er the green,
Grateful to fairy eyes ; they secret take
Their rest, and only wretched mortals wake.
This dead of day I fly to thee alone,
A world to me, a multitude in one.
Oh sweet as dew-drops on these flowery lawns,
When the sky opens, and the evening dawns !
Straight as the pink, that towers so high on air,
Soft as the blue-bell, as the daisy, fair !
Bless'd be the hour, when first I was convey'd
An infant captive to this blissful shade !
And bless'd the hand that did my form refine,
And shrunk my stature to a match with thine !

Glad I for thee renounce my royal birth,
And all the giant daughters of the earth.
Thou, if thy breast with equal ardour burn,
Renounce thy kind, and love for love return.
So from us two, combined by nuptial ties,
A race unknown of demi-gods shall rise.
Oh speak, my love! my vows with vows repay,
And sweetly swear my rising fears away."
　　To whom (the shining azure of her eyes
More brighten'd) thus th' enamour'd maid replies :
　　" By all the stars, and first the glorious moon,
I swear, and by the head of Oberon,
A dreadful oath! no prince of fairy line
Shall e'er in wedlock plight his vows with mine.
Where'er my footsteps in the dance are seen,
May toadstools rise, and mildews blast the green,
May the keen east-wind blight my fav'rite flowers,
And snakes and spotted adders haunt my bowers.
Confined whole ages in a hemlock shade,
There rather pine I a neglected maid ;
Or worse, exiled from Cynthia's gentle rays,
Parch in the sun a thousand summer-days,
Than any prince, a prince of fairy line,
In sacred wedlock plight his vows with mine."
　　She ended : and with lips of rosy hue
Dipp'd five times over in ambrosial dew,
Stifled his words.　When, from his covert rear'd,
The frowning brow of Oberon appear'd.
A sun-flower's trunk was near, whence (killing sight!)
The monarch issued, half an ell in height :
Full on the pair a furious look he cast,
Nor spake ; but gave his bugle-horn a blast,
That through the woodland echo'd far and wide,
And drew a swarm of subjects to his side.
A hundred chosen knights, in war renown'd,
Drive Albion banish'd from the sacred ground ;

And twice ten myriads guard the bright abodes,
Where the proud king, amidst his demi-gods,
For Kenna's sudden bridal bids prepare,
And to Azuriel gives the weeping fair.
　　If fame in arms, with ancient birth combined,
And faultless beauty, and a spotless mind,
To love and praise can generous souls incline,
That love, Azuriel, and that praise were thine.
Blood, only less than royal, fill'd thy veins,
Proud was the roof, and large thy fair domains.
Where now the skies high Holland-house invades
And short-lived Warwick sadden'd all the shades,
Thy dwelling stood: nor did in him afford
A nobler owner, or a lovelier lord.
For thee a hundred fields produced their store,
And by thy name ten thousand vassals swore,
So loved thy name, that, at their monarch's choice,
All Fairy shouted with a general voice.
　　Oriel alone a secret rage suppress'd,
That from his bosom heaved the golden vest.
Along the banks of Thame his empire ran,
Wide was his range, and populous his clan.
When cleanly servants, if we trust old tales,
Beside their wages had good fairy vails,
Whole heaps of silver tokens, nightly paid
The careful wife or the neat dairy-maid,
Sunk not his stores. 　With smiles and powerful bribes
He gain'd the leaders of his neighbour tribes,
And ere the night the face of heaven had changed,
Beneath his banners half the fairies ranged.
　　Mean-while driven back to earth, a lonely way
The cheerless Albion wander'd half the day,
A long, long journey, choked with brakes and thorns,
Ill-measured by ten thousand barley-corns.
Tired out at length, a spreading stream he spy'd
Fed by old Thame, a daughter of the tide:

'Twas then a spreading stream, though, now, its fame
Obscured, it bears the creek's inglorious name,
And creeps, as through contracted bounds it strays,
A leap for boys in these degenerate days.
  On the clear crystal's verdant bank he stood,
And thrice look'd back upon the fatal wood,
And thrice he groan'd, and thrice he beat his breast,
And thus in tears his kindred god address'd :
  " If true, ye watery powers, my lineage came
From Neptune mingling with a mortal dame ;
Down to his court, with coral garlands crown'd,
Through all your grottos waft my plaintive sound,
And urge the god, whose trident shakes the earth,
To grace his offspring and assert my birth."
  He said. A gentle Naiad heard his prayer,
And, touch'd with pity for a lover's care,
Shoots to the sea, where low beneath the tides
Old Neptune in th' unfathom'd deep resides.
Roused at the news the sea's stern sultan swore
Revenge, and scarce from present arms forbore,
But first the nymph his harbinger he sends,
And to her care the fav'rite boy commends.
  As through the Thames her backward course she
      guides,
Driven up his current by the refluent tides,
Along his banks the pigmy legions spread,
She spies, and haughty Oriel at their head.
Soon with wrong'd Albion's name the host she fires,
And counts the ocean's god among his sires ;
" The ocean's god, by whom shall be o'erthrown
(Styx heard his oath) the tyrant Oberon.
See here, beneath a toadstool's deadly gloom
Lies Albion : him the fates your leader doom.
Hear and obey ; 'tis Neptune's powerful call,
By him Azuriel and his king shall fall."

She said. They bow'd : and on their shields upbore,
With shouts, their new-saluted emperor.
Even Oriel smiled : at least to smile he strove,
And hopes of vengeance triumph'd over love.
　See now the mourner of the lonely shade
By gods protected, and by hosts obey'd,
A slave, a chief, by fickle Fortune's play,
In the short course of one revolving day.
What wonder if the youth, so strangely bless'd,
Felt his heart flutter in his little breast !
His thick embattled troops, with secret pride,
He views extended half an acre wide ;
More light he treads, more tall he seems to rise,
And struts a straw-breadth nearer to the skies.
　O for thy muse, great bard,[1] whose lofty strains
In battle join'd the pygmies and the cranes !
Each gaudy knight, had I that warmth divine,
Each colour'd legion in my verse should shine.
But simple I, and innocent of art,
The tale, that soothed my infant years, impart,
The tale I hear'd whole winter-eves, untired,
And sing the battles that my nurse inspired.
　Now the shrill corn-pipes, echoing loud to arms,
To rank and file reduce the straggling swarms.
Thick rows of spears at once, with sudden glare,
A grove of needles, glitter in the air ;
Loose in the winds small ribbon streamers flow,
Dipp'd in all colours of the heavenly bow,
And the gay host, that now its march pursues,
Gleams o'er the meadows in a thousand hues.
　Unseen and silent march the slow brigades
Through pathless wilds, and unfrequented shades.
In hope already vanquish'd by surprise,
In Albion's power the fairy empire lies ;

---

[1] Mr Addison.

Already has he seized on Kenna's charms,
And the glad beauty trembles in his arms.
The march concludes : and now in prospect near,
But fenced with arms, the hostile towers appear,
For Oberon, or druids falsely sing,
Wore his prime visor in a magic ring.
A subtle spright, that opening plots foretold
By sudden dimness on the beamy gold.
Hence, in a crescent form'd, his legions bright,
With beating bosoms, waited for the fight ;
To charge their foes they march, a glittering band,
And in their van doth bold Azuriel stand.
What rage that hour did Albion's soul possess,
Let chiefs imagine, and let lovers guess !
Forth issuing from his ranks, that strove in vain
To check his course, athwart the dreadful plain
He strides indignant : and with haughty cries
To single fight the fairy prince defies.
Forbear, rash youth, th' unequal war to try ;
Nor, sprung from mortals, with immortals vie.
No god stands ready to avert thy doom,
Nor yet thy grandsire of the waves is come.
My words are vain—no words the wretch can move,
By beauty dazzled and bewitch'd by love :
He longs, he burns, to win the glorious prize,
And sees no danger, while he sees her eyes.
Now from each host the eager warriors start,
And furious Albion flings his hasty dart :
'Twas feather'd from the bee's transparent wing,
And its shaft ended in a hornet's sting ;
But toss'd in rage, it flew without a wound,
High o'er the foe, and guiltless pierced the ground.
Not so Azuriel's : with unerring aim
Too near the needle-pointed javelin came,
Drove through the seven-fold shield and silken vest, .
And lightly rased the lover's ivory breast.

Roused at the smart, and rising to the blow,
With his keen sword he cleaves his fairy foe,
Sheer from the shoulder to the waist he cleaves,
And of one arm the tott'ring trunk bereaves.
   His useless steel brave Albion wields no more,
But sternly smiles, and thinks the combat o'er.
So had it been, had aught of mortal strain,
Or less than fairy felt the deadly pain.
But empyreal forms, howe'er in fight
Gash'd and dismember'd, easily unite.
As some frail cup of China's purest mold,
With azure varnish'd, and bedropp'd with gold,
Though broke, if cured by some nice virgin's hands,
In its old strength and pristine beauty stands;
The tumults of the boiling bohea braves,
And holds secure the coffee's sable waves:
So did Azuriel's arm, if fame say true,
Rejoin the vital trunk whence first it grew;
And, whilst in wonder fix'd poor Albion stood,
Plunged the cursed sabre in his heart's warm blood.
The golden broidery, tender Milhah wove,
The breast to Kenna sacred and to love,
Lie rent and mangled: and the gaping wound
Pours out a flood of purple on the ground.
The jetty lustre sickens in his eyes:
On his cold cheeks the bloomy freshness dies:
"Oh Kenna, Kenna," thrice he try'd to say
"Kenna, farewell:" and sigh'd his soul away.
   His fall the dryads with loud shrieks deplore,
By sister naiads echo'd from the shore,
Thence down to Neptune's secret realms convey'd,
Through grots, and glooms, and many a coral shade.
The sea's great sire, with looks denouncing war,
The trident shakes, and mounts the pearly car;
With one stern frown the wide-spread deep deforms,
And works the madding ocean into storms.

2 C

O'er foaming mountains, and through bursting tides,
Now high, now low, the bounding chariot rides,
'Till through the Thames in a loud whirlwind's roar
It shoots, and lands him on the destined shore.
　Now fix't on earth his towering stature stood,
Hung o'er the mountains, and o'erlooked the wood.
To Brompton's grove one ample stride he took,
(The valleys trembled, and the forests shook)
The next huge step reach'd the devoted shade,
Where choked in blood was wretched Albion laid :
Where now the vanquish'd with the victor's join'd,
Beneath the regal banners stood combined.
　Th' embattled dwarfs with rage and scorn he pass'd,
And on their town his eye vindictive cast.
Its deep foundations his strong trident cleaves,
And high in air th' uprooted empire heaves ;
On his broad engine the vast ruin hung,
Which on the foe with force divine he flung ;
Aghast the legions, in th' approaching shade,
Th' inverted spires and rocking domes survey'd
That downward tumbling on the host below
Crush'd the whole nation at one dreadful blow.
Towers, arms, nymphs, warriors, are together lost,
And a whole empire falls to sooth sad Albion's ghost.
　Such was the period, long restrain'd by Fate.
And such the downfall of the fairy state.
This dale, a pleasing region, not unbless'd,
This dale possess'd they ; and had still possess'd
Had not their monarch, with a father's pride,
Rent from her lord th' inviolable bride,
Rash to dissolve the contract seal'd above,
The solemn vows, and sacred bonds of love.
Now, where his elves so brightly danced the round,
No violet breathes, nor daisy paints the ground,
His towers and people fill one common grave,
A shapeless ruin, and a barren cave.

Beneath huge hills of smoking piles he lay
Stunn'd and confounded a whole summer's day.
At length awaked (for what can long restrain
Unbody'd spirits?) but awaked in pain:
And as he saw the desolated wood,
And the dark den where once his empire stood,
Grief chilled his heart: to his half-open'd eyes
In every oak a Neptune seemed to rise:
He fled: and left with all his trembling peers,
The long possession of a thousand years.
Through bush, through brake, through groves, and
    gloomy dales,
Through dank and dry, o'er streams and flowery
    vales,
Direct they fled; but often look'd behind,
And stopp'd and started at each rustling wind.
Wing'd with like fear his abdicated bands,
Disperse and wander into different lands,
Part did beneath the Peak's deep caverns lie,
In silent glooms impervious to the sky;
Part on fair Avon's margin seek repose,[1]
Whose stream o'er Britain's midmost region flows,
Where formidable Neptune never came,
And seas and oceans are but known by fame:
Some to dark woods and secret shades retreat,
And some on mountains choose their airy seat.
There haply by the ruddy damsel seen,
Or shepherd boy, they featly foot the green,
While from their steps a circling verdure springs;
But fly from towns, and dreads the court of kings.

---

[1] " Thou soft flowing Avon, by thy silver stream
    Of things more than mortal thy Shakspeare would dream
    The fairies by moonlight dance round his green bed,
    For hallow'd the turf is which pillow'd his head."
                          GARRICK.

Mean-while sad Kenna loth to quit the grove,
Hung o'er the body of her breathless love,
Try'd every art (vain arts !) to change his doom,
And vow'd (vain vows !) to join him in the tomb.
What could she do? the Fates alike deny
The dead to live, or fairy forms to die.
    An herb there grows (the same old Homer tells
Ulysses bore to rival Circe's spells) : [1]
Its root is ebon-black, but sends to light,
A stem that bends with flowerets milky white,
Holy the plant, which gods and fairies know,
But secret kept from mortal men below.
On his pale limbs its virtuous juice she shed,
And murmur'd mystic numbers o'er the dead,
When lo ! the little shape by magic power
Grew less and less, contracted to a flower,
A flower, that first in this sweet garden smiled,
To virgins sacred, and the snow-drop stiled.
    The new-born plant with sweet regret she view'd.
Warm'd with her sighs, and with her tears bedew'd,
Its ripened seeds from bank to bank convey'd
And with her lover whiten'd half the shade.
Thus won from death each spring she sees him grow
And glories in the vegetable snow,
Which now increased through wide Britannia's plains,
Its parent's warmth and spotless name retains ;
First leader of the flowery race aspires,
And foremost catches the sun's genial fires,
'Mid frosts and snows triumphant dares appear,
Mingles the seasons, and leads on the year.
    Deserted now of all the pigmy race,
Nor man nor fairy touch'd this guilty place.
In heaps on heaps for many a rolling age,
It lay accursed the mark of Neptune's rage ;

---

[1] *Odys.* B. 10.

'Till great Nassau recloth'd the desert shade
Thence sacred to Britannia's monarchs made.
'Twas then the green-robed nymph, fair Kenna, came,
(Kenna that gave the neighbouring town its name).
Proud when she saw th' ennobled garden shine
With nymphs and heroes of her lover's line.
She vow'd to grace the mansions once her own,
And picture out in plants the fairy town.
To far-famed Wise her flight unseen she sped,
And with gay prospects filled the craftsman's head,
Soft in his fancy drew a pleasing scheme,
And plann'd that landskip in a morning dream.
    With the sweet view the sire of gardens fired,
Attempts the labour by the nymph inspired,
The walls and streets in rows of yew designs,
And forms the town in all its ancient lines ;
The corner trees he lifts more high in air.
And girds the palace with a verdant square.
    With a sad pleasure the aërial maid
This image of her ancient realm surveyed ;
How changed, how fall'n from its primæval pride !
Yet here each moon, the hour her lover died,
Each moon his solemn obsequies she pays,
And leads the dance beneath pale Cynthia's rays ;
Pleased in these shades to head her fairy train,
And grace the groves where Albion's kinsmen reign.[1]

TALE XXVIII.

[From " A Pleasant Treatise of Witches," 12mo, Lond. 1673.]

SIARRA hath left us this notable relation, that there
lived in his time, in Spain, a [no]table and beauti-

---

[1] By Thomas Tickell.

ful virgin, but far more famous for her excellence
at her needle, insomuch that happy did that courtier
think himself, that could wear the smallest piece of
her work, though at a price almost invaluable.   It
happen'd one day, as this admirable seamstress sate
working in her garden, that, casting aside her eye on
some fair flower or tree, she saw, as she thought, a
little gentleman, yet one that shew'd great nobility by
his clothing, come riding toward her from behind a
bed of flowers ; thus surprised how any body should
come into her garden, but much more, at the stature
of the person, who, as he was on horseback, exceeded
not a foot's length in height, she had reason to suspect
that her eyes deceived her.   But the gallant, spurring
his horse up the garden, made it not long, though his
horse was little, before he came to her : then greeting
the lady in most decent manner, after some compliments passed, he acquaints her with the cause of his
bold arrival ; that, forasmuch as he was a prince
amongst the fairies, and did intend to celebrate his
marriage on such a day, he desired she would work
points for him and his princess against the time he
appointed.   The lady consented to his demands, and
he took his leave ; but whether the multitude of
business caused the lady to forget her promise, or the
strangeness of the thing made her neglect the work,
thinking her sight to have been deceived, I know not ;
yet so it fell out, that, when the appointed time came,
the work was not ready.   The hour, wherein she had
promised the fairy-prince some fruits of her needle,
happen'd to be one day as she was at dinner with many
noble persons, having quite forgot her promise ; when,
on a sudden, casting her eye to the door, she saw an
infinite train of fairies come in : so that fixing her
eyes on them, and, rememb'ring how she [had]
neglected her promise, she sate as one amazed, and

astonished the whole company. But, at last, the train had mounted upon the table, and as they were prancing on their horses round the brims of a large dish of white-broth, an officer that seemed too busy in making way before them, fell into the dish, which caused the lady to burst into a sudden fit of laughter, and thereby to recover her senses. When the whole fairy company was come upon the table, that the brims of every dish seemed fill'd with little horsemen, she saw the prince coming toward her, who hearing she had not done what she promised, seemed to go away displeased. The lady presently fell into a fit of melancholy, and, being asked by her friends the cause of these alterations and astonishments, related the whole matter; but, notwithstanding all their consolations, pined away, and died not long after.

'Tis reported likewise of a country girl, being sent out daily by her mother to look to a sow that was then big with pigs, that the sow always strayed out of the girl's sight, and yet always came safe home at night; this the maid often observing, resolved to watch her more narrowly, and followed her one day closely, till they both came to a fair green valley, where was laid a large bason full of milk and white bread. The sow having eaten her mess, returned home, and that night pigg'd eleven pigs. The good wife, rising early next morning to look to her beast, found on the threshold of the sty ten half-crowns, and entering in, saw but one pig; judging by these things, that the fairies had fed her sow, and bought her pigs.

A certain woman having put out her child to nurse in the country, found, when she came to take it home, that its form was so much altered that she scarce knew it; nevertheless, not knowing what time might do, took it home for her own. But when, after some years, it

could neither speak nor go, the poor woman was feign
to carry it, with much trouble, in her arms ; and, one
day, a poor man coming to the door, God bless you,
mistress, said he, and your poor child, be pleased to
bestow something on a poor man. Ah ! this child,
repli'd she, is the cause of all my sorrow ; and related what had happen'd ; adding, moreover, that she
thought it was changed, and none of her child. The
old man, whom years had render'd more prudent in
such matters, told her that to find out the truth, she
should make a clear fire, sweep the hearth very clean,
and place the child fast in his chair, that he might
not fall before it ; then break a dozen eggs, and
place the four and twenty half-shells before it ; then
go out and listen at the door, for if the child spoke,
it was certainly a changeling ; and then she should
carry it out, and leave it on the dunghill to cry, and
not to pity it, till she heard its voice no more. The
woman, having done all things according to these
words, heard the child say, Seven years old was I,
before I came to the nurse, and four years have I
lived since, and never saw so many milk-pans before.
So the woman took it up, and left it upon the dunghill
to cry, and not to be pitied, till at last she thought
the voice went up into the air ; and, coming out,
found there in the stead her own natural and well-
favoured child.

———

TALE XXIX.

[From MS. Harl. 6482.]

Of spirits called Hobgoblins, or Robin Goodfellowes.

THESE kinde of spirits are more familiar and
domestical than the others, and for some causes

to us unknown, abode in one place more then in another, so that some never almost depart from some particular houses, as though they were their proper mansions, making in them sundry noises, rumours, mockeries, gawds and jests, without doing any harme at all ; and some have heard them play at gitterns and Jews' harps, and ring bells and make answer to those that call them, and speake with certain signes, laughters and merry gestures, so that those of the house come at last to be so familiar and well acquainted with them that they fear them not at all. But in truth, if they had free power to put in execution their mallicious desire, we should finde these pranks of theirs not to be jests, but earnest indeed, tending to the destruction both of our body and soul, but their power is so restrained and tyed that they can passe no further then to jests and gawds, and if they do any harm at all, it is certainly very little, as by experience hath been founde.

[From MS. Rawl. Poet. 66.]

A farmer hired a grange commonly reported to be haunted with fairies, and paid a shrewd for it every half year. A gentleman asked him how he durst live in the house, and whether no spirits haunted him? Truth, quoth he, there be two saints in Heaven do vex me more than all the devills in hell, namely, the Virgin Mary and Michaell the Archangell ; on whose daies he paied his rent.

TALE XXX.

PARNELL'S FAIRY TALE.

In Britain's isle and Arthur's days,
When midnight fairies daunc'd the maze,
    Liv'd Edwin of the Green :
Edwin, I wis, a gentle youth,
Endow'd with courage, sense, and truth,
    Tho' badly shap'd he'd been.

His mountain back mote well be said
To measure height against his head,
    And lift itself above ;
Yet spite of all that nature did
To make his uncouth form forbid,
    This creature dar'd to love.

He felt the charms of Edith's eyes,
Nor wanted hope to gain the prize,
    Cou'd ladies look within ;
But one sir Topaz dress'd with art,
And, if a shape cou'd win a heart,
    He had a shape to win.

Edwin, if right I read my song,
With slighted passion pac'd along
    All in the moony light ;
'Twas near an old enchanted court,
Where sportive fairies made resort
    To revel out the night.

His heart was drear, his hope was cross'd,
'Twas late, 'twas far, the path was lost
    That reach'd the neighbour-town ;
With weary steps he quits the shades,
Resolv'd the darkling dome he treads,
    And drops his limbs adown.

But scant he lays him on the floor,
When hollow winds remove the door,
   A trembling rocks the ground:
And well I ween, to count aright,
At once a hundred tapers light
   On all the walls around.

Now sounding tongues assail his ear,
Now sounding feet approachen near,
   And now the sounds increase:
And from the corner where he lay,
He sees a train profusely gay
   Come prankling o'er the place.

But (trust me, gentles,) never yet
Was dight a masquing half so neat,
   Or half so rich, before;
The country lent the sweet perfumes,
The sea, the pearl, the sky, the plumes,
   The town its silken store.

Now, whilst he gaz'd, a gallant drest
In flaunting robes above the rest,
   With awful accent cry'd;
"What mortal of a wretched mind,
Whose sighs infect the balmy wind,
   Has here presum'd to hide?"

At this the swain, whose vent'rous soul
No fears of magic art controul,
   Advanc'd in open sight;
"Nor have I cause of dreed," he said,
"Who view by no presumption led,
   Your revels of the night.

"'Twas grief for scorn of faithful love,
Which made my steps unweeting rove

Amid the nightly dew."
" 'Tis well," the gallant cries again,
" We fairies never injure men
　　Who dare to tell us true.

" Exalt thy love-dejected heart,
Be mine the task, or ere we part,
　　To make thee grief resign ;
Now take the pleasure of thy chaunce ;
Whilst I with Mab, my part'ner, daunce,
　　Be little Mable thine."

He spoke, and all a sudden there
Light music floats in wanton air ;
　　The monarch leads the queen :
The rest their fairy part'ners found,
And Mable trimly tript the ground
　　With Edwin of the Green.

The dauncing past, the board was laid,
And siker such a feast was made
　　As heart and lip desire ;
Withouten hands the dishes fly,
The glasses with a wish come nigh,
　　And with a wish retire.

But now to please the fairy king,
Full ev'ry deal they laugh and sing,
　　And antic feats devise ;
Some wind and tumble like an ape,
And other some transmut their shape
　　In Edwin's wond'ring eyes.

'Till one at last that Robin hight,
Renown'd for pinching maids by night,
　　Has bent him up aloof ;
And full against the beam he flung,
Where by the back the youth he hung,
　　To spraul unneath the roof.

From thence, " Reverse my charm," he crys,
" And let it fairly now suffice
    The gambol has been shown."
But Oberon answers with a smile,
" Content thee, Edwin, for a while,
    The vantage is thine own."

Here ended all the phantom-play ;
They smelt the fresh approach of day,
    And heard a cock to crow ;
The whirling wind that bore the crowd
Has clapp'd the door, and whistled loud,
    To warn them all to go.

Then screaming all at once they fly,
And all at once the tapers dye ;
    Poor Edwin falls to floor.
Forlorn his state, and dark the place,
Was never wight in sike a case
    Thro' all the land before !

But soon as dan Apollo rose,
Full jolly creature home he goes,
    He feels his back the less ;
His honest tongue and steady mind
Had rid him of the lump behind,
    Which made him want success.

With lusty livelyhed he talks,
He seems a-dauncing as he walks,
    His story soon took wind ;
And beauteous Edith sees the youth,
Endow'd with courage, sense and truth,
    Without a bunch behind.

The story told, sir Topaz moved,
The youth of Edith erst apprev'd,

To see the revel scene :
At close of eve he leaves his home,
And wends to find the ruined dome,
All on the gloomy plain.

As there he bides, it so befell
The wind came rustling down a dell,
A shaking seiz'd the wall :
Up spring the tapers as before,
The fairies bragly foot the floor,
And music fills the hall.

But certes sorely sunk with woe,
Sir Topaz sees the elphin show,
His spirits in him dy :
When Oberon crys, "A man is near,
A mortal passion, cleeped fear,
Hangs flagging in the sky."

With that sir Topaz, hapless youth
In accents fault'ring, ay for ruth,
Intreats them pity graunt ;
For als he been a mister wight,
Betray'd by wand'ring in the night,
To tread the circled haunt.

"Ah losell vile," at once they roar,
"And little skill'd of fairie lore,
Thy cause to come we know :
Now has thy kestrell courage fell ;
And fairies, since a lye you tell,
Are free to work thee woe."

Then Will, who bears the wispy fire
To trail the swains among the mire,
The caitive upward flung ;
There like a tortoise in a shop

He dangled from the chamber top,
　Where whilome Edwin hung.

The revel now proceeds apace,
Deftly they frisk it o'er the place,
　They sit, they drink, and eat ;
The time with frolic mirth beguile,
And poor sir Topaz hangs the while,
　'Till all the route retreat.

By this the stars began to wink,
They shriek, they fly, the tapers sink,
　And down y-drops the knight ;
For never spell by fairie laid,
With strong enchantment bound a glade
　Beyond the length of night.

Chill, dark, alone, adreed, he lay,
Till up the welkin rose the day,
　They deem'd the dole was o'er :
But wot ye well his harder lot,
His seely back the bunch had got,
　Which Edwin lost afore !

This tale a Sybil nurse ared ;
She softly stroak'd my youngling head,
　And when the tale was done,
" Thus some are born, my son," she cries,
" With base impediments to rise,
　And some are born with none.

" But virtue can itself advance
To what the fav'rite fools of chance
　By fortune seem design'd ;
Virtue can gain the odds of fate,
And from itself shake off the weight
　Upon th'unworthy mind."

XXXII.

Fairy Songs.

—*o*—

SONG I.

TITANIAS LULLABY.

BY SHAKSPEARE.

YOU spotted snakes, with double tongue,
  Thorny hedge-hogs, be not seen;
  Newts, and blind-worms, do no wrong,
Come not near our fairy queen.

CHORUS.

Philomel, with melody,
  Sing in our sweet lullaby;
Lulla, lulla, lullaby; lulla, lulla, lullaby.

Weaving spiders come not here,
  Hence, you long-legg'd spinners, hence:
Beetles black, approach not near;
  Worm, nor snail, do no offence.

CHORUS.

Philomel, with melody, &c.

SONG II.

IMITATION.

Lo! here, beneath this hallow'd shade,
  Within a cowslip's blossom deep,
The lovely queen of elves is laid,
  May nought disturb her balmy sleep

Let not the snake, or baleful toad,
  Approach the silent mansion near,
Or newt profane the sweet abode,
  Or owl repeat her orgies here!

No snail or worm shall hither come,
  With noxious filth her bow'r to stain;
Hence be the beetle's sudden hum,
  And spider's disembowel'd train!

The love-lorn nightingale alone
  Shall through Titania's arbour stray,
To soothe her sleep with melting moan,
  And lull her with his sweetest lay.

SONG III.

PUCK'S NIGHT ADDRESS.

BY SHAKSPEARE.

Now the haughty lion roars,
  And the wolf behowls the moon;
Whilst the heavy ploughman snores,
  All with weary task fordone.

Now the wasted brands do glow,
  Whilst the screech-owl, screeching loud,

Puts the wretch, that lies in woe,
In remembrance of a shroud.

Now it is the time of night,
That the graves, all gaping wide,
. Every one let forth his sprite,
In the church-way path, to glide.

And we fairies, that do run,
By the triple Hecate's team,
From the presence of the sun,
Following darkness like a dream,
Now are frolic ; not a mouse
Shall disturb this hallow'd house :
I am sent, with broom, before,
To sweep the dust behind the door.[1]

SONG IV.

THE PRANKS OF ROBIN GOOD-FELLOW.[2]

FROM Oberon, in fairyland,
The king of ghosts and shadows there,
Mad Robin, I at his command,
Am sent to view the night-sports here ;
What revel-rout
Is kept about

---

[1] Midsummer-Night's Dream.
[2] This well-known song is attributed by Peck to Ben Jonson, and Mr Collier possesses a very early MS. copy of it, where the initials of that poet are found at the end. Mr Collier's MS. possesses many variations, some of which I have noted, and an additional stanza, also here given. In the old black-letter copies, it is directed to be sung to the tune of Dulcina.
—HALLIWELL.

In every corner where I go,
  I will o'ersee,
  And merry be,
And make good sport, with ho, ho, ho !

More swift than lightning can I fly
  About this airy welkin soon,
And, in a minute's space, decry
  Each thing that's done below the moon :
    There's not a hag,
    Nor ghost shall wag,
  Nor cry, ware Goblin ! where I go ;[1]
    But Robin I
    Their feats will spy,
  And fear them home, with ho, ho, ho !

If any wanderers I meet,
  That from their night-sport do trudge home,
With counterfeiting voice I greet,
  And cause them on with me to roam ;
    Through woods, through lakes,
    Through bogs, through brakes,
  O'er bush and brier, with them I go,
    I call upon
    Them to come on,[2]
  And wend me laughing, ho, ho, ho !

Sometimes I meet them like a man,
  Sometimes, an ox,[3] sometimes, a hound ;
And to a horse I turn me can,
  To trip and trot about them round ;

---

[1] "Nor any friend, where ere I goe."—Mr Collier's MS.
[2] "All in the nicke,
    To play some tricke."—PERCY.
[3] "A haste."—Mr Collier's MS.

But if, to ride,
My back they stride,
More swift than wind away I go ;
O'er hedge and lands,
Through pools and ponds,
I whinny laughing, ho, ho, ho !

When lads and lasses merry be,
With possets, and with junkets fine,
Unseen of all the company,
I eat their cates, and sip their wine ;
And to make sport,
I f—t and snort,
And out the candles do I blow ;
The maids I kiss ;
They shriek—who's this?
I answer nought, but ho, ho, ho !

Yet, now and then, the maids to please,
I card, at midnight, up their wool ;
And, while they sleep, snort, f—t, and fease,
With wheel to thread their flax I pull ;
I grind at mill,
Their malt up still,
I dress their hemp, I spin their tow ;
If any wake,
And would me take,
I wend me laughing, ho, ho, ho !

When house or hearth doth sluttish lie,
I pinch the maidens black and blue ;
And from the bed the bed-clothes I
Pull off, and lay them nak'd to view ;
'Twixt sleep and wake,
I do them take,

And on the "clay-cold" floor them throw,
  If out they cry,
  Then forth I fly,[1]
And loudly laugh I, ho, ho, ho!

Whenas my fellow-elves and I
  In circled ring do trip a round;
If that our sports by any eye
  Do happen to be seen or found;
    If that they
    No words do say,
  But *mum* continue as they go,
    Each night I do
    Put groat in shoe,
  And wind out laughing, ho, ho, ho![2]

When any need to borrow ought,
  We lend them what they do require;
And for the use demand we nought:
  Our own is all we do desire:
    If to repay
    They do delay,
  Abroad amongst them then I go;
    And night by night
    I them affright,
  With pinching, dreams, and ho, ho, ho!

When lazy queans have nought to do,
  But study how to cog and lie,
To make debate, and mischief too,
  'Twixt one another secretly,
    I mark their glose,
    And it disclose

---

[1] "And would me spie."—Mr Collier's MS.
[2] This stanza is peculiar to Mr Collier's MS.

To them that they have wronged so;
When I have done
I get me gone,
And leave them scolding, ho, ho, ho!

When men do traps and engines set
In loop-holes, where the vermin creep,
Who from their folds and houses fet
Their ducks and geese, and lambs and sheep,
I spy the gin,
And enter in,
And seem a vermin taken so;
But, when they there
Approach me near,
I leap out laughing, ho, ho, ho!

By wells, and gills, in meadows green,
We nightly dance our hey-day guise;
And, to our fairy king and queen,
We chant our moonlight minstrelsies:[1]
When larks 'gin sing
Away we fling,
And babes new-born steal as we go,
An elf in bed
We leave instead,
And wend us laughing, ho, ho, ho!

From hag-bred Merlin's time have I
Thus nightly revell'd to and fro;
And for my pranks men call me by
The name of Robin Good-fellow:

---

[1] Instead of these four lines, Mr Collier's MS. reads—

"Thus do we pass, and see unseen
The actions of mortality;
When to our fairy king and queen,
We chant our moonlight harmony."

Fiends, ghosts and sprites,
That haunt the nights,
The hags and goblins do me know;
And beldames old
My feats have told;
So *vale, vale!* ho, ho, ho!

SONG V.

THE FAIRYS FAREWELL.

FAREWELL rewards and fairies!
Good housewives now may say;
For now foul sluts in dairies,
Do fare as well as they.
And though they sweep their hearths no less
Than maids were wont to do,
Yet who of late for cleanliness
Finds six-pence in her shoe?

Lament, lament old abbies,
The fairies' lost command;
They did but change priests' babies,
But some have changed your land:
And all your children stol'n from thence
Are now grown puritanes,
Who live as changelings ever since,
For love of your demaines.

At morning and at evening both
You merry were and glad,
So little care of sleep and sloth,
These pretty ladies had.

When Tom came home from labour,
  Or Ciss to milking rose,
Then merrily went their tabour,
  And nimbly went their toes.

Witness those rings and roundelays
  Of theirs, which yet remain ;
Were footed in queen Mary's days
  On many a grassy plain.
But since of late Elizabeth,
  And later James came in,
They never danced on any heath,
  As when the time hath bin.

By which we note the fairies
  Were of the old profession ;
Their songs were *Ave Maries*,
  Their dances were procession.
But now, alas ! they all are dead,
  Or gone beyond the seas,
Or farther for religion fled,
  Or else to take their ease.

A tell-tale in their company,
  They never could endure ;
And whoso kept not secretly
  Their mirth was punish'd sure :
It was a just and christian deed
  To pinch such black and blue :
O how the commonwealth doth need
  Such justices as you !

Now they have left our quarters ;
  A register they have,
Who can preserve their charters ;
  A man both wise and grave.

An hundred of their merry pranks
By one that I could name
Are kept in store ; con twenty thanks
To William for the same.

To William Churne of Staffordshire
Give laud and praises due,
Who every meal can mend your chear
With tales both old and true :
To William all give audience,
And pray ye for his noddle :
For all the fairies' evidence
Were lost if it were addle.[1]

SONG VI.

The three following songs are taken from a very interesting
collection of madrigals by Mr Oliphant. The two first
are from a publication by Weelkes, and the third from
Ravenscroft. The last one is also given by Douce, in his
"Illustrations," vol. i. p. 83.

I.

On the plains,
Fairy trains
    Were a-treading measures ;
Satyrs play'd,
Fairies stray'd
    At the stops set leisures.

---

[1] By Richard Corbet, afterwards Bishop of Oxford and Nor-
wich, who died in 1635. Posterity would have been much more
indebted to this witty prelate for a few of gaffer Churn's fairy-
tales than for all the sermons his lordship ever wrote.

Nymphs begin
To come in
    Quickly thick and threefold ;
Now they dance,
Now they prance,
    Present there to behold.

II.

Come let's begin to revel't out,
And tread the hills and dales about ;
That hills and dales and woods may sound,
An echo to this warbling sound.
Lads, merry be with music sweet,
And, fairies, trip it with your feet,
That hills and dales and woods may sound
An echo to this warbling round.

III.

Dare you haunt our hallow'd green ?
None but fairies here are seen.
    Down and sleep;
    Wake and weep,
Pinch him black and pinch him blue,
That seeks to steal a lover true.
When you come to hear us sing,
Or to tread our fairy ring,
Pinch him black, and pinch him blue ;
O, thus our nails shall handle you !

PRINTED BY BALLANTYNE AND COMPANY
EDINBURGH AND LONDON

FRANK AND WILLIAM KERSLAKE'S PUBLICATIONS.

In old-fashioned red paper boards, edges uncut, one vol., foolscap 8vo. Price 6s.

TRADITIONAL TALES

OF THE

ENGLISH AND SCOTISH PEASANTRY.

By ALLAN CUNNINGHAM.

A NEW EDITION.

A singularly interesting collection of stories illustrative of the state and manners of Scotland, "'tis sixty years since." The book has long been scarce, and was highly esteemed by the Author of "*Waverley.*"

OPINIONS OF THE PRESS.

Glasgow Herald.

"It is a pleasant surprise to get a Reprint of this charming book. . . . His 'Tales of the English and Scotch Peasantry' are distinguished by all the best qualities of his writing, and the publishers have done a service to literature in reproducing them."

Spectator.

"We welcome, therefore, this Reprint of Mr Cunningham's stories, and thank Messrs Kerslake for plucking them from an untimely oblivion, and pre-senting them in the quaint and simple binding of forty or fifty years ago. Allan Cunningham's songs and stories are simple and vivid, and picturesque always, and his intense nationality, his impulsive warmth, and his youthful freshness, give the semblance and feeling of reality to his most romantic inventions."

Scotsman.

"Allan Cunningham's delightful Traditional Tales are not likely to be allowed to go out sight. They have charmed many readers, and it may be hoped will charm many more. To this end, a new edition will be welcomed. It is neatly printed and well got up."

Examiner.

"The volume is got up as neatly as book-lovers can wish, and will, no doubt, come to plenty of readers as a fresh revelation of peasant life."

In old-fashioned boards, edges uncut, 18s.

THE PLAYS, POEMS, AND LETTERS OF SIR JOHN SUCKLING.

Collated with the Early Copies, and Illustrated by a Copious Memoir, Portrait, Facsimile of Writing, and Appendix of Tracts relating to the Poet. Forming *two volumes* uniform with the *Traditional Tales.* Twenty-five copies are printed on large and thick paper *for private circulation, or Subscribers.*

This edition contains additional Poems and Letters from MSS. in the State Paper Office, British Museum, and Bodleian Library. It is strange that Suckling's Works should not have been reprinted since the edition published now more than a century ago (1770) in two duodecimo volumes. A selection from them appeared, indeed, in 1836, with a Memoir, by the Rev. A. Suckling ; but selections are always more or less unsatisfactory.

When we consider at how early an age Suckling died, it becomes remarkable that he should have left so much behind him worthy of preservation and of a lasting place in our literature. His songs have acquired a well-merited fame for their masterly gaiety and exquisite point ; his plays, though possibly ill-suited for representation, abound in capital passages ; and his prose works—the *Letters* and *Account of Religion*—manifest great correctness and solidity of judgment and admirable soundness of sense.

It should also be remembered, to Suckling's honour, that he was probably, after the editors of the first folio, the earliest person who interested himself in the revival and promotion of Shakespeare's reputation, and his own productions contain a large number of Shakespearian phrases and allusions, to say nothing of passages which are direct imitations of the great poet, for whom he appears to have entertained an ardent and sincere admiration.

Suckling was one of those men of precocious genius who, like his contemporaries Randolph and Carew, and (to go a little farther back in point of time) Beaumont and Browne, composed works of high and permanent value, at a period of life when many around them had scarcely completed their education, and who, again, had they lived longer, might have perhaps transmitted to us a larger, but not a richer, inheritance.

The Letters are valuable, not only for the wit and sense in which they abound, and their interesting allusions to persons and events, but for the closer glimpses which they often afford to us of the writer's individuality.

For *Opinions of the Press,* see the PUBLISHERS' CATALOGUE.

Preparing for Publication, uniform with Suckling's Works, in one volume, foolscap 8vo, old paper boards. Price 12s.

THE COMPLETE POEMS AND PLAYS OF THOMAS RANDOLPH.

NOW FIRST COLLECTED, WITH SOME ACCOUNT OF RANDOLPH, AND A PORTRAIT.

Much that Randolph has left behind him, shows him to have been a man of extraordinary genius, and had he not died so young, there is a great probability that of all our early writers, he would have ranked nearest to Shakespeare.

FRANK & WILLIAM KERSLAKE, 13 BOOKSELLERS ROW, W.C.

4

www.ingramcontent.com/pod-product-compliance
Lightning Source LLC
Chambersburg PA
CBHW030955110726
47900CB00004B/1281